Watcher of Skies

and other short stories

RB
Rossendale Books

Published by Rossendale Books
In association with Amazon KDP

Published in paperback 2022
Category: Crime Fiction
Copyright James Bowyer © 2022
ISBN : 9798809099240

Author Photograph, Justyna Wlostowska
Joe the Lion Artwork/ Photography, Utter Nutter
Front Cover and all other artwork Larry Flewers © 2022

The author can be contacted on Facebook : James Bowyer
Or by email   -   jamesbowyer67@gmail.com

All rights reserved, Copyright under Berne Copyright Convention and Pan American Convention. No part of this book may be reproduced, stored in a retrieval system, or transmitted in any form or by any means, electronic, mechanical, photocopying, recording or otherwise, without prior permission of the author. The author's moral rights have been asserted.

This is a work of fiction. Names, characters, corporations, institutions, organisations, events or locales in this novel are either the product of the author's imagination or, if real, used fictitiously. Any resemblance to actual persons (living or dead) is entirely coincidental

ACKNOWLEDGEMENTS

To say Larry (Lal) Flewers - one of my oldest and craziest of friends - had a part to play in the making of this collection would be quite an understatement not only has he provided amazing graphical artwork but his quiet and tenacious enthusiasm helped set sail the ship I'm now Happily adrift on.
I thank you buddy.

In no particular order, other kind thanks go out to the following family and friends;
Katerina Aydinoglu - Without doubt my biggest fan. Your immovable encouragement and conviction went above and beyond gracious compliments, so much so that I took it as *de facto* taking my scribbling's to the next level.

Gareth Witney - Whose innocuous comment made many moons ago started the ball rolling in the first place - I blame you for everything.
Sue Witney and Debra Bekker – All engines need a good service thanks for stepping in to do the tune up.

Lynda Yilmaz – Another early admirer and good friend.
Eshan Jarvis – The youngest of my test guinea pigs who not only survived but *enjoyed* the first draft of an earlier tale. What a brave lad.
Jessica Bowyer – My eldest daughter who has been with me throughout this arduous journey since day one. A true advocate and faithful confidant throughout.

Dean Rinaldi – For getting my backside into gear and lighting the way.
And last but not least special thanks go out to my beautiful wife Justyna, without whom none of this would have even been possible. Your patience, understanding and generosity in allowing me the time to roam into unchartered waters is simply priceless.

For Jessica - who believes

CONTENTS

Joe the Lion 9

The Boy Who Could Fix Things 93

Obsession 141

Watcher of the Skies 209

Joe the Lion

Chapter One

The pounding of footsteps raining down the stairs like a blitzkrieg of demented percussion alerted Janine Marshall to the fact that her son was going out.

"Don't be late Joe, I mean it. Be back by 6.30 latest, you hear me young man?" she called out, and then louder, so loud in fact she expected the neighbours would join in, *"YOU HEAR ME JOE MARSHALL!"*

"Yes mum!" Joe Marshall barely acceded, flying through the open front door as if his very life depended on it.

Janine managed to catch a flashing glimpse of her nine-year-old son clutching a toy; his brand-new Rapier 900 foam dart assault rifle, before he disappeared off the drive.

Just a flash. Blink and you'd have missed him.

Scooting hard left, hopping on one leg to make the turn, the sun's afternoon rays striking the toy gun, outlining its grey-metallic markings.

Just like a cartoon character; she almost laughed.

She knew where her son was heading. To the park: Henley's Park.

Still, a tsunami of apprehension washed over her. Flooding her with reasons why he should be accompanied, at least by an older child.

An imaginary mob of disgruntled parents brandishing banners and homemade placards descended on the property's driveway, the accusations screamed out in scarlet.

You're a bad parent!!
Janine Marshall has just let her nine-year son go to the park ALONE!
How could she do that?
She's not a fit parent!
OMG WHY, WHY, WHY?
Stone the BITCH!!

Janine tried to shut out the images of the jostling town folk baying for her to be lynched, but they continued to berate her. The park was literally two streets away and they backed onto its lake side. She would be able to see him arrive, and anyway, hadn't the last time been ok?

..........Ah Janine, who's to say that's ok, huh? You...? One overly determined mum protested, climbing out the drawer of dark consciousness........*so, you think it's ok to do that, let your son out on his own?*

No come on. I need, I need time on my own.

.....because you're not a fit parent is that why?

That's not fair, since his father... it's been hard...

...isn't that a slippery slope of sad excuses Janine...

I can't get anything done while he's under my feet!

......Oh excuses, excuses, Janine. You keep telling yourself that, can't you see that it's just plain WRONG?

Don't even go there, she shuddered, he'll be fine.

She knew he was meeting his new friends; it was all he had been talking about for the past week, and Henley's was mere minutes away. You could detect every badly pronounced syllable on a still day, squawking their little heads off, besides she'll never get anything done with him under her feet.

It's your one and only day off, remember! And you've done nothing except put a load of washing on! You should be lucky we live on top of such a popular park! He'll be fine.

Besides hadn't she been trying to prize him off that blasted PlayStation? Didn't that count for something? Jesus Christ, if it wasn't one thing it was another. If it's not the gaming then it's the nagging, if it's not the nagging then it's the tantrums, if it's not the tantrums, then it's the... 'It' goes on and on. At least one minor miracle had been accomplished: getting him off the evil black box of late. His fascination with one of the notoriously explicit games, what was it called, 'Call of War' or something? Enough to drive her insane all the explosions gunfire and the noise! How on earth do kids manage to endure without it.....*affecting them?* Damaging their health? The fact that she had acquiesced in giving him that game was bad enough.

My god! Maybe it was a reaction to his father's....! Janine sudden epiphany jolted her to a standstill.

No, no, he'll be fine......

With that last resolute thought, Janine Marshall shut the matter out of her mind completely. Doggedly focusing on the list of 'To-Dos' she'd mentally prepared for herself during the week. Opening the cupboard door under the stairs, she reached for the hoover.

*...it's always someone else's child you read about...*The voice called out of the drawer's dark recesses.

"OH, COME ON!"

She stabbed at the Electrolux 300 Super Glider's tiny on-button with her foot. It roared into life then died almost instantly. She jabbed it again and again.

Don't you fuck with me! Not today!

Janine quit sparring with the on button, took a deep breath, and slowly, with precision delicately tapped at the switch. This time the machine responded, humbly coming to life.

Ok! All's well with the world.

The decision to let her son out, sat down on the steps of justice, the jury still out, mulling it over.

At exactly 4.53pm, three hours and nine minutes after she'd last seen her son scamper out of the front door, Janine Marshall's life as she knew it would be forever splintered and fractured, like an earthquake demolishing a mountainside; shattered, never to be the same again.

***

Joe spotted the group of boys almost immediately. After scanning Henley's Park from just inside the main gate, he counted five, no four boys, two of whom had brought their bikes along for the ride.

All four lads had their Nerf guns either strapped to their backs or swinging loosely by their sides.

Joe guessed they were all around eleven or twelve years of age, maybe older, older than him anyway but that didn't concern him.

His own school friends were obsessed with Pokémon and its associated characters. As far as Joe was concerned those playing cards were for *babies*!

He'd spent many hours compulsively waiting for the boys to arrive in the park, vigilant by his bedroom window, knowing that they played regularly together on weekends at certain times.

Today was no exception.

Going be a great game today! He was so pleased with himself having caught the boys just at the right moment. His feet were tingling he was so excited. Once they saw his gun they would welcome him with open arms, in fact they would be ecstatic! *Wow is that a Rapier 900?* He could almost hear the admiration. *That is so cool!*

The noise of loud pattering water distracted his daydream. Laid out to the left, Henley's large glistening kidney-shaped lake reflected a silvery surface. Joe hadn't seen the fountain working before. He stared transfixed, admiring the gushing water, before resuming his search for the boys again, quickly spying the lads among the various groups of day-trippers.

He knew he'd been fortunate to spot the boys as early as he had. Henley's Park was enormous, huge in fact. In total, sixty-nine acres of glorious recreational landscape were to be savoured. To Joe, it seemed to have its own time zones, it was that big.

Henley Park's entrances divided the park neatly and precisely into the three districts which made up Sanford town. The West Gate entrance had Henley's, (known for its posh residential area and the given name of the park). At the North-West gate entrance was Wesley Park (posh but not as posh as Henley's) and finally the East gate, or the Main gate as it was commonly referred to, which was Sanford proper (not posh at all).

Along with the lake - something which could supply the town reservoir with enough water in case there was a severe drought - other choice features were eight tennis courts stationed near the West gate, cleverly designed in an elongated hollow, which meant the sound of thwacking balls and accompanied moans and groans were not heard by the casual observer.

Central to the park sat an old-fashioned style bandstand, looking tired and weathered but nevertheless still iconic in design; it drew Sanford's OAP contingency. Here they would congregate, ready to do battle. Armed with deck chairs and dripping ice-creams they would enjoy the silent symphonies.

In all his young years coming to the park, Joe had never once witnessed a single band play, or any other live performance, come to think of it. He had commandeered the bandstand organising his own legions of commandos and paratroopers to war, giving orders and issuing radio messages alike depending on the sway and outcome of the battle. He would pretend the old biddies were the enemy in tanks, converging on his position...and at the last minute, when all else failed he would call in an air strike

Two kiosks served the park's inhabitants *Wall's* ice cream, and lately - mostly down to millennials - burgers, fries, and other fast foods had manifested. These were strategically positioned on either side of the bandstand area. One high up on an elevation near a small, quaint aviary - some councilman's idea of nature and man co-existing – and its rival nearer the lower plateau in reach of the bandstand and lake.

Moving further and deeper into the park, a cricket pitch and pavilion served the town's aspiring Essex County batsmen. Positioned on a plateau near the West gate, the green divided a park keeper's forestry bordering one side and the tennis courts on the other.

Finally, and not lastly, the playground. Recently upgraded, kind of, this was Joe's favourite and the place where he was heading today. The playground was named Harry's Place; named after an RAF serviceman's dog; a handsome, soppy Golden Retriever. Apparently, he could be found on any given day running loose, chasing squirrels, and playing with children - so stated the commemorative brass plaque on the bench.

This was situated near the North-West gate area and one of the amenities furthest away if coming from the main entrance.

In between all of this were loving stretches of pathways, cycle routes and various open spaces to picnic, where glorious oaks flourished, and impossibly high pine trees towered. Joe loved to explore the various tracks that led to the playground area. Not only was the park enormous but it was also blessed with fabulous twisting slopes and convoluted trails to explore and a park ranger's habitat that even Joe hadn't dared venture into.

It was absolute bliss for a child of Joe's age.

Joe called out to the boys, but to no avail. The combination of street traffic, splashing water and several hundred people babbling away made it impossible for anyone to hear what was being said ten feet away, let alone one hundred.

Joe set off in pursuit.

From the main gate, the path forked; the left path meandered down to the lake, the right path stretched up to the aviary and the first ice cream pit stop. The boys were taking the lakeside route.

In a flash of cunning thought, Joe decided he would take the high ground, following along the top path covertly and spy on them from afar. They hadn't waited for him after all, and it would be fun to play.

Sprinting up the incline, he quickly reached the summit, losing sight of his prey briefly. They had passed behind the small thicket of trees that also housed the park's toilet amenities.

Even if they looked up when they emerged, he was now camouflaged by the ice cream brigade of hopeful children bellowing for treats.

He waited, hidden in the crowd, for the boys to round the bend a hundred feet below, and sure enough, he was rewarded. The boys drifted into view continuing their lakeside stroll. One bent and picked up a stone before launching it at an unsuspecting group of ducks.

Joe sniggered. *They have no idea! This is so much fun! I'm in 'Call of War', and no-one can see me....*

A little girl promptly bumped into him, falling onto her behind. The ice-cream cone she clung onto for dear life; which came with a double topping of soft scoop vanilla seasoned with crushed nuts prevailed, still held tightly in one hand but her nose was now decorated clown-like. She didn't cry, continuing her goal to systematically lick the ice cream to death.

See! That little girl didn't even know I was there!

Joe moved off, following a cycle route that led away from the kiosk. The path wound directly along the back fence of the park. He was able to utilise and hide behind every tree lining the path, checking the coast was clear before moving on to the next trunk. As things stood, they would converge at the 'mystery maze' (his own personal naming of the rock feature) but even then, a mere twenty feet away, he would remain hidden, obscured by the various rock formations that made up the maze.

That's if they take the maze route. They could decide to walk the long way around by the rangers' hut and forestry!

Joe cupped a hand lifting an imaginary radio 'comms' link to his ear.

"Chikkkkk..." Making the noise of static radio, Joe pretended to communicate with 'Headquarters'. "Charlie One, Charlie One, come in, over..."

He slung the Rapier 900 tightly across his chest. Peeking from behind the tree, he checked the position of the boys who were still in sight, but were now a lot closer, having reached the end of the lake's own pathway. Their direction would lead them up an incline towards the rock features, ending with a fork in the path and with it a decision would need to be made. The boys were only fifty feet away.

"Charlie One, come in, this is Delta leader. Do you copy, over?"

Joe switched voices.

"This is Charlie One receiving, over."

"Good to hear to you. I have the target in sight, repeat, I have the target in sight, over."

"Proceed with mission, I repeat, proceed with mission, over."

Two cyclists, dressed up to the nines in cycling attire, cruised pass the tree Joe was crouching beside. The lead rider smiled, realising the little boy with the toy gun was talking to himself. He nodded to his cycling partner, indicating Joe.

"Copy that Charlie One, over,"

"Good luck Delta Leader, over,"

"Over and out."

The second cyclist gave Joe a friendly parting smile.

Joe lowered his hand. *The mission was on.*

The Rapier 900 was raised; the sight of the barrel aimed at the departing rider's backs.

Blam! Blam!

Joe imagined both cyclists were smashed into the boundary fencing, the force of the blast not only sending the men flying but taking out their bikes as well. Both men were completely pulverised, body parts decorating the park railings in a bloody twisted mess.

Joe made the static noise of the radio.

"Chikkkkk…. Bogeys neutralised Charlie One, mission is still a go, over."

Checking the coast was clear, he dashed over to the rock formation that made up the spiralling maze twenty feet away, ducking down at the first outcrop. With heart racing and holding his breath he cocked the Rapier 900 just in case the boys suddenly appeared.

I'm not going to be surprised, not today. Today was special!

Listening intently, he strained to hear any sign of the boys' approach, there was nothing he could make out over the general hum of the park. Losing patience, Joe peered over the rocks up the path above; nothing, there was no sign of the boys.

They must have taken the longer route, bypassing the rock maze altogether!

Joe breathed easy. Still with hesitant steps, he circled stealthily around the outcrop and headed away from the maze, cutting back across the open grass to the cycle path. Following the direction the cyclists took, Joe carefully crept up the incline to the lip of the plateau that overlooked the cricket pitch. From here the tops of the tennis courts could be seen in the distance, four hundred metres away. Cutting diagonally across the pitch, now only twenty or thirty feet away, heading towards the tennis courts were the four boys. They were close enough for Joe to hear their conversation.

"You know The Mandalorian Season 2 is gonna be awesome!" one boy could be heard saying.

"Yeah well, I think it's overrated," another piped up.

"What does that mean?" the first boy asked.

"What do you think it means!"

"I dunno!"

"It means it's shit, dummy!" a third chimed.

The other boys immediately burst into harsh laughter. The first boy complained, but now they were too far away for Joe to hear what the response was. There was more laughter. He waited until they had covered some distance before continuing along the cycle path which ran adjacent to the field. The slight incline up into the green shielded his position, but still Joe wanted to maintain concealment as he raced along the path to the tennis courts and the playground beyond. Without breaking his stride, Joe called up headquarters.

"Chikkkkk, Charlie One come in, over."

"This is Charlie One, over."

"This is Delta Leader I have successfully reached the green. Permission to engage, over."

"Are you ready Delta one?"

"Affirmative, over."

"Proceed with caution over."

"Copy that, over and out."

Arriving at the start of the long line of tennis courts, Joe turned left, carrying on down the depressed path noting that only a few courts were taken this afternoon.

Not that it mattered. The mission, his mission, was to engage the enemy at the rendezvous point.

Chapter Two

Joe sat waiting on the swings, watching as the four boys approached Harry's Place.

He'd made it unseen ahead of the boy's arrival and now pretended to casually inspect the Rapier 900 whilst covertly checking their progress into the play area.

The playground sat in a depressed bowl, consisting of two sets of swings, one for toddlers and a second one for slightly older children. There was a miserable sand pit positioned at one end which had long since been abandoned; a convenient place for feral cats and dogs off their leads to defecate freely in. A hazardous climbing frame of brutal iron shaped into cubes and loops, designed for one purpose only; to maim and mangle. A roundabout meant for the little people, but so often had the older children claiming sovereignty and finally several 'arty-farty' (as Joe liked to call them) wooden structures that could only have been created by a town council lunatic; triangles, squares and tunnels placed in a haphazard kind of way for children to clamber over and generally hospitalize themselves on. These were all dotted around the playground, randomly placed, almost as if the organiser had dumped the structures off the back of a lorry and driven off.

It was normally quiet in the playground on a good day and today, Saturday, was no exception. Besides Joe there were a couple of noisy toddlers with their beleaguered parents playing on the swings. The parents looked and sounded bored. Enduring the impressive ruckus; waiting for the fun to wear off, so they could all venture down to the local pub, the main subject of their conversations.

The four boys entered the playground, completely ignoring Joe, heading instead over to the deadly climbing frame.

"What about him?" Joe overheard one of the boys asking. He glanced furtively over in their direction.

All four were watching him closely. Joe half smiled back, but looked away, he could feel his cheeks burning hot.

"Nah, he's too small," the dark-haired boy declared, "and it'll make the game unfair anyways." It was the boy who had called one of their number a dummy earlier, the group's vocal leader of sorts.

"Why's that? He looks like he wants to join in as well... Haven't we seen him around here before?"

"It'll be uneven dummy, *duh*...!"

"Yeah, but he's got a gun."

"So what...!"

Joe checked the boys again. Two were turning away, scouting the playground, but the freckled, slightly overweight boy who had inquired was still watching Joe intently. The older lad gave a little wave. Joe smiled back.

"Come on dummy...!" the dark-haired lad said, marching off towards the elongated wooden triangle, "I wanna win the first round!"

The chubby boy shrugged apologetically at Joe before skipping over to the triangle. The two other boys had also trudged off in the opposite direction, heading for one of the wooden tunnels.

Joe watched the group play their game of soldiers over and over.

The bored parents eventually prised their darlings away, with of promises of ice cream and maybe, *if they were very good children*, a trip to the lake to feed the ducks would be on the cards.

Joe was beginning to wish he was going along with them; the ice cream treat sounded good. The foam dart jabbing his back bought him back to the present, it fell to the ground, landing between his feet. It wasn't a hard jab; the boy who fired it ran over to collect it. He had been the one who Joe had overheard asking about The Mandalorian.

"Can I play?" Joe asked the boy.

"Err..." the older boy picked up the loose pellet before glancing over to the dark-haired boy.

"I have my own gun!" Joe showed off his gun enthusiastically, "it's a Rapier 900!"

"Come on Freddie!"

"He wants to play!" Freddie called back.

"We are playing!"

"I can be on your team if you like, I could be...I could be your base of operations," Joe persisted.

"Base of what?"

"Operations... you know, like Charlie One *'come in Charlie One, over.'* Joe lifted his hand to his ear, "Over and out."

"Oh, I see..." Freddie didn't really but played along, "I dunno...Rob kinda likes it the way it is at the moment. You see we got two aside and..."

"...that's ok..." Joe looked away, inspecting the ground.

Freddie's partner came jogging over to join them.

"Hi," Joe gave a quick wave at the newcomer.

"Hi,"

"This is George, I'm Freddie," Freddie introduced.

"I'm Joe,"

"He wants to join in," Freddie explained as if it wasn't obvious.

"We have two teams," George said.

"I told him,"

"I have a Rapier 900," Joe showed George his gun.

"Yeah, I used to have one of those, they break easily. We've all got Nerf guns; they're the best,"

"Mine's ok, it works really well. The loading chamber…"

"What's going on?" The dark-haired boy appeared, pushing his way into the group.

Staring at Joe, he quickly focused on the gun in Joe's hands

"They're rubbish and they're cheap, those bullets don't work in our guns either!"

Joe stared at his Rapier 900. He'd saved up his pocket money for six long months to purchase that gun and the first chance he'd had to show it off he was being told it was worthless.

"Come on Rob, why don't you let him join in," the freckled kid appeared behind Rob, smiling at Joe.

"Because, Russell, you dummy, he'll only get in the way and his gun isn't good enough, that's why."

"But he's here and we could always…" Russell protested feebly.

"I could collect all the bullets,"

All three boys stared at Joe.

Rob gawped.

"I could, you know, pick up the bullets for you," Joe waved at the foam pellets lying around, "save you having to do that."

Russell smiled at Joe, "yeah you could be…"

"No," everyone looked at Rob, "We don't want you to join in with us. Come on guys, let's go!" Rob turned away but still watched to see his friends' reactions, "Come on George!" he persisted, noticing that the others were deliberating.

George shrugged at Joe, "Gotta go," and he left too, scanning the ground for spent cartridges as he made his way back to the wooden tunnels.

Freddie looked to Russell before leaving. Once the three were together, Rob laughed loudly at a private joke with the others, giving Joe a sly backward glance.

Joe handed the foam dart over to the older boy.

"Maybe next time, Joe," Russell offered, accepting the bullet, "we could play…"

"That's ok…" Joe smiled meekly, He felt crushed though. Ever since he'd spotted the boys coming to Henley's Park, he'd wanted to play with them, join in with them, be one of them. All summer he'd been practicing his aiming, shooting tin cans off the little back wall in his garden, driving his mum insane with the clattering noise. He'd saved diligently, obsessed with owning the Rapier 900 after seeing the toy gun in Drake's Toy Shop window display, even begging his mum to bridge the short fall in costs. He was certain they would want him to join their gang after seeing his brand-new gun. He even had extra bullets! *Why wouldn't they let him play?* He was superfast on his feet, and he knew all the words for command control. He'd played *Call of War* on his PlayStation into the late hours, over and over until his game console practically overheated and blew itself up. But here they were rejecting him, pushing him away.

Russell turned away, "See ya Joe,"

For the next twenty minutes he watched the boys play out their games. No other children accompanied with parents came to the playground. The boys had the place all to themselves this afternoon and they took full advantage of the fact. Running up and down the full range the playground had to offer, using every nook and cranny to devise new strategies, screaming with glee and submission whenever they were shot.

All the while Joe watched silently, gently swinging on his seat.

Maybe if I tried harder, they would let me join in. They would have to let me then, wouldn't they?

Joe stood up, determined more than ever to join in.

Freddie peered over at George, "Can you see them?"

"No…they was over by the tree line last time… *ahhhhh!*" Foam bullets rained down from out of nowhere. Russell had just rushed over and sprayed several successful hits.

"Bugger…!" George moaned.

"Hey, what's he doing?" Freddie was watching Joe.

All three watched as Joe bent down and collected the spent bullets.

"He only wants to play with us," Russell stated. He too began collecting the loose pellets, offering a quick smile at Joe.

"GO AWAY!" Rob screamed at Joe, only feet away.

Joe remained rooted.

Rob fired his Annihilator point blank at Joe's face. The dart pellet hit Joe square on the forehead. A perfect shot. It was a miracle he hadn't been struck in the eye. Freddie and George turned to each other. A wicked gleam manifesting: both had the same idea.

They let rip their guns, pumping the action bolts again and again. All the shots hit Joe squarely and forcefully in the chest and body. The spent darts fell to the ground.

Russell looked on, appalled. His gun remained lowered. His heart went out Joe who had barely moved, only to flinch impulsively. Joe hadn't even cried out in pain although he knew from experience it would have hurt being fired upon from that close.

George laughed, Freddie grinned, and Rob sneered.

In a final act of cruelty, Rob walked up to Joe and snatched the Rapier from his grasp. Pulling back the cocking mechanism, he pulled the trigger whilst holding the chamber open. Again and again he rammed the action bolt until it jammed, permanently. The gun wouldn't fire anymore.

"Don't you get it, dummy? We don't want you to play,.......*NOW GO AWAY!*" The Rapier was discarded, hitting the ground hard. It bounced away coming to a final stop in the dirt. It looked broken.

The boys watched for a reaction but there was none. Joe remained stoic, too stunned to react.

"Come on," Rob led the shooting party back towards the swings.

"Maybe someone can fix it," Russell said. He picked up the Rapier and handed it back to Joe, who still hadn't moved an inch, "I'm sorry Joe, I gotta go ," he placed the gun gently at Joe's feet as if laying a wreath at a memorial.

The boys regrouped, occasionally glancing Joe's way.

Head resting on his chest, it was a while before Joe bent down and picked the Rapier up.

"IT'S NOT CHEAP!" He screamed at the boys.

The group, startled, stared back.

Joe turned and ran. He ran until his legs became blocks of lead and his sides hurt so bad that he couldn't breathe anymore.

Chapter Three

Wiping the tears from his eyes and with his cheeks stinging, Joe stood up. Slumped, dejected he began to walk again, the barrel of his Rapier 900 dragging on the ground as he made his way along the boundary fence opposite the tennis courts. Barely noticing where he was going, he was only dimly aware that he was still in the park. The arc of the afternoon sun, still holding a place in the sky, blazed its glorious late summer heat, colouring the ground a golden brown.

Joe hadn't been this far before and couldn't care less. He just walked where his feet led him. Finally, after a hundred metres or so he graced the surroundings with a weary squint.

Where am I?

He gazed left and right to find some semblance of bearing. Frowning, he realised he'd never been to this part of the park.

Was this somewhere near Wesley's gate? I must be...wait, where am I?

Joe took stock of where he actually was. He hadn't wandered out of Wesley's gate. Of that he was sure; the tree line that accompanied the boundary fence which he had been following, stretched on for an age. The tennis courts and playground were long gone. Spying a small gate close by, Joe headed over. Sure enough it was just that, a rusty old iron gate; dilapidated and seemingly no longer in use, wedged open. Joe squeezed through the gap. Overgrown thickets of sharp thorny bushes and ferns immediately flicked and tickled him. He distractedly brushed the leaves and twigs aside.

This must be one of the old, old entrances no longer in use or needed...

The path was visible and as he followed the dirt track away from the park, he felt a little excited as it might lead to a hidden part of the park that only he had discovered a consolation prize of sorts.

It could be my very own secret that no-one would know about! He'd never tell the boys...well, maybe Russell.

When Joe eventually broke through the brush into a quiet side street that ran the length of the park, his disappointment was incalculable. Once again he was crestfallen. It was nothing to get excited about. The old gate was nothing more than that, an old gate, not in use anymore. Another let down. There was no secret garden, no hidden gem. In fact, all he had now was a very long walk home, through unfamiliar side roads with nothing to look at. At least with the park he could have walked along the lake or something.

Joe debated whether to turn around, but the image of Rob taunting him in the park swayed his decision. He didn't want to see them ever again.

Just go home, forget it.

He kicked listlessly at some stones letting one pebble adjudicate, left or right. Either way would lead in the general direction of home. The pebble rolled left. The choice was settled.

Joe set off for home. He hadn't got very far when voices from out of nowhere descended rapidly, overtaking his thoughts.

We've all got Nerf guns, George laughed cruelly, pointing at the Rapier. *I used to have one of those, they break real easy...*

They're rubbish... Rob interrupted, emphasising... *and cheap!*

"Go away!" Joe shouted out to the taunts.

Those bullets don't work in our guns!!

Don't you get it dummy!

Rob's imaginary face shattered into a million pixels.

All three imaginary boys began to laugh and point cruelly at Joe. Russell joined the party picking up his Rapier.

Oh, Joe, it's broken, his face broke into a sneering smile.

You going to cry for your mmmmmmmmuuuuuuuuuuummmmmmmmmyyyyyyy he taunted.

He pointed a long bony finger.

He finished, bursting into a callous, haunting laugh.

"I hate you! I hate you," Joe screamed, *"I HATE YOU..."*

A man spoke suddenly, abruptly interrupting Joe's painful reflection.

"Those boys were just plain mean, weren't they?"

"Huh?" He snapped a suspicious look up at a man cleaning a shop door window, assuming it had to be him who had just spoken. Feeling more than a little embarrassed, Joe glanced away, breathing hard.

Where had he come from? Where am I?

The window cleaner had his back to Joe, standing just inside the shop's entrance, concentrating on the job at hand. If he had heard Joe's awful cry, he made no mention of it. Using long strokes up and down, he worked the windows of the front door like a man on a mission. They looked proper clean to Joe, sparkling fresh as the glass refracted, catching in the afternoon sun. Still, he worked that cloth.

Joe remained still, waiting for the man to speak again.

Did that man say something to him? Did I imagine it?

Joe took a moment to look up and down for anyone else in the vicinity, for anyone else who might have spoken. There was no-one else no-one was close enough.

He was aware of some movement across the street, a hunched over old lady was walking her dog, or rather dragging the poor mutt along without regard to the animal's welfare. Plain ignoring the dog to be precise. Every now and then the dog would detect a scent worth investigating, but was cruelly punished for daring to stop and check. The old woman cursed loudly, yanking on the lead with a vicious jolt. The dog scampered dutifully back in line, but not before giving what Joe thought was a quick look of resignation. *'This is my life'* it conveyed.

"Yeah, it was me talking to you."

Joe turned back to face the window cleaner who was now watching Joe curiously. He noticed the man's eyebrows had exploded with unchecked growth, giving him an owlish appearance. The old man's hands began folding the blue jay cloth. In a second it was folded expertly, vanishing from sight in the blink of an eye.

"Huh?" Joe blinked. He was still staring at the space where the cloth had once been.

The window cleaner broke into a warm smile.

"They were just plain mean weren't they, those boys," the window cleaner repeated, indicating with a nod the direction Joe had just come from.

Joe looked around again.

Where am I? He'd turned a couple of corners and now...

Am I on Lawrence Road, no wait this is Johnson Street, isn't it?

It kind of looked familiar but the roads in this part of town were all grid mapped, a concrete maze. It was so easy to lose your bearings, especially for a nine-year-old. He'd wandered farther than necessary; head down, he'd been kicking loose stones, dejected, fed up, lost in his own world barely holding his misery in check.

"Is this Johnson Street, Mister?"

The old man ignored Joe's question.

"Boys in gangs can be, well...just plain nasty!"

"Well yeah, they were," Joe admitted, "Do you know them?" he searched the old man's face suspiciously. He didn't recall seeing the old man at the park.

"The name's Jenkins and this is my shop," the man smiled again, again ignoring Joe's questions. He turned to appraise the shop's interior as if receiving the keys for the first time, "it's not much but it's all mine."

Joe followed the old man's gaze, taking in the property properly for the first time.

It was a converted corner shop that had once clearly been a house. The cheaply renovated exterior and concreted over front drive, disguised its original terraced style layout. Like dominos the houses stacked together.

The first floor served as a flat. From Joe's position staring up at the windows, the flat had much the same appearance as its lower floor cousin, tarnished and in need of some dedicated TLC.

The shop itself looked worn and tired; flaking paint spread like a rash across the doorframe. Childish graffiti decorated the lower panelling which couldn't hide the fact that it too was rotting to the core, destined for collapse. It looked proper old to Joe, just like the shopkeeper. The man had dyed his thinning hair brown at some point, combing back what was left. Lighter shades of various blondes competed with the dye, and over the ears, grey had won the day.

"Is your shop open?" Joe asked innocently.

In answer the old man spluttered a nicotine laced cackle.

Joe anticipated an accompanying cough to follow but was unrewarded.

"Of course it's open, boy! Seven days a week! Never missed a day in my entire life even when I was supposed to be in bed nursing a fever!"

"Oh, it's just..."

"Run down?" Old man Jenkins finished.

"Yeah, kind of."

"Do you know how hard it is to run a shop, young man? Day in day out, huh? Well do yah? Let me tell you something for free kiddo, it ain't easy. Being on your own has its downside."

Joe remained silent waiting for the old man to expand, but instead he returned to the window muttering an expletive at a mark only he could see.

"Do you know Rob and Russell?"

"I don't know them, but I know their kind!"

Feeling more confident, Joe judged the old man to be harmless.

"Is this a...charity shop?" Joe ventured, staring hard into shop's dark interior through the open doorway. He could just make out a counter to one side. Walls lined with plastic toys and general bric-a-brac. Boxes were placed together without really a thought. They were stacked haphazardly on top of white framed shelving.

"Yes it is. You are clever!" the man spun around pointing a finger at Joe, a look of wonder on his face. The look evaporated when spied the toy gun, "is that a Rapier 900?"

"It doesn't work," Joe lifted the toy gun half-heartedly, swinging the body of the gun away dejectedly.

"Really, are you sure?"

"Yeah, Rob broke it. It was working fine until he touched it. Now it's jammed or, I dunno…"

"Can I see…?"

"Err…"

Joe hesitated, looking down at the crippled toy. Even though he knew the rifle wasn't working, he felt loath to hand it over, and to a stranger at that.

"My grandson had the Rapier 500. The older version …" the old man confessed shaking his head sadly, "Now that was lethal!"

"Did he?" Joe's interest was immediately piqued. He looked closely at the man, suspecting a joke.

"Sure did. I remember he once hit a Heinz can from 30 yards! Shot it clean off its perch…boy, that gun was awesome!"

"That's what I said, but nobody believed me! They all bought the Nerf guns, but I knew that the Rapier was mental! My mum wouldn't let me have the Rapier 500, said I wasn't old enough, but I think the real reason was because it was so………. *powerful*."

"And you were right…here let me see," again the old man reached out, still standing inside the shop's shadows.

This time Joe handed over the gun without hesitation.

"Hmmm…looks alright," the man tried the cocking mechanism. It wouldn't budge.

"Told you so," Joe gifted the shopkeeper a smug look.

Without an explanation the shop keeper about-turned sharply, disappearing into the gloomy emporium.

For a split second all Joe did was… nothing. His mouth, though, went through a series of guppy gulps sucking in air.

What just happened?

"Err…" he stuttered, panicking, "hey…mister!"

From inside the old man called out, "I can fix this, come on in. I got a ton of toys and stuff you can look at,"

For Joe this was more irresistible than the last crumbled cookie in the pack. He crossed the threshold into the shop, keeping one eye on the old man with his prized possession, the other eye scanning the shop's second-hand treasures.

It was a sea of junk.

In one corner, coats and garments sagged precariously on a rail, desperately hanging on for dear life. Immediately above this were ancient looking framed works of landscapes and portraits. On another wall, white shelving units stacked to the brim with children's games and cuddly toys stared back.

The whole shop was cluttered, randomly organised. To Joe it looked a mess...and it was smelly. It reminded him of his Nan when she came to visit. He always held his breath when she gave him a hug. He couldn't resist the impulse to hold his nose whilst pulling a face. If the old man noticed, he ignored the gesture, now standing behind his equally cluttered glass counter, inspecting the gun closely.

"Do you think you can fix it?" Joe asked eagerly, now moving towards the counter, never taking his eyes off the man as he handled the rifle.

"I'll let you in on a secret," the man spoke softly, still focusing on the gun, "I can fix most things... things that need to be fixed," he glanced in Joe's direction and winked.

Joe frowned. He'd heard that before. The expression reminded him of something his dad would often say. He would initially come over and inspect whatever he'd dropped or broken, saying he'd fix it, but ultimately couldn't. Joe's heart sank. When grownups say stuff like that they were generally lying. It wasn't that they were being mean, they just said stuff like that to be kind, and now his dad would never fix anything again.

"Go have a look around and see if you spot anything you like; I might even let you have something for free!"

"Ok,"

Joe left the man to his fiddling. He wandered over to the nearest white wooden unit that presented itself. It had three shelves festooned with toy cars and plastic oddments from various long forgotten games. Most were in terrible condition, dust and rust covered the items like rancid chicken pox. Joe reached out, spying a Hot Wheels Mustang that looked in reasonable shape.

"Here, I think you'll find it's working now," the man announced, causing Joe to jump. The Rapier 900 rifle was held out for Joe to inspect, "Come and see."

"Really...?"

The man smiled as Joe took hold of his gun.

"That was real quick,"

"I've freed the spring here," the old man pointed at a spot along the undercarriage, "works just fine,"

Joe eagerly slid back the mechanism cocking the rifle.

It moved effortlessly, sliding like a dream into position with a resounding and satisfying loud clunk. Joe pulled the trigger and again was rewarded with the metallic sound, this time of a hammer snapping on an empty chamber.

CLICK

Joe's mouth dropped open faster than a magician's trap door.

He stared hard at the rifle, flabbergasted.

"Told yah," whispered the old man, his eyes narrowing to snake-like slits.

"Wow...how...how did you do it?" Joe asked incredulously.

Jenkins tapped his nose, "Can't tell you, trade secret, but trust me when I tell you it's been......upgraded!"

Joe turned the rifle over in his hands, gazing wonderingly at the toy. He knew instinctively it was the same gun, still his gun, and yet it even felt...different, heavier more...more like the real thing!

"Upgraded?"

"Uh huh, especially for you... Joe!"

"Awesome!"

"You'll be needing some of these to go with it," Like a trues salesman, a magazine of red foam bullets appeared from under his dirty rag, held in a plastic clip, "free of charge, ten pops in every mag."

"For me...?" Joe gently touched the first bullet resting on the top of the magazine. The cone tip felt like hardened plastic, similar in design to his old ones, only harder.

"I've never seen red ones before!"

"They slot in just like the old ones did," the shopkeeper passed over the mag. "But I must warn you, it'll kick like a mule, teach you a lesson you'll never forget if you're not careful..."

Joe inserted the magazine skilfully, slapping the clip so it snapped home. They too felt heavier.

Just like the real deal.

He beamed a huge smile of utter joy.

"Hey...!" the man tilted his head with a sly smile, "you look like you know what you're doing there, partner! You know what I think? I think you should go and teach those boys a lesson!" He leaned conspiratorially across his counter, his eyes gleaming with intensity, "Don't you?"

Joe hefted the gun feeling the weight for balance.

"Can you do that for me Joe? Can you teach boy?"

"I....I..." Joe blinked.

"Joe," The old man's voice caressed, "don't you wanna make things right?"

Like a deranged stereo signal oscillating in his head, panning inside to outside becoming one, the old man took control.

"It's a beautiful thing Joe, learning values.... like duty and sacrifice. Can you do that for me? Can you do what's right?"

"I , I want to.....I want to stop being... scared!" Joe whispered.

"Well you can, Joe, you can. Take a stand, go forth and deliver my message, make things right!"

Joe's eyes glazed, rolling white. Listening to the old man, he almost stopped breathing a trickle of salvia ran down his dirty chin.

Rob and the others shouldn't have been so mean! My all new Rapier 900 will kick their butts! Have them running, running for their lives!! I'll be the one now in charge now!!

"That's right Joe, you'll be the one!"

Rob shouldn't have broken my gun!

"No, he shouldn't have!" Old man Jenkins hissed.

They should be taught a lesson!

"That's right! What would your father think, Joe? What lesson would HE teach? Make your father proud, boy!"

Joe looked up at the shopkeeper, his eyes still pearly white.

"Payback time..." Joe dribbled in a trance.

The old man let out a terrible shriek, slapping the counter so hard it should have, by rights, smashed the glass into a thousand million pieces. Straightening up, the awful howl continued.

"You sure look good with that rifle boy! Don't fire it in here for goodness' sake, blow a hole clean through my wall, make no mistake!"

Joe slung the rifle over his shoulder. His eyes rolled back, focusing once more his face hardening, adopting a new found resolve.

"I'd wait until I caught up with those boys before you go shooting. Remember, you've got ten chances, ten shots to make things right...best not be wasting them."

"I won't." Joe gave the man his full attention, a look of reverence replacing the distrust from only minutes ago.

"Then you go get them... *Delta leader!*" the old man winked.

Joe nodded and left.

In the doorway he remembered his manners, half turning, he mumbled over his shoulder, "Thanks Mister," then he was gone.

The shopkeeper stopped smiling, his face contorting into a snarl, baring broken teeth decorated with yellow and brown nicotine stains, "You're welcome," he growled.

The shadows, already saturating the darkened aisles, spread their black curling tentacles over the shelving and clothes stands, enveloping the shopkeeper's body, spilling over the counter. Toys, clothes, et al, faded out of existence. Within seconds the shop was completely darkened save for a spot near the front door. The sunlight struggled to make an impression through the dirty glass.

The front door slammed shut, rattling the window to near oblivion. A toy Mister Potato Head, minus one eye and one arm, perched on the edge of the shelving unit. A lone survivor from the earlier culling wobbled with the vibration, and just when it looked like gravity would claim first prize, a wisp of a black finger, curled from around the aisle, popping the figurine back into place. The dark tentacle slithered back around the corner, merging with the shadowy recesses.

All was deathly quiet in the derelict shop.

Chapter Four

Rob squinted out the bars of the climbing frame, watching George and Freddy taking cover behind the children's roundabout. Unknowingly their heads bobbed up and down above the top of the frame.

So obvious, he thought, smirking, *they must think I'm an idiot! Dummies!!*

Beside him, Russell scrabbled nervously, reloading his Nerf Delta Trooper's magazine, fumbling in the process. Several of the foam bullets escaped his grasp. Russell ignored the fallen pellets and continued loading with a bunch in his hand.

Rob tutted loudly, "You ok there, fiddle sticks?"

Russell grinned back, "Yeah, yeah I got it... thank you!"

Rob's own Annihilator weapon was already fully loaded and ready to dish out its devastating and rapid-fire power.

"What took you so long...I mean come on!" he refrained from laughing and instead gave Russell a look of despair.

"Done!" Russell declared. He held the gun up proudly.

"Finally!"

"You ready?" Russell asked knowing the answer already.

"Oh yeah...since yesterday!"

"Where are they?"

"Where do you think? Only the most obvious place to hide!" Rob shook his head sadly.

"Behind the big tree...?"

"No...! The roundabout.... *obs*!"

"Oh...yeah that is obvious!" Russell grinned.

"Why didn't you say that then?"

Russell chanced a peek.

"Don't, they'll see us....!" Rob snapped.

"No, they won't. We gonna rush them or......?"

"No...! I got a better plan...you rush them and draw their attention while I attack from over there," Rob pointed back to the tree line facing them a little more than twenty feet away. The trees formed a wall of natural camouflage, circling three quarters of the playground. The other two boys were hiding at the entrance to the play area, exposed but for the roundabout. They were sitting ducks, only if he could flank them without being seen. Sacrificing Russell for the glory of victory was a small price to pay.

"Why can't I do that?" Russell protested.

"'Cause I just thought of it!"

"Oh."

Rob shook his head despairingly, giving Russell his best dummy look.

"Why don't we wait for them to rush us?"

"Cause I wanna win this one dummy!"

"We will,"

"Only because of my plan we will!"

"If you say so,"

"Yes I do, now when I go, count to 30…"

"Why thirty?"

"What?"

"Why thirty? You said thirty…"

"I know what I said!"

"So….?"

"Well, why not?"

"Why not twenty?"

Rob hung his head in exasperation, "Russell?"

"Yeah,"

"Can you count to thirty?"

"Yeah, course I can!"

"Then count to thirty!" Rob snapped.

"Alright…keep your hair on!" Russell laughed.

"What?"

"I said…"

"Forget it!" Rob checked his gun for the hundredth time, only there was no need. "Ready," he started.

"One, two, three," Russell began counting quickly.

"Wait!"

"But you said ready!"

"Wait until I go…. you dummy!"

"Oh…."

Rob paused, taking a breath……*how do I always end up with Russell?*

"Ready," he said, watching Russell's reaction carefully.

"Ready!"

Rob sprinted away, up towards the tree line; behind him he could hear Russell counting slowly. He ran with the lightning speed of a Ninja…no of a Superhero. He was The Flash out of the DC Comics. No-one could see him. He was so fast, time itself was slowing down everything became a blur. He made it to the trees in ½ second flat - actually 8 seconds in real time- Hugging the trunk with one hand, he pushed off, aiming for the adjacent tree, heading towards the roundabout. Without even looking in the direction of his friends he slammed into the next tree, panting with the exertion and nervous excitement. Only then did he coolly look around, searching the area below him. To his dismay, Russell could be seen and heard storming the roundabout, shouting blue bloody murder. The other two boys popped up from behind their hiding spot and let rip with their guns, spraying Russell with foam death.

Not now, Russell, you dummy! That wasn't even twenty!
"Hey Rob!"

He jerked, completely caught off guard at the voice. His brain had already calculated who the owner was, but his body reacted differently.

Doesn't this kid take no for an answer?

Joe stood before him, roughly ten feet away, holding the Rapier 900 in both hands.

Rob's eyes narrowed with instant distrust.

What's he doing back?

"Got my gun fixed," Joe swung the rifle nonchalantly.
"So what?"
"I wanna play now," Joe shrugged.
"Go away, I told you we don't want to play with you,"
"But it's been upgraded!"
"Upgraded?"
"Yeah, I'll show you," Joe cocked the rifle.

Rob stared, his eyes widening. *That didn't sound like no Rapier 900! That sounded like...*

"Told yah," Joe beamed, "you'll want to play with it now!"
"No, I won't. Never happen." Rob said.

Joe looked past Rob at the approach of the two other boys.

George and Freddy had collected their bikes, using both hands to push them up the incline. They were still a little way off, laughing at some joke, glancing back at Russell who was collecting the spent bullets. It was easy to see who the brunt of the joke was. Their own guns strapped across their backs, they laboured up the hill. Behind them two women with shrieking toddlers had commandeered the roundabout with quiet authority. Nosing their prams like battle ships clearing a path. The boys had left quickly, gathering their bikes, ordering Russell to collect all the spent bullets.

Aware of the others nearing, Rob spoke with gained confidence, "I don't care about your stupid gun, we don't want to play with you!" chin jutting out, he stood his ground, staring Joe down.

"Hi," Joe smiled at the other boys, lifting the Rapier. "Better than before," he said.

George and Freddie turned to one another, bemused. Leaning against their bikes they waited to see what would happen. *This should be fun*, their expressions read.

"Wanna see?"

George shrugged.

"No, we don…" Rob started. He never finished.

Joe pulled the trigger.

BLAMMMMMMM!

There was a white flash and an almighty roar from the Rapier 900, shutting Rob up completely. George screamed in pain as his bike was catapulted from him, spinning wildly away. Its back wheel disintegrated instantly, taking the bulk of the blast. He collapsed onto his backside, stunned and shocked.

The recoil had knocked Joe onto his back as well. The realisation that the kickback had knocked him off his feet and here he was looking at the tree tops made him let out a whoop of joy. He struggled to pick himself up. His head was buzzing with what sounded like a pack of flies swarming about his ears. His right arm and shoulder felt numb from where he had held the rifle. Shaking his head to clear the buzzing, he looked over to the where the boys had been standing. His eyes focussed.

"That was…AWESOME!" Joe shouted, staring at the Rapier 900 in utter amazement. He said it would kick like a mule and he was right! WOW!!

Rob and Freddie, eyes wide as saucers, stared at Joe's weapon.

"What… just… happened…?" Rob managed to speak, albeit slowly.

"I think that's a real gun!" Freddie stuttered.

"My bike!" George cried hoping his friends would notice.

"Can't be," Rob tried to grasp the situation and failing.

Joe cocked the rifle again.

He loved the sound of that gun loading, he loved it so much.

"On second thoughts," Joe began stroking his rifle, "I don't want to play with you anymore you should leave now…" his voice had dropped an octave.

Rob swallowed. If he left now then he would lose all credibility, even in the face of such adversity. *Stand your ground, he's only a kid*, "No," he managed, jutting his chin out even more defiantly.

Joe laughed back, only it came out as a terrible cackle.

Rob and Freddie stole a look at each other.

"Oh, you'll run alright, come into my shop...STEALING!" Joe snarled, his voice no longer his.

"Huh?" Freddie looked hard at Joe.

"Always the same boys, isn't it?" Joe tilted his head, looking from one boy to another, his voice cracking the syllables, "Think you can wind me up playing your silly games, don't you? *Oh, look its old Jenky, let's wind the old man up let's push him as hard as we CAN!*"

"What is he going on about?" George spoke up.

"I'll tell you what it's about Spotty," Joe lowered the rifle to waist level, "I want you to run."

"Now listen," Rob began, "You can't…"

BLAMMMMMMM!

Joe fired up into the branches of the tree.

Rob was gone. Running at full pelt down the hill towards the roundabout, screaming and yelling in high pitched juvenile alarm, as if not sure which vocal pitch to choose. George was still lying on the ground. Holding his side now, he started to cry miserably.

Freddie remained frozen stiff, a dark patch slowly expanding over his crotch and down his wobbling legs. His eyes still bright and wide, he gawped incredulously back at Joe, struggling to formulate words, "Uh err, uh…."

Russell, still by the roundabout, stared up transfixed, the look of bewilderment etched all over his young features. The foam cartridges he'd diligently collected now lay scattered on the ground.

The two women, after a short pause, leapt into action scooping up their complaining toddlers from the roundabout. Survival instincts activated they wasted no time in getting the hell out of there. Followed by Rob who overtook them, bounding up the slope leading into the playground.

"I told you Freddie, I told you it was upgraded," Joe lovingly caressed the Rapier 900 with gentle strokes, touching the gun as if for the very first time, his voice back to normal.

George whimpered, wiping tears and snot from his sodden face. His twisted, mangled, bike slid off his body as he manoeuvred into a sitting position, eyes glued to Joe.

"My body hurts," he stuttered.

Freddie managed a quick peek at his friend before facing Joe again.

"It wasn't me. It wasn't me. Joe, *right?* Your name is Joe? Yeah, I wanted to play with you, you know that right, you know…" he blurted as fast as he could.

Joe made the sound of static radio, cutting Freddie off.

"Chikkkkk, this is Delta Leader, over."

George turned to look up at Freddie, his desperate expression morphing into one of confusion, "What's he doing?"

"This is Charlie One, go ahead Delta Leader, over."

"Permission to engage target, over."

George and Freddie listened, dumbfounded.

"Delta Leader…permission granted, over."

"Copy that Charlie One, Delta Leader over and out, chikkkkk."

"Hey…" Freddie started.

"You gringos ain't welcome in this town no-more," Joe turned his head and spat. Only it wasn't forceful enough, dribbling sadly down his chin and onto his shirt. Ignoring the spit, Joe cracked a smile, cocking the Rapier once more. The barrel squared straight at Freddie's petrified face.

"RUN!" the old man was back.

Chapter Five

George scrambled to his feet faster than a March hare released from a trap. Pushing the smashed bike aside and ignoring the acute pain in his stomach, he pursued his friend down the slope.

"RUN!" Freddie screamed at a frozen Russell, "He's got a real GUN!"

The fleeing boys were upon their friend in seconds, zipping past the roundabout, they bounded up the steps.

Russell jolted into life. Forgetting his Nerf gun altogether, he too got up to speed, struggling up the short set of steps, he made chase after Freddie and George, all three headed towards the cricket pitch.

Way ahead across the green Rob was now a distant figure, with the two mums straggling behind, their weaving prams taking on lives of their own. It was all they could manage not to lose control.

Joe trotted onto the playground, slowing only to investigate the deserted roundabout. A Nerf gun lay discarded on one of the wooden seats. He recognised it as being Russell's. Prodding the other boy's gun as if inspecting an insect on the ground, Joe stepped back.

"Chikkk, target acquired,"

BLAMMMMMMMM!

This time he'd placed one leg back to steady himself in anticipation. The recoil, still potent and impressive, drove him back, but this time he managed to stay on his feet. The Rapier 900 jumped and almost flew from his hands. It took all his strength just to hold onto it. The devastation caused to the roundabout was impressive.

"Whoa!"

Only he'd missed the gun. Missed it entirely. A massive black hole now presented itself just behind where the Nerf gun still sat in defiance of the punishment it had just avoided. The steel bars surrounding the seat that children used to hang onto, were buckled and twisted out of shape. The carousel itself turned as if gently propelled.

"Huh?" Joe stared in disbelief at the carnage, "How's that possible?" his ringing ears muffling the words.

Are the sights out?

He squinted down the barrel.

Maybe these sights are for the foam darts and now I've got the real deal the sights are useless?

Joe checked the magazine clip, pulling it out fully for an inspection.

How many bullets did the shopkeeper say he had? Ten? Fifteen?

After the old man had handed him the repaired weapon it was all a bit of a blur. Like when his mum would wake him for school; the moment when reality conquered the dreams, vanquishing the sandman for good.

He remembered walking into the park confronting Rob, but before that......?

"Hey kid?" a man's voice called surprising him.

The two cyclists Joe had seen earlier were watching closely, not ten feet away. They had just pulled up. Alerted by the gunshots, they had sped over to see if the boy in the playground was alright. One was scanning the vicinity, both looked worried.

"What the hell happened here?" the man on the right asked, looking past Joe at the wrecked roundabout.

Joe stared back, impassive, ignoring the question.

"We'd better get out of here, Tom!" the man on the left glanced around nervously, "I can't see any..."

"Hey KID!" Tom asked again, interrupting his colleague, pressing Joe for an answer, "did you see what happened?"

Joe slapped the magazine clip back in place.

"Chikkkkk. Charlie One come in, over."

"This is Charlie One, over."

"What the hell," Tom frowned, "it's that kid from before, remember Michael?"

"This is Delta Leader. Please confirm new orders, over."

"You alright kid?" Tom shook his head at his friend, "Does he look ok to you?"

"New orders confirmed...seek and destroy all bogeys, over."

"Copy that, Charlie One, over and out."

"We can't just leave the kid Michael, what if something happens to him?" Tom appealed to his friend, "you'd never forgive yourself."

"Thought you could run me out of town, didn't you?" Joe's voice dropped again.

"What's the matter with that kid?" Michael looked hard at Joe. He was beginning to feel that maybe the boy wasn't the full ticket.

Joe cocked the Rapier 900, watching the men intently.

"Err...what's he doing?" Michael switched his attention.

"Kid come on that ain't gonna help, we need to leave now!" Tom turned to his friend, "Michael we can't just go! Help me get him away from here,"

Joe lifted the rifle and carefully adjusted his aim at Tom. He didn't use the sights.

"I know it was YOU!" Joe growled, "You fucking cowards! Smashing my windows along with those bastard kids...!"

"Tom something's definitely not..." Michael started. He never finished.

Joe pulled the trigger.

BLAMMMMMMM!

When the first gunshot rang out, ricocheting across the playground, both Julie Fennel and her friend Denise Hall jumped as if electrocuted. Their next reaction was to grab the toddlers off the carousel without thinking and pulling their babies to their bosoms protectively. The boy beside the carousel dropped his gun and foam pellets, he too had jumped as if cattle prodded. They had just literary just arrived laying the law down with dibs on the roundabout.

"What was THAT?" Julie managed to speak first, staring wildly in all directions.

"You mean the gunshot?" Denise snapped sarcastically.

The second gunshot had both women spinning around looking in the direction of the tree line. Of the four children that had been up there, one was now running helter-skelter down the slope towards them. Arms flailing, his face a picture of pure terror.

"Did you see where it came from?" gasped Denise, frantically searching the park beyond the kids.

"Over there, wasn't it?" Julie pointed towards the kids with a shaking hand.

"Jesus was that a real gunshot?"

Both ladies began hurriedly strapping their kids into their strollers.

"Let's get out of here!"

"Good idea."

Both the toddlers began to complain and wail.

"Shush darling its ok, Mummy's here..." Julie rammed a pacifier into her daughter's mouth.

"HE'S GOT A GUN! HE'S GOT A REAL GUN!!" Rob screamed as he flew past the women.

Julie and Denise wasted a precious second making eye contact, absolute fear mirrored their expressions.

"Go!" Julie was the first to swivel her stroller around, Denise's a close second.

"Which way?" Julie cried, her voice cracking. She paused momentarily after mounting the small incline, searching the large cricket green.

"That way!" Denise jabbed a finger at Rob's fleeing back.

Halfway across the green, Denise fumbled with her phone, "I'm calling Terry he can ring the police!"

Julie prayed her stroller would take the punishment. The green wasn't exactly flat, and the left rear wheel had been decidedly wobbly of late.

Please hold out, please hold out, she begged.

The third gunshot rang out.

BLAMMMMMMM!

"Ahhh...they're coming closer..." Denise's stroller teetered from the spasm. She struggled to stabilize the pram and hold on to the phone at the same time.

"Forget the bloody phone! We'll ring them when we get out of here!"

"Oh my god, what about those poor kids...?"

"What if it was those kids...!"

"Jesus! You think it was those kids?" Denise chanced a quick backward glance without somehow tripping the stroller.

"God knows, but we're not gonna hang around to find out!"

They made it to the far-side of the green with strollers intact. Hearts pounding, chests heaving, both nearly doubled over from the exertion and both holding onto their sides as if they were about to come undone.

Chelsea, Denise's 10-month-old baby leant precariously out over her pram to stare quizzically up at her mum, her pacifier pumping two-to-the-dozen; a tiny plastic piston working overtime. She pointed a tiny delicate finger at her mother. The mad dash across the green had been exciting. She wanted more of the same.

"Shit, I'm knackered!" Denise panted, sucking in large gulps of air.

"We should be safe."

"I don't think I can walk any further, let alone run!" Denise shook her head.

"You and me both!"

The fourth gunshot rang out.

BLAMMMMMMM!

The women vaulted back into action, pulling and pushing the prams whichever way they could and as fast as their tired legs could muster. It turned out they still had plenty of steam left in the engine room after all.

***

"Good return!" Stephen Benton called out across the tennis court. He still hadn't moved.

After taking the serve, following through, running up to the net, his serve had been for once perfect, an ace in the making. He certainly wasn't expecting a return ball to come whizzing past his head. It was still only a fluke, he conceded, but was Tony finally getting the hang of the game?

Tony Miller, his tennis partner, smiled appreciatively, "Thanks."

Getting a compliment from his Stephen made his heart soar. He knew it had been pure luck that he'd managed to swing the racket at the right moment, striking the ball for the return *and it was in!* If he did manage to connect with the ball, and this was a big if, it would normally end up being launched into the cage fencing that encompassed the courts.

Actually, that was exactly what would happen and although he was hopeless at tennis, it was also fair to say that Stephen took the game just a tad more seriously. Not only did he wear the latest designer outfits and shoes, his equipment was also top notch. The racket was made of carbon fibre as opposed to the aluminium ones sold in Sports Direct. A 'Wilson' carbon fibre graphite no less! Stephen had even taken to wearing a headband more recently. Tony assumed it was in honour of his idol John McEnroe, the flamboyant legendary tennis star. He looked a little ridiculous in Tony's eyes, although he would never say as much.

Their relationship was very much a one-sided affair for most of their time together. For Tony was in love with Stephen. He had been for years, going back to when they had been adolescents playing hide and seek and other innocent games. His awareness of this had come early in their relationship and now Tony was obsessed with being with his friend. Any time he could find to be with Stephen was bliss, and if that meant running around sweating after tennis balls then so be it. That was fine by him.

"40-15," Stephen called out, scooping a ball expertly with his foot and racket.

"Is it still 5-1 to you?"

"Oh yeah."

"Ok." Tony acknowledged with a smile.

He had no idea what the score was, Stephen usually handled those duties. He was content with allowing Stephen the role. A role in which he often fantasised being dominated in by his friend. At home, in the car...in bed.

Both men headed to their respective back lines, Stephen still managing to skip the distance back, readying for the next serve. They had been playing for over an hour now without a break, and his stamina was not even tested. If he was bluffing, he didn't show it. Tony, on the other hand, was knackered. He was totally worn out and craving a cigarette break. The last one had been ages ago. But he waited until Stephen called the break. He would never interrupt Stephen's flow.

They had arrived early to grab a court, only to find the place thankfully and unusually deserted. It could be murder on the weekend, mainly Sundays, sometimes impossible to bag a game. They settled on Court 6, Stephen's favourite, due to the fact it had been repainted recently and the netting was one of the better cared for ones. Some of the other nets were atrocious. Sagging and limp, a poor example of the standard Henley's had once offered. They had quickly warmed up. Serving balls diagonally until Stephen declared he'd warmed up enough.

For the next two hours they smashed away. Tony had only really come along for the ride to be with Stephen. Spending time with him was all he cared about. He was just so glad...

BLAMMMMMMM!

"What the fuck was that?" Stephen shouted, catching hold of the ball right in the middle of a serve.

"Sounded like a gun, a shotgun maybe!"

"My god that sounded close,"

Both men remained rooted to the spot, waiting.

The tennis courts were set ten feet lower, in a depression from the pathway on one side and a tree lined stretch of the park on the other. Only the other courts could be seen in opposite directions, so it was impossible to see 360 degrees. Impossible to see what was going on in the rest of the park.

"What should we do Stephen?"

"Shhh Tony, wait listen..."

Tony patiently waited, staring past his friend towards the children's play area. He couldn't make out much, there was too much fencing distorting the view. It appeared to be empty.

"I think we should go." Tony moved towards the net, "That sounded really close," he looked around, staring up at the high ground.

"Maybe it was a firework?"

"Firework...? Stephen that was hardly a firework!"

"Could have been!"

"I don't think so. Do you?

"I don't know what to think, bloody kids letting off...what they called these days? Bangers. No...air bombs?" Stephen waved the air with his racket.

"Stephen I really think we should go,"

BLAMMMMMMM!

"We should go!!" Stephen declared.

Both made for the exit gate in the fence. Forgetting the tennis balls entirely, Stephen shoved his beloved Wilson 'Flare' graphite racket into its side pocket. Quickly shouldering the designer bag, he left the court without a backward glance or care.

"Come on Tony, what are you waiting for?" he called back.

"What about the balls?"

"Forget the bloody balls!"

"But they're Wilson's!"

"I don't care!"

Stephen was up the stairs two at a time. He'd reached the top before realising his tennis partner was still on the court.

"It won't take long," Tony called up, running to each and every ball discarded about the court. They were everywhere, thirty balls to collect and he was only halfway through collecting them, his bag swinging open, nearly spilling out the collected balls.

Somebody will pinch them. Stephen paid a lot of money for these...

"TONY!" Stephen roared, he was beginning to lose patience rapidly, "What are you doing down there?"

BLAMMMMMMM!

"Oh my god...!" Tony started, literally jumping as the blast reverberated through the court.

"If you don't get up here now, I'm going! Come on."

"Nearly done...wait for me Stephen...wait," Tony ran to collect the last ball, turning, he ran as fast as he could to the exit. Just as he neared the gate, he spotted a lone green ball all the way in the corner.

How did I miss it!

Stephen spotted the look in his friend's eye, "Forget it Tony, it's not worth it mate!"

For a second it looked as if the ball would be abandoned: it should have been.

Tony changed direction and sped across the concrete.

"Won't take a second Stephen...!"

At £1.80 each he wasn't going to let one slip away. What.... and let somebody else profit? No, Stephen will appreciate the effort later.

It was on the far side away from the stairs. Finally reaching the tennis ball, Tony scooped it up and in the process, dropped half a dozen collected balls. They spilled out, bouncing madly as if making a break for freedom.

BLAMMMMMMM!

"Ohhhhh…" Tony moaned mournfully, scuttling around on hands and knees, frantically snatching at the balls, "come here, come here,"

Up on the pathway Stephen slapped his head in frustration.

What an idiot!

Out of the corner of his eye a movement snapped his head round. A boy was running towards him along the path from the direction of the playground. He was less than fifty feet away.

He squinted at the approaching kid. *What's he carrying? Golf club?*

"Someone's coming…," Stephen called out without looking down into the court, "it's ok…it's only a kid."

Tony stared up towards the path, he'd managed to collect all the balls and was now zipping the bag shut. He spotted the boy closing in on Stephen. He looked young, maybe eight years old, "I'm coming!" he called up. As he approached the exit, Tony adjusted his sports bag for the climb up the stairs, he was only three steps away…

BLAMMMMMMM!

"Ahhh!" Tony shrieked, falling back and collapsing completely, his legs useless from the shock.

The gunshot cannoned around the court.

A loud, sickening thud came next. Stephen's body had come crashing down the stairs, hitting the hard concrete of the court

Tony didn't want to look, had too though. Stephen's lifeless blues eyes stared right back at him.

At first all he could do was blink uncontrollably at the incomprehensible sight of his friend's bloody face.

"Stephen, oh Stephen…" Tony wailed, crawling closer to his friend, *"No, no, no…please god no!"*

In seconds, Tony's life had shattered utterly disintegrated he couldn't even begin to compute the situation.

"Wake up, Stephen! Wake up!" he managed to slide a trembling hand under his friend's head, parting the hair the way Stephen combed it back.

He began gently rocking back and forth, cuddling the head tightly. Blood from the gaping hole in Stephen's abdomen lapped blood at Tony like the gentle incoming tide on the beach.

"I love you…you knew that right? Of course you did. We would have been so happy, you know…so happy together…"

The tennis balls Tony had so diligently collected spilled back out, leaving scarlet streaks stretching across the court.

Chapter Six

BAMMMMMMM!

A flash of light and a wave of heat swept over Michael. He also felt his face peppered by some substance, his goggles instantly pebble dashed. The same sensation descended on his shoulders and upper body.

Blood! That was blood!

His brain raced to catch up, to calculate the impossible. Looking down at his torso confirmed what his brain struggled to admit. He was covered in bright red blood and…matter. His mouth dropped open in utter compounded amazement.

If that was blood then….

Michael looked to his right. The space where Tom had been standing was now empty.

But that wasn't completely true, was it? Tom and his bike were still standing. Tom's hands gripped the handlebars tightly. Only he was now minus a head.

A red gush of sprayed blood shot up out of the gruesome ruptured hole. Pulsing, it repeated the action. Tom's head was nowhere to be seen.

"Uh…uh…" Michael tried, but just couldn't formulate any words. He heard the little boy speaking, but it meant nothing. The words were incomprehensible.

Joe picked himself up off the floor. He'd slammed against the side of the roundabout, landing awkwardly on the little step. He winced, his back hurt as if someone had punched him hard and viciously. It hurt bad, worse than when he'd once fallen down the stairs at home. That had been bad enough. Being rushed to hospital, spending the night in that cold and lonely place was nearly as bad as the fall itself. Taking a slow, deep, breath he managed to stand properly.

"Chikkkkk, come in Charlie One, over."

"This is Charlie One receiving, over."

"I'm hit, need medical evac over."

"How bad is it Delta Leader…? Over."

"I'll live, over."

"Continue with mission over, I repeat continue with mission, we will airlift you after you complete the mission, over."

"Copy that."

Joe dropped his hand back down to his side, watching the other man shake and splutter incoherently. The man wasn't a threat to the mission. Curiously, he watched as the first cyclist's body toppled over. Shrugging, he turned and trotted for the steps, exiting Harry's Place without a backward glance.

After a brief scrutiny of the green and seeing no sign of the boys, he chose to head back the way he had entered the playground area, past the tennis courts. Gradually Joe picked up the pace until he was jogging.

Spying a man emerging from the depths of the courts, he held his course. As he drew closer, he could tell the man was aware of him, calling down to someone below in the court. Across the man's shoulders was a large bag, it had what appeared to be a rifle poking out of it.

Joe scowled.

A rifle! The enemy is everywhere now! No time to radio in for instructions, he would have to deal with the threat himself, quickly, before the man drew his weapon!

Joe cocked the Rapier, watching the man's reaction. Without breaking his stride, he positioned the butt of the rifle into his stomach.

"Hey kid did you see what's happening….?"

Joe ignored the question, pulling the trigger instead.

BLAMMMMMMMM!

The man catapulted out of sight back down the stairs, tumbling the last steps and sprawling back onto the tennis court. He was dead before he hit the ground.

Joe landed on his back, hitting the grass verge incline, the force of the landing knocking the wind clean out from his lungs. He hadn't had time to brace himself, letting the Rapier speak as he ran. Stars blinked and sparkled in front of his eyes. He'd never seen the spectacle before now.

Dazed and confused, he rolled over and crawled up the grassy slope, clawing and pulling at the grass with his free hand for purchase, the pain in his back now a constant throb. Upon reaching the top he collapsed, face down, breathing hard.

Just need to rest for a while

Joe closed his eyes gratefully.

You sleep boy, I need to have a word with chubs

Joe twitched then became still, saliva drooled from his mouth.

***

Rob hit the green sprinting and didn't let up. Not waiting for the others wasn't a choice.

He was naturally fast, gifted in fact. He would have been picked for the school athletic team if he'd had the right attitude. There had been the championships at Crystal Palace that summer and Coach Williams at Sandown Comprehensive had encouraged and coerced until he'd been blue in the face, all to no avail. Robert 'Robbo' Kent was a grade A slacker.

Always was and always would be.

What was the point of running around and around on a stupid field! Are you dummies? Huh......?"

He'd point this out to his equally inept crew, punching those that needed a physical reminder of his authority, *"Are you stupid dummies too?"*

No way was he hanging around to see the outcome even if it meant Freddie or George had been hurt. All for one and one for all! Those bozos wouldn't have waited for him, would they? What the hell was happening anyway? Where had that boy got that gun from? The kid was a lunatic, wasn't he? Aiming the gun at his head! Jesus he could have been killed! What have I done? Nothing! Not my fault the kid's a special needs case!

He could hear the desperate mothers panting and squawking behind him, the third blast of the Rapier came just as he reached the end of the green.

Surveying the park from the cricket green's elevated position, Rob took a moment to appreciate the spectacle before him.

Life in the park had come to a standstill; it was like a picture postcard, a snapshot taken for the Sanford tourism board.

A day out in the park! The caption would sparkle.

Except in this picture all the people were facing forward, alarmed statuettes staring into the sky, as if witnessing an aerial display or the second coming. Even the children had joined in the fun, mimicking the parents; the ones closest were gawping and pointing at him.

It's not me you dummies!

He was about to race on down onto the path that fed round to the lake when a thought occurred to him.

The police would be coming soon. They might think he had something to do with it, right? Oh yeah, they definitely would. Knowing the police, they would round up all the parties, guilty or not, and then what? They would dig up his little record of petty thieving in the town centre and then what? Another afternoon spent counting cracks in a cell. No thank you! I'll take my chances at the Wesley gate entrance.

Rob scanned the route to the Northwest entrance. That would mean cutting back along the edge of the cricket green. He'd be exposed if Joe chose to come that way.

Where to hide?

Spying the high walled wire fencing of the Rangers' Forestry, Rob afforded himself a cheeky little smile.

Maybe hide out in the Rangers' compound? Joe wouldn't come that way and he could definitely hide from the police. Yes, that's it! A brilliant idea Robbo! Besides, wouldn't the police surround the park anyways? Exiting the park would be virtually impossible. He'd be there in a minute. Slip inside the gate somewhere and hide deep inside the small, dark wood. The forest was a Nature reserve, after all. Perfect for the job! Let Joe and his wonder gun find him in there! And even if he did come in after him, we'll be waiting, won't we? He would have the advantage this time.

Rob immediately took off heading down the path towards the Rangers' lodgings without another thought, just as the fourth blast erupted.

***

"Hello? Hello?"

"This is the operator. Please state which emergency?"

"Police, I need the police now! Quickly...!"

"Transferring you now, please stay on the line, thank you."

Julie stared at her mobile.

"What is it?" Denise queried, seeing her friend's expression.

"She said thank you...? Why would she thank me?"

Denise shrugged, now watching the distant horizon for movement.

"Just courtesy, innit," she replied.

The two women had made it to the bandstand, halfway to exiting the park. A fair number of people, still unsure of what to do, had gathered there, milling about. There was safety in numbers.

Julie and Denise had joined them, parking their strollers against the far side, hidden from view. The gossip was buzzing. Worried faces were peering periodically over to the Northwest part of the park, now long deserted. The main topic from the crowd; did anybody see what happened?

Denise lit two cigarettes, passing one to her friend.

"Thanks babes,"

"Maybe we should just go, Jules?"

"Let's just..."

"You're through to the police, can you tell me what the emergency is?"

"Oh yes! Hello...erm we're in a park...err," Julie stuttered

"Henley's Park," Denise chipped in.

"Right...Henley's Park! There's been gunshots! Someone is firing a gun! You need to get over here as quick as possible!"

"Ok, slow down, Madam, which park is that again?"

"Henley's! It's in Sanford!"

"Is that Sanford, Essex?"

"YES! Isn't this Romford police station?"

"No madam, you've come through to Bow Station police call centre, we handle all calls for the area."

"Well, we're in Essex!"

"Ok. You can hear gunshots, is that right?"

"I just told you that!"

"Did you see the gun or gunman, madam?"

"No."

"Has anyone been shot?"

"I don't know do I...? We all just bloody ran!"

"I understand. Please remain calm. Can I take your name, Madam?" Julie obliged, "Please stay on the line."

"What did they say?" Denise drew hard on her cigarette.

"Stay on the bloody line!" Julie snapped back, shaking her head.

"Bloody useless...!"

"Whatever happened to, 'we'll be right there, thank you for your co-operation'.......!"

"Maybe we should go," Denise repeated, stubbing out the half-smoked cigarette, "what do you think?"

"Did you ring the police?" A man standing close by enquired. He'd been watching the women closely.

"I'm hanging on right now," Julie indicated her mobile phone sarcastically.

"Right, right, sorry," The man nodded apologetically, "Did I hear you say you saw the gunman?"

Denise shook her head, raising her eyes skywards irritably, "No, we just ran, there were children back there as well,"

"Wow, it's like something out of a movie!" the man nearly gushed.

"It's not funny! You wasn't up there!" Denise snapped, adjusting the pram.

"Err... No sorry...I didn't mean..." he stammered, looking quite contrite.

"Don't worry about her, she's just scared," Julie half smiled.

"Right...me too... You say you were up there? Wow...must have been quite scary being that close,"

"And some......!"

"Hey...who are they?" the man had caught sight of George and Freddie at the top of the hill.

BLAMMMMMMM!

Everybody stopped talking. The two boys started running down the slope towards the bandstand.

"IT'S THEM!" a voice shrieked.

Pandemonium ensued.

"It's those kids!" Denise calmly deduced, squinting hard.

"Shit I forgot about them, should we go with them?" Julie motioned at the rapidly departing crowd.

"Nah, I still haven't recovered and I'm still holding on, remember."

"Fair enough babes. Want another ciggie?"

"Go on then."

"You know what? I bet it's all a big joke, something to do with those kids!"

"You reckon?"

"Yeah, they were with us in the playground, remember?"

"And we've been right mugged off!"

"Little shits!"

***

The First Contact operator, Linda Hicks, clicked the hold switch, leaning back in her seat, "That's the second one, sir," she called over her shoulder to her supervisor, Sergeant PC Wallis, whilst typing the info into the Computer Aided Despatch (CAD) system the Metropolitan Police used to monitor and collate all calls.

The operator recorded the phone call as procedure. Once the CAD number was created, it immediately responded by pinging up the (I) Grade of response (Immediate response requirement) alerting police in the corresponding area that an officer was needed urgently at the location given. The monitor the operator was using indicated that an IRV (Incident Response Vehicle) had been tagged and was now on its way.

This would happen four more times in the next twenty seconds. Monitors were lighting up all over the wall.

Inspector Forbes, one of two Duty Officers in charge of Communication Operations at the Bow Police HQ for North and East London, studied the CCTV monitors lining the huge call centre walls and made a critical decision. Making his way over to the four pods utilised for despatching services, he called ahead to the despatch supervisor, "Where's the nearest ARV's?"

"Chelmsford sir, two are heading down the A12 as we speak,"

"Alert them,"

"Already done guv."

"Guv...?" Another operator called over. Unlike the first operator who was a civilian, she was a serving policewoman. PC Roberts had been in the post for three years. She sat four desks along to Hicks in a group of twelve First Contact operators.

"Tell me."

"I've got another one."

Another arm was raised, "Sir you should really listen to this!"

Forbes made his way over to the operator, taking the woman's headset, she tapped the replay button.

"Several shots have been fired...you should send someone."

"Did you see the gunman?"

"No, I didn't....but there's some ladies here who say..."

Before the man could finish, a distant gunshot could clearly be distinguished in the background.

"Oh my GOD! You need to get here quick!"

Forbes had spent time with an armed unit. His training buddy at Hendon had applied for the specialist unit. He knew the sound was genuine. This was for real.

"Did you hear that?"

"Jesus Christ!" Forbes threw the headset at the operator, "Get every Area car available up to the park to clear a path for Trojan 1 + 2, I want that main road blocked off as of yesterday!"

"Yes guv."

"All IRV's in the area to assist,"

"Yes guv,"

"Give me Sanford on screen will you," he called down to an operator, "A127, A12, all cameras, everything we got."

Eight monitors flickered in response.

Forbes snatched a phone up off his desk, "Get me the Super at Romford, right away."

Inspector Forbes spoke quickly.

"We have a possible 279 in progress, in Sanford, sir."
"Authentic?"
"Five...wait,"
Sergeant Wallis held up both hands.
"Ten contacts now sir."
"Whereabouts exactly?"
"Henley's Park."
"Christ that's huge."
The Superintendent cleared his desk.
Forbes' next call was to his superior upstairs.
"Sir, possible 279 in progress,"
"Where are we with it?"
Forbes gave everything so far.
"Trojan 1...?" He looked over at PC Roberts.
"...7 minutes guv,"
"Seven minutes away sir,"
"Is Romford aware?"
"Romford is sending everything they can spare as we speak, ETA 5 minutes."
"Let Chelmsford know as well, might as well have back up. Any Area cars, they have to be made available south of Brentwood, I want those park exits blocked, I want every inch of the park's perimeter covered, nobody move until we clear the park, understood?"
"Understood sir,"
"Inspector, get a team in the Command room, set up SOPs, we're taking it from there,"
"Understood."
Forbes surveyed the room, "Sergeant, get me four PC operators now, move to SOP's command centre now, we're running the show,"
"Yes guv."
"Clive you're in charge of comms here." Forbes nodded to his colleague before returning to his desk and snatching up his mobile. He messaged his wife about the 'good news' as he left the room.
Sergeant Wallis tapped PC Roberts on her shoulder, "You're with me. It's your lucky day constable!"

Chapter Seven

"Just run!" George cried, taking point. If his stomach hurt he was putting on a brave face.

The two boys headed out over the cricket green, in pursuit of the fleeing women. Sapped of energy from the initial sprint, and not known for their agility, the boys slowed down. The blast of the third gunshot cancelled out any doubt they might have had whether to hang around or not. They picked up the pace.

"He's gone mental!" Freddie managed a snapshot look behind.

"What is that thing, is it a real gun?" George called out.

"That ain't no Rapier 900!"

"Mine never did that," George declared, as if wishing some models were able to wield such devastating destruction.

"My mum would never allow me to have one if it did!" Freddie conceded.

The fourth blast came as they neared the edge of the green. The two women in front sprung back into action, dropping from view, practically dragging their strollers away. Their cursing continued down the incline towards the lake. Of Rob there was no sign.

"Where's he gone?" George panted, trying to catch his breath as well.

"Who, Robbo? He left us behind, remember? Who cares!" Freddie stared back across the cricket green searching for Joe.

"Didn't he used to say running was for dummies?"

"Yes he did!"

Both boys managed a quick snigger, a release of emotion more than anything else.

"I can't see Joe anywhere," Freddie gave up watching the green. Pulling his Nerf gun round to check for damage, "We lost all those bullets!" He sat down dejected.

"Bummer dude!" George checked his clip for bullets, "Oh no!"

"What?"

"Our bikes!"

Freddie suddenly pulled a face, "What happened to Russell, where's he got to?"

"Wasn't he behind us?" George joined Freddie on the ground, laying back.

"Last time I looked he was,"

"He is a dummy!"

Both boys let out a cruel laugh.

Below, the crowds were migrating mostly in one direction, towards the main gate entrance. Some had congregated by the bandstand, some were by the lakeside, and most were staring up in their direction. The two boys rested for a while, occasionally glancing back across the green.

"Look at all the people…"

"…Yeah, like ants!" Freddie finished, "if only they knew it was just a kid!"

"Hey," George pointed to the crowds below, "You don't think they think it's us, do you?"

"Nah, do these look like real guns?" Freddie lifted his toy gun.

"It might to them!"

Both boys looked down at the crowds and back to their guns.

"Oops…I didn't think of that!" Freddie waved his gun dramatically, "bang bang your dead!"

"Come on I'm tired, I wanna go home!"

"Yeah, me too. Let's get out of the park."

"Good idea."

"Wanna come over to my house? We can watch The Mandalorian."

"Ok."

Positioning their Nerf guns once more across their backs, the boys moved off.

"I'm not running anymore though," Freddie announced boldly, stepping onto the winding path.

"Me neither,"

"Can't be bothered."

"Me too."

With that declaration of independence, both boys swaggered down towards the lake, feeling tough and cocky.

They had survived, they had seen the gunman, they had laughed in the face of death…they had….

BLAMMMMMMM!

The two boys started running once more.

**

Russell let out a whimper, holding his ears tightly. Clamping down hard, even with his eyes screwed shut he couldn't stop the tears from seeping down his young cheeks. Taking shelter behind a large and seasoned oak tree, he cowered, pulling his legs tight within his arms, making himself as tiny as he possibly could. He was only forty feet away from Joe.

"He doesn't know you're here, he doesn't know you're here, he doesn't know you're here."

Over and over Russell mumbled the simple mantra, softly and quietly, willing the words to be true.

When Russell had fled the playground racing up the slope, he'd initially followed Freddie and George's fleeing backs, but his gut instinct kicked in and rather than choosing to escape across the cricket green he'd chosen to head towards the tennis courts. Split up! Screamed his brain, SPLIT UP!

There had been adults playing earlier, the thwack of tennis rackets smashing balls had been the background soundtrack all afternoon. Adults meant authority. So he doubled back, crossing the play area to the opposite side of the tennis courts. There were trees which he could hide behind potentially. As he made it to the embankment, from the corner of his eye, he could see Joe making his way down to the roundabout.

The echo of another blast rang out just as he made it to the first large tree. Freezing on the spot he hid behind the large oak, unable to move. A quick glance confirmed Joe was still in the playground staring at the roundabout.

Keeping his back to the playground, he sprinted to the next tree and then the next. The voices of two men floated up from the courts, their words were unintelligible, but he picked up the alarm in their voices. He'd paused by the tree nearest to the men. Jumping as the fourth blast ricocheted through the park he'd hunkered down, his legs shaking from fear. One of the men below had now climbed the steps and was calling for his friend. Russell clearly heard him say, "Someone's coming...its ok it's just a kid," then the gun roared again, this time so close he almost cried out in terror. Quelling the urge to cry he waited.

"Hey fatso……….!" Joe called out.

But it wasn't Joe's voice anymore. It was deep and raspy.

Russell stopped breathing.

Is he with someone now? Oh God no...he knows you're here!!

"I know you're behind that tree boy! Come out!!" Joe shouted again as if reading Russell's thoughts, "I won't shoot you I promise! It wasn't you who was stealing from my shop...it was your friends...I know that!"

Russell ignored the request. Quivering uncontrollably, his bursting bladder chose to empty its contents at that very moment.

"I saw you run over there, fat boy!"

Russell remained rooted to the spot. Joe would have to run a fair way round the courts just to get to him.

BLAMMMMMMM!

A sizeable clump of earth exploded to Russell's left. He let out a squeal of pure fear.

"I was your friend Joe!" He called out.

There was silence, then.

"There's no Joe here chubs...!" the deep voice growled back.

Russell gasped. How is he doing that?

A good five minutes passed before he dared to open his eyes again, listening for signs of life, of the men, of Joe.

All that could be heard now was a quiet, sorrowful, lament; a man softly crying, distressed and traumatized. It was coming from the tennis courts below.

Standing and finding his strength Russell shuffled around the old oak tree to gaze down into Court No 6. Two men lay stricken on the concrete floor. The muffled sobs he'd overheard were coming from one of them. He was stroking the head of the other, making cooing noises, accompanied by little whimpers. The ground surrounding the men was a carpet of red.

Of Joe there was no sign.

Russell backed away afraid the man might suddenly detect his presence and call out for help. There was nothing he could do to help anyway.

Get out of the park! You have to get out of the park! Now!!

Russell, terrified, turned and fled.

Where to go? The railings go on forever!

To the little boy, exhausted and terrorized, indeed they did go on. Looking left, they stretched as far as the eye could see back past the playground and into the hazy distance. To the right, the railings met with a right angle of the park. Large, detached houses with opulent gardens backed onto the park here, carrying on the perimeter past the cricket green and eventually onto the lake area. This would lead him to the West Gate entrance, but...

Joe might be that way? Wasn't he heading that way? He wouldn't head back to the playground, would he? Would he?!?!

The Park had turned into a prison. A prison with six-foot railings topped with lethal pointed spikes, designed to stop detainees. He had never climbed them before, wouldn't know how to. The extra pounds he carried had seen to that.

Russell let out a little whimper before turning left, heading for the Wesley's North West Gate entrance, praying that he wouldn't bump into Joe, all the while mentally kicking himself.

Should have followed George and Freddie, why didn't I just follow the boys? Stupid, stupid, stupid!

Now he really was on his own.

***

"Police are on their way madam," the operator spoke in Julie's ear.

"Finally!"

"They won't be long. Are you out of the park yet?"

"Yes, we've made our way to the entrance," Julie winked at Denise.

"Good, please do not go back inside. Stay away from the park, the police will seal off the entrances."

"I won't thank you."

"You've been great, thank you Julie." The line went dead.

"What'd they say?" Denise had lit another cigarette and was puffing furiously, pacing around her stroller with the look of a tormented soul. In her stroller Chelsea was taking a nap, now being as good as any time.

"They're on their way!" Julie mimicked, "and I've been great. It's alright for her sitting in a cushy office probably having a laugh right now!"

"Right...! Probably sending two bobbies straight out of Hendon, still wet behind the ears!"

"Hendon...?"

"Yeah, you know! Just finished their training, it's in Hendon, London."

"I didn't know that," Julie muttered, checking on her little darling, Maddie, who was studying the bandstand's occupants suspiciously.

The sound of wailing sirens could now clearly be detected, growing in volume, screaming through the neighbouring town. They appeared to be coming from all directions, overlapping with each other and forming a symphony of electronic alarm.

"That doesn't sound like a couple of wet backs just out of Hendon,"

"Bloody hell, sounds like they've brought the bleeding cavalry,"

"I think you're right."

"We should go, Jules!"

Denise swung her stroller in response, calling after her friend, "come on, it'll be murder getting out of here now!"

The two women swiftly joined the migration already exiting the park. Passing the deserted ice cream kiosk, Chelsea woke up as if by instinct pointing to the large 99 Chocolate Flake advertisement.

"Sorry babes! Ain't happening…!"

Chapter Eight

Joe rolled onto his back, allowing a little whimper to escape his dry lips. Blinking up at the blue heavens, he realised he had been asleep. *How long have I been laying here?* The throbbing pain he felt in his back was now constant and unabating. He stared up at the vast clear Essex sky tracking a high flying bird as it glided gracefully using thermals to conserve energy. The serene silence of the park was deafeningly quiet, not even the background hum of town traffic over a mile away breached the tranquillity. It was as if time itself was standing still in Henley's Park.

Maybe I could lay here just for a while longer. It's so peaceful and quiet.

Joe once again gratefully closed his eyes, letting the serenity aid his retreat from the pain, drifting away with...

Chikkkkk Delta leader, come in Delta leader, over!

Joe blinked, coming out of his slumber, confused. *Where was that coming from? He hadn't put his hand to his ear, calling for instructions. What...?*

Groaning with the effort he sat up, pulling the Rapier 900 across his lap. The gun was still impressively heavy, still so realistic.

Delta Leader, do you copy, over?

The voice of command centre, the one he'd used over and over invaded his thoughts again. Louder, clearer, pressing.

Joe slowly put his hand up to his ear.

"This is Delta Leader, over," he said tentatively.

Good to hear you're ok Delta Leader! Status update!

Joe looked around, staring wildly about the deserted cricket green.

Where was that coming from? Who was saying that? There was no-one around.

"I don't want to play no more...I just wanna go home now," he stuttered.

Mission is still a go over

"I just wanna go home now," Joe repeated, his eyes starting to blur.

Negative, I repeat, that's a negative. Complete the mission, I repeat, complete the MISSION!

"But my mum will be angry with me for being late..."

Delta Leader you need to finish the mission!

"But my back hurts real bad" Joe replied, tears formed threatening to spill over.

Then another voice joined in, coming from a long way, whispering like the wind.

Jooooooooooo......

He froze. Was that....*Dad?*

Jooooooooooo......

His father's voice, as he remembered it, now clear as a bell, brought goosebumps all over his body.

"Dad...?"

DON'T LISTEN TO HIM!! HE LEFT YOU BEHIND DIDN'T HE? WHAT KIND OF A FATHER DOES THAT!?!?

The voice of command screamed, overriding the whisper, slamming the door shut on his father's voice. Only now Joe recognised the other voice. The voice of command. How could it be him? How is he in my head?!?

You finish the mission NOW, BOY! Those miserable bastard kids need educating. They need to be brought to justice!! You get up and do as you're told!! You get up or I'll make sure your mummy gets her justice as well...Do you understand me BOY!

Without raising his hand this time and tears now falling freely, Joe responded, "Copy that Charlie One...mission still a go."

Maintain radio silence, over and out! The old man growled.

Wiping the tears and snot on the sleeve of his shirt, Joe struggled to his feet. Rubbing his lower back to alleviate the intense pain, he surveyed the immediate vicinity, confirming what he already knew. The place was deserted. His target had headed somewhere towards the East of the park, possibly already had left the park.

He had to find him... and finish the mission. Maybe he's down by the lake? Or hiding in the maze? Better get going...

If Joe heard the circling police sirens, he chose to ignore them. Holding the Rapier across his chest, he fell into a stumbling trot crossing the cricket green diagonally, heading for the lake.

***

Henley Park's main entrance resembled the grand opening of a visiting funfair on carnival night. Only there wasn't a single cheer, no applause welcoming the bandleader. Just a low pitch grumbling hum of concerned voices.

It hadn't seen numbers like that since the time an amateur woodwind quartet from Chelmsford commandeered the bandstand, treating the good people of Sanford to a performance of Tchaikovsky's Swan Lake. Fly-posters had littered the area only days prior to the concert. Billed as 'A Day in the Park' it had gone down rather well, a minor success that had never been capitalised on, mostly because it was impromptu at best. Now it was topped by another extemporised event.

Most of the people exiting the park had heard the gunshots to some degree, the park's elevated plateaus and heavily wooded sections muffled and distorted the impact of the noise, but the acoustics over the open terrain were mostly incredibly clear. Some people had just upped and left without needing encouragement; others packed away their picnic hampers, reeled in their fishing rods, gathered their little ones and some, well they just went with the flow, better safe than sorry. But all begged the same question: *What the hell is going on here?*

Instead of dispersing completely, intrigue and curiosity held the crowd, glued by their fascination. Their numbers swelling with passers-by joining the fun, generated from the common inquisitive nature that human beings possessed: to stand and stare.

The four promised police cars which had arrived from Romford Station strategically blocked the A118 main road that the park fronted. First on the scene, they quickly assessed the need for major back up. They got it.

The crowds were spilling onto the road, swelling in numbers. Fuelled by the traffic-jammed occupants, realising they weren't going anywhere soon, who were now exiting their vehicles rubbernecking for a better look.

Local residents, not satisfied with peering from behind lace curtains and blinds, braved the unknown and ventured out onto the street as well.

What's going on?
Is it a carnival?
Has there been an accident?
Has someone drowned?
Do you mind not leaning on my car? This is my driveway!

Police motorcycles, relieved of traffic duty, arrived next, struggling to re-route traffic back up at the junctions before it could join the already stricken drivers. If they could, it was chaotic. They were fighting a losing battle.

Joe's mum wandered through the fringes of the crowd, scanning faces, shapes and colours, desperate to spot her son. Pushing deeper and deeper into the throng of bodies, her anxiety growing by the second.

She had heard the sirens screaming past her house, only metres away from the main road. Maternal instinct had taken over. Dropping the screwdriver she had been using and wandering out into the back garden, she had seen a sight never witnessed before; the mass exodus of Henley's Park.

All along the lakeside, Janine joined residents lining their back gardens, staring across the water into the park's depths hoping to catch a glimpse of the gunman.

"What's happening?" she asked of her neighbour.

"Gunshots Janine, there's been gunshots!"

Snatching her mobile phone, the only necessity, she ran all the way to the park's entrance. Her earlier premonition of angry crowds chanting and calling for blood became all so real as she approached. All that was missing were the banners.

Why hasn't Joe come back! Is he in there somewhere? Oh God!

The babble of conversations she first encountered only heightened her growing apprehension; all were talking of gunshots, a rogue gunman, a serial killer, *a possible terrorist threat!* Of course, no-one knew, all were wildly gossiping, all misleading. The crowd was talking, taking over the construction, building a tower of uncertainty.

She had to find her son*, but where was he?*

Janine began calling out, rapidly resorting to indiscriminate cries of desperation, every salvo drawing attention, but not from her Joe.

The police were turning up in larger numbers, battling through the crowds and pushing back, holding the perimeter. Unsympathetic, methodical, and thorough, they formed a cordon from the entrance back to the road and adjoining pavement. A police BMW X5 ARV followed by a riot van swept through the gates, narrowly missing policemen and civilians alike.

"My son is in there!" Janine protested vehemently at the first policeman she came across holding the line.

"Madam I'm sure he's out by now," the constable replied, holding firm.

"I can't find him! He's in there, I know it!"

"You'll have to wait here, I can't let you pass,"

"Please, please I have to go in there!"

"Everyone is out now madam!"

"PLEASE!"

The cop ignored Janine's requests, easily distracted by the hustling deluge.

Frustrated, Janine continued her search, calling out for her son. She set off, making her way to the other side of the perimeter.

"JOOOOOOOOO...!"

Two boys turned to stare perplexed at Janine's disappearing back, now swallowed up by the pressing onlookers. They had hung back after exiting the park, excited by the arrival of the police and the growing intensity of the crowds. Being smaller, they easily held their ground by the perimeter but were now bored with the jostling and noise.

"Did she say Joe?" Freddie asked George.

"Yeah, she sure did!"

"You don't think...?" Both boys turned to stare incredulously at one another.

"That's his mum!" George spluttered.

"That's insane bro!"

"What are the odds?"

"Million to one.........!"

"Shall we tell the police?"

"Nah, they won't believe us, will they? Think about it...!"

"Yeah, you're probably right," George admitted. His face then lit up devilishly, "Hey, why don't we follow her and see what happens."

"Maybe she's a nutter as well!"

"Mental!"

"Come on!"

The two boys pushed their way through the crowd in pursuit, determined not to lose their quarry.

***

The Park Rangers' compound was ramshackle and a mess. There was no visible sign of life. Rob climbed over the top of the large metal gate easily, pausing to check the hut for movement. It was a cross between a wooden shack and a stone outbuilding. Still no Ranger appeared. If he was going to appear, now would be the moment to repel his advance. Rob was anticipating the man to suddenly appear, screaming his head off.

What are you doing here? Get out! This isn't part of the park, be off with you! Rob had had his fair share of authority yelling at him. But there was nobody.

Moving on, he crossed the clearing, a driveway of leaves and hard mud, passing an old Land Rover looking tired and in need of some major TLC.

Without wasting any more time, he left the compound, following the track that led into the woods. On both sides, the tall pine trees and conifers dominated the forest's interior, hugging the pathway oppressively. Before long he was deep into the canopy of evergreen.

Hah! This'll be perfect! I'll wait it out here!

Choosing a route going directly into the forest, off the track, Rob scanned his choices. It wouldn't really matter where he chose to hide. It all looked the same.

Maybe I should climb a tree?

Since arriving, his next move had eluded him.

Was it enough just to sit behind a tree? Sit it out and wait for the park to close? If that dummy wandered in here, he would definitely spot him first, or if he was luckier still, the Park Ranger would nab him and turf him out!

Rob decided to move deeper, further into the dark forest, taking the chance that deeper would be safer.

***

Hugging the fence line a good fifty feet away from the playground's outer rim, Russell could see it was devoid of life, Joe hadn't come back this way.

Looking beyond Harry's Place into the distance, to the Northwest the park opened up. The area was a deserted manicured open ground. He would easily be spotted if Joe turned his gaze on this part of the park. It would be far too dangerous to traverse this section. Russell knew only too well that he would be a sitting duck if he ventured out onto the grass.

Nowhere to hide. Better to stay close to the fence where he could see Joe coming at him from a distance... but where was Joe?

With worried feet, Russell set off, constantly glancing back, expecting the threat to re-manifest itself out of nowhere at any second.

He almost didn't register the old dilapidated gate as he trotted by. Barely open, the rusty gate had gone unnoticed in his first scan of the landscape, just another dark green section of the railings he'd not spotted.

What a stroke of luck! Oh, thank you! THANK YOU! A way out at last! Home!!

Peering cautiously into the thicket beyond, Russell tentatively stepped through the opening, brambles and thick overgrown bushes awaited. Leaving the park with one last sweep for Joe, of which there was no sign, Russell disappeared into the undergrowth. In a matter of moments he knew he would be homeward bound, safe and sound, regardless of where the gate led out, it would surely lead to a road he could use.

Chapter Nine

PC Gary Collins, part of the Road Traffic Unit, seconded out of Romford, parked his BMW RT 1250 police bike at the junction of Johnson Road and Wilmot Street. Kicking the stand out, he scanned left and right, and in the middle distance to his right he saw his colleague, PC Laurie Anderson, who had just cruised up and was doing the same thing, blocking the next adjacent road junction, preventing traffic from joining the long picturesque suburban park road that ran next to Henley's Park.

He'd received direct instructions from the Communications Command Centre at BOW to get his arse in gear over to the park. He cancelled the coffee break he was just about to enjoy at the BP's Soldier of Fortune service station he and his colleagues frequented regularly. In fact, he'd just pulled up and was just fancying which tasty pastry had his name on it. PC Anderson, laden with their coffees was about to divide up the sugar sachets when despatch relayed the call.

"Bollocks!" Anderson placed the large cappuccino takeaways on top of the waste bin outside the convenience shop's sliding doors, they both fell over. "That's the second time this week!" he said.

"Jinxed, that's you, fucking jinxed," Collins shook his head, mentally reminding himself to avoid parking up with Anderson for a couple of days.

"279? She did say 279?"

"Henley's Park," Collins confirmed.

Collins stared longingly at the abandoned coffee. A BP worker was staring at the mess.

"Jesus!" Anderson pulled on his helmet.

"Blue light run buddy."

Anderson shot out of the garage forecourt first, engaging his blues and twos. They cruised up the slip road in tandem, watching, then slowing, for the nearside traffic to acknowledge their presence. Almost immediately they were released, and the men unleashed the awesome power the RTs had at their disposal, accelerating up the busy arterial heading towards Sanford, their screaming sirens and flashing lights parting a channel down the fast lane.

Arriving at the chaotic A118/A127 junction, the men received new instructions to join and support a Trojan team advancing from Wesley's gate in the Northwest.

"Detain any person or persons exiting the park, no exceptions."

"Any updates?" Collins asked the commander..

"Only that the park...we think that the park has now been vacated and we're looking for the shooter or shooters only, but there may be stragglers or casualties and until the armed response boys have cleared the area you are to hold back." The commanding officer passed on the information.

"Should any suspects hop it over the railing you and Anderson will provide visible presence and if needed, chase down the culprits........ *now get going!*"

The two traffic cops sped off to join the team at the park. A Divisional transit van pulled up on Collins' left, joining a BMW X5 ARV already parked further along, depositing five constables before coasting to a stop in the middle of the road. This part of the park was covered. The police began to slowly fan out, all watching the railings from a safe distance.

Collins watched as a group of armed police clambered over the railings further down, before spreading out and heading for the interior.

He gave the neighbouring houses a once over, noting that already the occupants-come-ghosts were materializing in their first floor windows.

Alerted by the flashing blues, bewildered versus quizzical looks competed, Collins noticed.

Wouldn't be long before they ventured out, braving it to the front gardens. Then the enquiries would start.

Collins was prepared.

Oh Cappuccino, how cruel! It wasn't meant to have been...! If only he'd been ten minutes earlier coming to the garage!

Collins sighed, settling in for the inevitable wait. An image of the mouth-watering pastry that had his name on it joined the abandoned coffee...*bollocks, its bloody Anderson's fault!*

***

Joe checked his position at the cricket green's edge, overlooking the park. The vista below was an unusual one. Certainly he'd never seen it before, not like this. It was as if he had the park all to himself.

Awesome! But then...where was everyone? Was the park closed now? But it's not late... is it?

Looking down to the lower section of the park, the lake and bandstand areas were all deserted, devoid of people. There was no cyclists, no deck-chaired OAP's licking their dripping ice cream treats, no squawking children in prams demanding attention. There was... nobody, not a living soul. Not even a single annoying dog, hell bent on hunting down turbo-charged squirrels. Further afield still, he scanned the small thicket of trees that enclosed the public toilets. Nothing was moving.

From his position the trees obscured the main entrance from view. It was eerily quiet, but this was his park and even if it had closed early there was no problem, he could just climb over the gate if needed. Joe began to fantasize what it would be like to have the park all to himself every day. Just like this, just like it was right now.

That would be something wouldn't it? He could play Call of War all day every day! He would invite only the right friends to play here too! He could do anything he wanted...

Chikkkkk this is Charlie One come in, over

Joe tensed. Forgetting the view, forgetting his dream park fantasy. It evaporated, pushed rudely aside in an instant. His breathing accelerated: fear and apprehension growing.

Why won't he leave me alone?!?

Again the voice of command spoke, pressing for a response. The old man was back.

Come in Delta Leader

"This is Delta Leader, over," Joe replied impassively, his arms limp by his side.

We have new intel. Proceed immediately to the Park Rangers' compound. I repeat, we have new intel

"Copy that," Joe murmured.

Then another voice spoke, drifting with the breeze.

Joooooooooo..................

Joe spun around, "Dad?"

There was no-one there, he was all alone in the park.

Joooooooooo................

His father's voice, clear as the day was long, swept through, blurring reality; a reality already splintered struggling to not shatter completely.

How could this be, his dad talking to him right now, how was it possible?

Joe eyed the Rangers' compound not two hundred feet away, the throbbing pain in his back a reminder that all was not well.

Finish the mission. That's all he had to do. Then he could go home, and all the weird voices would go away. His mum must be looking out for him from across the lake by now, worried sick probably

Taking a deep breath, Joe hefted the Rapier 900, cocking the mechanism, he loaded a bullet.

"Let's finish this."

***

Janine had reached the end of her tether. There was no sign of Joe anywhere. She had screamed herself hoarse, pushed and elbowed her way through the other side of the crowd.

Now more determined than ever to be taken seriously by the police, Janine made it to the front line, tapping the shoulder of the nearest cop.

"Hey…," the constable snapped, zeroing in on her immediately, "I won't tell you again madam, do not…"

"MY SON IS IN THE PARK!" She screamed at the man.

A second cop appeared, backing his colleague up. He stared hard at Janine. The people nearest Janine had at first grumbled at her barging her way to the front, but shocked at the intensity of her emotional outburst, they watched this latest development unfold.

"MY SON…" Janine sobbed, unable to hold the tears back any longer.

"Alright miss… alright," the second cop interrupted raising his hands, "calm down. Wait there." He left to confer with a group of officers by the main gates.

"As if you're bleeding well going anywhere, honestly!" An old lady standing beside Janine tutted loudly, "they don't care, do they," she began kindly, before suddenly erupting, "Oi! Do you mind…?" The old lady gawped at George and Freddie as the boys barged their way to the front.

The second cop returned with his superior in tow.

"This lady says her children are in there still guv, very insistent she is too,"

"Please! It's my son…he's…he's still in the park! You have to believe me!"

"Madam," the officer began patiently, "there's nothing I can do until we apprehend the gunman."

Janine's eyes wavered, the heat, the stress…, it was all too much. She could feel her legs going.

"I suggest you wait…"

"She's telling the truth!" A young voice cut in.

Everybody looked down at the boy. Janine stared, amazed at the two boys standing beside her. She reached out and gently caressed George's Nerf gun strapped across his back.

Could these boys be Joe's friends?

"We know, because we left him in there," George added, giving Janine a strange look before pointing at the entrance, as if offering an idiot, directions to the park.

"You know Joe?" Janine asked George, her heart racing.

The Sergeant had heard enough. Turning away, he was about to head back when Freddie delivered the words the crowd never dreamed of hearing.

"Yeah, we know him. He's the one with the gun!"

All eyes descended on the lad.

***

A noise drew Collins' attention away from the kindly old gentleman offering him a cup of tea.

The man had appeared from the quaint well-kept property on the corner of Wilmot Street and as predicted, enquired *"what the hell was going on in his street?!"* He then produced a rattling tray with the beverage and a saucer full of hob-nobs. The old man had been waving to the constable from his garden gate for a full minute before Collins gave in and acknowledged the kind gesture.

"Excuse me officer, would you like some tea?"

"Please sir, go back inside. We'll inform you later…"

"Do you take sugar?"

The bush on the park side, no more than twenty feet away from the pair, began to rustle and move.

Collins moved quickly round his bike, forgetting the old man, forgetting the tea and biscuits.

What the hell?

A child appeared. A boy, no-more than twelve years old, looking wide-eyed and very much relieved, stepped hesitantly into the road. His clothes looked like they had been to hell and back his hair was much the same. It was as if the lad had been in a tumble dryer on long spin and managed to climb out somehow. He looked spaced out. And on top of that, what struck Collins the most was the fact that the boy didn't even seem to be aware of the large police force presence up and down the street.

Where had he come from? The park……..?

"Hey you! Kid!" Collins shouted, "Come here now!"

The boy blinked, registering Collins for the first time since appearing from the bush.

"Yes you! Get over here now!"

At first Collins thought the boy would comply, but instead he turned, looking back at the park.

"He's in there!" the boy shouted, his weak voice cracking

"Who's in there? Get over here now!"

"Joe! He's still in there!"

Collins moved fast for a big man carrying a few extra pounds he shouldn't really have. He leapt into action, moving before the boy could finish his sentence. Not surprisingly, the boy moved faster. Having a head start made all the difference.

The boy sped across the street, easily outmanoeuvring the large policeman.

"Oi, stop! *STOP NOW!*" Collins shouted at the boy's back.

But Russell didn't stop, wouldn't stop, in fact he wasn't going to stop for anything short of home.

Running past the resident on the corner still holding the rattling tray of crockery, he made it to the copse of trees behind the property, vanishing inside before PC Collins could swing the bike round.

"He's getting away!" the old boy declared.

"Shit!"

Collins sped on down the road, hoping to catch the boy on the other side.

***

Joe arrived at the forest past the Rangers' compound. The pines and conifers dominated the view, stretching impossibly high. He had to crane his neck just to see the tops. The track leading into the woodland disappeared from view almost immediately, twisting into obscurity.

Without so much as a glance in the direction of the Park Ranger's home, Joe squeezed his slim frame between the gate's iron bars, wincing as he straightened his back.

Why doesn't the pain go away?

Shuffling now, for each step cruelly reminded Joe of the injury to his back, he made a beeline for the forest track, entering its dark, evergreen canopy. The forest hummed with its own life-force, birds calling to each other near and far bounced throughout the wood as if from stereo speakers, panning from left to right.

Pausing to take in the contour of the land, Joe switched directions, choosing to leave the rough track and instead began ascending the incline into the trees. It was harder to proceed but he would have a better vantage point over the lay of the woodland.

His target could be anywhere, better to climb to higher ground.

Each step brought with it another small twinge of pain. He hadn't gone more than ten agonizing steps when the snap of a twig startled Joe; it was close, real close. Spinning round, he reacted, pulling the trigger without thinking.

BLAMMMMMMM!

The Rapier unleashed its cannon, blasting a massive chunk out of a large pine tree, not ten feet away, exposing the tree's yellowing flesh. For a second the tree seemed as if it would collapse.

Luckily for Joe there was an open space of soft earth and bark chippings to cushion his landing. It was still agonising. Slowly and laboriously, Joe managed to pick himself up, using the Rapier as leverage whilst listening out for any signs of the target. There was none; he'd simply panicked, the sound of the forest tricking his senses.

Jooooooooo.........

His father's voice whispered in his ears.

"Where is he, Dad?" Joe whispered back.

Silence answered.

Chapter Ten

Janine and the boys waited inside the park gate's entrance as instructed, watching the police officer walk up the short incline that led to the park keeper's drive. A dozen police officers huddled round a Divisional van, specially kitted out for communications and surveillance.

Two other vehicles were there, one a larger police van used for riot control, the other a police BMW X5 ARV with all its doors left wide open. Three heavily armed policemen stood by the vehicle waiting; adjusting their body kits, they looked serious, ready for anything. After a brief conference, all the men at the Divisional van turned to stare at the group. The Sergeant waved Janine and the boys to come forward.

"My name is Chief Inspector Carmichael, I'm in charge here," the police officer wearing a decorated cap spoke directly to Janine, glancing briefly at the boys.

"My officer here tells me that your son is still in the park is that right?"

Janine nodded.

"And you two," Carmichael now looked at the boys, "know who the gunman is...is that right?"

George and Freddie nodded back.

"Okay, tell me everything you know," the inspector fronted the two boys, watching their faces closely.

Freddie and George both began at once

"He's gone mental..."

"We didn't know..."

"He has a real gun..."

"But it looks like a toy gun..."

"Whoa you two slow down...one at a time...you," Carmichael pointed at George.

Taking a deep breath, George told him everything, beginning with the war game earlier in the afternoon, the arrival and dismissal of Joe, and finally the reappearance of Joe and the subsequent shootings.

Janine's head wobbled, computing George's words.

"Now listen carefully, young man," Carmichael had a hard stare, chiselled from years of working and dealing with uncompromising situations and he was employing it to its best effect right now, "You're telling me that there's a nine-year-old kid out there and he's got a high-powered rifle?"

"Yep, that's right," George nodded, giving his best hard stare back.

Janine gasped, "That is not true......! My Joe hasn't got a gun! What are you saying?"

George shrugged as if to say, *'not my problem'*.

"It's true, lady!" Freddie backed his friend up, "You didn't see it... he nearly killed US!"

Carmichael studied the group one by one. Time was running out fast, he'd wasted enough time here, holding back the Trojan unit when he should have released them into the park.

"Okay, that's enough, you can wait over there," he pointed to an ambulance further up the drive.

BLAMMMMMMM!

Faint, but still easily recognizable, the bark of a powerful weapon stunned everyone into silence.

They all heard it. They all stared into the park's interior.

"Sergeant, get these people out of here!"

"Yes sir," the officer turned to propel the group away, "Come on you lot, follow me,"

"WAIT!" Janine resisted the tug, "what about my son?" she said to the Chief Inspector's back.

Carmichael paused, but could only meet Janine's eyes in response.

"He's just a boy!"

He turned away, instantly surrounded by swarming staff and the armed response unit leader.

"Dylan!" The sergeant called to a colleague.

"Come on, you can wait here," the officer impatiently pointed up the drive.

"Oh God," Janine muttered. Now completely distraught, she felt sick and faint. She had a profound premonition that Joe was caught up in this somehow. Déjà vu tapped on her shoulder. Do you remember me, it asked?

The woman, PC Dylan joined the group escorting them to the ambulance, "This way madam, this way...c'mon let's go."

George and Freddie grinned at each other, barely able to keep their excitement in check. As far as they were concerned this was the best Saturday afternoon, ever!

The Trojan leader received his instructions, and without fanfare he jogged back to his men and all four piled back into their car without a word. In seconds it was ripping up tarmac, taking the right fork towards the aviary enclosure and the high ground.

***

At the last second Joe saw the branch coming. He only had to time to partially duck. Turning away wasn't enough to stop the impact. Sending him stumbling forward, the force still knocked the wind out of him and released his grip on the Rapier, which flew out of his shocked hands.

"HAH!" Rob screamed, pouncing on the loose rifle, "GOT IT!" He backed away, grinning insanely at Joe, "HAHA I got it, I GOT IT, you lose!"

The pain was so intense that Joe couldn't help but cry. There was no sound, but the tears easily flowed. He couldn't stand. He felt sick and it hurt so bad all over his upper body that now even his arms were failing him and even if he wanted to, he couldn't bring himself to stand, instead facing Rob on his hands and knees, he stared vacantly at the boy's midriff. Blood trickled past his eyebrow, the gash on his forehead opening up. He felt so tired he could sleep forever.

"Now it's your turn to see how it feels, huh! Not so clever now are you, you fucking freak!"

Rob cocked the rifle. The mechanism slid easily but with a subdued sound, the normal sound a plastic toy gun would make. Staring at the rifle in disbelief, Rob pulled the trigger.

Pfftt.

"WHAT?" he screamed at the gun, *"What's wrong with you?"*

Joe levelled his gaze at Rob, taking in the situation.

What happened? Was it broken? Had Rob broken it again?

Rob ran the short distance between them, releasing a vicious kick to Joe's stomach.

"You deserved that, you crazy little shit! Not my fault! NOT MY FAULT! You deserve it!"

Circling Joe's prostrate body, Rob surveyed the rifle, once more pulling and smacking the loading bolt.

"Why doesn't it work huh? Tell me the secret, freak! Why doesn't it work?!"

Rob swore continually with mounting frustration, still desperately trying and failing to operate the Rapier's bolt mechanism.

Joe ignored Rob's pacing and cursing. Lying curled up and inert on the pine carpet floor he stared ahead, not really seeing anything. Even the pain he was feeling had retreated to a numbing ache. He wondered if his mother was missing him and what she had prepared for tea. Chicken nuggets. He hoped it was chicken nuggets, chips, and beans.

A bush facing him shimmered as if disturbed by a gentle wind. Joe squinted hard at the bush; forgetting his pain, forgetting Rob, he tried to focus on the rustling plant.

For a second he could have sworn…..

Blinking rapidly, trying to clear blurry tears, Joe gasped in shock. His father, dressed in his army combat fatigues, sat across from him. There was no mistake now. It was exactly how Joe had remembered last seeing his father, the day before his deployment to Afghanistan two years ago.

"What's your favourite animal Joe?"

"Lions!"

"Really? Not the tiger? I thought you loved tigers."

"Uh uh, tigers don't roar."

"Is that right?"

"Uh huh. They have the biggest roars, Daddy! Raaaaarrrrrrrr!"

"That's right they do."

"I like lions!"

"My little man…….Joe the Lion!"

"When will you be back?"

"That's a really good question Joe. I need you to do something for me. Can you take care of mummy for me little man? Can you do that for me? Just until I return?"

"Is mummy sick?"

"No…she just needs you, and I need you to be a good boy and take care of her for me. Will you do that for me?"

"I will Daddy, I promise!"

"That's my boy."

"Raaaaarrrrrrrr……….!"

"Hah….! I love you Joe, remember that."

"I love you too, daddy."

His father broke the trance with a smile. The kind affectionate smile Joe remembered whenever his father acquiesced to his relentless demands, scooping him up or hunting him down and finally tickling him until Joe screamed for mercy. The same warm, fatherly smile that said, 'everything's alright'.

Joe returned the smile, "Daddy………" he murmured softly.

Another tear fell. This one was of joy. An all's well with the world kind of tear.

The Rapier 900 clicked loudly. The bolt mechanism abruptly loaded a bullet into its chamber. Rob let out a whoop of crazed glee. He stopped pacing around.

"YES! YES! *Finally! At last!*"

Joe's father nodded, holding the same treasured smile, I love you he mouthed silently.

"Let's see how you like it, huh! Freak..!" Rob shouted down at Joe. Raising the gun, he aimed the sights at his legs, *"I AIN'T NO DUMMY!"*

He pulled the trigger.

BLAMMMMMMM!

***

The Trojan unit raced towards the Rangers' compound. It reached the habitat in under a minute. The X5 skidded sideways to a halt near the gate. Exiting the car with guns drawn, the team divided, two men quickly dispersing through the clearing, circling the cabin. They split up, swiftly entering the building, kicking down the doors front and back.

"ARMED POLICE......!"

Sweeping the building in seconds the men called out directives.

"Clear!"

"Clear!"

The men reappeared, training their guns into the woodland.

"Charlie One proceed into the woods," a voice from operations commanded.

"Copy that."

Charlie One motioned his team to move on.

"Alpha One, I've got one body at the playground," Delta, the second Trojan unit checked in.

"Understood, proceed onto the Rangers' Compound from the Northwest."

"Copy that."

BLAMMMMMMM!

All the men crouched defensively at the report.

"What was that? Who fired?" Operations radioed.

"We got a gunshot coming from the forest."

"Can you see the gunman?"

"That's a negative."

"Proceed, sweep and clean."

"Copy that."

Charlie One motioned the team to move out. Standing as one, they quickly cut their way into the woodland. Scanning the terrain, Charlie One indicated they should fan out, pointing two fingers for his men to head down the path and into the woods on the left, motioning for his partner to follow his lead on the right. They wasted no time, combing the forest, clearing each tree.

"I got something," one of the team whispered into Charlie One's earpiece.

Charlie One halted his advance.

"Talk to me."

"Two kids, 2 o'clock."

Charlie One checked the vicinity, "I got nothing," he whispered back.

"Fifty feet...one is armed."

"Copy, wait for my signal."

"Copy that."

Charlie One motioned his man to follow, indicating the higher ground. Creeping stealthily, they covered the distance quickly, his scope soon picking out a boy that was pacing back and forth, holding what appeared to be a semi-automatic rifle.

He was no-more than thirty feet away. He was shouting to someone on the ground. They were too far away to hear what he was saying. Charlie One silently side stepped two feet to his left. He saw a second boy now, lying still, curled up on the ground.

"Target acquired." he whispered into his mic.

"Confirm gunman?" Operations asked.

Charlie One paused. In his sights the boy had a gun...*a boy!* He couldn't be more than fifteen.

"Charlie One, I repeat, confirm gunman!"

"Confirm," he whispered.

"What is the situation?"

"One boy down, condition unknown, immediate evac, second boy..." again Charlie One paused, swallowing, "second boy...threat."

There was silence, then;

"You are Green, I repeat, green light."

"Copy."

Charlie One watched as Rob lifted his rifle and took aim at Joe. Without hesitation he squeezed the trigger of his Heckler and Koch MP5 semiautomatic machine gun.

***

Russell turned a corner, chancing a glance back down the road. Nothing. The scary policeman with the bike hadn't pursued him down this road. He was alone. Granting himself a reprieve from running, Russell lent against the window display of a shop to catch his breath.

Where am I?

He took in his surroundings. Staring up and down the road, he looked for a familiar landmark, a building, a house, a signpost, anything that would reveal his location. After running from the policeman on the bike he'd kept his head down and run. Nothing here was recognizable. He was standing outside a corner shop though. Decrepit looking, Russell examined the name above the doorway.

Second Time Around

The dirty windows and flaking woodwork revealed an out of business, graffiti ridden derelict shop. An old lady walking her dog across the street appeared from behind a parked car, oblivious to his presence, she was practically dragging the poor mutt who would stop to smell a scent, only for the lead to yank its head before it could get a proper sniff in. As they passed, the dog stopped to stare over at him, checking him out, even though it must have been anticipating the cruel hand of the owner about to dish out another vicious snap.

"That was some adventure?" The old man's voice surprised him.

Russell spun round to see an old man admiring the shop's window display from inside the open doorway. He'd seemingly come from nowhere. Certainly it seemed that way to Russell. He hadn't been standing there moments ago.

"Am I right?" the man pressed, now facing Russell, his ancient face cracking a thin smile.

Russell turned to check behind; was he talking to me? There was nobody around. The old lady and the dog were long gone. He nodded carefully, rooted to the spot. Suspiciously checking the old man over, the sudden appearance had taken Russell by surprise, and he was fed up with surprises for one day.

"Phew wee, that gun was something else, wasn't it?" the old man continued, "I mean...WOW! That thing could blow a hole clean through a Sherman TANK!"

"Was you there in the park?" Russell found his voice.

"No, young man I was not! But I sure as hell heard it!"

Russell frowned, "But if you weren't there, how would...?"

"This is my shop," the old man said, proudly gesturing at the shop. Completely ignoring Russell, he produced a dirty white rag from his back pocket which he used to wipe aggressively at the tarnished windows.

Russell watched the old man work, unsure of what to say next, then remembering the time, announced, "I gotta go mister..."

"You want an Annihilator to replace the one you lost?" The old man continued to work the windows.

"What…….?"

"I've got a whole bunch of those Nerfy things in my shop…" the old man spun his hands and the cloth disappeared.

Russell stared, google-eyed at the spot where the cloth had been moments before.

Where did that go? Was that a trick?

"You wanna come inside and see?" The door to the shop was now fully open, revealing a darkened interior, "I got all the latest stuff! See?"

A rack of Nerf guns held centre stage inside the shop. All kinds of tantalizing colour matched weapons in all sizes presented themselves. The beautifully wicked adornment cried for attention.

The old man hadn't moved but was looking intently at Russell. A tiny pointy triangle appeared out of the old man's mouth, black and glistening, it caressed obscenely at the upper lip.

"See anything you like?"

"I gotta go mister," Russell mumbled, transfixed, but repelled by the sight, "My mum will be worried!" he took off running.

There was no looking back. Russell ran as hard as he had been running all day, maybe even harder. There had been something, something chilling and tangible stroking his back, a malevolent presence coercing him towards that doorway.

But he had been alone, hadn't he? There was no-one behind me!

There was no question in his mind that if he'd stayed there a second longer, he would have been through that door… *and that door hadn't been open when he arrived had it!*…well it would have shut behind him snappedy- snap as soon as he'd stepped in. Russell was sure of that, as sure as eggs are eggs. The old man scared the life out of Russell, more so than Joe and his terrifying gun, so he fled….*escaped…*

Russell knew deep down, he just knew……….. he had escaped someone or something of pure evil.

Chapter Eleven

"All units move in!" Charlie One ordered.

The men burst into the clearing, screaming their mantra, "ARMED POLICE! DROP IT!"

Rob froze, dropping the Rapier 900 instantly as if he'd been scalded. It clattered harmlessly onto the ground, just a cheap plastic toy rifle.

Charlie One grabbed Rob, spinning him around and forcing him onto his knees with a ruthless kick to the back of his calf, "Don't move!"

Rob cried out as the handcuffs tightened their hold, "It was him...... *IT WAS HIM!*" he pleaded.

"Shut up!"

The men covered the area, revealing they were alone.

"Clear!"

"Check the boy!"

"He's still breathing, just about."

"Call it in."

"Copy."

Charlie One picked up the toy gun. Inspecting it revealed what he had first suspected, *hoped* was a better word. When he'd first sighted the gun in Rob's hands he gambled the two were playing and this wasn't the real gunman. He'd aimed high.

A Toy! Jesus Christ...thank fuck he'd aimed high.

His radio cracked to life.

"This is Delta One. We got two dead bodies.......making our way to you."

"Copy,"

"Guv?" one of his men asked. They still had a job to do.

"The gunman's still out there," he announced, "you two with me. Charlie Two, wait here for Delta."

The men set off without question.

***

An armed policeman from Delta unit gently lowered Joe onto the bench seat in the back of the riot van, positioning him upright against the window.

"You'll be alright kid, your mum's here waiting," he informed Joe kindly, "won't be long now."

Joe stared ahead, if he heard the policeman he didn't respond. He hadn't said a word since being scooped up and carried out of the woods.

"Here take this with you," the Delta CO handed the officer the Rapier 900 before sliding the side door shut. The journey back through the park was a bumpy ride, but the policeman watched over Joe, mindful that he didn't slip off the seat.

Judging by the state of the boy, he wondered what kind of hell the kid had been through. The rest of his team had carried on the search, along with Charlie Unit, sweeping the park, still looking for the elusive gunman. The cop sat back turning the Rapier 900 over in his hands.

His own son, Adam, had an enviable collection, enough, in fact to supply a small battalion in the neighbourhood.

At weekends the carnage would start. Foam pellets carpeted the patio like an infestation. His wife hated the fact that Adam was playing war games, she hated the guns. The irony wasn't lost on the cop.

"This is Alpha One, come in Charlie One over."

From habit, he'd switched his earpiece to radio before getting into the riot van. The message was coming through loud and clear, bouncing around in the small metallic confines of the van.

"This is Charlie One, over," a voice responded.

"Proceed to operations for debriefing over."

"Copy that."

The policeman switched his radio off, giving Joe a conciliatory half smile, "like I said kid, it's all over now."

Joe raised his head to stare vacantly back.

"Is your dad here as well? Bet he'll be relieved to see you, huh?" he got no response, "My kid had one of these…well something like it, you know what I mean."

Joe continued to stare.

"Here, you can have this back." The policeman handed Joe's rifle over, suspecting the kid wanted his toy back. There was no reaction.

He sighed.

Kid's been through a lot what did you expect… gratitude?

"Delta Leader this is Charlie One, over."

The cop stared curiously at Joe. *What the hell was he doing? Is he mimicking the radio?*

Joe had raised his hand to his ear, staring intensely at the policeman.

"Mission is still a go. I repeat mission is still a go."

"Hey kid you alright?"

Joe reached for the Rapier 900 sitting beside him, sliding the mechanism back. It delivered the authentic locking sound of a real gun loading a bullet into the chamber.

The policeman started, sitting up, drawn to the sound of the gun loading. He stared incredulously at the toy gun.

"What the...?" he began.

"Mission still a go... copy that," Joe murmured dreamily, raising the rifle and aiming at the cop.

"Hey kid...." Delta Two sat bolt up..

"He won't let me go." Joe whispered.

"What did you say?"

Joe pulled the trigger.

***

PC Dave Collins cruised up and down the streets looking for the chubby kid. He'd got released from the park duty and wanted to give the area one last sweep before he clocked off. After hearing that some kids in the park had been in some way caught up in all the events, he'd realised his big mistake in letting this one slip away from him.

Little shit had taken off like a bat out of hell, definitely up to no good!

Pulling up outside the old charity shop on Johnson Avenue and Hamilton Drive, he dismounted, stretching his legs before the long ride home out of town. He had been cleared to clock off. The corner shop was good as any to stop for a cigarette.

It was a futile exercise anyway, looking for the runaway. Too many parked cars for the little urchin to hide behind. He'd be long gone by now. Playing hide-and-seek from a cop came easy for kids, especially with so many places to duck behind, but you never know, he might strike gold. They had no fear of authority, kids these days. They weren't afraid of the police.

Respectful? What a joke, more like resentful!

Collins wandered over to the shop's windows. Run down and poor condition, he remembered the place well, remembered him more like. Cantankerous old man at the best of times, he wasn't a likeable soul to many.

Removing his helmet, Collins peered through the dirty panes revealing a barren and vacated shop. Only smashed shelving units accompanying broken display stands could be seen.

Vandals disguised as children had rifled the property, leaving their business cards of urination and desecration. They had been generous throughout.

Collins stepped back. Lighting a cigarette, he scrutinized the upper floor windows. They looked much the same. Some, like the shop, had been boarded up.

Didn't the old man used to live in the flat above the shop? He couldn't be sure. It was so long ago now. The exact details eluded him. But he did remember what happened. Oh yeah, that one remained embedded. The gory aftermath: he remembered it like it was yesterday.

What was his name again? Jones, Jackson? No....Jenkins... that's it, old man Jenkins

Always the same, go check out the complaints, calls from both the public and the old man alike. He would comply with the request from despatch, heading out eventually to the shop, but knowing what to expect each time. He wasn't the only one that had to deal with the old timer, but he was the one most associated with the place. The one with preceding history that went way back.

"Those kids are stealing. They're always causing me trouble... what you gonna do about it? What you gonna do about those bloody kids, huh?"

Old man Jenkins would spit, literally, the corners of his mouth congealed with thick white spittle like glue holding the lips momentarily. Every sentence was destined to contain several projectiles. Jabbing his gnarled bony finger at Collins' chest, his face contorted with uncontrolled rage. He always wore the same clothes, or he did every time Collins visited, it would seem. Smelling of damp cardboard and worst things. If he stood too close the faint acid tang of urine and other delightful scents would waft over.

He always expected the old man to suddenly remember him from the early days, back in the day when he was a child, browsing the shop's wares. His own family home only two streets away, he would wander in, intrigued, and fascinated by the piles of junk. Back then it had had staff, atmosphere and even a splash of quirky charm. He'd felt welcomed.

But the recognition never came, the old man too consumed by his hate. A group of feral children in the area; nasty pieces of work, would harass the old man. Once they had got their juvenile claws sharpened, stealing and general troublemaking followed, slowly but surely eating away until they found his breaking point.

Laughing as he stumbled out of the shop screaming for blood, the kids would easily evade his efforts, taunting him further. It was like a pack of wild animals circling their prey, eventually going for the kill: The day of the accusations. Serious allegations of abuse that grew in voice and number. Collins hadn't believed it, personally couldn't see it being true. But somehow one outspoken, loudmouthed, brat, managed to shout louder than the rest, claiming to have been touched inappropriately. Probably in reality he had had his collar felt or at worst, a slap round the head, and deservedly no doubt. But these days you couldn't get away with that, and that was all that was needed. With the right momentum it had evolved into something far uglier.

Fuelled by the parent's demand for justice, they pursued their own retribution, turning up the heat on an already hot spot.

Bad news, they say, spreads the fastest and boy, did it spread. Like an out-of-control forest fire. Sweeping throughout the neighbouring streets, fuelled by misplaced hate and ignorance, the shop had gathered severe abuse and not just from the kids anymore. Parents whose own lifestyles could be morally questioned made themselves visible.

Graffiti would appear on a daily basis, just wanton nonsense at first, but the spelling would improve gradually, as would the artwork. Then the window breaking started; bricks and stones thrown by unseen cowards, perceived as rightful justice by vigilantes upholding the children's honour, the abuse continued unabated. The staff had abandoned ship, scared for their own welfare, leaving a drowning Jenkins to fight the cause alone.

The old man had taken as much as he could stand. It hadn't taken long for the rot to whittle away at him. A couple of weeks after the first incident, his shop didn't open. A friend raised the alarm, and with growing pressure the police had had to break the doors down. They went into the flat above the shop first. Finding no-one there the shop next. There they found him, hanging by the neck behind his counter he'd been dead for at least three days. The smell had been horrific.

He'd left no note. No surprise there, but to all parties concerned it didn't take a genius to put two and two together. In the following days someone had cleared out the shop. Another charity agency had 'helped out'. Stripping the shop of the prized assets, junk really, after all, it was a second-hand shop, and not a very good one at that. The place had never been taken over, certainly no-one in the area wanted to take over the premises knowing the situation. Again, bad news travels……

It was a sad ending to a human being's life, and although Collins hadn't known the old man personally, only met the man on call, he didn't deserve to go out like that. Driven to the only recourse available; full of loneliness, depression, certainly desperation, and possibly hate.

Collins stubbed his cigarette out, turning to leave, the memories of the past weighing heavy on his mind. Not an ideal place to be passing the time and on the way home for the weekend.

Had I done enough, had I helped in any way to prevent the outcome? Could I have done more?

In his hearts of hearts, he knew he hadn't bothered with getting to the bottom of the disturbances.

Strapping his helmet back on, Collins was halfway across the forecourt when the noise stopped him dead. To the cop it sounded like the latch of a door clicking as it opened, but maybe he'd misheard, the helmet muffling the sound. Across the street the houses showed no signs of life. There was no movement

Click

It came again. Clear as a bell. Clear as day.

But that would be impossible right? Because the shop was derelict.......

He turned to face the shop.

What the......?

The glass panelled shop door had swung open....

That's impossible, hadn't I checked...? Maybe I hadn't, after all I was only here to have a ciggy.

Collins approached the shop door expecting to see an estate agent or some other plausible explanation waltz out the doorway. Flicking his visor open he peered into the gloom.

The sun was dropping below the rooftops rapidly and visibility was poor this side of the road.

"Anyone about?" he called out, feeling more than a little foolish.

There's no-one here, just a coincidence I happened to be here when it clicked open

"Hello?"

There was no reply. Taking hold of the handle he was about to shut the door, when something he had missed the first time he'd looked through the window, caught his eye.

As if in cinemascope colour against the black and white, a toy Mr Potato Head sat perched all alone on a white shelving unit, as if caught in the spotlight. What was remarkable and odd was the fact that the shelving unit looked intact, new even.

How the hell had I not seen that?

The toy itself looked in reasonable condition as well.

Collins remembered when Toy Story, the first film of the series, had come out, how he had been a little more than obsessed with the clever, ground-breaking animation in general and with Pixar Animations in particular. Starting with Woody his collection grew; Buzz Light Year was acquired next, rapidly followed by the entire cast, he had to have every character. All but one was acquisitioned: Mr Potato Head. Somehow, and for whatever reason, this had been the one that had slipped the net. He'd moved on, unable to fully complete the set, bored, looking for new pursuits; football cards and Transformer sets, whatever the latest craze was, he'd grow out of Toy Story and Pixar films.

Collins stepped fully into the shop, compelled to investigate, his biker boots crunching noisily on the debris littering the shop.

"Hello," he called out again, taking hold of the toy. On inspection its condition was remarkably pristine.

How in all that is holy did this get left behind?

Now standing inside the shop, his relationship and connection with coming here on an almost weekly basis, flooded his thoughts, disturbing flashes projected, thrown back to a volatile time.

"What you gonna do about those kids huh copper!" Old man Jenkins spat the last word.

Collins shrugged for the umpteenth time.

"There's nothing I can do sir, if you install cameras, you know a CCTV system, we might be able to ident..."

"....I don't have bleeding money for that!" Jenkins spat some more.

Collins resisted the urge to wipe the tiny projectile of spit that had landed on his tunic.

"Can you describe them for me?"

"Little bastards..."

"Well, all I can..."

"....if I ever catch one of them, I'll make them pay! You wait and see!"

"If there's nothing else..."

"Hang on a minute......don't I know you copper? You came here too...didn't you?"

Collins blinked. That wasn't one he remembered, the old man had never let on, never once reminding him of then and now.

"Oh, but I did remember. You see I never let on, but I remember you copper, you used to come in as well!"

He gave the shop a quick scan, instinctively searching the rear for movement, for anything. Something...had he missed something?

"Yes...yes, I remember you, spotty little git, you came into my shop looking for Pixar Toys, didn't you?"

His hand twitched as if touched. Looking down he stared at Mr Potato Head.

The toy was now missing an arm and an eye.

Hold on a minute...wasn't the toy in perfect nick?

The remaining eye moved, turning to look at Collins.

No...! That didn't really happen...Did it?

Mesmerised, he stared hard at the toy.

"You was gonna steal me too, weren't you copper! But I wasn't mint enough for your taste. You thought about it though, didn't you? You're a despicable thief too! Just like the rest of those bastard kids!"

Jenkins voice sneered louder than before.

The large purple ears wriggled ever so slightly.

"Huh?" Collins dropped the toy, an involuntary reaction.

Backing away, he watched the toy come to rest face down.

Jesus!......The derelict shop, the toy, the voice

He could feel uneasiness mushrooming out of control. The dark shadowy room cultivating his fear seeding a dreadful terror about to flourish and explode.

Get a grip Gary this isn't real...this isn't happening!

The loud creaking noise stopped his heart beating. It continued as he turned to face the music.

Behind the smashed shop's counter, a body swayed, hanging from the ceiling, timing its orbit to coincide with the policeman's.

"Jesus Christ what the fuck....?" Gary Collins gulped for air, struggling to contain the rising claustrophobia in his motorcycle helmet.

Look at me! GARY! LOOK! Jenkins commanded.

Collins released a tiny whimper.

Look what those kids did to me!!

The old man's tilting head showed broken teeth, only his mouth wasn't moving. The eyes bulged, ready to pop from the pressure the noose employed, the black tongue, looking impossible long, lolled freely. Blood splashed, staining the old man's chest.

What you gonna do about those bastard kids, copper!!

All around the shop, black tentacles materialized, stretching and curling from the rear of the shop, lacing octopi arms committing to the hanging body.

The tentacles now raced towards the petrified Collins. He clutched his helmet, for there was nothing he could do but gulp terrified mouthfuls of air.

YOU DID NOTHING!! The old man bellowed, wriggling and twisting, a doomed worm on a fish hook

The shop door slammed firmly shut…
PC Gary Collins didn't hear it shut…
He didn't hear anything…
Anymore……

The Boy Who Could Fix Things

Chapter One

It began to rain, rain real hard. The type of rain that would, upon impact, explode, creating miniature water volcanoes, simultaneously erupting all across the playgrounds at Sandown's Comprehensive Upper School. The rain was dancing, a crazy beautiful rain dance.

The kids weren't interested in the dancing rain, they ran for cover.

Sam Williams ran too following the herd to the nearest refuge, the bicycle shed. Pushing past bodies, those selfish enough to linger just inside, he ignored the mutterings of complaints, finding a space near the back, away from the dripping entrance.

The shed was new, a large, elongated type. Built to house fifty bikes or so, it even came with a bespoke cowling, all fancy. It was bookended with ventilated shielding which barely fought back against the elements. Someone's clever idea of ingenuity but really, the school had overspent, justifying the inflated cost which sucked up half the year's budget commissioning the damn thing. Still, it had to be said it was a success of sorts. The students loved hanging around in there.

Spotting his best friend standing alone, Sam nodded acknowledgement.

"That is insane!" He indicated the downpour.

"You know!" Stu 'DJ' Philips laughed back without taking his eyes off the deluge.

Stu was Sam's friend, had been for the past year. They became brothers in every sense of the word; lived in each other's homes over the weekends and holidays. Went to school together, hung out together in town. Anyone who chanced upon them thought they were brothers, even the teachers when resorting to sarcasm, would refer to the pair as two peas in a pod. If the teacher was being especially disparaging, calling the two 'The Brothers Grimm'.

To say they were best friends would be an understatement. Their closeness inevitably garnered attention and some resentment with their peers and teachers alike, the two boys didn't care. They were unconcerned. To them their friendship was unique. A wonderful union glued together out of mutual respect for each other.

Stu had approached Sam one day out of the blue, declaring that they should hang out together, seeing as how they both lived on the same street, went to the same school.

It was Stu, a well-liked apologetic student who was the driving force behind their friendship. At first Sam had found the introduction a little peculiar; he couldn't remember Stu living on his street at all, couldn't remember the boy at school even. The aberrational feeling soon passed as the two grew close.

Sam was also well liked amongst his peers. One of the kids that seemed to breeze through school's hurdles of life, popular with girls and boys alike. Naturally gifted athletically and what he lacked up top, he made up for with swaggering charisma, confident in the knowledge he'd endure academia without too much effort.

"I read somewhere that we live in one of the driest parts of England," Stu began, "like it rains everywhere else more than here, well, apart from Scotland and Ireland. It rains there a lot as well, more than here, probably more than out in the oceans. In fact, did you know it rains less out at sea than it does on land?"

Sam smiled. Stu's nickname DJ came about from his habit of talking. A lot.

"No, I did not know that DJ! But how do they know, I mean it's not like there's measuring devices out in the oceans!"

"It's all about evaporation my friend!"

"Right, well now it feels like the opposite. Phew, man I am wet!" Sam slicked back his hair, rockabilly style.

Both boys surveyed the water carnage in silence, large pools were already beginning to amalgamate and unionize. The path home to the main block was treacherously wet and a decision that could wait.

"The power of nature, bro, never to be underestimated, should always be respected," Stu muttered in response but quietly, almost in reverence, nodding slowly, his eyes fixated on a spot somewhere only he could see.

Sam smiled at his best friend. Remembering how much of a dreamer he could be, a true Piscean. Always optimistic, ultimately a tragic romantic in waiting. He was also a joker.

Glancing over Stu's shoulder, Sam surveyed the crowd.

The Upper School consisted of years 10 and 11 and an annex for 6th form students. The tenth and eleventh grades rarely to spoke to one another and no-one spoke to the 6th formers. Both Sam and DJ were year 10 pupils. Both were 15 years old, their birthdays coming within a week of each other's was another sign their friendship was meant to be.

"Notice how the rain makes us all equals." Stu indicated the gaggle of students dripping and shivering.

"Yeah, I guess."

"See we got older girls dangerously close," Stu winked badly.

"Mate, it's raining!"

"Yeah, but we got wet T-shirts man."

"Ah of course…."

"Oh, come on Sammy boy, check it out."

Sam followed Stu's gaze to the two older girls standing next to them, their white shirts saturated, showing the curves of their generous chests.

His blatant stare was immediately exposed with a disgusted tut.

"Hah! Busted, mate!" Stu snapped his head back laughing over-loudly. He had quite a distinct extrovert laugh.

Sam shook his head but couldn't stop the smile from breaking loose.

"Who's that talking to Adams?" Sam frowned, peering through the maze of bodies at the couple, snuck in the corner at the back where there was extra cover from a side panel.

"Where…?"

"At the back over there, past the older kids," Sam indicated with his head.

"I don't see…" Stu glanced round, already suspicious, "Where? You ain't gonna get me busted mucker," he half laughed.

"There!" Sam took hold of his Stu's head and physically swivelled it in the right direction, pushing his friend forward slightly in the process.

Two boys sat huddled together, perched on the arches of the bike supports, deep in conversation, oblivious to the crowd around them. One boy held a notebook and pen, head down, scribbling intently, while the other boy, Gary Adams, spoke continuously.

"No idea." Stu muttered, losing interest, turning his attention back to the dreary wet vista. "I can only see Adams!"

"Eh? He's right there talking… ah forget it."

Sam continued to watch the boys covertly.

He recognised Adams from his Chemistry class. The boy was a bit of a loner, a swot who preferred his own company. He had a habit of quickly putting his hand up to be the first whenever answering a teacher's questions, then he would finger his glasses, pushing them up slightly before glancing furtively around the classroom.

Adams had few friends and those he did talk to were of the same breed. Awkward types, those who found it hard to fit in with the crowd: the types that got bullied.

"Maybe it's a 6th former, who knows." Stu casually added without taking his gaze from the rain. "Who cares anyway?"

"Yeah, but why's he talking to a 6th former?" Sam questioned, still staring.

The other boy's face remained hidden. All he could make out was the hair and hands. The pen he was holding never stopped moving and the boy never looked up.

Sam frowned just as Adams lifted his eyes and their gaze met. For the second time, Sam had been caught staring. He looked away, but not before he had witnessed what Adams always did, pushing his glasses up whilst giving the shed a nervous sweep.

"You know we're going to have to make a run for it." Stu inspected his sodden uniform.

"Huh?"

"Lunchtime's nearly over and we're soaked, got to find a radiator that's on, right?"

"Right…"

Stu turned to Sam.

"Stop staring at the melons man, its pervy!"

"Yeah, thanks for that." Sam laughed.

"Mate they better be putting the heaters on otherwise we're gonna be suffering. Know what I mean?"

"Why's he so nervous?"

"Huh?"

"Adams, what's he up to?"

"Who knows? Who cares?" Stu spat.

"And who's he with?"

"Mate if you're that interested why don't you just go over there and ask!"

Sam thought it over.

"You know what, I might just do that."

Stu sniggered, "I might just do that," he mimicked.

"Sod you!"

"No SOD YOU!" Stu laughed louder.

Everyone turned to stare. The girls nearest them screwed their faces up in disgust.

Sam shook his head at his friend.

"Man, you're so sad."

"I'm sad?" Stu turned to Sam while slowly backing out of the bicycle shed, "I'm sad?" he repeated.

Sam stopped smiling, realising his friend was up to something.

"I'M SAD," Stu was nearly shouting now, standing in the pouring rain, "Tell me brother, who's sad now!"

With that declaration Stu began kicking the pools of water into the bike shed, laughing his signature chortle, only wildly this time, aiming for the girls mostly, but the splashing ultimately claiming all the pupils in the firing line. The crowd of children began clamouring their disgust whilst exiting the shed.

Stu laughed even louder, his shoes scuffing the ground, finding the last of the puddles and victims.

Following his classmate's rapid exodus, Sam tried to spot Adams and though he thought he caught a glimpse of the boy he couldn't be sure. Of his scribe there was no sign.

"So, are you going to meet me here or come over to mine so we can go together?" Denise Matthews asked Sam. Emphasising heavily on the 'together'.

Speaking in the main corridor by the entrance where the lockers were housed, she had finally managed to corner her boyfriend.

Denise was a tall girl for her age, pretty, with natural good looks, her dark, almost raven black hair flowed over her shoulders, clipped at the sides in accordance with the school's policy. It was the now the afternoon, the rain outside having finally relented, allowing the pupils to mingle once more, wandering around the school grounds. Sandown's Halloween Disco that night was the topic of Denise's challenge.

"I dunno?"

"Come on Sam, it's not that hard a decision!"

"Okay, I'll meet you here." Sam shrugged. Turning away, he pulled out his math books before closing the locker and hopefully closing the subject as well.

"Huh!"

"Well, you asked. Anyway, aren't you going with Rachel and Tracy?"

"Well, we could all go together." Denise stated matter of factly.

Sam turned to his girlfriend of nine months. It had seemed recently that she had become more attached, more demanding more... *girlfriend*. He remembered their first encounter, that moment when they had first kissed. The school had been closing for the summer break and all season they had been flirting, bumping into each other laughing it off with lingering looks. Eventually Denise had one of her girlfriends pass him a note.

Do you like Denise?

That had been the spark to set their relationship alight. Fleeting moments in the corridors between classes; seeking each other out in the playground only to avoid confrontation at the last minute. All the taunting, playing round the bush was not enough anymore.

They had had a wonderful summer, discovering adolescent passion, meeting almost every day to wander the town, in the rain sometimes, just larking about. Exploring the usual haunts, making the most of the landmarks dotted about normally ignored but now an essential factor, spending even more time than necessary in recreational parks.

Stu had tagged along at times, happy to play gooseberry. His antics and tomfoolery were welcomed, filling the gaps between the tender affection, a clowning catalyst helping to pass the long days.

That summer holiday had been magical, an awakening of teenage angst. Sam had pursued Denise, but in reality, he had been the prey all along. She had taken the initiative. She had suggested the what, where, and why. She was in control.

"Sam."

He blinked, yanked out of his reverie.

"Babes, lately you've been miles away, like you don't care anymore."

Sam's eyes wandered.

"Are we good still?"

"Yeah of course," Sam smiled at a passing student.

"Well, it doesn't feel like it."

"Denise come on; nothing has changed. Just got a lot on my mind what with the exams, you know."

"You are my boyfriend, remember!"

"I know."

"Then prove it!" The jab hit him in the shoulder, hard enough to spin him off balance.

"Ouch!" Sam rubbed the spot feigning injury, "Denise!"

Denise was already gone, walking away rapidly, her back stiff and straight.

Sighing, Sam stared after his girlfriend. Sometimes he wondered if this was all part of a game that girls liked to play. It sure as hell didn't start off this way. Was he missing something?

Slamming his locker door and snapping the Chubb lock firmly in place, he was about to follow Denise to class. The image of Stu's face in the shed, looking away into the rain, denying the fact, sprung into his consciousness like an alarm on repeat and not dismissed.

I did see someone with Adams! I know I did. And so did DJ. Why is he lying?

Chapter Two

The Upper School Halloween disco was in full swing. The party was well attended, swelling the assembly hall with fancy dressed nightmares.

Having started at 7.30pm, the disco was now at its zenith, with only 30 minutes to go before all the ghouls, witches and zombies had to vacate the building and return to their crypts and coffins.

On the stage, Jason Coe, a 6th form student, delivered the tunes. He had approached the organisers with a generous offer, donating his services and equipment for the night. Eager to have some practice with his newly acquired decks, Jason dreamed of Ibiza nights and beyond. Dressed in a luminous skeleton costume complete with mask his wraparound Cyclops spotlight bobbed up and down in time to the beat. The night was a success, and it was mostly down to him.

Four teachers had gallantly volunteered as peacekeepers. Suffering the night's excursion with mild apprehension and trepidation, guards were up. It was well founded. Previous discos were notoriously inauspicious affairs and had nearly been banned altogether; recounts of drunken loutish behaviour (mostly outside the school, it had to be said) heavy petting hidden behind the main stage was reported, as well as smoking on school premises. Thankfully, no drugs had ever been discovered, which of course didn't mean they were not being ingested prior to entering. All of which were big no-no's and part of the goodwill agreement set in place at Friday morning's assembly by Mr Callaghan, the head of tenth year and the teacher in charge of the night's festivities.

"The main gates will be closed at precisely 8pm anybody and I mean anybody, turning up after this time will not be permitted to enter! The gates will then reopen at 9.45pm. Parents will be allowed in the grounds before and after for the purpose of dropping off and collecting, and the disco will finish at 10pm sharp! Please make sure, if you are attending the disco that everybody who is involved is aware of these restrictions. A letter giving full details and how to obtain tickets will be handed out to take home at reception." Mr Callaghan had intoned dispassionately; it was plainly obvious to the students he wasn't a fan.

Towards the end of the night, some teachers, it should be said, were apt to be pushing their own boundaries of compliance. Acquiescing in favour of a 'quiet' night, they yielded to the general good behaviour, their coffee mugs laced with vodka, partnered with a cheeky smoke, and ultimately turning a blind eye to some pupils' more questionable behaviour. So far it would seem it had gone without a hitch.

Sam had come as a Zombie, allowing his mother to do most of the art work, something which she had taken on enthusiastically.

"You look awesome, even if I say so myself!" she had enthused.

"You look about as scary as my guinea-pig," Tom, Sam's older brother giggled. "Is that left over Bolognese mum?"

"What!"

"Don't listen to him Sam, he's only jealous 'cause he's not going!"

From across the neon dance floor, Sam spied Adams gently swaying to the music, his back to the wall. Flashing strobes pierced dancing bodies, throwing intermittent images of display. Only his top half moved. From where he was standing it was hard to see if there was anybody with him.

Sam smiled, *who'd have thought Adams would come? He even had some moves, albeit questionable ones.*

"Wanna try the punch?" Denise held out her plastic cup, a cheeky smile giving the game away. She had waddled over with her troupe in tow.

"No way, I tried it earlier." Sam shook his head vehemently.

"Oh, go on babes." Denise persisted, her hooded eyes, accentuated by the heavy makeup, now joining the naughty smile. "For me?" she pouted.

Sam sighed.

Denise's girlfriends, Rachel Eden and Tracy Collins, both witches themselves, sipped their own illegal concoctions watching the dancers on the floor, swaying in unison.

Taking the offering, Sam sipped at the drink.

"Come on, all of it!" Denise insisted, tipping his hand.

It tasted sickly sweet, like cherry toothpaste. If there was alcohol in it, it was well hidden beneath the paste.

"That's my boy!" Denise laughed, her head wobbling. The strobe lighting flickered back into life, the effect producing a stuttered montage of flashing teeth, and her dark makeup now highlighted to reveal its excess.

She's drunk, Sam deduced accurately.

"Your mates have no imagination, do they?"

"We're the 'Witches of Eastwick', obs!"

"Of course you are."

"You tried the punch yet?" Stu appeared, holding two cups of his own bootleg. He was dressed as the 'Joker', Batman's nemesis. "Perkins has finally buggered off! It's not bad, to be fair!"

Mr Perkins, the year eleven Biology teacher, was tasked with the herculean role of the punch monitor. He had foolishly left said post, allowing a free-for-all of desperate ghouls to contaminate the bowl.

Stu offered Sam a cup, "Everyone is dumping their stash into it," he laughed wildly.

Denise studied Stu with poison eyes.

"Oh yeah, I wouldn't put it past him to try and catch everyone out!"

"Nah he's bored. Gone for a smoke I reckon!"

"What about the dance you promised me?" Denise pointed a wicked finger at Sam.

"Later." He begged off noticing one of Denise's friends eye-balling Stu.

"Later, later, later, that's all you promise me!"

Sam stuck to his guns, watching the crowd.

"I suppose you'll dance with your other girlfriend though!" Denise made a face at Stu.

"Err...." Stu stammered.

He was totally caught off guard. Turning to Sam brought no help.

"Urgh... you boys are boring, boring, boring!"

Up on the stage, Jason Coe showed off his improving skills by taking the music up a level; the timing of which was much appreciated, telling by the loud whooping on the dance floor.

"Thank you!" Denise grabbed a cup, sploshing half of it down Stu's front in the process.

"Hey!"

"You're... *welcome*," Denise lurched sideways before straightening up her trajectory. Leaving the two boys with a farewell cackle, her friends took up the call, their screeching easily competing with the music. The 'Witches of Eastwick' crashed onto the dance floor, their arms flailing wildly about, drinks spilling with abandon.

"Denise is..."

"Drunk." Sam finished.

"I was going to say happy."

"Very happy by the looks of it!"

Both boys instinctively high-fived.

"Did you see Rachel looking at you?" Sam nudged his friend. He knew a look when he saw one. And that was a look.

"That girl has eyes only for the mirror, my man."

"I think you're right but, she did look at you for at least a minute."

Stu made a face surveying the crowd, "I see Adams has made some new friends."

"Eh? What do you mean?"

Stu pointed with his cup.

Sam squinted over to where he'd last spotted Adams. At first the dancing bodies and flashing shards of light hid the boy, then Sam managed to zero in.

Adams wasn't throwing shapes to the music. He was being slapped! Sam could see the kid was trying desperately to avoid the beating.

Sam catapulted into action, pushing through the throng of dancing Werewolves and swaying Vampires, their protestations adding to their grotesque make-up.

"Really?" Stu sighed, accepting the inevitable.

Sam was upon the group in seconds.

"Oi...!" Oblivious to Sam's approach, both boys jumped visibly at Sam's shout. Even over the PA sound system it was loud: loud enough to make them start.

Sam recognised one of the boys; Martin Lucas, a troublemaker, mean and moody and always seemingly in detention. Sam shared PE with Lucas. He'd once witnessed Lucas punch a prop-forward in a rugby scrum, dirty tactics from a dirty player.

The other boy was his side kick, the faithful lieutenant Darren Wilkes: Lucas's clone, only uglier. Sam had seen him around the school, consciously avoiding any contact. The boy was trouble, real trouble. Even Sam's family connection at the school didn't guarantee immunity from Wilkes. Both boys were dressed casually, Halloween wasn't for them.

"What you doing?" Sam spoke to Lucas, ignoring the glaring Wilkes.

"Nothing..." Lucas smiled back all innocence.

"What's it got to do with you?" Lieutenant Wilkes stepped in.

Sam turned to face the boy; squaring up to the challenge, it was time to test that connection.

"He's with me."

The boy shrugged, *like I care.*

"Well ain't that cute!"

Lucas shook his head at his partner in crime. Wilkes gave his friend a questioning look in return. *What?*

"You don't wanna mess with Sam."

The other boy shrugged again.

Stu joined the shooting party. The tables were turning for the rescue squad.

"That's Tom Williams' brother." Lucas stated.

Wilkes looked Sam and Stu up and down, stopping to stare Sam out. He ground out a snarl, changing tactics, "What we got here, The Walking Dead?" He smirked.

"You ok Adams?" Stu ignored the jibe.

"Like he said," Sam squared up to Wilkes, "right?"

"You gotta love the older brother." Stu laughed, looking at Sam then back at Lucas, "don't you think?"

As if by divine intervention the music ceased, the timing biblical. There followed an annoying wall of crackling as Jason Coe switched on the microphone, creating distorted feedback. There was some ground to cover before perfecting his craft.

"HEY EVERYBODY! Err…so I've been told by Mr Callaghan we've gotta wind it down. I hope you've had a good time enjoying the tunes, I know I have…err, so we're gonna slow it down for the last ten minutes. For all of you lovers out there, this is for you!" The PA crackled again, signalling the changeover.

Mr Callaghan's disapproving face said it all, standing to one side behind Jason, he lent forward to remonstrate with the DJ.

Jason, with a reputation now in the making, pretended not to notice.

The music resumed with Take That's cover of the Bee Gees classic, *How Deep Is Your Love*.

Jason didn't know it at the time, but he had just produced the penultimate of finale songs. All future discos would end with this classic love song.

On the dance floor, a reshuffling of ghoulish bodies was slowly taking place. Off went the couples and groups of girls, replaced by a migration of slow shuffling boys plucking up the courage in a now or never moment. The time had come to get close and personal with the opposite sex without fear of repercussions. The chance to touch a girl.

"Now's your chance, boys…!" Stu winked dramatically at Lucas.

"Piss off Philpot!"

Stu made a face in return. Sam elbowed his friend, adding a quick smile of approval. Nice one mate.

"Come on Dal, let's leave these girls to their tea party." Lucas gave Adams one last caressing tap on the cheek, "Laters, Adi boy."

Darren the Clone held onto Sam's gaze. He wasn't used to such diplomacy. The kill was still fresh in his mind, and he hadn't had his fill. He faked a lunge at Adams before obediently following his captain. The pair sauntered away, parting the crowds as if by telekinesis. Lucas could be seen laughing and pointing at some of the other students' makeup.

"What was that all about?" Stu muttered with a shake of this head. He remembered he still had a cup full of alcohol.

"You ok?" Sam spoke to Adams who nodded humbly in return, "Are you mental taking on the chuckle brothers?" Stu probed.

"There you are!"

No-one had seen Denise appear, wobbling on the spot.

"Where have you been? Come on," she cooed, grabbing Sam's arm.

He managed an apologetic farewell shrug before the crowd swallowed them up.

"Girls, huh?" Stu motioned.

Realising he was alone, Adams had also slunk off, leaving without a word, Stu shrugged and finished his drink.

"Time for one more, me thinks," with that he headed off to the punch bowl hoping to get one for the road before the deception was exposed by Mr Perkins.

Chapter Three

The sound of the bell signalled a migration of bodies throughout the school's corridors. It was Monday morning. The usual gossip of Friday night's disco was being spread around the school with alternating accuracy. The highlight being the recant of Mr Perkins goof, and Mr Callaghan's wrath upon discovering the punch had been spiked under their watch.

Sam left his English class. He didn't notice or feel the touch at his elbow at first, only the sound of a soft voice repeating his name stopped him short.

"I want you to have this," the voice continued.

Sam stared down at Adam's out-stretched hand. He hadn't been aware of the other's presence; in fact it almost spooked him to think that the boy had been standing there obviously trying to get his attention. One second he was just there, he hadn't seen him approach but there he was all the same.

"Take it."

Sam slowly took hold of the gold cigarette lighter. Gingerly turning the piece over in his hand, he was surprised at the weight. An old-fashioned type, generally used by older men, suited types. There were grooves down the sides but otherwise it had no markings or brand. Still, it looked expensive.

"I've seen you smoking so I..." Adams trailed off.

"What's it for? I mean...why?"

"It's a... thank you."

Sam studied Adam's face which remained lowered. He flipped the lid, clicking the lighter into life. A flame flickered at the response.

Definitely on the expensive side, Sam concluded.

"Really? You want me to have this?"

"Yes, please take it...I want you to have it."

"Why?"

"Well, it's a thank you...for...you know, the other night."

"I see," Sam half smiled, now he understood, "Well ok, thanks," he pocketed the lighter, "don't worry about those clowns, they won't bother you no more."

Adams merely nodded and made to leave.

"Wait."

Adams paused looking up into Sam's face, finally locking onto his gaze, albeit briefly.

"I've wanted to talk with you."

"Me?" Adams looked nervously away.

Sam couldn't help but smile, "Yeah, you."

"Oh."

Looking around, Sam checked their privacy before continuing.

"I wanted to ask you about the other day...in the bike shed. You were talking to another boy."

Adams frowned, "I don't remember."

"Yeah, you do."

Again, Adams shook his head, looking even more concerned.

"You know it was raining...last Friday...I saw you with this boy. You were talking and he was writing or something?"

Adams' head lifted, his body stiffened as if lethally injected, but now straightening up, his self-conscious stoop dissolved in an instant.

"You saw him?" he gasped, his face burning bright with earnest wonder.

Sam nodded.

"Yeah I saw him alright...Who was he?"

Adams lowered his head back to its usual submissive position.

"What was that all about? I didn't recognise him. Was he from the lower school or something?"

Sam waited but the only response forthcoming was Adams whispering to himself, followed by mumblings.

"Wait...what, can it be true...so it's gonna happen?"

"Hey...hello...earth to Adams...anybody there?"

Adams continued to gibber away, a smile appearing momentarily on his face, before a frown displaced it.

"You ok?" Sam tapped the other boy gently on the shoulder. He jumped as if electrocuted, snapping his head back and visibly moving away from Sam. His face was troubled.

"Don't touch me!"

"Hey, I'm not the weirdo here."

Adams looked left and right. They were alone now; the other pupils having long dispersed to their next classes.

"He fixes things."

"He fixes things?" Sam spoke slowly, "Like what?"

"What needs fixing!" Adams hissed, meeting Sam's questioning gaze only for the second time.

"Right," Sam studied the other boy's face for an indication of mockery.

As far as he could tell Adams was serious, even so he prodded sarcastically, "What, like bicycles?"

"No, not stuff like that...like...personal stuff."

"Personal stuff...?" Sam repeated.

"Yeah..."

"What, like problems?"

"Problems...yeah he fixes problems."

"Look I've got English Lit...I gotta go," Sam indicated down the corridor.

Adams nodded in agreement, "Me too."

The two boys parted ways, awkwardly moving in opposite directions. Before he'd got two feet, Sam paused turning around, "Hey if I wanted to find him...how would I find him? I mean what class is he in?"

Adams had stopped as well, without looking around he replied quietly, almost matter-of-factly, "He's here, in the playground," before shuffling off.

Sam shook his head gently, "That boy has issues."

The hand holding the chalk paused in its progress across the blackboard, halted by the classroom door opening.

"Ah here he is...young Master Williams, why am I not surprised?"

"Sorry Miss, I was delayed," Sam remained by the entrance, awaiting his fate.

From the back of the room Stu smirked, shaking his head wonderingly.

"Of course you are. You're always...contrite. Pray tell the class what befell you this time. What manner of catastrophe stopped you from accomplishing the hundred yards from your last lesson to this very door you just struggled to find? I mean, surely there was an easier route than taking the Khyber Pass via Timbuktu!" Miss Deacons, his English Literature teacher turned to face Sam, her stern, no-nonsense attitude setting the tone for what leniency was forthcoming.

Sam remained still.

"No? Then was there a damsel in distress calling your name out from a tower?" she waved out the window, "Not seen on the school premises before, distracting you from the mundane and boring routine that you so obviously detest."

"Sorry Miss I was..."

"You have a mid-term exam paper coming up on Friday, this Friday, which will be included in your course work, and I don't have to tell you how important this will be." She paused, "Or maybe in your case I do, Sam."

There was audible snickering which ceased with a flick of her hand.

Sam couldn't help but fidget under her piercing gaze. The self-conscious feeling was immediate and damning. Miss Deacon was not a teacher to trifle with.

Handing Sam several pages, she commanded abruptly, "Sit down."

Making his way to the back of the class Sam slumped down dejectedly into his seat.

"Romeo and Juliet, page 19." Sam duly opened his book, whilst giving Stu a sideways look and half a smile. The smile vanished as he glanced at the grade and comments on the homework paper that had been handed out. He slumped further into his seat.

D. Did you even read the book??

Miss Deacons returned to the black board and drew a thick chalk line underneath the word LOVE.

"So, what are we to make of Romeo's dismissal of Rosaline, his love interest at the start of the play, when we are introduced to the..." Miss Deacons' voice droned away into the background.

He fixes things

Sam stared at the red writing streaked throughout his assignment, sighing loudly.

Stu held up his own homework result, C+. He flushed a cocky smile in celebratory cheekiness.

He fixes things

Sam blinked. Adams' words, repeating themselves like an insistent alarm clock echoing vociferously.

He's here...in the playground

The grade on his paper remained unchanged.

Surely Adams was a fruitcake, right? Could he be on to something? Sam stared at the red writing on the paper. Maybe, just maybe there is a way out. If this 'boy' that he spoke about was real, really was for real, then maybe he could fix this. Fix all his grades for that matter.

Chapter Four

Five days had passed. It was Friday afternoon and lunch break at Sandown's. For the past twenty minutes Sam had been scouring the grounds searching for the 'boy', as he had all week. He quickly inspected the school's canteen which adjoined the main assembly hall and had long been closed due to the decline in its popularity and the subsequent culling of budget costs. Still pupils would gather here eating their packed lunches or discussing various activity clubs, even though the kitchen was a modern-day museum now and out of bounds, the tables had been left as a reminder of the good old days.

No sign there.

His wandering had led to the various outbuildings, scouting around the new science block and back, even taking a trip out through the main entrance, onto the streets and back around through the south entrance.

No joy. Nothing of the mysterious kid Adams had spoken about so reverently. Frustratingly, Adams was also out of the loop, no-where to be found. After asking a few classmates that Adams talked to (few being the operative word) about his whereabouts, it turned out Adams was off, sick or something. So even if he could help, Sam was seriously beginning to wonder about the validity of his claim, in fact the niggling feeling that it was all a prank and that somehow he'd been tricked by Adams was sitting heavy on his scepticism shoulder.

Leaving Stu out of the mix had seemed to be a sensible idea, for the time being anyway. He'd decided that his best friend would remain oblivious. Explaining how he was going to have someone, a boy with no name, 'fix' his homework like a magician would produce a rabbit out of a hat, would be hard to justify. Not to mention where the recommendation was coming from. For now, he'd keep this to himself. He could visualise his friend laughing at the absurdity of it all.

You don't honestly believe a word from that knob, do you?
Nah of course not
Then tell me mate. Why are you looking for a pot of gold at the end of the rainbow, Sammy boy? Ain't nothing there... nothing there...but TROUBLE.

Sam found himself staring into the bike shed. The memory of Stu kicking the pools of rainwater at the girls, who were screaming out their disgust and exasperation, brought out a smile which changed quickly. A frown appeared, his thoughts of that day darkening suddenly. Adams had been talking to a boy that morning, deep in conspiratorial conversation. Sam pictured the scene, only now Adams was turning to smile at him. The smile turned into an evil monstrosity of a smile, mouth blackened and cavernous, the corners of the lips, pointy and sharp.

Sam shook his head, shaking off the cold shiver that rippled down his back at the same time.

Where had that come from?

A sound drew his attention, waking him from his musing. It came from the shed. The sound was of someone putting a bag between the supporting spokes, catching the metal as it scraped the sides.

Sam stared.

He was here!

The boy had his back to him, facing the school's perimeter wall. The 'bag' was in fact an old-fashioned style brown briefcase. It was tatty, well-worn and had definitely seen better days. Unbuckling the large strap, the boy pulled out a black A5 size notebook. Sam hadn't noticed before, but up close it too looked worn and frayed.

"Hey," he called out.

The boy ignored Sam's call, instead reaching down into his briefcase.

Walking closer, to within a few feet, Sam spoke again, only this time more forcefully.

"Excuse me!" Still the boy avoided any kind of acknowledgement.

"Do you know Adams?"

The boy opened a black notebook, pulling a pen out from an inside pocket of his jacket.

"He says you helped him." Sam continued, edging closer still, to within a couple of feet.

"You know, with…problems?"

The boy finally turned his head slightly, his features half obscured by a flop of black hair hanging over one eye.

"What is it you want?" His voice was surprising quiet, soft, almost effeminate.

"Sorry I don't to mean to…"

"What is it you need?" The boy stopped Sam short.

For a second, he wanted to apologise and walk away, the feeling of uncertainty pulling a big black blanket of anxiety into his consciousness.

This is ridiculous, what am I doing here?

He began to turn away before it was too late and before he'd made a fool of himself. Nearby, some pupils were laughing, one screamed almost in rapture. Two boys chased another across the playground. He didn't recognise them immediately and they ignored his presence.

"Tell me." The boy spoke again,

"Ok...ok, so I need some grades fixed! Can you do that huh?" Sam blurted forcefully, spinning around to face the boy.

The pen started moving across the notebook, rapidly crossing the page.

"You know, I got to improve my..." Sam dropped his voice, this time speaking gingerly, shrugging his shoulders as he did so, "course work and stuff."

"I understand. Is that all?"

"Err... yeah..."

"Are you sure?"

"Yeah ...I guess...what else is there? I need to fix my grades like yesterday..."

"I see," the boy cut in again, "now this is what I want."

Sam stopped short, completely stumped. Struggling to digest what the boy had said.

"I don't understand?" he managed.

The pen stopped moving, poised above the book, stilled by his words.

"I think you know exactly what I mean."

"No, I have no idea."

"What are you prepared to forfeit?"

"Forfeit? As in give up?" Sam wanted to laugh but some intuition saved him from doing that.

"Yes."

Looking over the boy's shoulder at the gardens that backed onto the school premises, Sam couldn't help the nagging feeling all wasn't well.

"I guess...mmmm...err..." he began.

"What about your girlfriend?"

"What??" Sam spat the word out explosively, finally unable to contain his emotions. He couldn't help himself; it just flew out. He waited for a reaction, but none was forthcoming,

"I thought you wanted money or something, you know, like maybe a favour."

"No."

"Look I really don't understand."

"I think you do."

Again, the contradiction, that annoying tone, the plain-spoken arrogance finally exhausted Sam's patience.

He's not joking!

Grimacing Sam stepped back, transfixed, staring wildly at the boy.

"What I require and for me to arrange, is for you to give up your girlfriend," the boy paused, "Denise."

"How did you know her name?" Sam stuttered.

"You won't have anything specific to do, informing her, nothing formal like that, a simple yes will suffice."

Who talks like that?

"She won't agree to this, I know she won't. No, it's not going to work." Sam managed to counter.

The boy turned and smiled without looking at Sam, "You have no idea, do you? Your life will change dramatically Sam Williams. Your girlfriend, whom I assume you are close to, won't even look at you again come the morning."

It was Sam's turn to smile. *This is nonsense, what you worried about?*

"Do we have an agreement?" The boy finally looked up. His eyes small, beady and unnaturally dark, fixed onto Sam's.

"You're not joking, are you?"

The boy was silent, watching.

Was that even a smile?

"Whatever, I need this done by Friday! My parents will go mental if I have flunked another exam," Sam relented, realising the futility in staring the boy out.

"Do We Have An Agreement?"

"YES!" Sam barked.

The boy lowered his penetrating gaze, returning to his scribbling.

"Then sign here." The notebook was swivelled to face Sam, held open with the pen offered invitingly. It was a fountain pen, the type with a little plastic ink cartridge which would be inserted into the body, the outer casing then screwed over the top.

Old fashioned, Sam noted.

"Thought you said a yes would suffice," Sam shot back sarcastically.

"This is next. Sign here at the bottom."

"Whatever," Sam shook his head dramatically, grabbing the pen, "You're weird mate."

He signed an impatient squiggle, noticing as he did so that there was an inscription on the pen, like an emblem.

"Now hold your hand out."

"What...?"

"Hold out your hand!" The boy commanded.

Sam did as he was told.

There was a blur of movement. The boy grabbed his hand, gripping it with vice-like strength. Sam grimaced at the state of the other boy's fingernails. He looked up into the black beady eyes.

"It's ok..." The boy whispered.

"Ouch!" Sam switched his gaze from the boy to his hand, his finger, now throbbing, dripped blood onto the page where he had just signed. The boy released his hand, "Hey did you do that?"

The book was instantly snapped shut and dropped into the boy's tatty satchel bag. Taking the pen from Sam, the boy dispensed with it the same way as the notebook.

"Jesus, you...you...you cut me!"

From the far side of the playground Stu appeared around one of the outbuildings, dribbling a football. He spotted Sam and called out, but was too far away to be heard.

"A small price to pay, I think you'll find." The boy stood up, buckling the satchel's strap.

Sucking his finger Sam muttered, "I gotta go."

"I know."

"What happens now?"

"Goodbye Sam."

"Is that it?"

Stu called his name again and this time Sam heard him.

"Oi Sammy boy!" this time the voice was closer. Sam turned to acknowledge his friend.

Waving a curt hello, he nodded back. Stu had closed the gap across the playground, the football rolling between his feet. Taking a quick swing he launched the ball at Sam who crouched to avoid the accurate kick from hitting him. The ball screamed into the back of the bicycle shed, smacking the garden wall with an impressive 'thwack' resonating loudly throughout the shed. The ball ricocheted back out almost as quickly and Sam caught the return, stopping it expertly beneath one shoe. It was a one in a million catch, the reaction unrepeatable.

He smiled back at Stu, "See that? Hah! That's what you call *skill!*"

Stu laughed back mockingly.

"Luck mate...pure luck."

Sam froze. His smile vanished, replaced with a look of bewilderment, his euphoria completely evaporated. Turning away he stared back into the shed. The football, now forgotten, rolled gently away, gradually picking up speed.

"Hey what's up?" Stu trapped the ball.

"Where's he gone?"

"Who?"

"The boy I was talking to!" Sam turned, indicating the area, "You saw him, right? He was behind me, here!"

Stu looked at the spot where Sam was pointing and back to his friend's face.

"Mate, there's no-one there."

"He was right here! I'm not joking!"

Stu shrugged. "Okay, there was a boy there. Hey, did you cut yourself?"

Sam scanned left to right, peering closely at the few children that were in the vicinity, none fit the description.

"Well, he's not here now." Stu picked up the ball, "I've been looking all over for you. Come on let's go down to Dino's, I'll buy you some chips. If we've got time that is, seeing as how you've been playing hide-n-seek all lunch break."

Sam, his face dark and troubled, followed his friend towards the entrance of the school gates. The pair made their way out, heading down the cul-de-sac in which the Sandown School resided before cutting left, walking the few hundred yards along the main road towards the small body of shops near the school.

Stu continuously played with the football, bouncing it against the garden's walls with annoying accuracy and dexterity. Reaching the chip shop, DJ paused, handing Sam the ball.

"Chip butty...?"

Your life will change dramatically Sam Williams.

Sam gasped. How had he missed that!

"Come on, its Freemans!" Stu laughed, misinterpreting Sam's look of shock.

"How did he know my name?"

"What?"

"The boy! He knew my name!"

Stu turned away, shaking his head, "You're seriously worrying me now," he said entering into the chip shop.

Sinking to his knees, Sam held the ball close to his chest squeezing it abstractedly.

"How did he know my name? I never told him my name! I know I didn't!"

He was still searching for an explanation when Stu reappeared with the hot food.

Taking one glance at his friend, Stu sighed, handing over Sam's portion.

"You know mate, that day, in the shed and rain, well, I got to tell you something."

Sam looked up, expecting a quip or some other one-liner gag.

"I never saw Adams talking with anyone," he paused before continuing, "I just agreed at the time, but actually I never saw this boy that you're banging on about."

"What, but you said..."

"Yeah, I know." Stu quickly attacked some chips, stuffing them into his mouth whilst looking at the traffic.

"Thanks for letting me know."

"Sorry mate."

They both continued to eat in silence. The afternoon traffic trundled past, the only constant noise.

"We better go back mate." Stu declared, squishing his chip bag.

"You go."

"I can't."

Sam looked up at his friend questioningly.

"Why's that?"

"Cause you got my football dude!"

Sam gave out a short, snorting laugh, "Fair enough," Standing, he surrendered the ball, "come on then, let's go."

The two boys trudged back to school, passing the football skilfully back and forth between parked cars and the feet of irritated shoppers; occasionally finding a wall to smack against. Neither boy noticed, nor cared, as overhead the sky darkened. Clouds absent until now began gathering quickly and ominously. Rapidly appearing from the east, they billowed all over the town suffocating the sunlight, squeezing out the afternoon rays until nothing was left but long dark projected shadows.

Chapter Five

Friday night had come and gone in a blur. All Sam remembered was walking through the front door and then...then nothing. 'Then' was a blank a complete blackout until now. Sleep had been a torturous night of tossing and turning. Strange dreams, evolving, devolving, none of it made sense. He'd slept in.

Upon waking, he'd ignored his best friend's texts, gambling that he wouldn't just turn up unannounced and discover the deceit. The fact was, he wanted to be alone. Even the thought of playing on his PlayStation failed to ignite his interest. Normally a sure way to pass the time if not dissolve it altogether. Only this morning it seemed alien to him.

What to say to Denise? Deciding the best course of action would be to wait until Monday to speak with his girlfriend. It would be best to let her know. After all, whatever the 'boy' had said, he'd fill her in with what had happened. It wouldn't be fair coming from someone else, especially a stranger. Besides, it really was just a prank, wasn't it? The more he thought about it the more absurd it seemed. What had he been thinking? Could Adams be mugging him off, like a joke? Was it all a practical joke?

How had he known my name?

He just couldn't shake that disturbing thought.

"Why don't you give Stuart a call?" His mother had suggested, sticking her head round the bedroom door noticing the morose and abstracted look painted on her son's face.

"Are you going to get out of bed today?"

He'd obliged, moping about from one room to another in a daze.

Saturday was a day for housework and her son was in the way, catatonic, moping about. She finally asked, "Is everything ok?

Sam mumbled an acknowledgement then turned abruptly.

"Where are Rich and Tom today?" he asked of his brothers

"Thomas is out playing tennis with your father at the club, and Richard has decided to remain in his lodgings at St George's for the weekend." His mother spoke slowly, emphasising the names of the two older siblings.

Tennis? Lodgings? What is she talking about?

Finally, his mother could no longer stand his brooding face and cornered her son in the kitchen.

"Okay, enough of this!" she asked, "Have you and Stuart fallen out?"

"No."

"Is it your upcoming exam results? Samuel?"

Sam turned again looking to his mother, "Since when do you call me Samuel?"

"You know I hate Sam or Sammy, darling." His mother finished folding the clothes she was holding and faced Sam, "Now, is this about your grades? Your father and I have a lot of faith in you keeping up the standard you've set all year. At the parents' meeting last term, Miss Deacons for one was completely brimming with admiration at your ability. I know the homework load has doubled but..." She stopped short, caught off guard by her son's sudden change of expression.

"What is it?"

"Miss Deacons said what?"

"Samuel, we discussed this only last week, don't you remember? Mr Perkins brought up the possibility of you going to St. George's College a year early. They forwarded your averages, and we have that interview with the Dean...darling, are you alright? You look positively queer!"

Now this is what I want, the words echoed, suddenly and loudly.

In a trance he sat down heavily on the breakfast stool, only the chair began sliding away from him. He held on to the table for support.

"Oh Samuel, stop this. I've got enough to do today without you and your silly games," his mother muttered, turning away, clearly annoyed, "and bring your washing down please, its piling up."

"Yeah...yeah...ok mum..."

Upstairs Sam sought out his phone, scrolling through the contacts list, searching. He had to know. The haunting premonition that was, up until now just a distraction, had become, it seemed, a screaming reality. Sam checked and double checked and finally checked one last time. He stopped looking. The name was not listed.

Could it really be happening?

Again he searched, this time the recent activity call list. Nothing. There was no sign of the name or number. Clicking the Facebook icon he waited, fixated on the glowing mobile. He searched, tapping frantically for recent posts and pictures, nothing. There was no mention of her. They weren't even friends. It was as if she didn't exist. Denise, his girlfriend of the last six months was no more; at least not on his phone.

Now this is what I want

DJ would know, Sam decided. He quickly searched out his friend's number, fidgeting as he waited for the call to connect.

"Ah there you are!" His friend's voice, suddenly reassuring and normal spoke in his ear, "Was wondering when you'd get back to me!"

"Yeah, yeah... sorry about that mate, look, I've got probably a strange question to ask, so don't laugh or anything but...," Sam paused, taking a moment.

"What is it Prof?"

Sam stopped, this time stumped, "What did you call me?"

Stu laughed.

"You know what, mate. Everyone calls you that."

"DJ I'm beginning to freak out here, mate, and I need you to be straight with me. Honestly this is going to sound weird but..."

"Who's DJ when he's at home?" Stu laughed, cutting in.

"What? You are, mate. That's your nickname."

"You're right this is beginning to sound weird. You're the one with the nickname. Professor.......!"

Sam stopped pacing about his bedroom, "What did you call me?"

"Professor..."

Sam froze, still holding the mobile, unable to respond. Professor?

"You still there, Prof?"

"Stop calling me that DJ. Listen, your nickname is DJ, I call you that because you blab on and on like a bloody disk jockey. I've called you that since we first met. Stop winding me up mate! Plus, now listen, and this will blow your mind. I don't have Denise's phone number anymore! It's vanished, like someone deleted it while I slept or something. We're not even friends on Facebook anymore! No Snapchat, no Instagram, no nothing!"

Stu remained silent.

"You there, mate?" Sam checked the connection on his mobile, "Stu?"

"I'm here."

"That's proper weird right?"

Again there was that ominous silence, then.

"Samuel, since when was Denise ever your girlfriend? You wouldn't have her as a friend on Facebook because Gary would pulverise you for just thinking about it! Do I have to say it out loud? Think about it, she's not in your league!"

It was Sam's turn to be quiet. Only it was in complete and utter stupor.

Not my girlfriend? Not in my league? What the hell is he talking about!

"Wait a minute. You said, Gary? Gary who...?"

Before Stu could reply, Sam knew the answer; knew what was coming. The final piece clicked and the fractured jig-saw puzzle was finally complete.

Stu sighed, "Adams, Gary Adams."

***

Sam ended the phone call. His mobile slipped from his hand thudding on the carpeted floor saw to that; bouncing softly, it landed face up revealing the connection was lost. He remained still, unable to move, not *daring* to move. He stayed like that for a while, his mouth moved without the companion of words.

Slowly Sam bent down to retrieve his phone; having ignored the four calls, he ignored the text message as well. It was from Stu: *Are you alright? Come over for a game of chess you'll feel better*

Feeling nauseous and faint, Sam sat on his bed staring trance-like about his room, only now becoming fully aware of the changes. Subtle nuances here and there, little changes that had been waiting to be discovered. Like a crime scene, his very own personal Agatha Christie *whodunit* was set out before him. All the answers were here, he just had to spot the crime. But unlike Christie some were now blatantly, glaringly obvious; beginning with his clothes, he pulled drawers open. At first the colours seemed right but pulling out the various t-shirts and pullovers revealed hidden changes that wouldn't be picked up until they were worn.

Gone were the heavy rock staples of AC/DC and Guns N' Roses. Now when unfolded, the t-shirts had prints of bands such as Coldplay and Dire Straits. There was even one from the Royal Albert Hall; The London Symphony Orchestra presents An Evening with John Williams.

Are you kidding me!

The wardrobe was next. Swishing garments revealed sensible attire replacing the bomber and leather jackets he once owned and loved.

Next, a quick scan over the IKEA Billy bookcase still exhibited books, but hardbacks had hi-jacked the paperbacks. Classic names like Shelley, Poe and Wyndham stared back, the copies of Herbert, King and Barker had ceased to exist. Even the bookends; a Lego bust of Boba Fett and a Stormtrooper from Star Wars were gone, replaced by a black onyx statue of Octavius Augustus Caesar and a grey painted clay cast of the Trojan Horse from the great War of Troy propped up the novels.

The walls were decorated differently too. The same large picture frames were still present but instead of his favourite flashy blockbusters,

Transformers and Alien, Steve Jobs glared across the room holding the very first iconic Apple iPhone.

Isn't this what you wanted? Isn't this exactly *what you wanted!*

"I wanted to….." he began to answer himself.

What are you prepared to forfeit?

Sam held his hands to his head, turning 360 degrees in utter bewilderment.

Adams, the 'boy', this transformation, Denise, his life! How was it even possible?

"No, this can't be," Sam muttered out loud, "This is not happening, this is not happening! I didn't want any of this! I only wanted to change my grades, not my LIFE!"

Breathing deeply, he swallowed volumes of air, trying to stop the panic from erupting from its hidden depths.

"This cannot be! I WANT MY LIFE BACK!"

Sam couldn't help the outburst, couldn't stop the hysteria in his voice. Monday couldn't come fast enough for Sam.

Chapter Six

The doorbell rang, "Stuart's here!" his mother called out.

Sam was ready and waiting. Had been for the past 20 minutes; Standing sentry in the living room looking out through the front windows.

"Morning," Sam grumbled.

"Morning," Stu replied. He was dressed in a hooded duffel coat, smart but sensible. Sam couldn't help the little smile from forming. His own coat was an old, faded puffer jacket; the closest he could find to being fashionable.

"Everything alright?" Stuart leaned in to look at his friend.

"Groovy."

"Nice jacket! Not seen it before?"

"It's my brother's."

"Guess he doesn't need it anymore, huh, being lodged at St George's,"

The two boys headed out. Across the road some neighbours were organising their brood, another was dumping his rubbish for the bin men. One of them waved cheerily at Sam.

That's never happened before! Jesus, what next? Offerings from strangers!

Finally, Stu could no longer contain himself.

"Want to talk about Saturday? You know…."

"Not really." Sam shut Stu down.

"Ok."

Continuing their journey to school in silence for a bit, Sam was happy not to converse.

Their breaths expelled the cold autumn air, cold and crisp it was a typical late October morning. It wasn't long before Stu, the one Sam knew from before opened up.

"You know my parents are organising a bonfire next weekend. Want to come over? I've already asked, they said it would be ok. There'll be fireworks and a bar-b-q. It'll be awesome! Dad's been saving wood since, forever!" Stuart quickly rattled out the invitation.

"Sure, sounds good." Sam smiled appreciatively at Stu. *It seemed some things never changed.*

"You won't believe how much wood my dad has gathered. I honestly don't know where he gets it from. I bet one of our neighbours calls the fire brigade. It happened last year, we never found out who it was, but my mum thinks it was the old cow two doors down. She's proper nosy. You should have seen their faces, the Firemen, that is, they were ready to hose our house down they were so annoyed!"

Sam listened to Stu babble away, content not having to speak or think too much about what he was going to say, what he was going to do when he got to school. But his thoughts soon drifted to the matter in hand; *how he was going to deal with Adams, what approach to use, would he even be in school? What of Denise? One thing at a time...... She'll understand once he explained the whole stupid story. Wouldn't she? What if......*

"HEY WATCH OUT!" Stu's arm snapped across Sam's chest, jolting him to a stop. Just in time as a car swooshed past, inches away from serious casualty.

"Careful Samuel... That was close!"

They were at a zebra crossing. He had just stepped out into the road without noticing the danger, neither had the motorist.

Stu checked both ways before continuing, releasing his protective arm.

"You awake yet?"

"Sorry. I was miles away," Sam mumbled

"It's ok. Come on."

The rest of the journey to school was made in silence.

At the gates, Stu pulled his friend aside.

"You're not going to do anything stupid are you?"

"Like what?"

"I dunno, like walk up to Denise Matthews and say, 'why haven't I got your phone number? *That kind of stupid?"* Stu laughed awkwardly but his eyes were serious.

Sam scanned the school grounds checking out the pupils as they wandered in. Just a typical Monday morning, only it was anything but. Stu looked genuinely concerned.

"Don't worry I won't."

Did he look scared? Sam pondered.

"Good, because..." Stu never finished. Three boys, all older students, barged between the two friends, knocking Stu off balance. Sam held his ground and was shoved aside for good measure.

"Hey!" Sam immediately protested, instantly inflamed with astonishment.

"WHAT?" The lead boy spun around, wearing his battle face, "What you gonna do about it, huh?" Placing himself in Sam's personal space, the two boys now stood inches apart, boxers at a pre-match weigh-in, psyching it out. "You got something to say FAGGOTBREATH!"

"We're good, we're good." Stu interrupted, pulling Sam away. He grabbed an arm before pushing his friend ahead. "Sorry about that."

The three older boys laughed, one slapping the lead boy on the back. Suddenly the third boy made a lunge at the two friends, but it was only a feint and he pulled back. Still Stu flinched, producing another burst of laughter.

"What the hell?" Sam exclaimed pulling out of Stu's grasp. The two boys were clear, now stepping through the main doors. "How dare they? Don't they know who I am?"

"Do you have a death wish?" Stu countered shaking his head.

"They'll regret that. Just wait until I speak to my brother!"

"Your brother? Who's that, Dwayne 'The Rock' Johnson?"

"Tom! My brother Tom, he'll sort them out." Sam opened his locker door throwing his rucksack inside.

"Right...Tom? You mean Thomas?" Stu asked.

Sam found his locker and punched the combination.

"This is the same Tom who organises chess classes and other after school activities? The same Tom who is a Prefect... that the Tom you mean?

Sam stared blankly.

"Did you fall down and bang your head?"

"No."

"Sam, we got Maths next, try and focus."

"So what...?"

Stu shut his locker door and turning to his friend "Exams! We have exams all day!"

"Shit!"

"Come on."

Entering the classroom, Sam and Stu took their places, the desks now separated slightly in acknowledgement of the exam's conditions. Sam checked the pupils whilst taking a seat, catching Denise's friend, Rachel Eden's eye. He smiled a greeting, expecting likewise in return. Only, Rachel stared, frowning in response, her expression turning into a grimace. With a shake of her head, she leaned over to the girl nearest to her and whispered something. Both looked back at Sam. The second girl made a face, poking her tongue out nastily.

"Okay you have 90 minutes to complete the paper in front of you," Mr Wright addressed his class, looking stern and serious, "there'll be no talking, no conferring, no whispering any answers to your buddies, and no cheating. The last one is very serious! Anyone caught doing the last one will be expelled! Are we clear? Yes? Then turn over your paper. You have," he checked the clock on the wall, "90 minutes, starting now."

Sam turned over his paper. He picked up his pen and…started writing. The answers came quick and easy, the thought process was fluid. He understood the equations. Trigonometry and geometry were immediate and comprehensible. In no time at all the first two pages were finished, there were no gaps, no problems to return to.

How is this possible?

Reading and answering were the same, there was no pause, it was as if he had the answers to hand and was merely copying down someone else's work. Each question was answered, each page finished.

This is almost enjoyable!

At 49 minutes and 26 seconds Sam put down his pen and sat back. He was the first to finish. Shuffling the papers, he put them together neatly, still mesmerised by what had just happened.

Stu, sitting to his left, looked up and smiled, "Really?" he mouthed.

Sam shrugged.

"Err…hmmm." Mr Wight coughed, looking at Sam.

Sam waited then put his hand up. Several of the class looked up, including Rachel Eden.

Mr Wight frowned and came over.

"Can I go? I've finished." Sam whispered.

"I'm afraid not Samuel. You'll have to wait until the end."

There it was again

Sam nodded, trying not to watch the others reactions.

"Are you sure you're done?"

Sam nodded again.

"Ok." Mr Wight gathered up Sam's exam papers, "I'll take those, but you'll have to wait until the end."

The next 30 minutes passed inordinately slowly; it was as though time was dragging every second out of every minute. Sam thought about what he would say when he confronted Adams. That was all he could think about.

The bell rang, releasing the class from the exam. The pupils filed out, handing in their papers, some reluctantly. Sam was ahead of the crowd standing to one side waiting for Stu in the corridor.

"Looks like you breezed that one Pro…" Stu caught himself, but not in time.

Sam shook his head, "You know I'm really not that clever mate."

"Yeah, right."

"What's next?"

"Well, I've got Biology and you have Physics my friend," Stu said.

"Better get to it I suppose."

"You suppose, do you? It'll be a walk in the park for you!"

The two boys parted ways, promising to meet up by the doors to head out for lunch. For the next two and a half hours Sam had to contend himself with the dealings of energy, matter and gravitational forces. Adams would have to wait.

***

"How did it go? No wait don't tell me, I already know the answer to that!" Stu ribbed Sam before he could utter a word. The two had caught up. It was lunch break and as planned they were heading for the canteen. "Oh bugger!" he suddenly exclaimed.

"What!"

"Don't look now, but Martin Lucas is over there."

"So?"

"Don't you remember? He hasn't forgiven you since that incident at the Halloween disco party! Don't you remember?" Stu stared at his friend. "Anyway, Gary Adams stepped in and made him look a fool in front of his mates, not to mention half the school!"

"That was me…" Sam started, but drifted off, the memory of that night refusing to manifest properly, "I stopped Lucas from…"

"In your dreams! Come on let's go before he sees you, and me, come to think of it."

Both boys about turned, heading smartly for the exit doors that lead directly out onto the playground. They almost made it. The door swung open, surprising them both. Filling the gap, a smiling Darren Wilkes and friend blocked the two boys' flight.

Behind them Martin Lucas cooed, "There you are Willy!"

Chapter Seven

Sam turned to face Lucas, who was accompanied by another boy.
"What are you gay boys up to, huh?"

Wilkes sniggered appropriately "Going outside to *play?*" he added viciously.

Stu looked desperate, now they were cornered, his head dropped, searching the ground for some lost dignity.

Sam stuck up for both of them.

"What's up Lucas?"

"We got some unfinished business Willy haven't we...?"

"Really, such as...?"

"Oh, you remember...Halloween disco, you spilling my drink!"

Sam looked over Lucas' shoulder, theatrically cocking his head.

"Actually, would you believe I don't...now if you don't mind," Sam indicated the door and salvation, "We were leaving,"

"Not so fast Professor Bung." Lucas sneered. "You and your..."

"Assistant Plug!" added Wilkes loudly.

Everyone looked at Wilkes.

"Well, it sounds good, don't it?" he responded to the strange looks.

"Anyway," Lucas shook his head at Wilkes, before turning back to Sam, "after school, outside the gates, we're gonna finish this," he jabbed his finger on Sam's chest, "and don't try and get out of it!"

"Wouldn't dream of it...."

"Come on let's go." The Lucas gang all tramped off, leaving Sam and Stu alone.

"Phew, for a minute there I thought we were in trouble!"

Sam rounded on his friend, "I am in trouble DJ!" he snapped.

Leaning back against the wall for support, he caught his breath. The incident had left him strangely apprehensive and fearful.

"Well...not until after school." Stu pointed out, trying to be helpful.

At that moment Denise and company appeared, marching past the two boys, heading for the exit door. The small troupe were focused, their strides synchronised. It screamed 'you don't want to mess with us!'

"Denise!" Sam called out.

All three girls turned their heads in unison. Tina and Rachel, the two girlfriends on either side of Denise stared back, their expressions horrified and outraged. They didn't break their stride.

"Wait! I need to talk to you!" Sam pleaded.

Denise said nothing and the three girls were gone. Out of the door seconds later, only Rachel stole a look, laughing. It was a cruel, hurtful, laugh, meant to cut deep. It implied loser.

Stu picked up his rucksack. "You honestly believe you and Denise are going out together don't you!"

Sam watched the exit doors swinging shut, "We are…were."

"Well, unless you've been keeping this from me, say for the last six months, I'd have to tell you…you're deluding yourself…big time! It's not healthy Samuel, I read somewhere…"

"DJ…."

"Not forgetting the fact that she's seeing Adams…has been for like forever…"

"DJ, please!"

"Sorry…"

"Listen Stu, I got to tell you something," turning to his friend, Sam pulled on Stu's arm, "Come on, I'll tell you everything."

Once outside he proceeded to explain the whole story, beginning with the day in the rain two weeks ago, his discussion with Adams and subsequent encounter with 'the boy', finishing with today's exams and his now apparently high intellectual abilities.

For a few seconds Stu was silent, an eternity for him, his face a picture of confusion. Eventually he managed, "That is quite a story Samuel!"

All around them pupils mingled, some shouting, others playing. Stu walked a little way ahead. Head bowed, scuffing the sole of his shoes distractedly.

"So, what do you think?"

"What do I think? Well…err… Samuel, I don't know what to say is what I think."

"You could start by saying I believe you! That would be nice coming from my best friend don't you think? And stop calling me Samuel! Can you at least try to do that!"

"Of course…I would like to…"

"Come on Stu, you play in the football team, not the chess team!!" Sam implored, desperate to find a connection with his old friend. He could still remember the past but it was slipping away, like he was grasping at straws.

Across the playground he spotted a figure in the distance that made him stop and stare.

Stu followed his gaze.

"Is that who I think it is?" Sam squinted, "It is...!"

"Uh-uh not a good idea," Stu started, but his friend was already heading across the tarmac. "Samuel! Wait I've got something I want to tell you too...!"

Sam stopped as if shot, "What now DJ? Suddenly remembered who you are...?"

His friend stared hard, his eyes widening, large as saucers.

"Stu...what do you know?"

"I think.... I think I know what's going on."

"Go on."

"Adams, the 'boy' who fixes things...me, we're all connected...."

"What?"

"I ...I couldn't say anything..."

"What are you saying? What do you mean you're all connected?"

"I'm trying to tell you!"

"Then tell me. Now!"

Stu searched Sam's face trying to speak, the angst conflicting with the desire to unleash a secret.

"If I...if I say anything then..." he trailed off.

"Then what DJ...then what...?"

Sam shook his head, disgusted, "I knew you were involved; I just knew it!" With that he stormed off, heading in the direction that he had last seen Adams.

***

"Gary!"

Gary Adams stopped at the sound of his name, slowly turning to face the caller. The familiar posture that had so personified Adams before was completely gone now. The boy that stood before Sam was unrecognisable. Standing straight he was as tall, if not taller than Sam, the shoulders no longer sagging, but square and strong. The uniform he wore was smart, fitted, and overly clean looking. His eyes were bright, the blue iris' almost electric blue with clarity.

Adams smiled sardonically, holding his hands aloft, "you got me."

Sam looked the other boy up and down.

"I don't even recognise you...how?"

"Like the new me?"

"Well..."

"Come on admit it, it kind of suits me doesn't it...and you... look at you. Do you like the new you?"

Sam ignored the question.

"What has happened? What has happened to me, Gary? My life is ruined! I don't have the same friends, the same clothes. I don't…I don't even have a girlfriend anymore!"

Smiling in a sad, sympathetic way, Adams put his hand on Sam's shoulder.

"You had it all didn't you? The attitude, the girlfriend, the life. Oh, everyone loves Sammy boy Williams!" Adams snarled. "But there was one itsy bitsy teeny weeny aspect blotting the perfect landscape, one little chink in that sparkling armour, eh! Of course, you know what I'm talking about don't you!"

"I…"

"A little bit of a thickie, aren't we? Or was, I should say now." Adams mocked, tilting his head.

Sam could only gawk.

"Come on mate, admit it. It's true. Don't act all coy with me. I'm not one of your girlfriends after all!" Adams let out a short snorting laugh.

Sam's head whipped up. Surely not. *That laugh it's…it's mine!*

As if reading his thoughts, Adams smile curled larger, the left eyebrow raised in perfect unison.

"Which leads us to Denise. Shame she doesn't remember you, huh? She remembers me though, didn't I mention that when I told you?" Adams paused, calmly walking around Sam, waiting for the penny to drop, "You know, in the bicycle shed."

"Wait…what?"

"You know, when the boy told you. Remember what he said, Sammy? 'What are you prepared to forfeit?'" Adams mimicked the voice, lowering his tone.

Sam stared hard, his head swimming with confusion, "You! You knew the boy would do this!"

"Ha, yes, yes, brilliant… brilliant Sam."

I only see Adams, Stu had said.

"Did you ever see me and 'the boy' together? Of course you didn't. That's because we was the same." Adams sighed. "I gotta admit the makeup alone took hours to…you never suspected, did you? Well, I must say I did a good job…eh matey?"

"I did see you!"

"Did yah? Did you really see me?"

Sam looked away confused.

"You were…….*different?*"

"Had to be Sammy boy, had to be, otherwise you'd never believe the prophecy."

"Prophecy...?" Sam repeated the word as if hearing it for the first time.

"Good God! I'm beginning to wonder if it has worked or not!" Adams let out the familiar snorting laugh. "Yes, the prophecy Sammy!"

"But you gave me a gold lighter I helped you from getting..."

"Bullied?" Adams finished the sentence before continuing, "Well thank you very much, but that was only once Sammy boy, and nothing compared to the daily crap I've had to deal with all my life. You have NO idea what it's like to be me. NO IDEA!" he screamed.

"Is this what it's all about then? You being bullied?"

Adams merely smiled in response.

"And what is this prophecy...?"

"Ah a good magician rarely exposing the tricks he plays.........fuck it, seeing as you won't remember much in a couple of weeks, you see it's really *Necromancy* when it boils right down to it. Good old fashioned 'black arts'. You see, I've been studying the ancient religious practice of Vodun or Voodoo as we know it over here. Did you know it originated in West Africa? I doubt it. Probably thought it was all down to Hollywood. Well, they adopted it and dramatized it with their hocus pocus stuff. A brief history of it is that it migrated around the seventeenth century from Africa to the West Indies Island of Hispaniola with the help of French colonial slavery adding a dollop of Catholic icing on top. You keeping up with me?"

Sam could only stare.

"Used to be called Saint-Domingue by the Frenchies, the island that is, now it's better known as Haiti, no? Well, now you've acquired some more of the old grey matter you can look it up and do your own homework for a change. It might even stick this time, eh!" Adams let out another snigger, "The think is it *works, it actually works*....you're not the first and you're not gonna be the last.....there's a queue forming!"

"Why go to all this bother?"

"Why? Isn't it obvious matey? No? I wanted to be like YOU! Sam Williams the boy who has it all. The attitude, the physique... *the girls.*" Adams spat.

Sam would have laughed in another life but felt sick instead.

"Me?"

"Yeah you! I wanted what you had. Do you have any idea what it's like to be me? Well, the old me that is. Well, you're gonna find out now, ain't yah."

Stu appeared, now standing behind Sam, staring from one boy to the other, transfixed.

"Please we got to reverse this...whatever it is you've done! You're going take it back... whatever this is... this curse!"

"Is that right mate?"

"Please, Gary." Sam implored the other boy.

"Sam...." Stu mumbled.

"Sorry Samuel," Adams interrupted, but it's taken a lot more than you can possibly imagine. The time, blah blah blah, I can't divulge it all but believe me I've made sacrifices too. Once you go down this road there ain't no going back."

From his pocket Sam produced the gold cigarette lighter.

Adams eyes narrowed instantly, but only for a split second before he recovered his composure. Not before Sam had noticed though.

"You gave me this didn't you? This has something to do with it."

Adams just smiled.

"Thought so..."

Still Adams said nothing.

"I'm right, aren't I?" it was Sam's turn to shout, finally finding his voice and confidence.

"Steady on. Remember, you're not the same Sam you once were!"

"Oh, you mean I don't remember how to fight? Well that's one thing that hasn't left me."

Before Adams could react, Sam quickly swung a right hook at the other boy's head. His aim was good, but slow, far too slow.

Adams easily swatted the effort aside, replying with a hard left-hand slap. The blow caught Sam perfectly across his face, knocking him completely off balance. Undeterred, Sam moved back in for another attempt.

"Don't Samuel!" Stu cried out, nearly getting in the way.

But Sam wasn't listening. Launching himself forward, he rugby tackled Adams' midriff, bundling the pair back, the momentum producing enough force for the two boys to tumble over with Sam on top.

"Get off me, get off me!" Adams cried, his previous cockiness gone.

Each boy now scrambling to grab the other's arms in a rapid display of flaying limbs. A small crowd had gathered on the fringes, like moths to a flame. The anticipation of a fight had been noticed early on with the commotion, and the crowd multiplying in numbers was now being rewarded.

"Fight, fight, fight, fight!" the crowd chanted.

"Take the curse back!" Sam managed between breaths. He had secured Adams, pinning him back on the ground, sitting on his chest, "Take it back!"

"I can't! I CAN'T!" Adams screamed. He'd lost that cocky composure, the swagger of the coolest kid in town. The geek wasn't quite back, but it was poking its spotty head around the corner again.

Sam ripped Adams' rucksack open. Feeling inside, he plucked out a black book. The black book he recognised as being the one in the bike shed.

"Got yah…!"

More pupils arrived, along with a concerned Mr Callaghan who had spotted the fighting from his classroom window.

"Stop this! Stop fighting right now!"

Sam, ignoring the teacher's request, leaned in close to Adams' face.

"Take it back or I'll curse YOU!"

"Too late Sam…you're too late!" Adams managed to spit with an actual tongue's worth of spit. But his eyes betrayed him, already they were dancing wildly from Sam to the book in his hands.

"We'll see about that!"

Adams laughed back hysterically, but this changed into a girlish high-pitched scream as the clump of hair in Sam's hand was yanked out of his head. Mr Callaghan, losing his patience, pulled Sam bodily away and in doing so helped perpetrate the loss of hair.

"Ok Williams, that's enough. Get off now!"

Adams struggled to his feet, the crowd parting as he staggered a few steps.

"You pulled my fucking hair out!"

Sam held the gold lighter to the black book.

"What are you doing, Williams?" Mr Callaghan gasped, seeing the lighter.

"Let's see, shall we?" Sam flicked the lighter.

"Nooooooooooo……!" Screamed Adams.

With a flash the book ignited, flames enveloped the worn cover almost instantly.

Two things happened next; the first was Adams collapsing, dropping like a stone, moaning and writhing, holding his head where the hair had been; the second was Stu suddenly shrieking in falsetto, a terrible noise of pain

Sam stared dumbfounded along with everyone else: stunned.

"DJ...?"

Students backed away gawping, their mouths dropping open. Some began to point, others were laughing.

"Philips? You ok?" Mr Callaghan leaned over Stu, reaching out a concerned hand.

Stu's head snapped up at the light touch. Everyone gasped.

"DJ what ...?"

"Don't look at me! Don't look at me!!" Stu cowered again, hiding his face from the crowd, but the slight exposure had revealed enough. His voice and his hair were unrecognisable.

"DJ, you're a... *girl!?!*" Sam gasped.

Stu was up in a second, sprinting away as if propelled, still holding his hands to his face. Wailing a miserable song as he went.

Mr Callaghan ran as well, chasing down the crying student, his face a picture of utter astonishment.

Chapter Eight

Across the playing fields, way out by the perimeter fencing, a majestic oak tree resided. It had matured over one hundred years and whilst all around there had been desecration in the name of profit, amazingly, it had survived the many attempts to hack down the natural beauty made by various headmasters and groundsmen over the years. It was the only tree on the school grounds now. It was also the last of its kind as far as the eye could see in any direction, possibly even further.

It was here that Sam found his best friend. He hunkered down, resting his back against the broad trunk. Sitting side by side, the two students gazed back towards the school buildings. Watching the scenes of calamity unfold in the distance.

"So, what's your real name?" Sam eventually asked, picking up a twig before throwing it away after inspecting its texture.

"Susan, Susan Bennett."

Sam smiled, *of course it is.* The name didn't ring any bells though.

"So all this time you've been faking. You knew all along."

Susan nodded.

"Wow!" They sat in silence for a little while. Sam frowned, "But you changed from DJ into...someone else?"

"I guess after you got 'Fixed' we all evolved again."

"Makes sense. Actually none of this makes sense." Sam shook his head.

"You were always asking the right questions. I couldn't say anything for fear the prophecy...you know, would revert back. I wanted to explain so badly you know...when you..."

Sam held up his hand silencing Susan.

"I just wanna know why?" he asked kindly, "Why you did it?"

Susan released a deep sigh; the kind that released a whole tanker's worth from the shoulders kind of sigh, "I've watched you for a long time, I knew you would never want to be my friend or make me your girlfriend, and after you started dating Denise I..."

"Hold on, how would you know that?"

"Come on Sam, you're the school jock, right? *Sam Williams!* You didn't even notice me...I had no chance. I can't compete with the likes of Denise Matthews!"

"I see, so..."

"So when Adams told me about the boy who could fix things...well I jumped at it. I became a boy to be close to you...I had no idea what a mess it would create."

Sam couldn't stop the laugh from coming, a release of emotion that needed to escape. Susan waited until he calmed down before asking.

"What's so funny?"

"Well it's just that...well, I thought I'd caused all this mess, up until you screamed."

"I see."

"Burning the book Gary had of everyone's blood signature must have undone the prophecy."

"I wonder how many were in that book? How is it I remembered my past life as well?"

"The thing is you do, remember that is...at least for a while, then it kinda becomes normal not to remember...I've been changed for nearly six months now....."

"Wow."

"Yeah...do you remember when we first met?

"Sort of."

"Well I had just changed the day before..."

"Yeah I remember now...you said we should be friends..."

"....cause we live on the same street." Susan finished.

"Right."

High above them the tree's branches and twigs swayed on the boughs, their leaves rustling a consonance of swishing sounds gifted by a gentle uplift from the wind.

"What now?" Sam turned to Susan.

"Tomorrow...tomorrow everyone will have forgotten all about this. It will be as if nothing has happened, I guess, slowly slowly back to normal. That's how it was for me... I hope...I hope we'll be friends."

Sam turned to look at Susan, breaking into a smile.

"Me too..."

"Hey, by the way, how did you know the book would be in Adams' bag?"

"To be honest I didn't. I recognised the satchel though, and hoped it was there. Who knew that Adams was the 'boy' who could fix things?" he pondered out loud.

Susan caught his arm, alarmed, "He wasn't."

"What?"

"Adams wasn't the 'fixer' Sam! That was his twin brother!"

"Holy shit...!"

***

Alone in the bicycle shed, two boys sat talking, huddled at the back.

"Hey, did you see that?" one of them exclaimed excitedly, pointing to the crowd that had gathered by the New Science block. In the distance a teacher could be seen running from a group of students. One was sitting on the floor, writhing around in pain. The other students could be seen pointing and laughing. Mr Callaghan was definitely not laughing. A horrified expression haunted his features as he chased another student across the playground.

"Someone must have got hurt! Look at Callaghan's face! That is so funny! He's such a dick!"

The other boy looked up momentarily, his jet-black floppy hair parted, partially revealing more of the pasty white skin. He returned his attention to the little black book. The writing continued, fast.

"How long is this gonna take anyway?" the student asked aggressively. He'd turned back to the scribe, "and what are you writing about?"

The pen never stopped moving.

"Hey, I asked you a question!"

"It won't take long..." the boy spoke quietly.

"Good 'cause I gotta meet someone...know what I mean?"

"What is it you want?"

"Huh?"

"What is it you want?"

"Listen pal I'm the one that serves up in this school...you want anything, and I mean anything, I'm the man, you get me?"

"What is it you want me to do?"

"Oh yeah, right......I wanna punish those that I hate...yeah!"

"I see...who are they? I need to know who..."

"The teachers, fool! All those condescending fuckers that have made me feel stupid, every last one of them. I hate them, I hate them all...telling me I'm an idiot...you know Miss Deacons threatened to expel me! The miserable bitch..."

The boy stopped writing, a wicked smile curled from nowhere, splitting open the face, "what are you prepared to forfeit?" he asked.

"Forfeit? As in give up...?"

"Yes."

"Whatever it takes buddy, I don't care! Whatever it takes. I'll sell my soul to the goddam devil, if that's what it's gotta take!"

The boy breathed and expelled loudly, turning his black beady eyes on the student. The eyes were tinged with red, glowing brighter by the second. He produced a rusty looking knife from within the dark folds of his jacket. Only it wasn't rust that decorated the blade.

"Finally, it's about time," he growled.

Obsession

Chapter One

Ping!
    54 likes

"Yesssss!" Carly Watson responded.

Her mobile had just come to life, lighting up and alerting her of the incoming message.

"Mum!" she shouted out excitedly without taking her eyes off the screen, "I've got another like!"

"That's great, dear," the response came from the adjoining room, slightly delayed. Carly's mum having endured repeated updates for the past two hours.

"Yes it is," Carly agreed, speaking to herself quietly.

"How many is that now?"

"54!"

"Wow! Well done!"

"I know, right? And it's only been a couple of hours!"

Carly looked down at the sleeping dog at her feet.

"54, Star. 54 already!"

Star looked up at the sound of her name, instantly attentive. Big brown eyes searching her owner's face, before looking to the bedroom door then back again at Carly.

"Hah! I know what you're thinking girl, sorry, later."

Star's head dropped to the floor.

"Come on, let's have one more..."

Carly resumed her vigil. Staring at the mobile, waiting, waiting, willing the phone, daring the phone to repeat the notification...nothing, "I guess it's not going to happen, huh..."

The mobile's screen went blank, switching itself off, time out reached.

"Carly, can you bring your dirty washing down if you've got anything you want especially done for the weekend..." her mother called out.

"Ok, sure, mum." Carly yelled back.

With obvious reluctance she stood and stretched her back, "Wow, how long has it been?" the bedside clock's digital face provided the answer.

11.47am

"What! Where'd the time go? The morning's gone already!" Carly yelped.

Gathering up a bundle of clothes from the top of the laundry bin, mostly t-shirts and a pair of jeans that she had put there the night before, she left the bedroom. Star stood as well, stretching her front legs and arching her back, exposing her healthy bone-white canines, she gave an impressive yawn. She too left the bedroom, padding dutifully behind her lady and master.

Carly returned seconds later, scooping up the mobile while balancing the laundry in the other hand, "You're coming with me!" She slipped the phone into the back pocket of her jeans.

It had all begun as a joke, well... not as a joke, but as something to do. Even though she knew in her heart of hearts winning was not part of her life, Carly Watson had entered Star, her three-year-old Japanese Akita into the 'The Best Looking Dog' competition, at the,

Paws and Claws Care Home Centre

It was a place where she gladly volunteered some of her free time, walking dogs, feeding the cats, disinfecting the kennels. *'General dog's body'* she would joke with the full-time staff; the pun never growing old.

She'd entered dog competitions before but had never won anything; coming third grabbed a pretty rosette it had to be said, but never winning outright.

This time it had felt different. This time somehow the genuine encouragement, the appeal, the timing, hell maybe the planets were in alignment or something, but this time it felt... destined! She couldn't believe she had been allowed to enter for a second year running. Maybe that was it, The Second Coming.

"I expect you'll to be entering Star into the competition this coming Saturday, Carly?" enquired Sheila Thompson, the owner of the centre, one morning. Spotting the part-time helper in the play pen, she approached and popped the question.

"I don't know. We did it last year remember...and, well, Star's three now, and..." Carly had started, looking shyly up at her boss.

"I won't hear of it," Shelia interrupted in her no-nonsense commanding voice, "put her name down and bring her in on Friday as well. Richard is organising the photo shoot, I'd give Star the groom of her life if I was you. Come by after school."

"Alright I will, thank you Sheila. Thank you!"

"You're more than welcome Carly You know how much I appreciate your help round here. The contest runs for two weeks. Oh, and remember to tell everyone to vote for the picture in the competition and not the competition web page, catches a lot of people out that one, for some reason."

"Ok I will!"

And she did just that, bringing Star straight round the next day after school, remembering at the last minute to brush her down.

***

"Hi, it's Carly, right? Good to see you." Richard Dawson finished adjusting the window's blinds, giving a nervous half smile, "just getting the light right."

He picked up the Canon Eos 5d Mark IV camera that lay on the table, switching the little on/off button at the same time.

Carly nodded in return, her head bowed slightly, already feeling a little awkward in the man's presence. She'd only seen him around once or twice, but instantly recognized who he was.

"And this must be Star. Wow, what a gorgeous dog. And so big! I didn't realise how big she is. I've seen her around before but up close makes all the difference. Aren't you gorgeous?"

Richard made as if to approach Star. His outstretched hand was deftly avoided, Star turning away before contact was made. It was obvious the feeling wasn't reciprocated. Star completely ignored Richard.

"She's a little shy around strangers," Carly answered by way of explanation, "It's in their nature."

"No worries. So, you're here for the shoot, yes?"

"Yes."

"Good, good…" Richard watched Carly, switching his gaze to Star after what seemed like an age, then back to Carly.

"So…over here?" she indicated the area near a corner which had a white sheet backdrop.

"That's right, yep." Richard came alive, adjusting his camera., "If you could bring Star over…good, yes…sit her down and that's it. If you could get her to look my way."

Star looked the other way.

"Star…over here girl," Carly encouraged; it was in vain. Star promptly got up walked over to her.

"No girl, stay. Stay!"

Star froze before giving a body shake, then decided what she really wanted to do was to sit down. She yawned, checked the door, then walked back to Carly.

"I'm sorry. Come on Star, there's a good girl. Here!" Carly led Star back, pointing to the white mat.

"It's ok, Carly, I get used to it…why don't you stay there with her, and I'll fire a few shots off?"

"Ok."

"Great."

The camera whirred and clicked. Richard adjusted the aperture.

"That's it lovely…lovely…If you could look this way," the camera flashed this time. "Great, a couple more. Okay, if you could come to me Carly, that's it, nice and slow, let's see if Star will sit still."

This time Star behaved; she even gave the camera a glance which was captured just in time.

"Got it!"

Carly was relieved, an uneasy feeling was beginning to gnaw. Richard's eyes were….. shifty. She just wanted to get it over with and get out of there now. Spending time in his presence was…there was something that she couldn't quite put her finger on. Something wrong.

"Let me show you," Richard lent towards Carly, holding the camera with the digital face showing, offering the image to her. Their bodies touched.

Star got up immediately, nosing her way between the pair.

"Oh, someone wants to see them as well," Richard laughed nervously, backing away slightly.

Star wasn't happy. Her head lowered, eyes trained looking up said otherwise. Dogs were not known to hold eye contact but Stars were locked onto Richard's. Carly recognised the pose though. She was on alert…….

***

There had been one time when Carly's family had visited their local pub for an impromptu Sunday afternoon drink, Star, being a regular, was allowed in. It helped that the land lady was a fan, had been from day one. It had been raining, only a slight, annoying drizzle but enough for the family to go inside rather than hang about in the beer garden. Star was only a mature puppy at the time but fully grown. All the patrons had fawned as she excitedly went from one kind, petting hand to the next. Everything had gone well until one man had entered with two pals. Star had gone from carnival parade to guard dog in a blink; ready to attack, her bark when it came, was epic, and in a closed space, it nearly took the roof off. Carly had rushed over to calm Star who wouldn't take her eyes off this one man. The dog's heightened senses had picked up something……….*something bad.*

After the man laughed it off with his pals, he'd retreated to another part of the pub, and only when he was out of eyesight did Star switch off.

Apologising profusely to a bar maid who had come over to mediate, Carly added, "Something's wrong with that guy, just letting you know Star wouldn't normally react that way."

The barmaid lent into whisper, "Your dog's spot on. He's proper dodgy that one!"

***

Star remained fixated on Richard.

"Come on girl, its ok, he's a friend."

Star remained rooted.

"Err...is she okay?" Richard's voice wavered.

"Star, that's enough. I think we'll go now. That's fine, the picture's fine," Carly said hurriedly.

"Okay, sure, I'll be putting up the all the photos tonight on the Paws and Claws website. You can view them before the competition goes live Saturday morning." Richard backed further away from the pair. He studied the camera's controls, fiddling with a button or two, and then added, "You can see them on my personal business site," he reached into his back pocket for a card, handing it over to Carly.

Star growled.

"That's enough, Star!" Carly accepted the card.

With the daylight space between the two now at an acceptable distance, Star switched off, padding to the door.

"Thanks again," Carly mumbled.

"No problem, no problem."

Outside Carly cuddled Star in the courtyard, "What was all that about girl? You didn't like him?"

Behind them, the window blinds rippled before settling back into place.

"Nor did I girl, nor did I."

And that was that. Star was in the competition for a second year running. Everyone who met Star would say she was handsome; a stunning, handsome dog.

"Not handsome, that's for boys," Carly would correct, "she's beautiful!"

Other glowing compliments garnered from around the neighbourhood when Carly proudly walked Star, were mostly positive.

"She's gorgeous!"
"Wow, what a lovely looking dog"
"Isn't she big for her age?"

Of course not everybody was as gracious and complimentary. The odd moment when a person happened to round a corner at the wrong time was a hoot to see, or not depending on the side of the road you walked down.

Star had the classic sesame coloured coat, favoured by a lot of owners of the Akita Inu breed. She was also true to having all the characteristics associated with the pedigree; loyal, composed, intelligent, faithful, and powerful.

Star was no exception. In fact, she was exemplary, growing slightly larger than the average female Japanese Akita. With Carly's slight build and height, the pair, when out walking, made for an impressive sight.

Carly dedicated her time, *heck, her life is she new it*, to the upbringing and wellbeing of Star. She didn't need friends. Friends let you down, friends lied to you, friends could hurt you. But Star never let her down, never complained. Not once. She was always there, always ready with a wagging tail, always happy to see her.

But it nearly never happened…….

Chapter Two

While researching dog breeders and other sources, the Watson's had primarily been thinking of the Golden Retriever breed to come and join the family.

"This family needs a dog!" Mr Watson had declared totally out the blue one Sunday afternoon as the family enjoyed a stroll through Benson's Park, walking off a mighty Sunday roast they had all just consumed at *The Fat Turk* pub.

"Oh, what a great idea, Eric," Mrs Watson cooed.

"I think so," Mr Watson agreed, looking very pleased with himself.

"I can help Daddy! Please, please, please can I help?" Carly had bounced up and down, tugging at her father's sleeve, "Please, Daddy!"

"Sure, Carly you can help," laughed Mr Watson, grabbing his twelve-year-old daughter around the waist, failing to contain her youthful excitement in the process.

"What kind of dog are we going to get, Dad?"

Alan, Carly's older brother, spoke up. Alan was three years older than his sister and he took the job of being the older sibling seriously.

"I'm thinking Retriever, Golden Retriever."

"What do they look like Daddy?" Carly asked excitedly, still bouncing.

"Just like that!" Mr Watson pointed at a dog walking with its owner across the park.

"Yes!" Alan nodded happily.

Carly stopped bouncing, the sudden explosive joy she had struggled to contain now vanished equally fast, like a balloon popping, instantly deflated.

"Of course we'll have to find a breeder, suitably nearby, what I mean by that kids is, one that doesn't break the bank getting too!"

Carly wasn't paying attention. That dog wasn't what she had envisaged.

Alan offered his sister a smug sideward glance.

Tough luck, it conveyed.

As the family made their way home, Carly began to scheme. She wasn't going to let her brother have his way, not while there was a chance. She still had time, plus she had an ace up her sleeve. Carly was still Daddy's girl, and she knew how to play him. If there was going to be a dog in the house, then it would be of her choosing, but she would have to act. Fast.

Back at home, she set about focusing on the job at hand. Disappearing upstairs she trawled the internet looking on her tablet at the hundreds of different breeds of canines.

We are not having a girlie dog in this house! No siree!!

Then Carly had come across an Akita. It was love at first sight. She'd never heard of one before, let alone seen one. The dog looked dignified, proud, and completely and utterly majestic. To Carly, the image of the dog on her tablet was literally calling out to her, choosing her, not the other way round. It was meant to be. There was only the small matter of finding a breeder, and one not too far from home.

Within a matter of hours Carly had not only found the dog of her dreams but also a suitable breeder relatively nearby. The gamble was if relatively nearby was what her dad considered 'suitably nearby'. It was crunch time. She just had to sell it right. Again, she knew just how to play it.

"Oh my God, look at the puppies! Aren't they gorgeous?"

Everyone looked up at the mention of puppies.

The Watsons were all convened in the L-shaped kitchen-come-dining room.

"Is that even a dog?" Alan asked, rather unkindly, peering over her shoulder.

"Mum, come and have a look!" Carly ignored her older brother. "Take a look at the Akita's."

"I don't know, Carly, I kinda had my heart set on a Labby honey!" Mr Watson called over from where he was sitting in the living room.

"Show me," Mrs Watson wandered past, "Oh, they do look cute, gotta say. Go show your father," she winked at her daughter.

"Daddy look, aren't they just adorable?"

"Hmm…"

"Oh, come on, look at those babies… what about these then? I know we talked about Golden Retrievers, but…Mum?"

"Well…"

"I think we should stick with Golden Retrievers, right, Dad?"

Carly made a face at her brother, and it wasn't a particular nice look.

"Atika's…how big do they get?" Mr Watson quizzed.

"Akita's," Carly corrected, "says here in height around 60cm in females, and about 70cm in males. The girls weigh about 25-35 kg, so roughly the same as Retrievers."

"Hmm…" The questions came thick and fast; what do they eat, are they friendly, will they be easily trained, are you prepared to look after it???

"Mum?" Carly called for backup.

"I think you should look into it a bit more and let's see, shall we." Mrs Watson cautioned.

"Your mum's right, I've never heard of the Atika's."

"*Akita's* Daddy……!" Carly corrected her father again, showing him another set of endearing pictures; puppies running loose in a perfect garden. Whoever had taken the photos was a professional, they looked stunning. It was an easy sell. Carly could almost taste success.

"Right, Akita. Gotta say they do look cute. Okay, sell it to me Carly."

"Dad…!" Alan moaned, he couldn't believe his sister had hoodwinked his father so succinctly, hadn't taken into the account his sister's determination. To Alan the writing was almost on the wall; it wasn't set yet, but the marker pens were poised and ready.

Carly didn't waste any time. Seizing the moment, she renewed her efforts and was quickly rewarded. Researching the breed had unearthed a little nutmeg, a deal winner to win all deals…which she was only too happy to impart later that evening at the dinner table.

"So, everyone I've been researching the bred and there's a lovely tale of a dog called Hachiko, a Japanese Akita, who waited for his owner to return from work at the train station every day," Carly began.

"…not exactly Lassie Comes Home, is it!" interjected Alan sarcastically, "What?" he responded to both parents in response to their glaring look, "I saw it advertised on Netflix!"

"They would both travel to the station," Carly continued staring hard at her brother, "every day and then the dog would wait for him to return. They did this for several years until one day the man didn't come home…he died." Carly looked around the table.

Mr Watson paused as he was about to take a large mouthful of Mrs Watson's delicious homemade shepherd's pie, "Well go on, what happened to the dog?"

"The story goes that the dog continued to wait at the station hoping for his owner to return…for nine years!"

"Oh my, that is so sweet!" Mrs Watson exclaimed.

"Nine years daddy!"

"Is that true Carly, what, like for real?" Mr Watson fed the pie to its final destination.

"Oh, come on! Who would believe that?" Alan implored, staring at his parents, "wouldn't there have been a film or something if it was that believable?"

"Actually, there were. Two films! And Richard Gere starred in one of them and that's probably on Netflix too!"

"Pleassssssse." Alan slumped on the couch.

"And there's a statue in his honour in his home town," Carly finished defiantly.

"Wow, is that true, Carly?" Mrs Watson called out.

"Yes, absolutely. Dad?"

Mr Watson stared into his twelve-year-old daughter's eyes. New the signs: the contract was draw up ready to sign. She just had to capitalise the moment.

"That is quite a story Carly, quite a story."

"I know, right? I've been reading up on them. They're loyal, faithful, affectionate, and they can be a bit stubborn, a bit like you Dad," Mrs Watson stifled a laugh, "but they're also strong, powerful and brilliant guard dogs."

"Are you kidding me? They look like overgrown foxes!" Alan pointed at Carly's phone.

"They were also bred as hunting dogs!"

"What for, rabbits?"

"Bears actually!"

Alan made a face, *"Bears actually,"* he mimicked.

"What were Golden Retrievers bred for huh? Retrieving sheep!"

"Alright, enough you two," Mrs Watson stepped in, defusing the situation.

Everyone looked to Mr Watson.

Carly waited. She daren't breathe.

Mr Watson looked over at his wife, who nodded.

"Ok Carly, you sold it to me."

"Yesssssss...!" Carly pulled a double fist.

"She always gets what she wants!" Alan complained, bolting from the couch, "It's not fair!" he added, storming out of the room.

"Alan, come back son," Mrs Watson called after him.

"Don't worry, he'll come round." Mr Watson changed the channel on the TV.

But Carly wasn't worried, she was in heaven.

"What we looking at cost wise, Carly, you got that far yet?" her father asked, still watching the TV.

Carly told him.

"HOW MUCH......!!"

***

Carly had willingly surrendered her Christmas and next birthday presents as down payments, even pulling extra chores around the house. Although that only lasted a couple of weeks; her mother struggled to find suitable jobs that a twelve-year-old could undertake effectively, let alone efficiently on top of her usual allotment. Fixing electrical wiring, painting and other repair work was a cut above her pay grade.

Alan slowly came around, slowly. Time, the eternal healer, did its part. Glaring looks and moody silences gradually dissipated, making way for conventional sibling rivalry. Back to normal in other words.

They met with the breeder the next weekend. Mr Watson had conceded the 'relatively nearby' that Carly professed was in fact close enough.... just. An hour's drive away was tolerable when all was said and done. Crossing the Thames via the Queen Elizabeth Bridge; a short jaunt into Kent's glorious countryside, reaching the little hamlet posted just outside Rochester. Alan chose not to come, funny enough, excusing himself with an appointment with a game of footie with friends over at the park.

"We can check out Rochester Castle afterwards," ventured Mr Watson, reading the sign on the approach. He got no takers for that.

The breeder's home smelled strongly of dogs, which were literally everywhere. A litter of eight pups along with the mum and dad were in a stifling, unventilated, front room. It was late autumn, and the owners had the central heating on already.

The makeshift pen set up in the front room was not really a deterrent, rather an obstacle course the pups thrived at overcoming. The pups' mum and dad running riot with excitement, or maybe worry, added to the mayhem.

In all the commotion, one of the pups had gone unnoticed. Being placed on the sofa for safe keeping, it had found refuge under a cushion. It had then emerged, crawling into Carly's lap, where it nestled its head between her neck and shoulder, remaining there quite content.

Carly got everyone's attention by waving a hand. "This one!" she declared with quivering lip.

After placing the deposit and with the promise to stay in touch, the Watsons had come away with high expectations of what family life would be like, come six weeks later, when they were proud owners of a Japanese Akita.

"You want to name her then, Carly?" Mrs Watson asked on the drive home.

"Can I?"

"Yes darling. She seems to have chosen you after all!"

In all her preparations, Carly had forgotten this simple but deciding factor.

Of course, the name!

"You got any ideas?"

"Not yet, but I will."

"I'm sure you will."

"How about Luna.?" Mr Watson broached.

"NO!" both Carly and her mum said at the same time, laughing together.

"I kinda like it." Mr Watson's appeal was again ignored.

Still, Carly would subconsciously return to the name, it had a ring to it.

In the interim, the breeder sent weekly pictures of the pup's development, with every update bringing more ooh's and aah's. The eight-week probation period needed for the pup's inoculation period to finish, passed excruciatingly slowly for one person.

Finally, the day arrived. The Watsons set off as a family this time to collect their newest member.

"What are you going to name her, Carly, have you settled on a name yet?" Mr Watson asked in the car on the journey back home.

Carly cuddled the pup in the back seat of the car, rubbing their noses together.

"Star! Her name is Star!" she declared, staring into the pup's eyes, "Because that's what you are, a beautiful shining light in my life."

Mr and Mrs Watson locked eyes, smiling together at the beautiful words.

"Still think it looks like a fox," grumbled Alan.

That had been three and a half years ago.

Chapter Three

Ping

Carly pulled her phone out of her back pocket. Turning the mobile on quickly and deftly with one hand, a habit she had picked up whilst walking Star, she opened the notifications.

61 likes

"Got a few more!" she spoke to Star who had accompanied her to the kitchen. After dumping the laundry into a basket on the floor, she inspected the fridge, searching for a drink. Star watched her every move.

Taking a can of Coke, she sat at the kitchen breakfast bar and scrolled through the website containing the other entries and their photos. The competition had eight contestants, and as of this very moment it was very tight; there were no discernible leaders. There was a Poodle (black), a Border Collie (black and white), an Alaskan Malamute (white and black), a Beagle (tricolour), a Cavalier King Charles Spaniel (tricolour) and a Jack Russell Terrier (tricolour).

Hate them all, she mused.

Carly had met a couple of the participants at the centre, mostly only on nodding terms. Nothing that had led to meet ups or dog walks. She preferred solitary rambling. Carly mostly kept herself to herself and was quite happy that way. On the couple of occasions she had been drawn into conversation by customers dropping their pooches off for a groom or an extended stay, she'd tended to dry up, finding an excuse to wander away.

Choosing to stay away from other dog owners was easier and preferable, *just because I'm a dog owner too doesn't mean I got to be friends* she would repeat the mantra on certain days to herself, besides some were just plain weird. It was said that some owners were like a mirror of their dogs, Carly had heard that more than once slung around the centre. Some too full of themselves, like that portly, narcissistic lady who visited once in while with her overfed Chihuahua, 'Little Bow Wow', nasty little shit who yapped and snapped at everybody who came close. Holding the mutt like it was a prize possession; *oh yeah, best to stay out the way of some owners.*

Taking a sip of Coke, Carly was about to log out when she noticed a dog she'd never seen before.

"Roxy - Airedale Terrier," she read out loud, "Roxy! What a stupid name. Not like yours Star." In the bottom corner she noticed the terrier had a total of 36 likes. Carly dismissed the Airedale. "Better keep an eye on that Malamute, eh Star, she's got 62 likes!"

Star looked up, hopefully. Carly checked the time, smiling down at the dog.

"Come on then girl."

Star was up and ready, tail charged.

"Walkies"

Star paced the kitchen in a tight circle waiting for the harness to arrive.

"Mum, I'm taking Star for a walk, ok?"

"Alright, don't be late for dinner," came the reply.

"Since when have we ever been late?" Carly muttered to Star, rubbing the dog's head, before clipping the K-9 body harness around her back.

"Who's a good girl then, huh?" Star immediately turned, leading the way to the front door. Checking she had a couple of poop scoop bags and a doggy treat in the bum-bag she favoured for walking, she picked up Star's lead, clipping it to the harness.

Star looked up, gave a big toothy grin, and pawed once at the front door.

"I know, I know, Star." The door was barely open before Star nosed herself through the opening, pulling strongly on the lead.

As they made their way through the quiet streets Carly instinctively watched out for other dogs and their owners. Especially the owners. It was second nature now. You could tell a lot from the behaviour of a person walking their dog, what to expect.

Star wasn't formally trained. She had been cage trained growing up, but by the time she was twelve months old she was fully grown, and she'd outgrown the first one. The Watsons had made the mistake of buying an adequate cage, soon realising that the impulsive buy was just that, impulsive. They learned fast. Carly bought books and read up on everything she could about the Akita Inu, so the surprises were kept to a minimum. Still, basic training was needed, and Star was an eager pupil in the field of education. The progress and attainment was simple and quick and before she hit twelve months old, Star was easily manageable and well behaved. If told off she would retreat to the cage, if she could have she would have shut the door herself.

Their late afternoon walk eventually took them past a short parade of shops, a typical collection of suburban franchises, isolated from the main town. The traditional newsagents had been taken over by a Tesco Metro, the Fish and Chip shop had now evolved into a glaring kebab take away/ restaurant and the general convenience store was now a glossy Nisa; but there was one shop that had resisted progress.

Riley & Sons

The butcher shop had quite literally managed the impossible, surviving the great takeover that almost every independent retailer had succumbed to. Without selling out they simply did what they did best and delivered the goods. Or maybe it had just been a demographical phenomenon that kept them alive. Stan Riley the second generation owner would say he knew his clientele, and hung in there, weathering every economic storm. Their 'old school' shop front also survived, its originality intact, only once being completely overhauled in its forty-five-year life span and even then, it was a carbon copy of what had been before. T   he original pavement sign had stayed. Cleaned up and rehung, swinging on new brass and iron fittings.

"No need to fix something that ain't broken, am I right?!" Old man Riley would cackle to one of his mates every time the conversation was brought up. *"My old man put it up and I ain't gonna be the fucker that brings it down!"*

Carly hated them, she resented the fact that they were the only store around that could supply what she needed, bones and offcuts for Star. The emotion stemmed from a loathing generated by the fact that every time she entered the shop, she was made to feel unwanted, a nuisance, *an annoying little girl.* She sensed Stan didn't like her, or was it women in general? Could it be he was just plain intimidated. For the last three walks he had been promising her some bones, but nothing had materialized. It was beginning to feel like a wind up and the joke was on her.

Outside Carly approached the butcher shop warily.

"Wait here girl," Star reluctantly sat back on her haunches, "Good girl." She bent over and squeezed Star around the neck.

"Hello there," Stan greeted Carly in his usual loud, over-the-top intonation. A cockney boy no longer in the sound of St. Mary's bells.

He spoke without bothering to look up from trimming the bloody joint in his hands.

Carly nodded and tried to smile, but it came out like a grimace.

"You after some bones, missy?" Stan's voice was like his stare, direct.

"Would you believe?" Carly found a little courage, her eyes wandered over the cut meat in the glass counter display.

"Fancy anything you see?" He slammed the knife he was holding down onto the bloody board.

Carly made a face in response, her nose twitched.

Stan's eyes narrowed slightly.

"Come back tomorrow missy, I'll have some for you tomorrow, okay?"

Carly lifted her gaze, "You said that yesterday."

Stan shrugged.

"….and the day before that."

Stan turned to the only other person in the shop, Vic Bennett, who had wandered in half-an-hour ago and was still loitering in the corner. His excuse was The Red Lion, the local pub wasn't open yet due to a funny gas smell. They hoped to have it opened as soon as they could. He'd had nothing to do so paying Stan a visit was the next best thing Vic could manage, talk some crap for a while.

"What can I say, Vic here pinched the last lot, didn't you, Vic?"

Vic wasn't the fastest gun in town, but for once he was just quick enough to catch Stan's meaning.

"Err…yeah that's right, sorry love," he gave Carly a condescending half smile.

Carly ignored Vic altogether.

"I used to have dog, did you know that Vic?" Stan began trimming again, "No? It was an Alsatian, beautiful boy, now that was a *real dog,* not one of your new-fangled breeds they love to import these days." He smirked to himself.

"Tomorrow…?" She stared vacantly at the packaged meat under the counter. Blood was dripping out of the cellophane, collecting into a little pool of red liquid.

The butcher frowned, throwing Vic a look….*She alright?*

"Yeah…I'll have some lovely ribs for yah," Stan's loud, over the top, cockney accent, even more pronounced, broke the trance.

Carly nodded, looked as if she was going to say something, then turned and left.

Vic waited until Carly passed by the window before asking, "What was all that about then Stan?"

Pointing to the open door, Stan muttered, "Fucking family never buy anything, not once in all the time I've been here, fuck 'em," Stan continued busying himself trimming the lamb he was about to mince, "I was going to give her bones the other day, but I fancied a laugh, thought she might have got the hint by now."

"She seems nice enough," Vic foolishly replied.

"Vic?"

"Yes Stan?"

"Shut up."

***

Carly collapsed on her bed. Star followed her into the room, circled her favourite spot once, twice, and after the third time decided the spot was adequate. She too collapsed, letting out a grunt as she settled down. She watched her owner briefly, then, hearing someone approach, turned to face the door.

"How's the competition going?" Alan poked his head round the bedroom door. His enquiry was anything but encouraging.

Carly checked; the phone was in her hand anyway.

85 likes

She told him.

"Is that all?" he mocked.

"Go away!" Carly fell back onto the bed staring up at the ceiling. She'd had enough for one day. It was school tomorrow and just thinking about it was depressing enough.

"She'll never win."

"Oh yeah, why's that?" Carly took the bait.

"'Cause you don't take it seriously, that's why."

Deep down she knew he was right, but coming from her brother, who had never taken to Star, never even offered to walk Star, it was an annoying observation.

Alan shrugged, "I can help if you'd like."

Carly made a face in return.

"Suit yourself." Alan turned to go.

"You've never liked Star!"

"Not true."

"Wait, do you mean that?"

"Yeah, yeah I do."

Carly sat up, "Really? You want to help? Why?"

Alan entered the room watching Star, "Hey girl." Star's tail lifted giving the briefest of wags.

Sitting down next to his sister, Alan surveyed the room as if for the first time.

"I always wanted this bedroom."

Carly frowned, looking around the bedroom as well.

"Eh?"

"When we moved here, I asked Dad if I could have this room."

"Did you?" Carly watched her brother's face, "I never knew."

"Yeah, he said that you needed it because when you got older you'd need the space, plus you're..." Alan trailed off.

"I'm what?"

"You're his favourite."

"Shut up!"

"It's true. You're always getting your own way. You got Star, remember? Dad was set on getting the Retriever and look how that turned out."

"Alan, I'm not Dad's favourite. It's crazy to say that!"

"What about the time when we all went to Disneyland, Paris."

"What about it?"

"Come on, Carly, you really think that was because I wanted to go? That wasn't for my benefit, was it?"

"Yeah, but you enjoyed it right?"

Alan looked at his sister as if to say, really?

"Anyway, I've said it now, but that's why you'll never win."

Carly shook her head.

"I don't get it?"

"It's always been given to you, don't you see? You kind of expect it."

"No I don't! That's rubbish!"

Again, her brother gave the look.

"Well, maybe, I...I don't know." Carly sat back, mulling over her brothers admission, "I never thought of it like that."

"If you want to win, you gotta get serious, and I mean serious....When I was playing football at school, if I wanted to be in the school team playing then I had to perform. Every match, every practice. The coach wasn't going to say Alan it's ok you're in the squad whatever happens. If I didn't show passion and work hard, I was dropped, I mean, I'm on the bench you know, but it happens, I had days where he looked at me and I know he's thinking you're not trying. Bang! On the bench. Side lined."

Carly stared into space, contemplating her brother's words. Star stood up, stretched, gave a body shake then after observing nothing much was happening sat back down again, still watching the two siblings.

"What do I need to do then?"

Alan stood up. He gave Star a pat on her head, then, turning to his sister he gave her a mischievous smile.

"You gotta go to war sis!"

Chapter Four

P^{ing}

Without thinking Carly picked up her phone, half expecting to see the usual notification dominating the screen's wallpaper.

It wasn't what she was expecting.

Hi Carly

"Hello yourself," she muttered, noticing the text was anonymous. The number was just that, a phone number. No name or miniature picture icon accompanied the message.

"Who are you?" she wondered aloud. The sender had used Messenger as a means to contact her.

There was no more from the undisclosed sender, just the greeting. Was it a friend? Someone from the dog centre? A prank?

Ping

How are you?

This time she couldn't resist.

Fine, who is this? Carly typed back.

The screen remained blank. She even had to tap the phone from switching itself off. Still there was no response.

"Huh, don't you just hate that Star?" From across the room Star looked up from her grooming, realising no command or directive was forthcoming and returned to the job at hand.

Ping

A friend

"Really, is that so," again Carly spoke to herself before typing,

My friends have names.

Ping

How's Star doing in the competition?

Carly stared back at the screen.

Ping

Actually, that's a bit of a rhetorical question on my part, I can see how's she's doing. Not bad. 89 likes

Carly nodded, "I know, not bad,"

She thought about it then typed.

Yeah, not bad, we've picked up some points over the weekend. Still got a long way to go!

Ping
I can help you.

"Can you now?" Carly muttered to herself. She waited to see if there was anything more forthcoming.

The screen remained blank. Whoever had sent those messages had called it a night, it would seem.

"Don't you just hate that Star….!"

Carly got ready for bed. She stripped quickly while brushing her teeth and then threw on the extra-large 'New York Knicks' basketball t-shirt that doubled as a pyjama top before checking to see how the other dogs were faring in the competition. Everyone had average numbers, the least being the Jack Russell with 31, the highest being…

WHAT?

She stared at the number at the bottom of the picture. She did a double take.

That's impossible, surely not.

But the numbers didn't lie. *124 likes*

She looked at the Airedale Terrier's picture and then back at the number.

How the hell has it managed to get so many votes!! It was only 50 or so this afternoon! I don't believe it!

"Can you believe that, Star? All this time we were worried about the bloody Maly and in through the back door comes this sneaky big nose!"

Star raised her head briefly from her own bed at the foot of Carly's.

She'll never win.

"Shut up Alan," Carly muttered to herself.

Roxy the Airedale Terrier was clearly taking the lead over the group, and by some margin. Star was in second place and in third place was Bear, the Malamute.

Because you never take it seriously

"You know what, Star? This is serious! I want you to win. You are going to win and that is that…WE ARE GOING TO WIN!"

Star ignored her.

"Typical. Here I am all hyped up and ready for battle and you're…you're ready for bed!"

Ping
Let me help

"Our mystery friend is back Star! Not going to turn help down, are we girl?"

I'd appreciate anything you can do to help Star, she typed back.

You got it Carly

For a long time she tossed and turned in bed; unable to relax, suddenly sitting bolt upright. *Of course!* Jumping out of bed, careful not to clip Star snoring away, she switched on her computer. It didn't take long to organise the poster. Uploading the dog centre picture, she soon had the script down as well.

She breathed a sigh of relief as the first of the copies ejected onto the flap.

Thank God I changed that ink cartridge!

Back in bed she planned the next stage. It was a while before sleep stopped avoiding her, deliberately and cruelly. Finally and gratefully, she slipped away into the blackness of dreams...

Walking Star in the garden, the fence impossibly long, stretching out as far as the eye can see, a tug from behind, you gotta go to war sis... her brother laughing, pulling, pulling on her arm... on the main road, Star leading, barking at everyone she sees... running fast... Star now galloping away, her stride impossibly fast, difficult just to keep up with her...now flying through the air, zipping round street corners...

Let me help...a voice coming from nowhere...

I don't know you! Where are you?

Turn around, Carly!

Star barking louder now, pulling, pulling....

Come back next week miss...I'll have some meat for you then...black goo dripped from Stan Riley's crazy eyes...do you like anything you see? The butcher stroked a massive cleaver parked in his cranium...tomorrow, come see me tomorrow...Star licking the puddle of liquid at her feet...coughing, coughing before vomiting up a still beating heart...I'll never let you down sis...Alan stepping in with a pair of defibrillator clamps spitting black sparks...machinery whining

Charged!

Clear?

Clear!

No Alan.........Noooooooooooooooooooooooooooo!

***

Monday morning; the students filed through the main gates of Sandown's Comprehensive School Upper School, where Carly walked alone, studying the pavement's crack as they appeared, in a world of her own. There were no friends to catch up with, no gossip that needed urgent spreading. She appeared oblivious to her surroundings. At the lockers she pulled an A4 ring binder filled with plastic envelopes out of her rucksack., The first one contained several copies of the work she'd been doing on the computer. Pulling out the top sheet, she gazed at the picture as if for the first time. She'd never done anything like this before. It felt like she was searching for a lost pet, posting a mug shot, *"Missing: Have you seen…"*

"Hey Carly,"

She turned around, caught off guard for a second.

"Hey Grace," she immediately recognised the girl from several of her lessons.

"What's that?" Grace stared questioningly at the paper in Carly's hands.

Carly held the picture up, searching the other girl's face.

"Huh…" Grace read the caption, "good idea! Here, tell you what, I'm gonna do it right now!"

Carly smiled anxiously, "Really? Wow…thank you!"

"Shut up!" Grace tapped away on her phone, "Done."

"Thank you so much"

"You are such a nerd, Carly, get the picture on the notice board!"

"I will!"

Grace skipped away, joining another friend waiting by the main entrance.

Both the girls looked back at Carly after a brief conferring of heads.

Carly busied herself with the coloured drawing pins on the board. Quite aware of the looks she was generating from passing students, the back of her neck felt as if someone was pressing a hot iron against it. Some of the children passing by glanced her way, some could be heard commenting. Stepping back, she admired her handiwork.

There, it's done!

"Hey what's that all about?" A voice, ever so close, asked.

Carly visibly jumped for the second time.

Two boys, who were standing just behind her, shifted to see better, the taller one of them had been the one piping up. He inspected the poster.

She didn't know them by name, they looked familiar though. Having the privilege of not having to wear uniforms, she guessed they were 6th formers. "That your dog?" the tall one asked kindly. He had to to be over six foot, Carly imagined.

"Yep," she replied defensively, determined to stand up to whatever these boys may throw at her.

"Cool looking dog!" he smiled, giving a Carly a nod.

"Thank you," she mumbled, clearly caught off guard. A shy smile followed next.

"What is it......a Husky?"

"Nah it's...it's a ...Malamute," the other boy added, "Right?"

"Akita, she's a Japanese Akita," Carly corrected them both.

"Never heard of an Aki..." the first boy grinned, struggling with the name.

"Akita," Carly smiled too.

"Right, Akita...cool dog, cool name too, Star...," he peered at the poster again, "...Carly," he flashed another warm smile.

Carly began to blush. She couldn't help the rush of heat that had suddenly decided to cook her cheeks.

The boys moved away, already discussing something else.

"Are you going to like my picture?" she blurted out, "I mean Star's... like Star's picture I meant," Carly shook her head, embarrassed by the faux pas.

The first boy stopped his friend, giving Carly a quizzical look over his shoulder.

He came back, holding Carly's gaze.

"I meant Star...*of course*, I meant Star!"

Reaching inside his bomber jacket the boy produced his mobile phone, swiping a password silently and swiftly.

Carly noticed it looked fancy, iPhone10, something or the other.

Without saying anything, he glanced at the poster checking the website details and tapped away.

"Remember to..." she began.

"Like the dog picture, not the site picture," the boy finished.

"Yeah, right...I usually have to mention that one."

"Done."

"Thank you."

"You're welcome," again that smile, "I'll tell my mates to do the same."

"Great"

"See you around, Carly,"

Carly returned the smile, this time it didn't feel awkward at all.

***

Lunch break was a light year away and every time Carly checked the clock, she cursed the man who invented the blasted timepiece. Her impatience didn't go unnoticed.

"Have you got somewhere else you want to be Carly Watson?" Miss Deacons admonished.

"Sorry miss...erm not really,"

"Well, that's good. For a minute there I was wondering who this girl was sitting front of me, doing a rather authentic Dorothy impersonation for the school play."

Carly blushed, not for the first time today.

"You're not Dorothy in the school play by any chance? No, I didn't think so? Right, well, if you've quite finished acting like *Dorothy* looking for Toto on the Yellow Brick Road...*SILENCE!*" she barked viciously at the other students sniggering, "I'd like you to read the next passage out loud."

Carly fumbled with the pages, totally lost.

"Page 45, from the top if it helps,"

"Yes, miss."

"Give me strength..."

Carly read the passage. The words held no meaning for her, and it showed.

Finally, the bell signalling break sounded; students filed out heading across the school grounds and beyond. Carly headed for the lockers. All she could think about was if the poster had had any effect. She checked for updates from the Dog Centres web page, overshooting the page in her haste and having to swipe the page back again.

93 likes

"Is that it? Come on........"!

Resignedly she swiped to the dreaded page with the image of Roxy.

140

Taking a deep breath, she switched the phone off and replaced it in her locker.

That's when she noticed the graffiti on her poster. Crossing over to the board, her mouth dropped open. Someone had drawn a top hat and sunglasses with a black felt tip pen, a parody over Star's mask, adding a cigar. They had also drawn between her back legs a penis, exaggerating the size.

Carly tore the poster down, clawing the paper off the notice board.

Her eyes glazed in a flash, tears welling up uncontrollably. They would have spilled down her cheeks, but the same emotion veered course and anger took the helm.

Bastards! Bastards! BASTARDS!

She did an about turn, heading purposefully back to her locker, throwing the crumpled paper inside. She pulled another poster out from the ring-binder. Defiantly slamming the locker door with force, it rebounded open. She didn't pause and gave the door another vicious slam.

Bastards!

Returning to the board and stabbing the pins into the cork, she imagined the face of whoever did it.

"Carly Watson!"

Who would do that?

"Carly Watson, do not slam your locker door!"

If she found out who did it, she would stick the pins into their……

"CARLY WATSON!"

She spun around in shock. Deputy Head Clarke was standing before her, his red blotched face, troubled and angry, radiating a deeper red than usual. He glared at her through thick rimmed glasses. He was notorious for two things throughout the school; one, his intolerance of disorder and retention, the second was his ruthlessness in dishing out the appropriate punishment. If you found yourself talking to Deputy Clarke outside of class, there was only one thing coming your way.

"That is school property young lady!" he boomed, pointing to the locker.

"I'm … I'm sorry sir," Carly swallowed, barely able to speak.

"So you should be, young lady. Your parents will be paying for it if it's damaged."

Carly could only sink deeper into acquiescence.

"What do you think about that?" he leaned a little closer, his body odour as bad as his reputation for leniency.

Carly tried to ignore the smell.

"Is everything alright, girl?" Deputy Clarke continued to probe his student; his voice still louder than necessary.

Carly nodded.

"What are you doing here?" He pointed at the board.

"It's a poster of my dog. I've entered her…" she began, "someone graffitied over…"

"Well, you'd better run along now," he suddenly interrupted, dismissing her.

"Yes sir."

Carly did just that. Head bowed she didn't waste time hanging around. Still clutching the ring binder, she disappeared around a corner and out of sight.

Deputy Clarke peered closely at the poster, "Hmm, handsome boy."

Chapter Five

For the next couple of days Carly drifted through the corridors and halls of school in much her usual inhibited way and after school she took Star out for her routine afternoon walks. The familiar pavements led the way until she ended up back at home. The competition was all she could focus on.

Her mother noticing her daughter's complete lack of interest in anything lately had tried involving Carly in anything other than the competition but finding it a near impossible task had backed off giving Carly the space she needed.

Carly sat on her bed, contemplating. The competition and Star's chances of winning it were slipping away,

"Time to go to war," she grinned at Star before opening the Messenger app on her phone.

She began tapping away, reaching out.

Hey how's it going? I've entered my dog, Star, into a 'Best Dog Competition' and was wondering if you would vote for my dog? You will! Great, Thank you so much. Oh, by the way, make sure you 'like' the picture not the competition web site, you know? Yeah, sometimes I have to...you know already? Ok, no problem....it ends next week, so don't... Okay, thank you so much!!

Carly texted everyone she knew and then some, resending the message over and over. The site page allowed her to see who had voted and who had not, so after texting, she could check to see if they had kept their word. Some did, some didn't. It was frustrating to see, but what can you do but hope that they eventually tapped that icon. She thought that it would be a simple yes, of course, but people can be mighty funny, especially when messaging. It was so easy to say 'of course'. Occasionally, someone wouldn't reply to the message, they would read it, but then nothing. Just ignore the request completely.

She'd spent the rest of the week chasing kids around the school playground. If it hadn't been for Star's competition, she would never have had the courage to talk to, let alone approach kids, and at home up in her room she would chase up the ones that had said they would but then hadn't.

By Thursday she had 150 likes and by Friday she had reached a satisfying 198. By now she'd drained the reservoir of potential votes at the school. A number normally that high would be sufficient to close the deal, but she didn't have the luxury of relaxing. Roxy was still in the lead, still ahead, still maintaining the gap. It felt as if they were playing a cat and mouse game, theirs alone. Ridiculous to think that way of course, she knew that was absurd, but as the days passed, she began to wonder who the owner was. *Had she seen them around the centre? Did they in fact know Star, and had they seen her as well?*

The feeling of suspicion began to fester. It was all consuming.

The latest update revealed a milestone.

200 likes

"Can you believe it Star, two hundred...! We've reached two hundred!"

Star ignored her, ignored the jubilant statistical outburst.

"You know a little appreciation would go a long way, girl!"

Star rolled over, getting more comfortable.

"Huh! I know someone who would appreciate the effort! But first, let's check the enemy."

Jumping off the bed she hurriedly left the bedroom, heading downstairs, "Mum...Mum! where are you?"

"Here in the kitchen!"

"You won't believe it but we're closing the gap,"

"That's great dear!" Mrs Watson paused in her reading, putting the book to one side.

"I know right? It's finally paying off,"

"What is?"

"All the hard work..."

"Gosh you sound like it's a task you've got to fulfil."

"Mum, this is serious! We have a chance to win... don't you realise how important this is to me!"

"And Star? This is about Star remember!"

"Well of course. I mean yes, Star, it's about Star."

"Are you sure? For a minute there it seemed like you were in the competition yourself," Mrs Watson gave her daughter a sideways look.

"Well, I have to do all the blasted work, chasing 'likes', ringing people I don't really talk to anymore after all. It's not as if Star is a pop idol and doesn't have to do anything!"

"Hmm yeah I guess," Mrs Watson conceded, "and who is the other competitor? I take it there's one in the running with you?"

"It's an Airedale Terrier called, Roxy, and yes, we're the only two with a chance of winning...at the moment."

"You seem pretty certain of that."

"Ugly mutt it is too," Carly wandered over to the kitchen window, staring out into the back garden.

Mrs Watson contemplated watching her daughter.

"Where's Dad?"

"Out with your brother looking at an old banger or something they said. Alan is relentless in his pursuit of a car."

"When will they be back?"

"Err...probably in an hour or so, we were thinking of going shopping together. Your dad is looking to buy a new Laptop." Mrs Watson watched Carly at the window. "You know, Carly I don't want you to get too worked up over this."

"What?"

"Well, what happens if Star doesn't win?"

Carly sat down next to her mum, holding her gaze, "We are going to win mum, and you're going to help!" she spoke with careful deliberation.

"Oh ...*right.*"

"Pick up your phone and start texting people."

"What, now?" Mrs Watson looked perplexed.

"Yes now...!"

"Ok. What do I say?"

"Come here, I'll show you." Carly proceeded to tap out the message, "All you have to do is copy and paste this to everyone in your contacts list in Messenger."

"Everyone?"

Carly gave her mum chiding look, "Everyone!"

"Ok, where do I start?"

Carly made a face.

"I'd best put the kettle on first."

"Good idea mum!"

For the next hour, Carly orchestrated the job, guiding her mum with answers and questions, ultimately mentoring the responses. The coffee helped, a lot.

Without them really noticing, the front door had opened but both ignored the return of father and brother. With typical fancy, Mr Watson called out as he did every time with annoying predictability, *"Honey, I'm home!"*

With no reply forthcoming, Mr Watson dropped his man bag in the hall, and giving Alan a strange look, he entered the kitchen. Star padded into the room through the open garden patio door, tail wagging. She was glad to see the boys arrive. Maybe one of them would pay her some attention for a change.

"Hello," he said with a tinge of sarcasm, "at least Star is happy to see me!"

Mrs Watson and Carly waved hands back in unison but continued to stare at the phone in Mrs Watson's hand.

"She did it!"

"Yes!"

"I can't believe Maggie responded!"

"Told you mum, just keep asking."

Alan shook his head sadly and went upstairs, already suspecting the reason.

"What's going on here then?"

Mrs Watson turned to her husband with wide excited eyes, "Star has 249 likes!"

"My god, has she got you involved now?" Mr Watson checked the cafetiere's coffee dregs hopefully.

"Eric, this is important, Star has to win! She's nearly level with Roxy!"

"Who the bloody hell is Roxy!"

"Star's nemesis!"

"Oh, that explains everything," he filled the kettle with water, "Hold on, is this to do with that competition you've entered Star in Carly?"

"Yes dad," Carly got up and showed him the results on her mobile, "we're this close to overtaking the ugly mutt."

Mr Watson studied the phone, then his daughter. "All a bit serious, isn't it?"

"Too right, this time Star is going to win!"

"What's Roxy got then?"

"253!" Carly spat.

Mr Watson raised his eyebrows, "It's really got the two of you going...this competition."

"Eric it's important. Sit down, I'll make you a lovely fresh pot of coffee, and you'll start messaging your friends."

"What now? I thought we were going to town...?"

"We are and we will, but first you need to help your daughter claim that prize!"

"Righto," Mr Watson checked to see where his son was hiding, "two against one, looks like I'm snookered!"

"Exactly darling, don't argue."

"Come on Dad let's do this, think of Star."

Mr Watson sat down next to his daughter. Looking from one to the other he sighed a conquered sigh, "Okay, show me."

The two women crowded the table, discussing possible contacts to approach and annoy.

"Dad, just paste this message and post it on to everyone, simpler than typing it repeatedly."

"Right."

After twenty minutes the return messages came pouring in, Mr Watson found he was busy explaining the situation over and over. After an hour he realised with silent certainty that there wasn't going to be an afternoon outing as promised, but that was okay. He was now hooked on the mission in hand. He was actually enjoying the experience. The hard work was paying off; the 'likes' started to accumulate, building steadily and with continued success. He chased every lead down thoroughly until there was a result. Mrs Watson supplied several rounds of cheese and ham toasties, pointing out possible sources to be exploited.

"Can you believe Roberts hasn't 'liked' the picture…!" He muttered to no-one in particular, "after saying he would! So annoying!!"

Carly sat back watching her parent with glowing pride. Star wandered in from the garden occasionally, seeing the cheers were nothing to be concerned with, she wandered back out.

"So, we have 309!" Mr Watson declared, "and our rival has…295!"

"Champions!" all three high-fived, excited exhausted and thrilled.

"I need a break," Mrs Watson sighed, excusing herself, she wandered away heading for the stairs, "I'm going for a lay down."

"You know she won't rest Dad," Carly was almost morose.

"How do you know it's a 'she'?"

"I don't…just a feeling,"

"Well, there's one person we haven't tapped," Mr Watson declared. Father and daughter locked eyes.

"ALAN!" they both shouted simultaneously.

***

Ping

Carly grabbed her phone from the bedroom desk. Could it be more 'likes'?

Hello Carly, I see you're doing okay in the competition.

"Huh, guess who's back Star!"

Star watched her owner from across the bedroom with hooded eyes.

"Don't look at me like that, girl!"

Yeah, we're neck and neck. Can't believe we've caught up Carly typed back

Silence

Ping

I've started the ball rolling

"You have?" she muttered to herself, "Well okay, actions speak louder than words friend!"

She then realised she had spoken the words and not typed them.

Great thank you so much. Every vote counts. I never win anything

But this time you will. I'll help you.

Carly smiled at the encouragement.

Thank you

No problem, glad to help. I've got some friends I haven't contacted yet, some you know from the old days back when we was following that band, you remember Toolkit don't you?

Carly sat back, transported to a distant time and place.

Oh my God Toolkit!

She quickly tapped away, speaking the words as she did, "Wow, I haven't thought about those days in like ages!

Ping

Crazy times loved every minute I remember you dancing on the stage, preaching with the singer!

For a second Carly was back there on the stage with Dean Moffatt, the singer of the grunge band Toolkit, at *The Pit,* a club she and Alan would hang out at on Thursday nights. They managed to get in using fake ID's. The bouncers were laid back on Thursdays as it was a promoted night for teenagers and garage bands. As such there was a never much agro, in fact the two doormen had easy nights mostly. That night she had drunk so much, crashing into strangers at the bar one minute, then she was on the stage egged on by a friend, head banging. The last thing she remembered was being carried out by a bouncer.

Ping

You was amazing that night, everyone thought you was so wild

I was out of control, typed Carly smiling.

You were flying girl!

Carly stopped smiling. Her recollection of that night taking a darker route, one that had to be retold by others for she had no memory, only flashes, images that danced away. What she did know was that Alan had frantically called their father, confessing the deception that he and his sister had pulled. While a friend sat with Carly keeping her upright, airways open, free from the vomit she'd been violently spewing, keeping her from passing out until he arrived. Her father scooped her up and rushed to Emergency at St Edward's Hospital where they had wasted no time in triage, straight through into the doctor's ward, pumping the drugs someone had slipped into her drink, out of her stomach. It had been the last time she was allowed out, unaccompanied. She had been a wild child, only just thirteen, going on eighteen. Alan had been grounded indefinitely as well.

Who are you? she typed quickly.

Nothing… then finally.

Ping

A friend from the old days

"Huh. Still the mystery… Ok…play it your way." Carly glanced over at Star, "Let's see if they're as good as their word, right girl?"

Star blinked back.

Who are you? She asked herself.

***

"Good morning sleepy head," Mrs Watson watched as Carly yawned her way around the kitchen. "What time did you go to sleep last night?"

"I dunno, late I guess."

"You're telling me!"

Carly bumped into a chair, dragging it out and collapsing heavily. Her head hit the kitchen table, only it was cushioned by her arms.

"What time is it, anyway?" she mumbled.

"Pardon?"

"I said what time is it?"

Mrs Watson ignored the question and ran the kitchen tap, filling the kettle.

"Want some tea?"

"Okay, yeah that would be nice."

For a minute Mrs Watson busied herself with the tea brewing, opening cupboards and general tidying up.

"Do you have to make so much noise!" Carly announced.

"Oh, I'm sorry sweetie," Mrs Watson's tone was mockingly burlesque, "Sunday roast doesn't magically appear on the table."

"What?"

"It is after midday, young lady!"

"I'm sorry mum, I didn't get much sleep last night."

"I'm not blind. Here's your tea."

"Thanks."

Mrs Watson studied her daughter while blowing into her own cup.

"How's Star doing?"

"I haven't looked yet."

"Well don't keep me in suspense! I'm involved now, aren't I?"

Carly groaned, "I'll be right back," and with that she disappeared up the stairs to collect her phone.

Seconds later there was a cry of disbelief.

"OH MY GOD.........!"

Carly came flying back down the stairs, into the kitchen, phone held in front of her as if holding the Holy Grail, tears welling up.

"You're not gonna believe it," she cried, eyes as wide as saucers.

Mrs Watson held onto the table waiting for the collision that never happened, "what...what is it?"

"She's only taken back the lead!"

"Oh Carly, I'm so sorry!"

"Look! Look!" Carly held her phone out for her mother to inspect.

339 vs 355

"After everything we've done!" Carly threw the phone down on the kitchen worktop in disgust.

Pulling her close, Mrs Watson hugged her daughter, "There's plenty of time still...it doesn't finish until next Friday right?"

"Actually, it finishes on the Saturday at midday."

"See, plenty of time."

"Just when you think you've got it covered...*bam!*"

"You're letting this take over your life."

"Mum, Star is my life and now I'm finally taking something seriously I want to do well. I want to win!"

Mrs Watson hugged her daughter in response.

"Look, why don't you take Star out for walkies, get some air, and when you come back, I'll have the dinner nearly ready, and we can all work out how to get more likes."

Carly squeezed her mum back tightly. "Thanks mum....... you're the best."

Star groaned loudly as dogs do when wanting attention. She was sitting beside the pair, unnoticed, but had heard the magic word, walkies.

Mother and daughter both laughed.

Chapter Six

Star walked ahead, leading the way, a big, grinning, toothy smile decorating her face for all to see, although to some people walking towards the pair it could be described as something entirely different.

Being a girl dog, she didn't stop at every lamppost, tree, dustbin, or anything else that required investigating and urinating on. She would come across a patch of grass en route and squat. Carly was so glad she hadn't picked a male dog, for even though they would empty their bladders after a short distance, boy dogs would still sniff at everything and go through the motion of leaving their scent, even if the tank was empty.

They crossed the street heading to the park. So far, no other dog walkers appeared on the horizon. Carly's thoughts drifted to the competition.

How is it she's managing to keep doing that, beating us? Every time we beat or get near her, she bloody well comes to life and bing! Takes off again. So annoying, I hate her, I hate Roxy and I hate HER!

Without realising it, Carly bumped into Star, who had come to a stop.
"Oops! Sorry girl."

She looked around at her surroundings, realising that they had wandered onto the street which housed the parade of shops. Benson's Park was only a matter of a few hundred yards further down, the West gate entrance was in sight.

Star had pulled up, not because they needed to cross a road, which she had been trained not to attempt unless commanded, but because they had turned the corner and literally walked into a woman and her friend gossiping.

Both ladies turned to stare irritably at the intrusion.

"Sorry," Carly mumbled.

One of the women looked as if she was going to say something but the sight of Star shut her open mouth instantly.

"That's okay," the other woman managed, equally stunned by the sight of Star. Both ladies shifted out the way, "Gosh that's a big dog!"

"She's friendly," Carly said, by way of explanation.

With the ladies out of the way, she could now see the parade was full of people milling around in several groups chatting around a yellow taped barrier that the police had set up.

The Do Not Cross-Crime Scene tape surrounded a large, cordoned off area of pavement in front of a shop. As Carly lead Star between the congregated people, it became clear which shop was sectioned off. Riley & Sons

The crowd was talking, but all Carly could make out were people discussing their daily nonsense, nothing to do with the shop. Spotting the man who had been in the shop a few days back chatting with another man, she edged closer hoping to overhear something of interest. Both the men had their backs to Carly.

"God knows Al, I just can't believe it. It seems…" Vic struggled with a suitable description, "Surreal, it seems bloody surreal, mate, that's what it is!" Vic shook his head wonderingly.

Al nodded back, half listening.

"I mean I was only in there yesterday," Vic shuddered.

"To be fair Vic, you're always in there," Al pointed out.

"Fair enough geeze, I'll give you that," Vic turned to his mate and in doing so, spotted Carly and Star. He squinted at the pair, before recognising the dog first, then Carly by association.

"Hey, you were there the other day as well." He nodded at the shop.

Vic's mate, Al, stepped back to get a better look at Carly, looking her up and down.

"Nice doggy," he remarked without smiling.

Carly stared at the shop, "What happened?" she murmured.

"Old Stan killed…" Al started.

"….It would appear," Vic interrupted, wanting to be the deliverer of the bad news, "that Stan topped himself."

Carly blinked.

"Oh my God, that's awful."

"And some," Vic smiled sadly, "He didn't open all last week, only discovered yesterday,"

"Choked on one of his own sausages!" Al proclaimed.

"What? No, he didn't, you burke!" Vic turned to his mate his face incredulous with annoyance. "He was found hanging in the kitchen. Nasty way to go, if you ask me!"

"I heard it was a sausage that done him!"

"Don't be stupid! Who told you that?"

"Fran at the pub, she said…"

"Fran doesn't know shit!"

"Well, that's what I heard."

"Well, what you heard is bollocks!" Al jabbed with a finger.

Vic muttered something unintelligible.

"Anyway, miss, miss?" Al looked around for Carly, but she and Star had left.

"Huh, don't say goodbye then!" Vic muttered. He turned back to face the shop, "Gonna miss you, Stanley," he said shaking his head sadly, "Gonna miss his sausages too."

"Vic?"

"Yeah."

"Shut up!"

"But I really liked them," Vic complained miserably.

Al shook his head again, "Burke!"

Carly headed away from the parade, choosing to not go to the park, but rather heading for the Paws & Claws Dog Centre Trust. Equally disturbed and confused, she headed back along the main road. The centre was 15 minutes' walk away, the feeling of needing to be with familiar people was strong.

They made good time and got there quickly.

"Carly! How lovely to see you," Sheila called out. She had been leaving the reception building, crossing the courtyard to check out the store's outbuilding, but had spotted Carly at the main gate. "Come to help out?" Sheila waited until Carly had let Star off her lead, before continuing to the outbuilding.

"Hi Sheila."

"Hello Star!" Sheila gave Star a cuddle. "We had a delivery yesterday and something's not right." Molly had signed the invoice but there was a niggling feeling that wouldn't leave her, so she wanted to double check the inventory.

"You here to help?" Shelia pressed again.

"Ah no, not really, just a social visit."

"That's a shame, could do with the big guys having a walk. By the way, congratulations with the competition, you're in the lead last time I looked."

"I wish. Roxy is back in front," Carly mumbled.

"Really? Huh. You know it's turning into a real humdinger this time around; I don't think I've ever seen such high numbers voting and it's only half way!"

Carly smiled weakly, looking around the centre.

"I guess I could help out for a little bit," she acquiesced.

"Atta girl, thanks Carly. Listen, you go ahead and we'll catch up in a bit?" Carly nodded, "You ok? You seem a little distracted?"

"I'm ok," Carly forced a smile.

"Great. See you in a bit then." Sheila carried on to the stores building.

After tying Star to a gatepost near the main office, she busied herself with letting the centre's two heavy weights out of their kennels. The dogs, having heard Carly's voice, were already pacing their pens with anticipation.

"Hey boy," she let Prince, the 4-year-old French Mastiff out first, letting him sniff her, knowing he was looking for Star. "She's tied up, Prince!" Next, she opened the pen holding Sally, the mixed breed German Shepherd. Both dogs immediately got to investigating each other before Sally scooted off with Prince lumbering behind.

Carly watched them play, looking for the ball normally located near the pens. She became aware of someone's presence, watching her.

"Hi Carly."

She looked over at the man watching her from the play area's gate.

"Hi."

"Love those big guys, especially the Bulldog."

"French Mastiff," Carly corrected him.

"Right, right, Mastiff." Richard adjusted his camera.

Carly collected the ball, calling to Sally who immediately zeroed in, focusing on the ball in Carly's hand, "Here girl," the ball arced over and Sally collected it, snatching the ball before the other dog could pounce. She taunted Prince who tried muscling it out of her possession, without success.

"How's the competition going?" Richard enquired, lifting the Canon Sure Shot, aiming the camera at Carly.

"Good."

Star began to bark.

"You're winning, no?"

Click. He snapped a shot.

"No, not at the moment."

"Huh. Well, keep it up, you're looking good. Did you like my picture of Star?"

Click.

Carly hid a frown, staring at the two dogs playing.

He's taking pictures of me I know it

Click. Click

Star gave another salvo of barks.

"Excuse me," Carly lifted the latch to the pen, checking the two big dogs were busy, she opened the gate, forcing Richard to back off.

"Hey girl, what's up?"

Click

Carly whirled round, "Are you...?"

"Richard!" Sheila called out from across the courtyard, "you got a minute?"

"Hello Sheila, thought I'd pop over and take some shots of the dogs in action."

"That's very kind of you,"

"No worries. Just in time, as it happens. Carly here was playing with them."

"Yes I know. Can I have a word with you in the office?"

Carly settled Star down, who was straining at her lead.

"Of course," Richard said amicably, switching the camera off.

"Hey girl, what's up? You wanna play with the others?" she watched as Sheila and Richard headed for the main building.

"I don't like him either," she whispered into Star's ear.

She finished playing with the big dogs, cutting the time short. Collecting Star and avoiding the office, she didn't bother saying goodbye.

***

After dinner the Watsons settled down to watch TV. They all agreed that Carly was doing exceptionally well in the competition and for the most part it was all down to her hard work.

Now it was time to take it easy, take stock and enjoy the moment.

"Are you joking?" Carly spluttered.

"Carly," her father began, "it's becoming a bit of an obsession with you and it's rubbing off on all of us. Look at what happened yesterday!"

"What? My family finally helping me to win something!"

"Carly..." Mrs Watson warned.

"I don't believe this, you were all for it, now... now I'm on my own again!"

"No-one said you were on your own, where did that come from?" her mother reached over to console her.

"Don't," Carly snapped her arm back, "you said you would help me when I got back! Now it's 'let's forget everything I said'!!"

"And I will help."

Mr Watson frowned at the escalating dispute, deciding it best to stay out of the action.

"I can't stop for a minute. She's never gonna stop either. DON'T YOU GET IT?"

"WE HAVE BEEN HELPING YOU!" Alan shouted across the room, unable to stop himself.

"Alan..." Mr Watson changed his mind, reprimanding his son.

"YOU DON'T GIVE A SHIT WHAT HAPPENS!" Carly jabbed a finger at her brother, who held his hands up mockingly.

"Everyone, calm down," Mrs Watson chose not to shout, trying to mediate the situation.

"You're the nutter!" Alan sneered.

"Alan that's a bit unkind!" Mrs Watson turned on her son.

"You're an arsehole!"

"CARLY!!" Mrs Watson gasped.

"I HATE THIS FAMILY!" Carly screamed, storming out of the living room.

"Carly!" Mr Watson called out after her.

"Why did you say that?" Mrs Watson glared at her son.

Alan shrugged in return, "It's driving us all nuts, isn't it?"

Mr Watson sighed resignedly, slowly getting up, he handed the remote to his son.

"Don't. Leave her for a minute to calm down," Mrs Watson decided, "you've both done enough damage as it is!"

"What did I do?" Mr Watson bleated.

***

Ping

Hi

Carly stared at the phone. *Not now*

Ping

Are you there?

"No," she muttered sarcastically.

Ping

Told you I would help

Carly sat up in bed.

What do you mean, she tapped back angrily.

For a minute there was no reply then,

Ping

You know what I mean

Carly just stared at the message frowning. She typed back,

You've been helping with votes? I appreciate the help, thank you. I've been a bit preoccupied lately

Ping
No, not that.
"Then what you talking about?" Carly looked over at Star in her bed, who was watching her closely,

"Don't ask me Star, it's my fan... they talk in riddles!"

Ping

For a long time all she could do was try and digest the words that glowed up at her. They shouldn't be there. She shouldn't have read those words.

I took care of that bastard old man

With slow precise typing she asked the question, but already she was piecing the answer together.

Who do you mean?

Ping

You know very well who, the lying bastard butcher

Carly gasped, holding a hand to her open mouth. Again she typed slowly,

You're just saying that, you didn't really kill him

The mobile remained blank, then,

Ping

They haven't released any information yet; the police don't want to scare the public about how he died

Carly waited, but couldn't hold back, she had to ask.

How did he die?

Ping

I chopped him up good and proper then fed him to my dog.

The phone tumbled from her hands, unable to support the weight. It fell to the floor with a thud.

Chapter Seven

"Come on, I'll walk to school with you sis," Alan waited for his sister to collect her rucksack, "You ok?"

"Yeah, why shouldn't I be?" Carly pushed past her brother, not bothering to wait. From the kitchen doorway their mother watched them leave.

"Okay," Alan muttered, closing the front door, "Gonna be a long walk," he sighed.

His prediction was pretty damn accurate. The journey to school was mostly in silence. The only communication was when he ventured some small talk about how the competition was going.

"Fine," Carly snapped, leaving him for dust at the gates of the school.

"Suit yourself."

Throughout the day Carly kept her head down, concentrating on her schooling. She listened intently to the teacher's questions, ignored the casual joking washing around her, discouraging the distraction. All in all, she was an attentive pupil.

It was only at lunch break that she dropped her guard, remembering the notice board and the poster. With trepidation she wandered over to the main entrance. Two girls were milling about at the board. From her approach Carly couldn't see who they were or what they were doing, but it soon became clear.

"What are you doing?" she spluttered, her mouth suddenly drying up, as her emotions all exploded at the same time.

"Oh!" Both girls spun around, the one with the marker pen looking the most surprised. They had been caught red handed, still defacing the picture.

"Busted!" the other girl laughed.

"Shut up Grace!" she laughed cruelly but not at her friend.

Carly remembered them from the other day, it was the same girl who had encouraged her to put the poster up, had 'liked' her picture. The other girl was the also the same girl she had run over to meet. She remembered the other girl's name now, Tracy Collins. Looking from one to the other, Carly felt a heat launching itself from the pit of her stomach.

"What... what are you doing?" she stammered, her breathing all caught up.

Tracy stared back defiantly, "Well can't you see?" she turned to the poster, replacing the lid on the pen.

Star's face was now sporting large glasses. There was also a crude image, depicting a pile of excrement and a stick man, and the penis was also back. Carly had interrupted the girls before the cartoon could be finished.

"I think it looks better, don't you, Grace?"

The other girl didn't answer, she merely stared vacantly back at Carly.

Carly pushed past the two girls, ripping the poster down violently.

"Hey, what you doing?" Tracy complained.

She shoved Carly back hard tripping her over with her own feet. She landed awkwardly. Both girls burst into another barrel of cruel laughter. Grace even pushed Tracy playfully back against the wall mimicking her friend's actions.

Carly was ready to scream, the rage inside boiled to the surface. It only needed one provocation, one more, *and she would*...scrabbling to get up she looked up to see Miles, the 6th former, the same boy from the other day, offering his hand, a concerned look etched on his kind face.

"What's going on here?" Mr Callaghan bellowed behind them all. No-one had seen the science teacher arrive.

Carly took Miles' hand, standing awkwardly, their bodies bumping briefly.

"Are you ok?" he searched her face.

Carly barely nodded.

Tracy Collins fidgeted under Miles' glaring attention, switching his glare to the other girl. Grace managed to pull a contorted clown face back.

"Miles what's going on, hmm?" Callaghan stepped between the two groups of children.

"It would appear, Sir, that these two," he motioned at Tracy and Grace, "have been the culprits we've been looking for, our graffiti artists," he gently took the poster from Carly's hands, showing it to the science teacher.

"Let me see," Callaghan accepted the poster, peered for a second at the image, then at Carly and finally at the other two girls, "Hmm, show me your hands Tracy Collins," he demanded.

Tracy's head sank but she produced as asked, one of the hands held the marker pen.

"Right, you two," he indicated sternly, "Headmaster's office. Now."

"WHAT?" Tracy shouted, "For that?"

"You can explain "that", and all the rest of your artistic talent that has been popping up round the school to the headmaster," he motioned for the girls to leave.

Both girls remained rooted.

"NOW!" Callaghan barked.

Tracy scowled at Carly before brushing past her. Grace obeyed the command as well, slowly making her way to the office, Callaghan followed.

"You got another poster?" Miles asked Carly.

The pair walked over to the lockers, where Carly produced another poster.

"How's it going?" he asked, studying the picture. He smiled at the image, "I like your dog. Whoever took that has a killer eye for a shot."

Carly blinked.

"What did you say?"

"I said, 'How's it going? You know, the competition," Miles laughed.

"No after that."

"Oh," Miles spoke deliberately slowly, "I like your dog. Whoever took that has a killer eye for a shot!"

"Oh my God!" Carly exclaimed holding on to Miles' arm, "Oh my God! I know who killed Old man Riley!"

"Who?" It was Miles' turn to look puzzled.

Making their way through the school Carly explained everything that had happened right up until the moment Miles had stepped in, leaving out the mystery fan's horrific admission. She didn't know why she was opening up to Miles, but it felt right. Studying his reaction, the decision seemed a wise one, although she didn't want to scare her new found friend away.

Oh, by the way, I'm in contact with a murderer don't you know
Really.....?
Oh yeah, we share late night chats via Messenger, and I get to hear all the grim details

Not something that she needed to pass on, she decided, especially in a developing relationship. The two students had taken to the tables outside the school's unused cafeteria, having the pick of seats as the place was practically deserted.

"Wow, Carly," Miles shook his head, "that is intense stuff."

But Carly wasn't listening, "I've got to warn her!" she stared into the distance.

"Who are we talking about now?" Miles asked, confused.

Carly shook her head. Instead she quickly dialled a number in her contacts list.

"She's not answering! Why isn't she answering?"

"I don't know," Miles answered her with a smile.

"She's always there!"

Carly looked at the phone for a time, "I've got to go and warn her," she stood up.

"What, now?"

"Yes, now, Miles,"

"I've got a bike if that'll help."

Carly stopped pacing, "I could kiss you! Come on then, let's go!" she was already running out of the hall.

"I wouldn't mind," Miles mumbled to himself before setting off after her.

From across the hall, Alan watched unnoticed as his sister leapt up and ran out of the room, followed by the boy at the table. He recognised the boy, a 6th former. His face darkened with smouldering outrage.

At the bicycle shed Miles unlocked the chain, pulling the racing bike out for Carly, who grabbed it.

"You might have a little problem…" he began but trailed off as Carly lent the bike, swinging her leg over as if she had owned it all her life, "…with the seat height being…" he trailed off again, "Here let me help," he finished, steadying Carly with an arm.

"Got it!" Carly hoisted herself up with his help, back pedalled expertly, before swinging the bike out and around, heading for the main entrance.

"I could come as well…" he started.

Carly was already gone.

"…if you wanted," he finished lamely.

***

Arriving at Paws and Claws in record time, Carly scanned the entrance before dismounting.

Wheeling the bicycle through the gate, she parked it inside, leaning it against the wall that ran the length of the centre.

In the reception office, Molly, the only other full time staff member, sat twirling her hair whilst chatting on the phone. At the sight of Carly, she gave a huge smile and a nod.

Ignoring the pretty receptionist, Carly walked through to Sheila's adjoining office without bothering to knock. She was still catching her breath.

"Carly! Do knock, why don't you," she began shuffling some paperwork on her desk.

"I've got to talk to you! You didn't answer your phone."

"Slow down," the older woman laughed, "Shouldn't you be at school?"

"It's about Richard! You need to know something!" Carly didn't slow down.

"Richard?"

"Yeah,"

"Ok...what have you heard?" she sat back, studying Carly.

"It's more ... intuition, than anything,"

"Uh huh... go on then, let's hear it,"

"Please take me seriously, Sheila. He's weird. He was taking photos of *me* the other day, not Star, and I bet he's been doing this a long time as well. If you check his camera, you'll find pictures…" Carly blurted. She wanted to say more, wanted to show her the phone messages but that was no proof that it was him, merely a conversation with a madman.

Sheila was silent for a second, still watching Carly's features. She got up and checked the door was closed properly before sitting back down.

"What I'm about to tell you goes no further, understand, young lady?" Shelia gave Carly a stern look.

Carly nodded.

Taking a deep breath, she placed her hands on the desk.

"I've let Richard go."

"What do you mean, let him go?"

"He no longer works for us, i.e. taking photos of the dogs."

"Why did you do that Sheila?"

Sighing, Sheila gazed out of the window, "Molly approached me several days ago complaining of ...there's no other word for it ... sexual harassment. You know me, I took this very seriously and we documented everything. It was enough for me to go to the police for advice."

"You believed her?"

"Let's just say Molly has a tendency to exaggerate so I wanted to do things right."

Carly was silent.

"He's gone now, Carly he won't be bothering you no more I promise you." Sheila smiled reassuringly.

"I think he's done a lot worse," Carly said.

"Pardon?"

"I think we need to get the police to check his laptop out, go to his house and...and take evidence and stuff," Carly said.

"Whoa Carly! Do you know something I don't?" Sheila leaned forward across the desk, "Did he touch you as well?"

"No."

"Ok, well that's a relief."

"But I have pretty good information that he might have done something dreadful. Something really bad."

"Carly if you know something, tell me!" Sheila implored. She could see the young girl was terribly distressed, this obviously wasn't just about sexual harassment.

"I have to go!"

"Wait Carly, can't you tell me?"

Standing, she excused herself, "I better get back to school." Upon reaching the door Carly paused, "I just really wanted to make sure you were okay," she said over her shoulder, and then was gone, shutting the door quietly behind her.

Sheila stared at the office door, contemplating the words,

I just wanted to make sure you were okay... Me? What on earth was she talking about?

She walked around the desk, opened her door, and leaned out, catching her assistant's attention, "Molly?"

"Yes,"

"Does Carly seem different to you?"

"Want do you mean.......?"

"I don't know, I can't put my finger on it,"

Molly shrugged, "Seems fine to me. Is she alright Sheila?"

"Hmm," Sheila shook her head, "it's nothing, don't worry."

***

"So, your mother and I have been discussing how to help you get more votes," Mr Watson addressed his daughter at dinner time, watching Carly play with her food. She'd been in a world of her own since he'd come home. Apparently, she'd been like that since getting home from school.

Mrs Watson had prompted him with her eyes to get on with it.

Carly looked up at her father reluctantly.

"Right, well, I'm going to use some of those posters you designed and put them on the counter. You know there's a lot of people who come in that I talk to." Mr Watson was Trade Manager at a local builders merchants *Sanford Builders Supplies*, "I must see fifty people at least every day who I can ask," he looked at his wife.

"What's the count now Carly?" Mrs Watson enquired gently.

"410."

"Good God, that's amazing Carly, really well done!" Mr Watson leant over and patted her on the shoulder.

"Against 429,"

"Ah…"

"Exactly. I told you. She's not gonna give up!"

"And nor are you. Remember, you're special." Mr Watson returned to his food, dissecting the fish slowly.

"I just feel so tired."

"Oh Carly." Mrs Watson, turned to her son, "Alan, can you walk Star tonight?"

"Yeah, no problem."

"No, she's my responsibility."

Alan shrugged *'I tried'* it said. Mrs Watson gave him a look of encouragement.

"I'll chase down some of my friends as well." Alan suggested.

"Good boy!" Mr Watson pointed a loaded fork at his son, "That's the spirit."

"Come on girl." Carly took Star for a short walk. In the cool evening afterglow she daydreamed, switching off as she wandered down familiar paths. Star decided, unusually for her, to defecate outside a neighbour's driveway.

"Bad girl, bad girl" Star looked suitably chastised, head bowed, eyes looking left and right. Sighing, Carly reached for a plastic bag in the pouch. Checking the windows of the house in case they wanted an explanation, she scooped up the mess.

"Guess it was coming out huh, Star."

Again Star looked everywhere but at her master.

"Come on Star, let's go."

The route was a simple trip around the block. Not wanting to visit the parade had meant sacrificing the park. Star had to go where she could.

Ping

Carly hesitated; her first impulse was to turn the mobile on without thinking. It was a habit, but she knew deep down this wasn't a Facebook notification.

He's not going to simply go away
Carly swiped the phone's surface.
Hi
Carly braced herself before responding.
Hello
How are we doing in the competition? Don't answer that, I already know.
Choosing her words carefully, Carly typed.
I think you've done enough, really, but thanks for all your help the competition is nearly over
Nothing came back, Carly waited and waited and just when she thought they had gone.
Ping
Doesn't it finish on Saturday morning?
Yes
Don't be afraid of me Carly, I want to help, remember
She swallowed.
But you killed someone
The response when it can made Carly wince, it was brutal.
What, that useless prick? Believe me the world's better off without him Carly. Some of his meat was rancid, wasn't fit for a dog. He had it coming
I gotta go
Carly switched off the phone, holding it like a prayer book.
My God what have I started? Am I to blame? Who was this person......

Chapter Eight

Tuesday was a blur. At school Carly dragged herself through the classes, she had to. Following the daily routine doled out by the school she was able to keep her head down, focusing on each lesson as they presented themselves, wandering the school's corridors mindlessly between classes. She had no real friends anyway, nobody to talk to.

Checking the updates at break time was the only interaction with the outside world she allowed, switching the phone off immediately after seeing the latest scores.

440 vs 465

Roxy was maintaining the lead, still ahead. At home was much the same. There was only the need to interact at dinner, after which she sloped off to her bedroom, shutting the door.

At school she hadn't bumped into Miles, in fact she avoided him. When she happened to spy the 6th former in the playground with his friend, Ethan, she'd hid. His searchlight gaze scanning the grounds, always watching. When the boys moved, so did she, in the opposite direction.

The same happened the next day. It was only a matter of time before they would turn a corner and bump into each other. Fortunately, his curriculum only required a certain amount of attendance. Still, it was only a matter of time. By Thursday lunch break that time was up.

"There you are!"

Carly stopped dead in her tracks.

"I've been looking everywhere for you!" Miles walked around to face Carly, "Have you been off school?" he asked gently.

"No, no, I've, well, I've been concentrating on studies, that's all," to Carly it sounded lame, but Miles merely nodded, still smiling.

"Hey how's the competition going?"

"Yeah, it's ok, I guess,"

"What? You were mental for it the other day."

"I am…" Carly broke out in a smile of her own, realising the goof she'd just made, "I mean, you know what I mean!"

"Hahaha, you're so funny, Carly. That's what I like about you,"

Carly began to blush; she couldn't help it.

"Wanna get some chips at Dino's? I'll pay."

Carly hesitated, "Erm…"

"Oh, come on."

"Ok," she gave in, "You're buying."

"Let's go then."

The pair headed out of the school, through the gates, onto the main road.

"I didn't thank you for lending me your bike the other day," Carly managed to say between mouthfuls of hot salty chips. They had bagged the only outside table Dino's supplied their patrons, watching the world go by.

"I'm just glad you brought it back."

"Of course, you didn't think I'd steal it?"

Miles grinned a chip filled smile, "I'd have hunted you down don't you worry…..so did you get to meet whoever….?"

"Yes….it turns out I might be onto something…maybe…I don't know…"

They ate in silence for a while, car watching.

Miles stole a look at Carly, "So what's the latest update with the competition?"

Before Carly could answer, a black Vauxhall Cavalier pulled up, screeching to a standstill, killing their conversation. Several cars behind had to brake hard, one driver tooted angrily.

A man leaped out already giving the students a furious glare.

Miles frowned, "Do you know him?"

"Oh shit," Carly mumbled.

"What did you say?" the man began shouting as he rounded his car, *"Huh?"*

Miles stood up. He was six foot two, and although lean and yet to fill out, he still carried 155 pounds to his name. Watching the man approach, he braced himself.

"It's him, the guy at the centre….."

"Who………?" Miles started.

"What did you say, Carly?" Richard was on top of them in seconds, his face screwed up in outrage, *"to Sheila! She's threatened me with the fucking police!"*

Carly could only stare back, silenced by Richard's temper.

"It was you, wasn't it? I know it was! She didn't say, but I'm not stupid! I never touched you!" he screamed.

"You better calm down mate!" Miles spoke up, moving stiffly towards the man, shielding Carly.

"I thought we were friends, I thought…what do you want? Fuck off!" Richard turned to Miles before dismissing the student with a look of contempt.

"NO!" a loud booming voice overrode them all, "YOU fuck off!"

Everyone turned to see Dino himself standing in the shop's doorway. Dino had seen everything from the beginning; the car arriving dramatically, the man jumping out, screaming his head off. He'd swung into action. Unlike Miles, Dino had filled out, weighed 300 pounds and looked every ounce of it. For a large man he could move quickly when he needed to.

Richard stared at the owner then back at Carly, jabbing a finger at her, "I won't…"

"Now fuckface, before I do something I'll regret!" Dino interrupted, making a move on Richard, his fists clenched, each one looking the size of a small football.

"Bitch….!" Richard screamed shrilly, back pedalling, keeping an eye on Dino.

"My God what a nutter!" Miles spluttered, after the black Vauxhall had careened back out into hooting traffic.

Dino nodded at Carly before heading back into his shop.

"What was that all about?" Miles turned to Carly, "How do you know that guy?"

Blinking back to life, Carly looked gratefully up at Miles, who was still standing.

"He was the guy that took the photos of all the dogs in the competition. He worked at the centre."

"No way, that guy?"

Carly nodded.

"Jeez what a nutter! I'm still stunned."

"He was touching the receptionist and I think I was next."

"Oh shit…"

"Sheila kicked him out, and I guess she must have mentioned the police."

"Why was he angry at you?"

"Who knows, he must have thought there was a connection between us."

The two students sat in silence for a while longer, ignoring the last of the chips.

"We should be getting back, I guess," Miles picked up the trash, looking for the bin.

"Yeah, look, sorry for that, it was..."

"Hey hey, don't apologise, it was not your fault. That guy has serious issues..."

"Yeah."

As they made their way up the street, Miles watched as Carly pulled out a business card from her jacket, turning it over to read the details. She put it away without a word and he didn't question her about it. He did manage, however, to see one small detail printed on the laminated card before she returned it to her pocket: an image of a camera.

***

Mr Watson tapped on his daughter's door, "Hey, you in there," He wasn't going to let another night go by without interaction, plus he'd had a directive from the boss.

The door opened; a miserable looking Carly stood waiting.

"I've been calling...."

Carly shrugged in response.

"How's the competition going?" Another shrug, "So you wanna come with me for a ride?" Mr Watson ventured, "It's Friday night remember, take away night, I've ordered, so all we have to do is pick it up."

"Do I have to come?"

"You know what? Yes, you do. Come on."

The drive over to the Lotus Garden Chinese restaurant they preferred was a short jaunt. Just as well, Mr Watson thought, his attempt to prise anything out of his daughter drew single syllable answers along with a grunt or two.

"Just a second, it nearly ready, sir," the Chinese lady smiled, before, during and after the conversation.

Mr Watson picked up the newspaper on the counter, giving each page a cursory glance. A tiny TV screen, as old as the hills, angled itself in the corner of the takeaway shop, displaying the 6 o'clock news.

"We go live to where Jane Winters, our correspondent, is coming to from Romford. Jane can you tell us, how is the mood with the local residents where you are ..."

Both Watsons looked up at the mention of the town. Romford only a stone's throw away in terms of neighbouring towns, heading west, literally a couple of miles away.

"...as you can see behind me, Sophie, there is still a gathering of concerned people here. The police have cordoned off the block of flats asking residents to confine themselves to their homes as they continue their investigations into this appalling crime..."

"...and are there anymore updates about what happened...?"

"...yes Sophie. Joining me now is Detective Constable Iain Banks of the Metropolitan Police who is leading the investigation. Detective can you tell us any more about what might be the motive and who the victim was?"

"Unfortunately I cannot release that information yet, but what I can tell you is we are taking every precaution and making every effort to follow up all leads and as you can see we are doing just that..."

"...can you confirm if there is a connection with this and the murder of Stanley Riley only a couple of miles away in Sanford four days ago?"

"...unfortunately that is still an on-going investigation, but I can tell you that Essex police, who are in charge of that case are doing everything possible..."

"Your order sir here ready!" the old lady interrupted, snapping the Watsons out of the news update.

"Thanks. Come on Carly."

In the car Mr Watson shivered involuntarily. "Wow, can you believe that? Two murders only a few miles from here! Gives me the creeps. No long walks with Star at night, you hear me, Carly?"

"Yes Dad, no long walks."

"I mean it, no going out after seven o'clock!"

"Dad I have Star with me, remember."

"Even so," Mr Watson checked on his daughter, "Got it?"

"Got it."

Dinner was a subdued affair, the Watsons eating quietly as if at a family wake.

"How's the competition going Carly?" Mrs Watson broached. After dividing up the Chinese food cartons, the silence had to be broken. Mr Watson, upon returning, had informed her of the terrible news gleaned at the Chinese takeaway.

"Still losing,"

"Oh well, one last push everybody, let's..." Mrs Watson rallied the family.

"...doesn't matter," Carly mumbled.

Alan watched his sister with a veiled look.

"Come on Carly, we're close to winning surely, what's Roxy got?" Mrs Watson sighed.

"I don't care..."

The fact was, Carly didn't know how many votes Roxy had. The last time she had managed a quick peep, the scores were neck and neck, to the last minute it would be down to the wire. Or so she predicted. She did care about the competition. Deep down she still wanted to win, still wanted to claim the prize. It was all so tragically tainted now. Turning on her phone was not an option.

After taking Star for a quick walk around the block, she excused herself and went straight up to her room, citing tiredness and wanting an early night. Tomorrow would be a big day however it ended.

Once she had closed the door, she took a deep breath. Picking up her phone she mentally prepared herself.

Please not tonight, closing her eyes and praying, praying for everything to go away. In her usual spot, Star whined softly.

"Here goes girl."

She turned it on.

Ping

A notification was waiting.

Ping

And another........

Ping, Ping, Ping

Carly's hand shook as she opened the Messenger App.

Hi Carly

You there

Please don't ignore me!

Carly!!

Someone had been busy.

I'm here, she typed back.

Ping

There you are! I was really worried about you!

I'm ok.

So, I see we are doing really well, 501 vs 509. Just can't quite overtake them, can we?

"No." Carly mumbled.

Still time, I think if we push just a little bit harder, we'll do it, probably be right down to the finish line...photo finish lol

Yes

Are you ok, you're not very talkative?

I'm just tired, really tired.

Are you upset with me?

Carly stared at the screen for a few seconds, before typing,

Why would I be?

I don't know, because of Richard maybe

Carly gasped, clamping a hand to her mouth, "No," she said, "No, no, no!"

Star stood up and began pacing the room, her whining unnoticed.

What about Richard? Carly found the courage to ask.

He had to go didn't he... dirty fucking paedo

Trembling, Carly typed with tears falling.

Why did you do it?

Carly are you serious? The bastard had it coming, he would have groomed you ...don't you know that?

He didn't deserve to die...he was sacked from the dog centre after all

Listen Carly...that fucker had stuff on his laptop, you know he did. He would have tricked you. He would have...touched you...molested you.

But you killed him!

I chopped him up good and fucking proper!! Fed that crying baby to my dog!!

He cried like a fucking baby Carly!!! Cried dying for his fucking MUMMY!!

Carly screamed, throwing the phone away. It bounced twice, nearly hitting Star, who watched it suspiciously, before turning to study her master again, big brown eyes unblinking, watching.

***

"Oh, come on!" Alan gripped the Xbox hand controller with both hands, shaking the contraption violently, his face contorted with rage, *"Give me a break!"* he demanded, ripping the headphones off his head. The controller was about to be launched when he became aware of somebody's presence standing in the doorway.

"Yeah, I know, I know. Not exactly good for the health, right?" he smiled weakly back at his sister. He did a double take, "You ok sis, you look weird?"

Carly stared at the TV screen, hypnotised.

"Hello, earth to Carly, come home!"

Carly's eyes flickered to Alan, then to the floor.

Discarding the game altogether, he stood and approached his sister.

"If I tell you something, promise me you won't say anything to Mum or Dad!"

"What's all this about?" he glanced behind her to make sure they were alone.

"You got to promise me first. Promise me!" He waited, leaning against the door frame nonchalantly.

"Alan!"

He waved a hand, "Okay, I promise…what's this all about?"

"You can't say anything to anybody," she pleaded.

"I said I promise. Now…What are you banging on about?"

Carly took a deep breath.

"The killings… you heard, right? About the killing in town……?" Carly paused, searching her brother's face.

He frowned. Whatever he'd been expecting, this wasn't it.

"I've been talking to the killer."

He shook his head, "What are you talking about Carly? For God's sake! What a thing to say."

Carly held up her mobile.

"On here, it's all here in print!"

He stared at the mobile and then at his sister's imploring eyes.

"I didn't know what to think at first, 'cause he was saying he was helping me with getting likes for Star in the competition. Then he told me about killing those men. He said things only someone would know if they…he knew. He did it Alan, *he killed those men!!*"

Alan held out his hand, "Show me," he said, his voice wavering.

Carly did as she was asked.

"You gotta believe me, I had no idea he'd do this…"

Taking the mobile he scrolled down the page, looking up at his sister and back down again, finally he questioned, "Where?"

"It's there."

"I don't see it."

"It's there! It's all there, everything he said…about killing them…I'm telling the truth!"

"Carly, there's nothing there, nothing of what you said. Nothing."

"Give it back," she snatched the phone out of his hands. Alan watched as she frantically scrolled the phone's pages.

"All I saw was your texting, no replies."

"It's right here!" Tears that had threatened to spill over began to fall freely now.

"I didn't see any texts but yours, sis," his voice genuinely anxious.

"I talked with him, I answered his questions, he…he…"

"Carly,"

"It's all here…" Carly moaned, "Why isn't it here?" she implored, finally looking up at her brother, searching his face with wide frightened eyes.

"Carly…" he smiled sadly.

"Alan…why isn't…"

"Come here," he pulled her in close, hugging her tight, "It's ok, it's ok," he tried to shush the sobs, now racking against his body. They stood like that for a while. Brother and sister, the closest they had ever been.

"You're special, Carly, don't let anyone tell you otherwise," he whispered gently into her ear, "I'll never let anyone hurt you, never."

Eventually he led her to her bed, helping her collapse onto the soft covers. She curled up immediately, turning her body away, quietly jerking, the tears silent but still coming.

He stood over her for a bit before pulling her trainers off. Taking the duvet cover, he placed it gently over her body. Next, he picked up her clothes from out of the laundry basket, inspecting the jeans and hoodie he remembered she must have worn the other night. He gave the items a quick sniff. Pausing, he bent down and collected the trainers she always wore as well.

Star settled down in her spot, yawning, but still monitored Alan as he left the room, switching off the light as he did so. In the doorway he hesitated, thought about shutting the door then remembering Star he left it ajar.

"I'll take care of it, sis." he whispered.

Checking the coast was clear in the kitchen, Alan pulled out a black bin liner from under the sink cupboard, stuffing the clothes and trainers inside before tying a quick knot.

"I'm just catching up with Tommy for a game at his place, mum," he poked his head around the door to where his parents were watching TV.

His father looked up, checking his watch. Mrs Watson shook her head at her husband.

"Don't be late darling, back by 12, ok?" they both went back to poring over her phone. He wondered what they were up to.

"Ok mum." He would be back long before then.

Opening the garage door, he wheeled his bike out, pulling the door down quietly behind him. The town centre was a short distance away and Alan made good time, cutting through a couple of overgrown cycle paths that ran parallel behind the gardens. Emerging out of the back roads and into the town's main streets, his route quickly leading him to subways that fed the large marketplace. The smell of rotting garbage floated up long before he was in sight of the square, along with the clamouring songs of the clean-up crews. The night was filled with nocturnal comings and goings; night buses, the odd car and a distant police siren. The town's one way system that circled the market was still busy. A few night crawlers were picking their way through the remains of the day. The barrow boy's rejects. Sniffing the fruit and veg, they hoped for a winner. A refuse lorry crawled down the centre on the square behind two workers, as they collected the black bags already previously gathered by a third. Alan picked his moment, cycling slowly behind and when the time was right, using the driver's blind side, rode in close. He hoisted the bag he was carrying high into the metal jaws of the crusher.

The cycle home now leisurely, he weaved slowly around the islands of rubbish and trash, taking his time. Tractor boys adjusting a market stall nearby dropped a scaffold brace, clanking and rolling. The sight of the metal bar jogged his memory of the horrendous night three years ago...that night at 'The Pit' venue, when Carly's drink had been spiked with drugs.

***

Sitting in the back seat of their father's car, Alan held his sister's head in his lap as they cut through the square. The car speed on down to an exit, his father shouting at the market boys, "Get out the way, *GET OUT THE WAY!*" One boy had let slip the brace he was holding, headlights illuminating his surprised face as the car bore down on him. Thinking his time had come, the boy could only await his fate. Mr Watson swerved just in time, missing the boy but riding the car straight over the pole without braking, smashing through a pile of collected garbage.

"How could you let your sister down, Alan?" His father's crying face at the hospital, wet from the tears, pleading, begging, and ultimately casting him away. A last barely audible whisper, "How could you let her...down...!"

"She's going into cardiac...!" A worried voice said, the speaker hidden from view.

The hospital curtains rippled as the doctors and nurses scurried and scrambled about the lifeless body of his sister. A whine of machinery stirred, growing to a steady hum.

"Charged...!"

"Clear?"

"Clear!"

ZAP

Obscured by the fabric, he still felt the body kick against the hospital cot. It felt as though he'd been kicked.

"AGAIN..." the machinery whirred to life again.

"Clear?

"Clear!"

ZAP

Ping

"Carly?" he breathed.

The curtain pulled back, revealing his sister's prone body, the wires, the mess. A nurse detached herself from the crowd.

"Please, you must wait outside," she was pulling on his arm, "we're doing everything we can young man, please…she's responding…"

Alan pushed the bike back into the garage, leaning it against the wall. He stared out into the black sky, hoping to shut out the memories, but they weren't done with him yet.

His father, pulling him aside, so close that he could tell what his father had eaten for dinner "Don't you ever let your sister down! Do you hear me, Alan?" *Don't you EVER let her down again!!"*.

He'd heard alright.

Carly had died that night. For a full minute she had been brain dead, but they had fought hard to resuscitate her, bringing her back. Only she wasn't the same Carly, the same sister he'd known for thirteen years. Something had come back with her, something dark.

Chapter Nine

"She's not up yet mum!"

"Well, wake her up then!"

Carly cracked her eyes open, groaning, sleep still clinging to her unconsciousness. Reality and light vanquishing the fantasy cushion of fading dreams, she groaned some more.

"Hey, you awake sis?"

"Well, I am now!" she moaned.

"It's past midday! You need to come downstairs,"

"Ok, ok, go away,"

"Don't be long mum's got something for you!"

Alan disappeared from view, his heavy steps retreating down the hallway.

Carly sat up, looking for Star. The room was empty, there was no sign of her. She already knew her dog was not there; it was a like a sixth sense.

Throwing the duvet cover off she zombie walked her way into the family bathroom. Staring at her reflection she made a face before dealing with the morning routine.

"Good morning!" Mrs Watson beamed with alarming cheerfulness.

"Morning, Princess!" Mr Watson followed up the greeting, equally bright and slightly annoying. Carly wasn't fully awake and ready for the world yet.

Alan gave his usual smirk.

Carly sat down, warily watching her family, who were all staring back at her.

"What?" Carly started.

"Tea?"

Carly nodded carefully, looking from one family member to the next.

"So, you know what today is right?" Mrs Watson placed a cup of tea in front of her daughter, taking a seat as well.

"Yeah, it's Saturday..." the penny finally dropped from a great height, "the competition!" Carly wailed, smacking her forehead.

The Watsons all laughed simultaneously; her expression was priceless.

"Thought you'd never remember!" Mr Watson shook his head wonderingly. He glanced over at his wife, "So we have some news for you." he paused for dramatic effect.

Carly caught her breath, waiting.

No-one could speak, although they were bursting at the seams.

"Oh for god sakes tell….." Carly began.

"……You're a winner! Star WON!" Mrs Watson gushed, grabbing her daughter's hands.

Carly's mouth dropped open. She looked from one parent to the next, stopping to look at her brother who nodded kindly, a rare smile coming from him.

"Holy shit! Holy shit!………*Shit really? We won?*""

"You won Carly! You really won!" Mr Watson came over and patted her on the shoulder.

"Hold on. We was losing, I remember the scores from last night. Star was still behind Roxy…"

"Ah, she was, but your mother and I spent all night…well, not all night you know what I mean…chasing up people who hadn't voted…" Mr Watson started.

"…and some people we hadn't contacted. This morning we monitored the site just in case, but it was all over. There wasn't any need. Not in the end" Mrs Watson finished.

Star padded into the house from the garden, looking hopefully from one family member to the next. The smells from the cooking were too much for her. Hearing Carly's voice she had wandered in hoping for a treat…and the morning walk.

"Really…you did that for Star?"

"And for you! We did it for you darling," Mrs Watson held her hand tightly, holding her daughter's gaze. "I could see it was taking its toll on you, so your father and I did what was needed. Go on, check your phone!" she beamed proudly.

"I will," Carly stood up, "I can't believe it, I can't believe we WON!" she jumped up, giving her mother a long hug. Star whined, so she reached down and squeezed Star around the neck, hugging the dog tightly too. "You hear that, Star, you won! You're a winner!"

"Come straight back, I'm doing a special breakfast, then you'll be wanting to go to see Sheila I expect. Your father will drive you there."

"Well done, sis," Alan called after his sister. She paused and smiled back over her shoulder before racing up the stairs.

It was true, all true. Star had won by a narrow margin, 559 to 548. On her phone the Paws and Claw website named her the winner. It had been close, fought all the way to the bitter end. The competition was finally over.

At the dog centre, Star was presented with the No.1 rosette and a humble silver trophy which was a first for the centre to award, with Star also grabbing a big hamper of doggy treats. It was a small, closed affair, only Molly and Sheila from the centre administering the spoils.

"I'll be taking the winner's photo," Sheila winked at Carly knowingly.

Carly thought about mentioning what she had seen last night in the Chinese, it would appear that Sheila hadn't seen or heard the news update. Neither had Molly, which came as no surprise. Molly wasn't exactly famed for her acumen when it came to current affairs.

Still, a major blessing. Carly breathed thankfully, deciding she wouldn't be the one to inform Sheila. No doubt the police would be making a call very soon, following up his last movements and connection to the centre. This was her moment after all.

"Never had a doubt, Carly," Sheila nudged her helper playfully, bringing Carly back to the real world. "Don't suppose you got time to help out? Gonna be a busy day," Sheila gave Carly a sly look.

"Go on, I'll take these back," her father stepped in, taking the prizes, "See you and Star back home."

"Thanks Dad," she watched as he loaded the car. Then on impulse she ran after him, "Dad!" she called out.

He looked round quizzically, caught off guard.

She hugged him tightly, "Thanks, thanks for everything," tears began to fall, she couldn't help it, it was all too much.

"You're welcome darling," he whispered in her ear, "You're special, remember? Don't ever forget that."

Chapter Ten

At Sandown School Miles and his best friend Josh, sitting in the bicycle shed, shared a playground joke, one that had been circulating and slowly evolving. The punch line was much the same, having altered course before reaching the end but it still produced the groan effect. Now it was their turn to hear it and pass it on.

Josh nodded with his head, indicating where he'd just spied Carly entering the school grounds. Miles' eyes lit up. He eagerly waved over at her across the way, catching her eye. She acknowledged with a smile, waving back eagerly. As she approached, he appraised the way she moved, the sheepish glance she let slip looking back, even the way she fidgeted with her long hair. He was beginning to like that, like that a lot. Josh made his excuses, sensing like a good friend would, the right moment to bail out.

"Good morning," Miles nudged Carly playfully when they caught up.

"Good morning you," she blushed.

The pair strolled slowly towards the science block, not really caring which way they wandered, neither worried about talking.

Miles stole a look at Carly. It felt so good to be around her, he couldn't get enough of being with her. From out of nowhere, he was suddenly the happiest boy in school, and it was unreal how quickly they had bonded.

Carly squeezed his arm as if reading his thoughts.

The timing of that, Miles thought, even that, was just perfect, magical.

Carly informed him of the news.

"So you're a winner, and Star is a champion. Best looking dog no less!" He declared warmly.

He got another squeeze in response.

"Come on... how does it feel? Must be a good feeling after all that hard work you put in...!"

"Yeah, it is," Carly admitted, smiling up at him, "glad it's finally over though.....it's been emotional!"

"I bet! You deserve it Carly, well done."

"Thanks," again that sheepish look he couldn't get enough of.

They continued the walk of young romantics, unsure of what to say, but also content not to say anything. For Miles it was perfect, and like that first time when he couldn't fully understand what was happening, he didn't care what anyone said...

"Oh," she interrupted his daydreaming, "you know what? Wait here a second, I just need to say something to someone, I'll be right back."

"Ok," he nodded amiably, looking around for the person in question.

Carly had spied Tracy Collins all alone, leaning against the wall engrossed with her phone and made a beeline for her.

"Hi Tracy."

Tracy looked around at the sound of her name being called, still smiling from the photo she had just posted, another pouting pose. The smile dropped instantly at the sight of Carly.

She glanced suspiciously around, expecting a trap. Seeing nothing to concern herself with, she turned on the charm.

"What do you want, dogface?"

Carly ignored the insult, "Where's your girlfriend?"

"Very funny, what do you want?"

"Oh, nothing from you, but..." Carly leaned in close to whisper, "If you ever cross me again," she gave Tracy a quick glimpse of the enormous kitchen knife she had tucked inside her jacket, "I'll cut your fucking tits off and cover your pathetic parent's faces with them! After I slit their throats and bleed them like little piggies!"

Tracy Collins' eyes bulged wide.

"The same goes for your bitch girlfriend. I'll chop that cunt up good and proper and feed her to my dog!" Carly sniffed the air theatrically, "Have you...have you just urinated?" she could see the other girl's legs wobbling with pure fear.

"Bad girl, *bad girl*," she chided, "Better go and clean yourself up!"

"What was that all about?" Miles asked when Carly caught back up with him.

"Oh nothing, really, I just apologised for the other day, said if she wanted...you know, we could be friends," she smiled coyly back at him.

"Really, you said that?"

Carly nodded giving Miles one of her modest looks, the two continued their walk, pavement watching.

"You know what, Carly Watson?" He stopped to give her a little tug, "You're something special," He declared leaning in for a kiss.

Carly looked up into Miles' blue eyes, "Yeah I hear that a lot."

Watcher of the Skies

Chapter One

"He's doing it again!" Thomas 'Tommy' Martin spoke aloud but to no-one. He was alone. Sitting by the bedroom window; staring down at his neighbour, the object of his fascination.

"What a weirdo!" saying the words slowly, he half expected the man to turn and look up and wave, *'Hello, yes, it's me, your friendly neighbourhood Mr Weirdo!'*

Swivelling on the computer chair he frantically searched his desk.

"Where is it…?"

Papers, pens, everything went flying. Jumping down he fell, landing awkwardly in his attempt to grab his phone, which had been launched in the process.

"Shit!"

Come on! Where is it? Ah, there!!

Snatching up the mobile with both hands he returned to his vigil by the window, carefully adjusting the curtain with the phone poking through.

Click, click, click, and finally click.

"Got yah!" Tommy checked the gallery app of the phone, swiping through the images deftly, hesitating for a second before returning to the window, this time hitting the record button.

"Oh yeah," *Definitely got yah now*, he thought, *YouTube for you now, Mr Weirdo.*

"What you doing?" Tommy spun round, startled by Abby, his eight-year-old sister, watching him from the bedroom door.

Sleepy eyed, still with hair all akimbo she was a picture of innocence. Only a couple of years away from discovering herself, the age of innocence soon to be just a memory in a picture book.

"Shhhh!" Tommy dismissed her irritably with a flick of his hand, but then turned back with a mischievous grin, "I'm watching the bogie man……!" He spoke in a creepy voice to accompany his mask.

"No, you're not."

"Wanna bet?"

Abby thought about it for a second, "I'm telling mummy!"

Tommy sighed, giving his sister a reproachful look, "Alright, but be quiet."

Waving her over to the window, they both peered out. Abby immediately frowned, suspicious of a trap.

"There's no bogie man!"

"There...look!" Tommy persisted.

Abby stared again, "But that's Mr Carty."

"Yes, that's him alright."

Abby looked at her brother, "He's the bogie man?"

Tommy nodded gravely. They both turned to look out of the window again.

Mr Cartwright, their neighbour, 68, and happily retired, prided himself on keeping the small, elongated garden, well kempt and fastidiously tidy. Make no mistake it was an award winning effort. Healthy flower beds abundantly flourishing, multi-coloured and trimmed, sat along the neighbouring fencing. Two sheds bookended the plot and, in the middle, 'The Lawn', as his mother would say of the grass.

Immaculate, so green and composite it could have been painted. Fit for a glossy magazine like *'Gardener's Weekly'*; the image would have had had reviewers complaining of fake.

In the middle of this dedication was Mr Cartwright, with his lawnmower.

Abby turned to her brother with a charming expression of alarm only eight-year-olds could possibly possess.

"Why is he standing still?"

Tommy shook his head in wonder.

"I have no idea, Abby. No idea."

Mr Cartwright had been standing still for the last ten minutes. Dead still. Not waiting still, not thinking *'Oh, I think I've just pulled a muscle'* still, but...frozen still.

Both hands gripped the lawn mower, his head lowered as if concentrating on the patch of lawn before him; left foot and calf raised, poised to finish the act of walking, but now, like the rest of his body, unmoving. From their position it was impossible to see Mr Cartwright's expression.

Tommy wondered what it would look like. Was he smiling? Crying? Laughing? Was he dead?

"He looks funny, like those statue people we saw in London, remember?"

"I sure do Abby, I sure do."

One Sunday afternoon, last summer, there had been a family day out by the Thames in London on the Southbank promenade. A popular walk festooned with a kaleidoscope of colour and cultural festivities, day trippers and South Londoners alike. It was here the family had come across the statue people, lots of them.

Abby had chosen one particularly authentic looking human sculpture to peer at. He was painted in gold from top to bottom and stood on a gold box.

The man, a caricature of Charlie Chaplin, splendidly perfect with bowler hat and cane, poised and frozen in the classic pose; as if waddling down a high street, at the start or ending of one of his iconic movies.

With coin in hand she had approached, unable to take her eyes off the man. Staring intently into his face while dropping the money into the collection hat, but just missing the mark. The coin had rolled away. Abby turned to pick up the runaway coin, only for the man to move suddenly and unexpectedly, causing her to scream in delicious fright.

"I'm going to tell Mummy!" Abby announced.

Tommy rounded on his little sister, horrified, "No you're not. You won't say anything! This'll be our little secret...right?"

Abby mulled it over; her eyes rolling up, searching the ceiling.

"Abby, promise me?" Tommy pressed.

"Promise!"

"Pinkie promise...?

Abby giggled.

"Come on, promise!"

Tommy squinted at his younger sibling.

"Are you crossing your fingers behind your back?" Tommy reproached, playfully pulling her close. He peered over her shoulder at the hidden hands.

"You are! Why you little..."

"No I'm not, no I'm not." Giggling hysterically with imp-like glee, Abby jumped away from her brother, spinning on the spot and sprinting for the door, "You can't catch me, you can't catch me."

Tommy made as if to chase after his sister, feinting the move. He watched her disappear out of the room, smiling at her playfulness.

"I'm telling mummy!" she shouted, now out of sight. The smile evaporated instantly.

"Whatever," Tommy shook his head, resigned.

A noise from outside drew him back to the window. Mr Cartwright was moving again, already on the return phase of mowing his horizontal lines to annoying perfection. Skilfully pivoting the mower as it reached the edge of the small patio near the house and off again back down the garden.

On reaching the bottom, he stopped.

Tommy leaned a little closer, anticipating a repeat performance. Mr Cartwright stared ahead, seeming to freeze again, but then stretched, arching his back slowly, both hands rubbing a point near the lower end. Shaking his head he propelled the lawnmower into the lower shed, only for it to catch on the concrete lip. He tilted the machine back and finally disappeared inside.

Tommy sat back thoughtfully.

Statue people... good name Abby...Statue People.

He checked his mobile once more, replaying the footage over and over. There was no denying he had caught something very peculiar and disturbing on film.

Blip

He checked the message. It was from Ray, his best friend.

Wanna go to the movies this weekend?

Sure, Tommy replied.

My turn to choose

You chose last time!

No I didn't

Yes you did matey

I think you'll find it was you!!

Well Trashcan Man 2 is showing, we gotta go see it

Isn't it rated 15?

Yeah, so what?

Dude we're 13 not 16! Remember we might get asked for ID

I'm actually 14, and anyway we both look older, so my mum reckons

What about Teri?

What about Teri??

She'll want to come, let her decide

Are you joking? She'll probably pick Legally Blonde or some other girl flick

We are talking about Teri here

Actually you're right it's still my turn to choose

Whatever

Laters

"Tommy! His mother called up, "It's 8.15! You'll be late for school. Come down.....NOW!"

He tapped a final message: *See you in assembly doughnut*
Tommy grabbed his rucksack, "Coming Mum!"

***

To some pupils Friday morning's school assembly was a source of entertainment; a chance to show off some 'dare' skillsets. To see how far the dare could go before inevitable expulsion from the hall and definitely detention. For the last player not to get caught, well, at Sandown's, it was immortality.

The coughing gag was always a winner. The coughing gag was the game where someone started to cough, which then got louder and louder as each participant raised the ante until the teachers could stand it no longer and zeroed in on the culprits. Of course, they had to catch you at it and that was the thrill. One kid would start the game and then, as if by telepathy, random coughs would coalesce, in an ever rising crescendo. With five hundred+ heads to monitor, the chance of you being caught was roughly 50-50. Still, those were pretty good odds. The excitement of getting away with it and being the champion antagonist was at times addictive; to others, such as Tommy Martin, it was a drag.

Ray Watkins sat down next to his best friend and playfully nudged him.

The two had been friends before joining Sandown, meeting through association of others whilst in Henley's Park, the largest park in Sanford, during one long hot summer many moons ago.

Ray, the foil of Tommy's indifference, was outspoken and direct, he would normally speak his mind whether or not the occasion asked for it, questioning rather than contemplating. The pair made a good team, bonding quickly, each having their own strengths and attributes respected and recognized by the other. It was a friendship that could last beyond school.

"Good morning, squire!"

"Morning. Going to join in today?" Tommy asked his friend.

"Err...let's just see who's orchestrating the Oscars, shall we? I mean there's teachers and then there's teachers, right?"

Tommy smiled. Some teachers were definitely a soft touch and Ray was no fool when it came to the game. He'd managed to win the academy award at least three times since the start of term and they were only into week five. He was totally revered in some corners of the playground.

The two boys watched as the hall filled up, both checking out the girls mostly. Another nudge from Ray he'd spied Tracy Collins and her legally blonde troupe, prancing their way into the crowd and most boys dreams. Tommy spotted Teri enter the hall, quickly taking a seat under the disapproving eye of a teacher.

Today's speaker and dare defier was none other than Geography and Head of Year 9, Mr Gray, a no-nonsense old school archetypical teacher, complete with eternal tweed suit and bow tie. Striding past teachers and children alike, his approach to the stage was reminiscent of a 4 Star general about to address his staff and troops for the big push into the theatre of war. Mr Gray was on a mission. God help those who stood in his way.

"It has unfortunately..." Mr Gray began, letting the words ring out strategically and with effect, "come to my attention...the disgusting, unbelievable and vulgar behaviour that a few boys have displayed at dinnertime in the playground yesterday," he gazed out at the sea of faces with a sweeping glare, pausing for effect.

"I am, of course, referring to the incident by the steps of the boiler room. Disgusting! There's no other word for it! DISGUSTING!" he shouted, barely containing the rage that so wanted to nuke the whole room.

An immediate ripple of tittering from a group of girls had teachers that lined the hall move into action, positioning themselves to stare out the guilty culprits.

Shaking their heads at those fool enough to make eye contact, some pressing fingers to their lips, an indication for silence, or face the consequences.

"I have never, NEVER, in all my days, witnessed such appalling and filthy acts of vile behaviour...... Spitting! SPITTING on each other's heads, in some sick and twisted game."

There would be no dare game today. All the 'would be' players were transfixed, along with the rest of the assembly, at the geography teacher's wrath.

"SLUGS!" bellowed Mr Gray, spraying out phlegm in his own version of the event.

The first two rows of pupils jumped out of their skins.

Tracy Collins, seated in the front row, stared disbelievingly at the goblet which had alighted on her skirt, narrowly missing her long, bare leg. Her friend, Rachel Eden sitting next to her, gagged audibly.

"Dirty, disgusting slugs the lot of you. There will NOT...... there will not be a repeat of this! I will not tolerate this kind of behaviour... it's filthy, it's dirty and it's unhygienic. If any of you are caught doing this again, and let me be clear on this, you will be receiving detention for a week! Do I make myself CLEAR?"

Tommy leaned discreetly over and whispered, "But he can spit though!"

Ray sniggered, unfortunately for him, too loudly. A teacher caught his eye, shaking his head indicating detention.

Mr Gray zeroed in on Ray as well, with lighthouse glaring eyes. For a second Ray died.

With assembly finished, the children dispersed from the main hall, making their way to their respective classes, for some a chance to catch up with friends and the last chance to catch up with the latest gossip before break time. For others it was a chance to drag out the inevitable, Tommy included.

"Sorry about that mate," he nudged his friend.

"Yeah, cheers buddy! I owe you one," Ray made as if to spit on Tommy.

A little spit did manage to make its way out onto his lip before dangling over. Tommy watched in disgust, pulling a face.

"That was gross, wasn't it? Glad I don't play it anymore," Ray declared.

"What, 'Gobbing Chamber'?"

The game Mr Gray had been referring to involved spitting on the head of some unfortunate soul who had the unenviable task of retrieving a ball that had descended into the janitor's basement stairwell, before the heavens opened with a blitzkrieg attack of aerial phlegm.

"Yeah, you can say that again! Never played though, did you?" Tommy challenged.

"Yes I did!"

"Ray, you've never played that game. You know how I know dude?"

"Go on,"

"You've never played football…ever!"

Ray thought about it, playfully cocking his head, "Yeah you're right, I never did."

"Listen, I've got something to show you." Tommy said, changing the subject, and began pulling his mobile out.

"Dude your phone should be locked away."

Ray immediately scanned the local vicinity and beyond. The teachers had a zero-tolerance policy when it came to mobile phones on one's person during lessons. Detention: no excuses and no exceptions.

"I know, I know, but you got to see this now!"

"It's not some wacky porn, is it? You know I'm not down with that!"

"No, it's not porn, but it sure is wacky bro!"

Ray studied the brief footage quietly, "Is that your neighbour?"

"Yeah, that's him alright."

"Man, you've got a problem, filming your neighbour!" Ray looked aghast pushing the phone away.

"What! Wait.....look again. Tell me what you see!" Tommy insisted, holding his phone out once more.

Ray sighed, slowly taking the mobile again, begrudgingly.

"I see...your neighbour standing still!"

"Exactly, dude."

"Wait," Ray did a double take, watching the time frame, "how is he...? That is wacky weird dude!"

Tommy nodded, "I know, right?"

"Anyways...I got to go," Ray backed away in the opposite direction, "Let me know if the lawnmower starts moving again anytime soon, Spielberg."

"Come on Ray."

"See you at break. You know what we can do this lunch time? Film the caretaker...brushing the leaves!"

Tommy showed Ray the finger.

"That wouldn't be a mobile phone I see in your hand, Tommy Martin?" Coach Williams had materialized undetected behind Tommy, "Oh dear, oh dear! Hand it over."

Ray shook his head mockingly, "I'll save you a seat!"

"But sir, class hasn't started yet." Tommy pleaded valiantly.

"You know the rules Tommy, no exceptions!"

He dutifully handed the phone over to the teacher, watching as it disappeared into Coach William's tracksuit pocket.

"You can collect it from reception after detention. Now, both of you get to class! Now......!"

Great just great, Tommy thought.

***

Dropping his rucksack, Tommy collapsed heavily onto his computer chair, pirouetting with the forced landing. Ray followed his friend into the bedroom, walking across the room to peer out of the window. Seeing nothing of interest, he too parked himself, laying-back on Tommy's bed, staring up at the ceiling.

"No sign of weirdo then," he muttered sadly.

Both boys had suffered detention, an hour-long incarceration in the company of Coach Williams, whose nickname, 'The Rat Catcher', thought up by one cocky year 8 student, was well founded and deserved due to his unnerving ability to snare offenders in the school halls.

When Coach Williams found out he'd been honoured with the unflattering mantle, he chose to accept it, rather than flush out the culprits. He had even taken to wearing a makeshift badge with a picture of Roland Rat in bold defiance, mocking the instigators. Of course, he then stepped up his recourse to Stasi levels; the old East German dreaded secret police, just to even the playing field. Williams' other occupation at the school, apart from being the number one pain in the butt for the children, was teaching year 8 History. This detention's delight, typical of Coach's punishment, had entailed a brief essay summarising the backlash and subsequent reprisal for the burning down of the White House by the British in 1814.

Oh, Coach knew how to have fun, nothing too taxing for Friday detention. On the blackboard was written:

SILENCE......NO TALKING

Other detainees included David Mitchell; a year 7 pupil, quiet and unassuming, the boy was in for the spitting incident last week that Mr Gray had so eloquently captured. Only David had been the victim.

With spit plastering his clothes and hair, reminiscent of a punk rock guitarist of old, he'd emerged from the stairwell still managing a victorious smile, duly holding the ball aloft.

As were three boys that had taken the brunt of the crime, Darren Hall, Kevin Masters and Neil Velour. All sitting apart at the back of the classroom; all three looking despondent, miserable, and angry. They had reason to be, they had a week of it to come.

The only girl and the enigma in the whole shooting party was Tracy Collins. Having complained to one of the assembly teachers regarding the spit and stain from Mr Gray, she'd received her punishment after expressing dissent and discord quite loudly with a string of un-lady like profanity.

The detention had passed without incident and now the boys were back at Tommy's, albeit chastised.

Picking up his PlayStation controller from the desk, Tommy waved at the window, "He only comes out in the mornings and weekends. Wanna play?"

Ray rolled his head on the bed contemplating the offer, "Nah."

"What you wanna do then?"

"I dunno." Ray sighed, "That detention sucked. What a waste of time."

"Okay, I know it was my fault, right." Tommy admitted.

Ray sat up, suddenly rejuvenated.

"Show me that clip of your neighbour again."

Tommy obliged, offering the phone and sitting next to his friend on the bed.

They both watched the short recording of Mr Cartwright doing his remarkable statue person act once again. However many times Tommy watched the clip, it still sent shivers down his spine.

"Statue people, that's what my little sister calls him!"

"Pretty accurate description, bro! I think she's hit on a name! Do you think he knew you were watching him?" Ray wondered.

"Don't think so. No, he couldn't have."

"Why?"

Tommy thought this over, "Well, I had the curtains drawn to a minimum for one thing and he never even once glanced my way," Tommy shrugged, "Even when he started moving again."

"Can I look something up on your computer?"

"Sure. What you thinking?"

"Well..." Ray began, "I'm wondering if this has been filmed before?"

"I doubt it bro."

"Well, let's have a look see."

For the next 20 minutes they scanned the internet, giving Google different search parameters. Each time nothing came up that was remotely close or relevant. They were presented with an abundant horde of clips with the real statue people from all over the world, some quite extraordinary and funny.

Mostly people being caught out and unaware of the prank being played; but then a YouTube clip caught Tommy's eye.

"Maybe we're looking in the wrong place."

"Go on..." Ray stopped looking at the screen, rubbing his tired eyes.

"We're never gonna find it here, well, not without the right questions. What if we searched through this sort of stuff..." Tommy stood up to retrieve a book off the shelf behind his computer.

The book in question was titled; 'The Mysterious & Unexplained'. His mother had picked it up for Tommy one day browsing the local charity shop. He'd hardly given it the time of day since. On the cover was a picture of the Pyramids with a crude UFO beaming a light down over the top. Tiny stick-like people surrounded the base, raising their arms up towards the spaceship, heads tilted, staring up. The illustrator had depicted the figures with smiling faces.

"I don't remember anything quite like it in here, but it's given me an idea."

"Really?" Rays face said it all.

"Come on, have an open mind," Tommy smirked back.

For the next hour they trawled the internet, alternating from the screen to Tommy's book arguing over what was the best research and lead. Abby popped her head round the door periodically, distracting Tommy and Ray alike with her giggles and nonsensical child talk, finally disappearing for good but not after testing the boy's patience to the max.

"You know what?" Ray suddenly proclaimed, looking defeated.

"Yeah, what?"

"I'm going home dude."

Tommy stretched, still staring at the screen, "I'm gonna carry on...got to be something in here somewhere."

"You do that, Sherlock, and be sure to let me know when the Aliens are coming will yah."

"Bugger off." Tommy laughed at his departing friend's back.

"Dinner time, Thomas," Tommy's mother called up from the depths of the house.

"Who's Thomas?" Ray wondered aloud.

"Piss off home."

He could hear a brief conversation as Ray left the house.

Sighing, Tommy gave up his search, pushing back in his chair, "Coming mum."

It was later that night after the Martin household had retired for the evening, that Tommy was lying on his bed, scrolling through his social media apps, flitting from one chat to another whilst competing in an online quiz game, when up Pinged a message. For a second he stared at the icon, contemplating its source and meaning.

Of course, cookies. He smiled; they get you every time. Click.

For the next two hours, and with almost hypnotic dedication, Tommy scanned and digested each disturbing montage of film, subscribing to the sender's channel and 'liking' the pages periodically. Shadows flickered on the bedroom walls as he continually soldiered on, exploring the unknown, out of this world and unexplained. Just when he had reached even his breaking point and with his stamina waning, he discovered an unnerving and disconcerting recording.

"Holy crap..." Tommy gasped out loud, "I've found something."

For a second all he could do was stare unblinking at the scene captured by one YouTuber's mobile phone, even after the clip was played back again and again, Tommy struggled to believe what he was seeing. Finally, he quickly downloaded the clip to his phone's memory, before sending it on to another domain.

Ping

Tommy sent an attached message: *I think I've found something dude*

Chapter Two

Tommy watched Ray and Teri Walker saunter into 'Popeye's' from the cafeteria's seating area. He waved them over, making room for them to sit beside him on the American style bench seats. Popeye's was located in Sanford's town centre. It was an all-in-one entertainment centre for kids which, at the time, was the largest in the county of Essex. Built only three years ago, the appeal and novelty still drew large numbers, even on weekdays. Management ran a tight ship; amenities and general hygiene throughout were maintained to a high standard. The joke running around town was that the staff were employed for being able to produce the insane smiles that hung onto their faces. Sometimes long after they had left. Either that or they needed prescription drugs to work there.

Divided into four main quadrants, the centre offered a ten-lane bowling alley, a gaming corner with state-of-the-art VR systems, an amusement arcade loaded with coin operated machines and other money sucking games, and of course, the café. There was even a small section in the café designated for adults to drink and watch live sport on large well placed screens. Great for the dads, who could spend their time watching their charges 'responsibly' from afar with a pint of beer and one eye on the football, or whatever happened to be televised, usually sport. Perennially busy, a place for the kids to meet and play, a place to get away, a place to hide. And it was Saturday, the busiest day of the week.

"Hey Teri….! Alright Ray?" Tommy greeted his friends coolly, one arm draped casually over the top of the faux leather seats.

"Alright mate."

"Hey, Tommy…" Teri Walker smiled a big toothy grin.

Tommy smiled back warmly. He liked Teri. Having joined the 'gang' a year ago, her laid-back personality and attitude totally suited the boys. She also dressed like the boys, casual, normally sporting a baseball cap, and similar sporty clothes. Never a distraction, Teri was cool. Plus, she lived two streets away from Tommy. Their friendship had formed slowly, a gradual acknowledgement in the corridors of Sandown Comprehensive and then in the street when passing, to eventually walking to school together in the mornings and hanging out in the evenings. She also played football for the school team, talked football, wanted to be a footballer and ultimately drove everybody she knew mad with her incessant babbling…about football.

"You want some chicken? Something to eat?" Ray asked Teri.

"Yeah sure, what you having...?"

"I'll get us Popeye's famous family bucket of fat me thinks."

"Here, take this," Teri handed over some cash laughing.

"You good Tommy?"

"Yeah, I've eaten dude."

Tommy and Teri watched the sports screen while Ray ordered, making small talk, glancing around occasionally, checking out who was entering the arcade. Seeing who was who and who was not.

Ray returned with a smile, "I ordered gut bucket and fat boy chips, sound good?"

"Mmm... Yummy, yummy in my tummy," again Teri laughed easily.

"You'll love it!" Ray spoke comically as if from a cartoon, "So, Tommy boy, you going to fill Teri in, or shall I? I haven't said a word by the way." Ray leaned across the table motioning with crossing arms, emphasising his commitment.

"Yeah, what's this all about, I'm dying to know," Teri leaned on the table folding her arms expectantly, eyes twinkling.

Looking across at his friends, Tommy suddenly didn't want to say anything about the strange sight of his neighbour, Mr Cartwright, crystallizing on his lawnmower. He wanted to forget his midnight discovery and definitely wanted to forget his crazy theory of what the hell it all meant. At the bar end of the cafeteria a father belched loudly.

"Excuse me," the man smiled, looking over at the group, realising his monumental burp had been overheard.

"Eugh......! Gross!" Ray laughed with Teri.

"I think we're living in a Matrix." Tommy blurted.

Both his friends turned and stared blankly back.

"A matrix type existence to be ... Well, something like that."

"Ok..." Ray said slowly, nodding to Teri, "Maybe I should have given you a heads up before we got here."

"What do you mean, Tommy?" Teri ignored Ray.

Ray started to say something, couldn't formulate his words properly, and sat back, closing his mouth in silent exasperation.

Tommy then proceeded to explain everything. Starting with Mr Cartwright, including the first time the neighbour had been spotted acting weird, the midnight reading of mysteries unexplained with the additional new clip and ending with his wild card synopsis.

"The more you dig up on this stuff the more you uncover! Did you show Teri the clip I sent last night?"

"No not yet." Ray scrolled through his videos, passing the phone so Teri could see the picture better. The video Tommy had downloaded showed an airplane captured, frozen still in the sky as if someone had paused the frame, only when played back, did it become somewhat more unsettling. Almost unbelievable viewing. Whoever took the footage was travelling in a car, complete with passing lampposts and other vehicles. It just didn't make any sense.

Teri looked hard at the screen, "Could be edited."

"Yeah maybe, but why haven't we heard about it before?" Ray took his phone back, looking to Tommy for a response.

"Maybe we missed it. Maybe its old and forgotten news," Tommy shrugged.

"Maybe...it is two years old on here......maybe," Ray leaned in close, searching the nearby booths for eavesdroppers; "they forgot to delete it!" he finished with a whisper and a wink.

"It is weird, I'll give you that," Teri smiled.

"Yeah, but who would do such scary crap like that, and why?" Ray asked.

"Because, I don't know, maybe it's real?" Tommy replied.

Just then their food arrived. Both his friends gladly turned to the smiling waitress.

"Family feast for four...?"

"Yup that's us," Ray proclaimed a bit over-loudly.

"Really Ray!" Teri raised her eyebrows, "Four?"

"Ok, here you go guys" the waitress placed the tray on the table.

"Thank you..." Ray checked the girl's name badge, "Hattie."

"Pleasure. Enjoy," Hattie smiled sweetly and left.

"Is it part of the job to smile all the time around here?" Ray wondered with a shake of his head, "Or is it just that good a place to work? Ok, tuck in Teri. Tommy, you want some? Got plenty here buddy."

Tommy shook his head, patiently waiting while his friends set about their lunch, picking up his mobile, checking the latest news, and then bored of doing that, people watching. By the entrance a large group of kids arrived with mothers. Immediately the children began jumping excitedly as if someone had switched on the batteries for imaginary pogo sticks. Scattering themselves around the fitting stall, grabbing bowling shoes without prompting, chaos ensued. Finally, Tommy could no longer contain his impatience.

"So, what do you think?"

"That was sick, and I think I'm gonna be SICK too! Coach would have a fit if he knew!" Teri swiped her hands with a scented wipe.

"Guy's come on...!" Tommy groaned.

Ray wiped his mouth, without a tissue, studying his best friend. Grabbing a handful of chips which he dipped slowly and deliberately into his second tub of barbeque sauce.

"What if," Ray leaned across the table giving both his friends a hooded look, "it's a government conspiracy, huh?"

"Are you serious right now?" Tommy asked.

"Well, my dad says that if it's bad and this looks bad, right? Then it all leads back to the government somehow, some way!"

"It's not the government, Ray."

"Could be…."

"Look, trust me this isn't the government."

"I think we should, you know, keep it in the bag of options just in case some suit turns up to cart us off to the funny farm?" Ray shrugged at Teri for support.

"This is too weird for the government," Teri muttered.

"The government has some pretty weird shit tucked its sleeves!"

"It that your Dad talking again?"

"Ok so, we're living in a matrix, a matrix game, controlled by extra-terrestrials probably played by some spotty teenager with hygiene issues and well, loves Popeye's," Ray finally let out, waving a chicken leg.

Teri laughed, "Yeah, doesn't get out much and hates football as well."

Tommy looked from one friend to another.

"Or we're just a simulation that's playing out to see if we can cure cancer?" Teri suggested, devouring a hot wing.

Both boys turned to stare.

"And once we do it's…curtains!" Teri finished matter-of-factly, rummaging through the party box for another hot wing. "These are soooo good! Then there's all the wars that's ever occurred over all the centuries, right? I mean they could be different levels or something in the game. Sort of like 'War of Ages' with Nintendo or whatever." Teri found another wing, "You want this?" Ray shook his head, raising his eyebrows and smirking at Tommy.

"What about those strange looking magicians who blow your minds with their insane tricks? Can you explain those weirdo's, huh? Remember that one? Can't recall his name, eyes like an albino, skinny as a rake what about him? He could be an alien here to monitor us."

"Glad I brought it up!" Tommy looked at Ray.

Teri expertly sucked the meat off the bone with one attempt, "Of course now that you've discovered their dirty little secret, Tommy, what do you think will happen next? To you, I mean," Teri wagged the last wing at him.

"What do you mean?"

"Isn't it obvious, dude?" Teri whispered, leaning forward conspiratorially.

Tommy and Ray both waited.

"Good night, sleep tight." She drew a line with her finger across her neck, topped with a clucking noise.

Ray sucked noisily on his drink. "Sorry..."

"Thanks for that Teri. I guess that's cleared everything up. Glad I asked..." Tommy frowned.

Teri shrugged nonchalantly, "You asked."

Tommy turned to watch the gamers. He recognised some of them from school, younger kids out on the town together, having fun.

"What you guy's doing tonight?" Ray ventured, giving the party box a last sweep for leftovers, "Wanna hang out later, go to the movies or something? You know, lighten the mood maybe?"

"I've got practice with my dad. You know how dedicated he is," Teri sighed, "Would love to hang out."

"You got anything planned, Tommy, apart from star gazing?" Ray smiled at his friend.

Tommy shook his head, "I'm skint."

"No probs buddy, I'll pay, you can sort me out next time."

"Ah... I'm feeling the loooove," Teri laughed.

"Yeah, ok then."

Teri gathered the mess left on the table, sweeping the tray into the litter cubicle on their way out, "I'll be mother, boys!"

"Thanks Mummy!" Ray laughed.

"What's on at the movies anyway?" Tommy asked.

"Trashcan Man 2! I told you!! Who cares what's on. Better than sitting at home dude!"

Chapter Three

Saturday afternoon passed quickly, stretching into a glorious late Indian summer evening. One of those September nights that drags on forever. The weather forecast for the week ahead and foreseeable future was much of the same. The town people of Sanford mostly enjoying the last of the long days and golden sunsets. Smoky barbeques drifting their mouth-watering aromas throughout the district, mingling with wood smoke and freshly cut grass. The afternoon traffic was dissipating from the A-roads and other capillaries, reducing the drone of background interference to a calmer stillness. Children's laughter could be heard louder and clearer now, instead of passing cars and rumbling delivery trucks. Suburbia was settling down for the second half of the hot weekend ahead.

At home Tommy watched as his sister pulled a face at her food.

"If you're going to the cinema later, can you tidy up your room and bring down your dirty laundry, please Thomas? Tommy, did you hear me?" Mrs Martin interrupted Tommy's reverie, putting a plate of steaming pasta in front of him.

"What?"

"Not what, *pardon*, young man." Mrs Martin tutted loudly, "Abigail, stop playing with your food!"

Abby poked her tongue out a little rebelliously, the small triangle of pink flesh protruding momentarily, darting back before her mother spotted the daring insubordination.

"Pardon..." Tommy acquiesced.

"I said bring down your laundry and tidy your room It's a state, I honestly don't know how you get it into such a mess," his sister wagged her head, mimicking her mother. Again this was missed, or ignored, or both.

"How have you got the money to go to the pictures anyway, Tommy?" His mother continued.

"Ray's paying. Plus, I've sold some of the PS3 games I didn't want anymore."

"The ones your father gave you? Really? Well, let's hope he doesn't find out next time he visits and asks, hmm?"

"And he gives me some money, remember. Anyway, Ray's paying."

"Wish he'd give me some more! Doesn't really cover what he gives me, looking after the two of you and running this household!" Mrs Martin grumbled.

Tommy joined his sister in pushing and poking his food.

"Mummy, Tommy says that Mr Carty is the boogieman!" Abby blurted watching her brother's reaction.

"Tommy! For God's sake! Stop putting nonsense into Abigail's head! It's bad enough that you've got your head in the clouds these days. And please, can both of you stop playing with your food!" Mrs Martin folded her cleaning cloth, "He may be old and a little eccentric but he's a good neighbour. Look how well he keeps his garden!" Mrs Martin returned to the kitchen counter muttering under her breath.

Tommy shook his head slowly at Abby.

I'm going to kill you, he mouthed silently.

"Mummy!"

After finishing his food, Tommy scooped up the discarded clothes as promised, throwing the garments into the laundry basket. A loud crack coming from the open window that faced his neighbour halted his chores. Carefully peering around the curtain and at the same time not wanting to appear too suspicious, he looked down into the garden below. At first it seemed to be empty, there was no sign of life. Whatever or whoever had made the sound was nowhere to be seen. He was about to return to his tidying up when his neighbour, Mr Cartwright, emerged from the bottom shed.

Dressed in his usual attire for gardening; faded jeans creased, never to be washed or ironed ever again in their life. He was wearing a familiar grey plain shirt, open almost to the navel, showing off his bony white skin, the red V-shaped sunburn tan around his collar and face in stark contrast to the exposed body.

Tommy held his vigil, deducing that the sound he'd heard must have come from inside the shed and caused by whatever Mr Cartwright had been doing inside.

Tinkering around with his crap no doubt, Tommy thought.

It housed all the old man's tools and junk, a lifetime's collection of hardware. He was about to turn away, and that was the moment, the instant that Tommy had another shock of his life.

Mr Cartwright turned to close the shed door, stooping slightly, holding the keys in his hand, fiddling loudly with the bunch to find the right one. His body moved forward to put the key in the lock, and as he did so, Tommy saw a face clearly in the shed window.

It was looking straight back at him!
A white oval face.
Black opaque eyes.
Unblinking.
Staring.

Tommy jerked away from the window, body twitching, the shock-jolt had sent him falling back, brushing the bed. Landing heavily, the laundry basket slipped from his trembling hands, bouncing on the floor and sending clothes flying. Cold tingling sensations took hold, flowing from the neck down to the base of his spine. The startled gasp that had escaped his lips was the only sound he could muster.

What the hell! Jesus, what was that??

Looking back up at the window in disbelief, Mr Cartwright could be heard locking the shed door, whistling an ancient tune.

Tommy crawled away from the window, unable to bring himself to stand.

PING

His mobile phone came to life, vibrating on the desk. Tommy jumped at the noise.

"Shit!"

The message was from Teri.

Need to discuss something I've found out you still meeting Ray right?

Tommy grasped the computer chair, pulling himself slowly up. From where he was positioned, all he could see were distant neighbouring gardens and roof top skylines.

The crack in the lace curtain gave away nothing of his neighbour's garden. Still holding the phone, Tommy inched towards the window, hunched over, choosing the corner as the vantage point. The top of the shed came into view, followed by the walls, and slowly the outline of the shed's window frame materialized. It was empty, clear, nothing to be seen.

Tommy straightened up. Taking a deep breath, he collected the washing before texting a reply to Teri.

Yeah. Ok see you there

With a last backward shudder at the window Tommy left for the town.

Did I really see that...that face...? What the hell is going on?

***

The movie theatre was located next to Popeye's, part of the main complex and adjacent to the entertainment arcade in the heart of the town centre's shopping precinct. The foyer to the cinema, already busy with the remaining shoppers and movie goers alike who mostly gazed up at the neon display monitors flashing the latest releases and timetables. Tommy lounged to one side of the entrance, watching the crowds come and go. He checked his phone for updates, clicking on a social media site at one friend's notification.

In the distance, a man with ill-fitting clothes flitted across the shopping precinct's concourse, stopping to stare up and down in equal measure. Speaking to no-one but looking to address anyone, his actions causing mums and dads to pull their children away sharply and abruptly changing direction, finding a new course to steer. Tommy recognised the man, Lenny Budgie, who was well known throughout the town as the local eccentric.

None of the kids in town knew the real story of Lenny, or if that was even his real name. A local character someone that both children and adults ridiculed alike. Always dressed in the same dark blue crumpled suit; trousers way too short, exposing his shins. Even the grimy white socks he preferred, pulled up high, couldn't hide the flesh. The jacket, too large and baggy for his emaciated frame, the once white shirt now a decidedly off-white-kind-of-yellow-shade buttoned up to the top, but without a tie, completed the outfit.

Some spoke of Lenny once being a successful businessman, devastated by grief after losing his wife to another man being caught in the act. His business suffered as a consequence, and he finally lost everything he once held dear. Now, he lived in a bedsit somewhere, his mind blown beyond the reach of conventional society rules, unwanted, ungoverned and unloved. Others relate a tale saying he was simply a nutcase, struggling with the rigours of life and by the time he reached his twenties, took the easy route. Dropping out, not caring anymore in appearance or behaviour. His hair now virtually gone, trailing wisps of dirty blond strands occasionally brushed with the comb he always carried, topped a pointy parrot like face, made even more so by his constant tilting as if listening to someone standing beside him. The green eyes though, were alive and well, flickering at everything and nothing; always unsettling when they converged, albeit for only a second, focusing tightly on whoever was brave enough to speak to him.

Tommy suspected Lenny's surname was born from a nickname chosen by the way he looked and acted. A free spirit was Lenny Budgie; troubled but free.

"Hey Tommy!" Teri appeared suddenly by his side, smiling.

"Jesus Teri! You made me jump!"

"Ha-ha! You were away with the fairies!"

"Yeah, thanks."

"Where's Ray?"

"Dunno, he should be here." Tommy checked his phone. "Anytime now."

"Good," Teri scanned the entrance.

"What is it you wanted to talk about?"

"Ah, let's wait for Ray, shall we?" Teri smiled another one of her easy smiles.

"Fair enough." Tommy was beginning to like those smiles.

"Oh God, it's Lenny!" Teri turned away in disgust.

Tommy smiled sensing an opportunity, "Hey Lenny, come here!"

"Don't, Tommy!"

Lenny spun around upon hearing his name called. He beamed a crazy grin, the two plastic carrier bags he carried twirled, reminding Tommy of buoys on a boat as he swivelled precariously, head tilted as if listening to some distant sound.

"Hello Tommy!" Lenny spoke with a comically high-pitched falsetto voice which complemented his persona. His smile never altered. Once delivered, it was institutionalized.

"Hello Lenny, you alright?" Tommy repaid Lenny with a large smile in return.

"Yeah," Lenny began twitching, "Lenny good!"

"What you doing?"

"Going home, silly!" The smile broadened, exposing a gummy mouth. Lenny's teeth had given up the ghost long ago.

"Hey Lenny, dance for me."

"No...."

Lenny wiggled his signature wiggle checking the foyer for spectators.

"Oh, go on..., I've got a penny!"

Lenny zapped his face back, whippet fast. His green eyes piercingly sharp.

"Have you?"

"Yeah, here." Tommy produced the promised coin, throwing it at the man's feet, "Go on, dance for me, Lenny."

"Oh, alright then," Lenny scooped the penny up without dropping the bags. He then proceeded to jitterbug, gyrating and twisting his body in a rocking motion, his legs started kicking as if playing football or doing an impromptu Scottish Highland fling for the mentally disturbed.

Teri stared in disbelief at the spectacle, closing her eyes in disgust.

"Dance Lenny...dance...!"

"Hah hah...hah hah...I'm dancing!"

"Nice one Lenny."

"Yeah..."

The dance stopped as quickly as it had started. Lenny distracted by something only he could see.

"You go home now, mate." Tommy spoke earnestly, giving Lenny a serious look.

"Yeah, Lenny go now, bye-bye." He turned to leave but instead paused with his back to Tommy and Teri, who both waited expectantly for something to happen. Teri began to ask if everything was alright, but then Lenny surprised them both.

"I've seen them, you know." he said over his shoulder before launching into his chaotic walk, dispersing groups of shoppers. Tommy and Teri watched his departure down the precinct with muted perplexity.

"It's cruel," Teri shook her head, "What you guys do. It's cruel."

"Hey Lenny, SEEN WHO?" Tommy shouted at the departing man's back.

Several people queuing stared back frowning one middle-aged lady muttering her disapproval.

Tommy ignored the complaining woman.

"What did he mean, *'I've seen them'*, seen who?"

Teri shook her head. "You shouldn't do that to him, it's cruel."

"What? Oh yeah, I know, you're probably right. Sorry, habit."

"There's Ray," Teri nodded down the precinct's concourse.

"What happened with your father and practice?" Tommy asked, remembering the promise.

"Well Dad got called into work, and I got bored sitting around on my own."

"That sucks."

"Doesn't matter, I get to hang with you guys now."

The two friends fell silent until Ray joined them, looking quizzically over his shoulder.

"Did I see Lenny Budgie?"

"Sure did, buddy, the one and only."

"Did he dance?" Ray mimicked Lenny with a little jig of his own.

"Jeez! You boys!" Teri moaned, taking off, heading away towards Popeye's.

"Thought she wanted to watch a film?" Ray looked at Tommy, who shrugged.

"Me too, come on. Let's see what this is all about."

"But Trashcan Man 2 is showing! I'll pay!"

"Sorry dude."

Ray dejected, wondered if he'd ever get to see the film.

Chapter Four

"So, we're back here again!" Ray sulked, sitting heavily next to Teri in Popeye's café, "Can't we go somewhere else today?"

"I asked to meet you guys at the cinema because I knew you wouldn't come here again," Teri admitted.

"We could go over to the park?" Tommy suggested helpfully.

"Park.......!" Ray spat.

"Yeah, you know, 'The Park', as in playing fields, swings, open spaces etc."

"I know what the park is. It could it be that you're both having withdrawal symptoms.......?"

"Yeah, like I eat as much as you do here, GUT BUCKET!"

"I've seen something too, guys," Teri spoke up, interrupting the sparring match.

Both boys turned to stare at Teri, Tommy wide-eyed.

"Not you as well!" Ray sat back, looking miserable.

"What have you seen?" Tommy asked quietly.

For an answer, Teri pulled out her mobile, tapping the screen and scrolling through her gallery of pictures.

"Here," she surrendered her phone to Tommy.

Ray shook his head, turning to look elsewhere in the café, settling on the TV monitor above the bar; a repeat game of rugby was showing that afternoon's highlights. He was having serious thoughts about sneaking off on his own to watch Trashcan Man.

"I got to thinking about what you said and, well, I couldn't help myself. I started taking pictures on the way home, just random pics. I don't know why, but the idea just came into my head."

"Yeah, like what a nutter!" Ray chimed in.

Tommy shot his best friend a look, who shrugged back.

"What am I looking at?"

Tommy returned his attention to the phone. In the image, Sanford's shopping concourse with its long line of shops could be seen. Shoppers oblivious to the cheeky snap carried their purchases, captured in various poses of still life; children caught running, some jumping and some climbing up chrome barriers that lined the car park. Even a pigeon had made the grade.

Teri had turned around, taking a shot of everyday life on a typical Saturday afternoon, just another day in good old Sanford town.

"Do you see it?" Teri asked.

Tommy stared hard at the picture.

"Do you see him?" Teri pressed.

Tommy blinked.

"Youse two can't be serious!" Ray moaned.

Both his friends continued to stare at the photo.

"Oh, come on!"

"I thought you were interested, dude," Tommy started, "You helped…"

"Listen, I was interested, because one," Ray held up a finger, "You're my friend. Two," another finger, "it was mildly interesting, and three," a third finger joined the others, "I needed to see if you was a full blown nutter, trying for the Lenny Budgie crown!"

Tommy sighed, "Thanks for understanding bro."

"Anytime pal, anytime."

Tommy returned to the image on the phone. He saw it instantly now; he didn't know how he hadn't spotted it before. Saw *him*.

In the picture, mostly obscured by a low-walled flower bed feature that decorated the concourse, was a man around fifty feet away from where Teri had stood taking the photograph. He was captured mid-stride, walking around the sandwich-board sign outside Greggs the bakers. He was looking directly at Teri. A blank expression, a balding head with non-descript features, his age indeterminable. Certainly not over fifty, but otherwise it was impossible to tell.

"I've seen him too." Tommy stated, still studying the image.

"Really, dude?" Ray smirked, "On your laptop late at night perhaps?"

"No, in my neighbour's shed. Mr Cartwright's shed."

"What?"

Teri stared quietly at the boys, taking back her phone and scrolling once more.

"Today I was in my bedroom, tidying up, when I saw him. Mr Cartwright was locking up and in the shed window *that* face appeared," Tommy explained, pointing to Teri's phone.

"Could have been a reflection or something?" Ray grumbled.

"Yeah, could have, until now."

"So what, the man was locked up in this old man's shed and now he's walking around stalking Teri?"

Tommy shrugged, "What is also weird when you think about it, is that Mr Cartwright came out of the shed when this guy was in it and acted like nothing unusual was happening, like locking a weird looking dude up for the night."

"Then there's this," Teri handed the phone back so both boys could see the image.

Again, she had taken a still life picture, this time in the car park, looking back at the shopping centre. Dozens of people in the process of finding their vehicles or loading up their car boots with shopping bags were in the frame. This time there no mistaking him; the man was there once more. Only he was turning away, as if heading back to the shopping centre, almost as if he'd been recognised, or discovered.

"He knew you were on to him!"

"Ok, now that is disturbing, guys," Ray admitted.

"Do you think he followed you back home?" Tommy asked Teri.

"Could have, I guess," she put her phone down on the table, lost in thought.

"A bit late for that, right, seeing as how he knows Tommy was perving at the neighbour! He knows exactly where Tommy lives!"

Tommy sat back contemplating.

"Hi! Are you guys going to order anything?" The same waitress from earlier in the day, Hattie, now stood by their booth holding a menu, smiling the award-winning smile.

"Err...no," Ray stood up, "I'm going over there," he pointed to the gaming section, "to clear my head and have some fun."

"How about you two?"

"Can we just order some Coke?" Teri responded, smiling sweetly back at Hattie whose own smile wavered ever so slightly.

"No probs. I'll bring them over."

"Thank you."

Tommy surveyed the café.

"Didn't notice how busy it is now," he muttered to Teri who was watching Ray sitting down in the VR 'experience' chair. He placed a set of goggles over his head while a worker adjusted the computer's simulation programming.

"What's it all mean, Tommy?" Teri asked quietly.

Tommy shook his head. "I really don't know what to think."

***

Ray collected the goggles from the attendant, handing over the money before settling into the custom-made sensor chair and strapping in. He asked for the jet fighter simulation after studying the list of preferred options.

"You played this before?" asked the attendant.

"Oh yeah!"

The gaming seat, balanced on the latest hydraulic platform that the latest VROS system had to offer, clicked and adjusted, coming to life with the computer programming. A faint humming noise accompanying the tinniest of vibrations could be heard as the final settings synchronised.

"Here we go, bro," Ray laughed out loud.

The attendant smiled knowingly and hit the start key.

Are you Ready?

Flashed up in Ray's peripheral vision, inching slowly across to the centre of the screen where it hesitated, then made its way to the other side, before disappearing out of sight. A cockpit full of dials and digital readings materialised, taking the place of the initiation, illuminated as if in a real pilot's cockpit canopy.

Ray's sense of reality was disappearing rapidly. Turning his head left and right 180 degrees checking out the landscape, it mimicked what a person would see if actually in this universe.

"Oh yeah, hit it!"

The programme sequencing began. Ray's fighter jet 'launched' itself off an aircraft carrier, accelerating at an insane speed, climbing almost vertically into the clouds and up into the stratosphere in no time. The dials' numbers raced as the fighter jet climbed and climbed. His seat reacted to the simulation, jerking backwards then tilting sharply as the steep ascent began.

"Woohoo!" Ray hooted, totally absorbed, and now in the zone, "Come on!"

The fighter jet levelled out, attaining the ceiling height; above, only the infinite blackness of space, ahead in the distance the majestic curvature of the Earth. A hazy mirage of white and blue ozone separated the floating mirage.

Cruising for a few seconds at the max height allowed the gamer to appreciate the incredible electromechanical technology, the Dolby 7.1 surround sound panning insanely in his ears. Indistinct radio chatter played along, the seat vibrating softly.

Enemy detected... Engage!

Flashed up.

"Let's go!" Ray searched the horizon, looking for the bogie.

The chair jerked hard left, catching Ray off guard, his head wobbling from the effect of stabilising. In the game, the fighter jet was now pitching at an acute angle. He was heading for a tiny speck several miles ahead and gaining ground.

Missiles armed

"Do it!" Ray shouted, totally lost in the game now. Suddenly the simulation was fuzzy and rippled with distortion, flickering momentarily before the screen went totally blank.

"What the………?" Ray turned his head left and right, frantically searching. Everywhere he turned there was nothing but darkness.

"Hey mister, it's not working!"

Turning his body fully in the cockpit chair, he was about to remove the goggles, when a small orange stick figure around two inches high appeared, walking across the darkness in front of his eyes. It paused, the head moving left to right. Ray watched as the strange figure began moving again. He removed the goggles, blinking from the contrast. In the Gaming Centre and the rest of the entertainment building, everything appeared normal. Placing the goggles back on, the orange stick figure remained in the darkness, glowing. Ray slowly removed the glasses. The orange man was real, a real man. It was the same man in Teri's picture, and he was walking into Popeye's.

***

Holy crap! Ray jumped out of the VR simulation seat.

He had to warn the others!!

"Hey, you alright?" the attendant called after Ray, but he was long gone, jumping up the steps that led to the gaming area like a kangaroo released into the wild.

The bowling section was what greeted customers first in Popeye's, a large oval island centred in the entrance also served as a customer service booth for all of Popeye's facilities as well as a storeroom for the bowling shoes. Opposite the bowling alley were the slot machines and children's play area, with the café and gaming sections to the rear completing the quadrant.

Ray knew instinctively the man wouldn't spot him immediately; the place was full; Saturday night crowds of children and adults in equal numbers all mingling around, watching, playing, and eating.

Ray vaulted the low chrome guardrail that surrounded the café and bar in an attempt to short cut his run. Landing awkwardly, he nearly sent a small group of youngsters sprawling.

"HEY! Watch it!" the dad encircled the kids protectively.

"Sorry!"

Tommy and Teri both looked up at the sound of the commotion just as Ray slid into their booth.

"You alright, Ray?" Tommy half smiled

"He's here!"

"Who?"

"Him!" Ray pointed to Teri's phone, "He's by the bowling alley, looking. We gotta get out of here, now!"

"What? Looking for who?" Tommy spoke, alarmed.

"Goldilocks and the three bears! Who do you think!"

"Where can we go? If he's by the entrance now, how are we going to get out of here without being seen?" Teri scanned the bowling section, looking for the bald man.

Tommy pointed to the back of the quadrant, "What about there!"

The back wall was covered from top to bottom with a large, heavy duty, black tarpaulin. A sign hanging in the middle proclaimed:

Rock climbing coming soon! How high can YOU go!!

The group stood up as one, crouching over, scuttling their way towards the back of the café. A group at the table next to theirs sniggered at the sight.

A man at the bar stared as the group passed him, still hunched over, shaking his head.

"Hey Hattie? The man called out, "what's in these drinks you're serving me?"

The tarp lifted with some effort by Tommy and Ray, and Teri slid underneath without waiting. The boys both hunkered down, dragging themselves underneath the heavy plastic partition.

Inside, the room was gloomy dark, smelling metal and plastic. The trio had to wait for their eyes to adjust before delicately inching forward as if blindfolded.

"I can't see anything, guys!" Ray squinted ahead.

Slowly the shape of a half built climbing wall loomed into view. Sections needing to be connected lay leaning up against the wall or discarded, as if the workers had simply vanished mid-construction. Boxes with multi-coloured hand and feet grips presented themselves among other boxes of connecting brackets. A workman's tower stood ready for the next stage; the remaining interlocking chrome guard rails lay about carelessly. It was a mess. The cavern was quite compact and relatively small, and the far walls appeared to be only several metres away.

"What we going to do? There's no-where to hide!" Teri cried.

"We just have to wait it out for a bit until he goes." Tommy spoke reassuringly, touching her shoulder. He even managed a small smile. "It'll be alright Teri, okay?" she leant up against him in response.

Ray raised his eyebrows, looking away. Now wasn't the time to smile.

"What do you think he wants?" Ray asked, whispering.

"Well, whatever it is, I don't want to find out," Teri whispered back. Moving away from Tommy, she stepped carefully around the hardware strewed about the floor, heading to the opposite side of the room, "There's a door, an exit. Look!"

Both boys peered at the far wall. Their eyes were now getting accustomed to the dark. The faint outline of an emergency exit door presented itself. The sign was lit but ever so faintly, and definitely a way out. Focusing on the dim light above the EXIT door they could begin to make out all the walls now.

"It must lead to the service corridor that runs around inside the building. Come on!" She whispered.

Tommy followed Teri, picking his way over the obstacles, galvanised with hope and the thought of safety. Teri was already at the door, holding it ajar. The fluorescent lights from inside the service corridor flooded into the room, lifting the ceiling up from the shadows.

"I was right!" Teri cried, her voice louder, delighted with her discovery. Tommy joined her looking through the gap.

"Let's go. It's got to lead back to the shopping centre," he glanced back looking for Ray.

"Ray, where…?" Tommy's voice broke. His eyes huge.

"Tommy!" Ray mumbled, standing petrified, staring back at his friends.

An unnaturally white hand rested on his shoulder, poking through the unbroken tarpaulin, a magician's optical illusion in full play.

Chapter Five

Gavin Danby watched the kids rush past, scrambling beneath the black tarp. The scene they set was comical.

What are they up to?

He smiled to himself, assuming it must be a game, either that or they were running from trouble. Up to no good won the vote. They reminded him of a time long past; memories stirred up from murky times when he was around their age, ducking and diving, causing mayhem with his pals. Jesus, the things he had got away with then would be front page news now.

Good luck to you kids

Draining the frothy dregs of his glass he called out to Agneta, the Polish bar waitress. Slurred would be a more accurate representation but to Gavin it was clear as the day was long.

Having propped up the bar since it had opened he'd watched Harlequins wipe the floor from under Saracens, beating them 45 – 19. Then, as if needing an excuse to drink more - drowning his sorrows so to speak - he'd continued the session, alternating his attention from ogling the waitress to the TV. The beer glasses won the contest his fantasies with the Polish girl took front stage.

"How do I say, 'Good morning' in Polish?" he asked sweetly for the umpteenth time.

Agneta groaned, turning away to find something to do. It had been kinda cute the first time now, now it was just boorish.

The strange looking man dressed in a flappy grey boiler suit and funny looking shoes caught Gavin's attention even before he crossed into the bar. Such a peculiar looking individual was apt to make a mark. Making a beeline straight to where the children had just disappeared, Gavin took an instant disliking to the stranger. *Baldy just didn't look right!*

"Hey pal!" Gavin gave out, "they went that way," he pointed in the opposite direction. Boiler man ignored his advice, ignored him totally - instead, he leant against the tarpaulin to listen.

"Hey! I said they went that way, PAL!" Gavin pushed himself off the bar, puffing out his chest in his best George of the Jungle impression, but really coming across as Gavin the Pisshead. He hoped Agneta was watching.

So what if I've had a few, he thought, *bleeding weirdo man chasing kids*

Boiler man then did something unexpected. Raising his arm he pushed his hand through the plastic barrier, there was no resistance. His arm just simply vanished up to his elbow.

What the fuck?

"Hey fella, leave those kids alone." Now unsure of himself, but committed all the same, Gavin reached out for Boiler Man. His intention was to whip the weirdo round and slap him hard, sending him on his way. That was what he wanted to do, but in the end was suddenly faced with the stranger spinning round to confront him.

"You're..." Gavin recoiled horrified, *"What are you? Jesus!"* Repulsed he staggered back.

Boiler man's mouth was rippling, as if vibrating to an unheard frequency the hooded eyes were dark and had no pupils. No natural pupils that Gavin could see anyway, blinking shut like a reptiles would. The bald head, which had at first seemed clean shaven, shiny and clean was in fact now beginning to glow, spaghetti-like pulsating veins, streaked back over the forehead to the base of the creature's skull.

"Ah man..." Gavin could only manage, his mind unable to digest the image in front of him

Boiler Man responded with a language only God and the universe shared. A black forked tongue flickered with each mysterious syllable between the rippling lips, before turning back to the tarpaulin and simply parting the black plastic as if moving a lace curtain aside. It stepped through the gap and was gone.

Gavin spluttered uncontrollably, a reflex of gagging due to his now dry throat and sheer relief.

"Agneta! I need another drink NOW!"

***

Tommy stared helplessly back at Ray, transfixed at the hand lying on his friend's shoulder, paralysed, unable to help or say anything.

How has he found us? Tommy struggled with the thought of the man simply being able to get to them so quickly.

"RAY!" screamed Teri, "Move!"

One second the hand was there then it was gone, retracted. Ray bolted, released without notice or fanfare, he ran for his life. Vaulting the workman's obstacle course in two awarding winning jumps, he was by the exit door in seconds.

Teri was already gone, heading down the access corridor, instinctively heading back towards the shopping precinct. Tommy followed with Ray tight on his heels. The three didn't stop running until they burst through the emergency exit onto the concourse. Slamming the door behind them; unconcerned with the curious looks they attracted, the three friends shot off, heading out of the centre, dodging the crowds heading for the cinema without stopping. Only in the car park did they slow down, unsure of which direction to take.

"This way…….!" Tommy took charge, pointing to the right, Teri and Ray followed without argument.

Several shoppers stopped to gawk at the running children, expecting to see a security guard or two in tow - suspecting shoplifting as the cause. A couple pushed their child bodily against their car thinking the worst.

The route Tommy took led the trio out of the car park towards the old part of town and onto the pathway by the canal. They crossed the dual carriage way that ran past the shopping centre. Hurdling the barriers and over the other side, narrowly avoiding the early evening traffic. A few cars honked angrily at the jaywalkers but the kids were already away heading down a junction road.

Only then did Teri glance back, too afraid of what she might see to do it before. No sign of Boiler Man, but it was now dusk, the streetlights were on, and the traffic headlights were distracting. It was difficult to see much other than what was 50 feet away.

"I can't see him?" Teri panted.

"Yeah, doesn't mean to say he ain't there!" Ray peered around worriedly, "What we going to do, I mean, where can we go?" he finished, staring wildly at his friends.

"Tommy?" Teri asked." Tommy, what?"

"I'm thinking!"

"Well, we gotta move somewhere…now!"

Ray jogged off, carrying on in the same direction.

The others picked up the pace behind Ray, heading away from the shopping centre.

"What about the canal?" Ray called back, "We can get to it from here."

"Okay, go for it!" Tommy agreed, giving the street a sweeping look, "Go."

All three children turned onto a sloping footpath leading to the town's river, bouncing down the large concrete steps. At the bottom they were greeted with some metal barriers meant to slow cyclists down, the group slipped through these and raced on.

The River Sanford wasn't really a river anymore; in reality it was a stream at best, especially in the summer. The council had deemed it necessary to construct a storm drain in case of flooding. In most places the pathway was five feet above the water level. Once upon a time it had been a working canal, fully functional, bringing the coal and wheat down from the mining communities via the Grand Union Canal and waterways network. There had been talk of it being refurbished and reopened due to the popularity in the Midlands revival, hence the major initiative and drive to reclaim it from decay. But the funding from private investors had never realised, the council lost interest in the project after the general complaints over public spending. Now it was deteriorating; a favourite spot for druggies and unsavoury types who preyed on the innocents who wandered in. Not a nice place to be at night.

"Which way now?" Teri checked both options. To head north would lead them further away from the town centre; South would wind in and out under the roads and through the tunnels of the centre, eventually petering out to the back roads and on to East London.

"This way. GO!" Tommy led the way, heading north.

As the group sped away along the pathway, a figure appeared on the path that bridged the canal opposite the slope they had vacated moments before.

Boiler man was joined by a second identical figure. They watched the progression of the children running along the footpath impassively, waiting until they had disappeared from view.

Boiler man #1 spluttered quietly. They both turned and left.

***

"Wait...! Wait!" Teri pulled up, out of breath. "I can't run anymore!" she looked knackered. The children had been running now for a full ten minutes.

"And I thought you were supposed to be fit!" Ray responded, glad to have stopped anyway, the adrenaline kick was wearing off. The group had clocked up a mile and were now presented with a dilemma.

Tommy checked to see if the coast was clear, clearly tired.

"We gotta keep moving," he managed to gasp.

"But where to, Tommy, where...?" Teri appealed, holding her sides with both arms.

The block paving pathway with stuttered illuminated lighting and galvanised guardrails they had been running along was long gone, a precarious dirt track dangerously close to the canal taking its place. Draping foliage hindered their progress. The dirt track continued winding into darkness, the black water with it.

"If he found us that easily then…" Teri trailed off, waving a tired arm.

"…Nowhere is safe." Ray finished the sentence.

Tommy turned to his friends, catching his breath before responding.

"I think I know where we might be safe. Or at least somewhere to go for now anyways."

Teri and Ray waited, looking around nervously at the undergrowth.

"It's not far from here. We got to get off the canal though."

"Suits me bro, this place is getting super creepy," Ray nodded into the darkness.

"You ok, Teri?"

"No," she managed to smile back.

"Ok let's go then. There's a break near here where we can climb out."

Sure enough, after another couple of minutes of walking, a clearing appeared on the embankment and the group scrambled up the muddy slope. Before they left the embankment, Tommy grabbed some leaves off one bush, then more from a different kind.

Teri shook her head at him questioningly.

Tommy waved it away.

"Where are we?" Ray looked around wonderingly as they arose out onto a back road, "Ah yeah, I know now."

The children had emerged from the canal a couple of miles from the centre, the streetlamps revealing a slightly more dilapidated side of Sanford. The mainly low-rise council flats sat next to out-of-business shops interspersed with some surviving shops. Garbage bags piled high, littered the parade's corner shop like dirty black bonfires ready to be lit. The rotting smells emanating up added to the texture of the area. The place was deserted.

"Better watch it round here," Ray added.

"Better here than back there!" Teri almost laughed.

"Come on," Tommy led the way past the low-rise block of flats and shops. A woman watching them approach the building from a second-floor balcony sat in darkness smoking a cigarette.

"Here…" Tommy pointed down a dingy alleyway that fed onto a side road. A 'No Access' sign swung on a chain, guarding the lane. They passed several cars, all looking past their sell by date. One was an old, red, '50s American Plymouth Fury, looming large and out of place among the

British assemblage. Its grill and twin front lights glaring and menacing. Strangely, it looked in good condition.

Tommy stopped suddenly outside a huge decrepit building, the others bumping into him.

The gate leading into the property had a dirty placard barely hanging onto its moorings. 'Private'. On the building itself a printed sign competed with graffiti disclosing the words:

Charles Barnard's Residential Home

In smaller writing underneath: **High Fields Care Home, District of Sanford**

"You got to be joking!" Ray let out.

"No, I'm not."

"Where are we Ray?" Teri peered into the garden after reading the sign.

"High Fields," Tommy responded.

The path led to a red brick, Georgian style building, the front door now converted, having a disabled slope and safety rail dividing the once opulent entrance. A keypad entry system that had once glowed with efficiency and pride was dark, tarnished and broken.

Ray just shook his head wonderingly.

"Come on but be quiet."

Tommy stepped onto the premises, watching the upper windows for signs of tenants.

Sanford's lowlifes loved hanging out here, using the building for selling and drug taking. The authorities had all but abandoned the site.

Knowing the doorbell wouldn't work, he pushed the fireproof front door inwards, again seeming to know it was unlocked and useless. Ignoring the stairs completely, Tommy led the group into the grotty dwelling. The smell of urine and other nauseating delights hit their senses immediately; they were strong enough to make Teri's eyes water. Tommy followed the passageway around to the left, past white grainy front doors towards the back. He stopped at number 4.

Without a word he knocked gently, leaning in close to hear the response. There was only silence.

Teri and Ray glanced at each other; Ray shook his head. *Don't ask me*, it indicated.

Tommy knocked again, a little louder, checking his phone for the time.

"Who is it?" A squeaky voice asked.

"Tommy."

"Yeah, it's Tommy," the voice repeated.

There was a slight pause and then the door opened slightly.

In the gloom an old man squinted through the crack looking at the group questioningly.

"Hello Tommy."

"Hello Lenny."

Chapter Six

"Can we come in?" Tommy asked softly.

"I'm not supposed to have more than one friend," Lenny's head moved slightly around the door, checking the shadowy outlines of the other two friends. Teri gave her sweetest smile.

"Especially girls..." he squeaked.

"Yeah, but you know me Lenny, I've always been a good friend, haven't I?"

"Yeah..."

The door didn't budge.

"You know me Lenny," Tommy persisted.

"Yeah..."

"I have some of that special tea for you." Tommy delivered the trump card.

"Do you? Do you really?" The door inched open ever so slightly, as Lenny leaned forward, searching Tommy's hands with his eyes.

"Oh yeah...here, look," Tommy produced the leaves he'd picked down by the embankment for Lenny to see.

"Ooooh..." Lenny cooed, "Are they for me?" his voice even squeakier than normal.

"Absolutely Lenny, can my friends come in too?"

"Of course, of course, come in, come in." The door flew open.

"Thanks Lenny."

"Yeah."

Tommy motioned the others to follow him in. Lenny backed away, watching as the trio of friends entered the room. With lowered eyes, his body suddenly released an uncontrolled spasm.

Tommy handed over the leaves.

"Ah thank you, Tommy. Tommy, my friend!" Lenny leant in for an awkward hug.

"You bet Lenny. This is Ray and Teri. They're your friends too."

"Yeah...!"

Lenny twirled on the spot, his lack of dancing prowess making the manoeuvre stiff and yet perfectly normal.

The three teenagers had time to take in Lenny's bedsit while he rummaged in a corner of the room which housed the compact kitchenette. Finding a jar, he unscrewed the lid and deposited the leaves inside, quickly replacing the lid and squinting at the contents.

All around, the room was absolute chaos. A small couch had newspapers and magazines, anything with printed articles piled high. One small cushion lay bare, relatively clean, like a desert island in a sea of pollution.

The floor was similarly a mess. It was a domestic bombsite. Cartons and packaging, empty bottles, general rubbish, months, if not years old, littered the grotty sticky carpet. Bin liners filled to the brim with various collections of editorials sat between boxes of junk. The walls were a patchwork of newspaper clippings, pictures and silver cooking foil, plastering every conceivable space available. There once was a window, but not anymore. It had befallen the same fate as the walls.

A basic dining table and two chairs could have taken the mantel for the most unhygienic piece in the room, if there hadn't been a kitchen. The sink was piled high with dirty utensils and plates, the draining board much the same but more so. Hazarding a guess when the last time anyone cleaned would be the equivalent of winning the lottery.

Near the door was the single bed, unmade, the pillows a dirty pale grey as were the sheets. After the initial viewing of the layout, what greeted the trio was the overpowering and clogging smell of decay sprinkled with body odour and unwashed feet, mainly feet. The temperature in the room was stifling, uncomfortably so, and the urge to turnaround and head out was compelling.

Teri held a hand to her mouth, holding back her desire to gag. Tommy shook his head and she dropped the hand resignedly. Ray also struggled to maintain a straight face, looking to Tommy for answers.

"Ooooh...you want a drink, Tommy?" Lenny's eyes sparkled with happiness.

"No, thank you Lenny, appreciate the offer, though."

"Yeah..."

"Lenny, can I ask you what you meant when you said, 'You'd seen them' earlier today."

Lenny dropped his head one way then another.

"Did I?"

"Yes you did."

Lenny shook his head, "No I didn't."

"By the cinema, when you danced for me."

"Yes I did, didn't I!"

"That's right, you danced, and when you left you said, *'You'd seen them'*"

"Did I?"

Tommy sighed, resisting the urge to hang his head.

"Yes you did."

Ray, on impulse, produced a coin, "Wanna dance Lenny?"

Lenny stared at the coin in Ray's hand, "No."

Tommy shot Ray a glaring look, who shrugged back at both Teri and Tommy.

"What are all these for Lenny?" Teri indicated the clippings on the wall.

"Oooooh...they're my collection." Lenny jerked into action, heading for the ones Teri had looked at.

"You've done a real good job collecting them," she continued.

"Yeah..."

Ray nudged Tommy, raising his eyebrows.

"What are they all about?" Teri pressed.

"My collections...?"

"Yes, what are they?" Teri joined Lenny, staring at the picture of one article.

Lenny studied the paper before gently stroking the picture.

"Lenny, why do you collect them?" Teri persisted.

"They remind me."

"Of what?"

Lenny looked down, his face pained, his twitching started again.

"My mummy used to collect them," he said finally.

Teri glanced back at the boys. Tommy nodded, encouraging her to keep going.

"Where's your mummy now?"

Lenny continued to stare at the floor, "Don't know."

Teri read one clip. In the picture a man was holding a massive fish he'd caught, beaming with pride, but obviously struggling with the sheer weight of the brute.

The headline announced:

Local man lands a whopper!

The boys joined Teri at the wall. Ray read the article out loud.

"It says here that the fish was caught in the River Sanford?"

"What? But that's impossible," Tommy turned to look at Ray's article.

"Why's that?" Teri asked.

"You saw the canal, didn't you? There is no river!"

"Yeah…" Lenny joined the discussion.

"Never has been, not since I've known anyway."

"Nor me." Tommy conceded, "Certainly not when this printed."

"This was printed two years ago," Ray read the date, "2017!"

The three friends split up, looking at various articles and news items.

Essex/Suffolk Divided Over Proposed Link

The story read of a major road works connecting the two counties' countryside and to the city, which, according to the paper, had started on the 22nd of April last year to be completed by 2025.

"Well, that never happened," muttered Tommy.

Kia Comes to Town

The county was welcoming the car giant's manufacturing works plant, opening in May 1995, down by the Thames estuary, near Tilbury. The picture showed a Korean team of managers and their British counterparts. All smiling faces surrounded by balloons, fanfare, etc, in front of the monolith construction plant.

"Have we got a Kia car factory here?" Ray shook his head, "Don't think we do," he moved onto the next one.

Tragedy As Tunnel Collapses

On the 3rd of June 1985 a national paper reported the collapse of Tunnel A at the Dartford crossing, resulting in the deaths of at least 200 people. It occurred during rush hour when the tunnel was at maximum capacity. Tunnel B was subsequently closed with the whole area and operation sealed off for good.

Teri stared, shocked. She had used the tunnel only a week ago, visiting the Bluewater Shopping Centre.

"Hey guys, look at this," Tommy waved the others over.

Ray and Teri stared at the clipping. A man and an older lady stood smiling at the cameras.

The date on the paper read 19th December 1998. It was Lenny, twenty years ago, happy and youthful, unrecognisable. The older lady by his side was his mother. Their names were printed under the photograph, 'Leonard Barnard and Mrs Marcie Barnard'. There was no sign or mention of Lenny's father. They appeared to be standing in their garden by the front gate. A second smaller photograph showed a huge telescope mounted on a makeshift table, presumably set in the converted loft of the house.

Lenny stood by the apparatus smiling proudly, his hand touching the telescope.

The article read:

Local Man Wins 'Scholarship'

"Leonard Barnard, 25, from Runwell Avenue, High Fields, Sanford, has won the prestigious and coveted 'Watcher of the Skies' Award, from the University of Bristol. His discovery of a new satellite, which until now has been undetected, has amazed and astounded astronomers and scientists alike from around the world. Using the latest Meade LXX900-DRF 20" telescope (pictured), which comes with Star Lock as standard, Leonard has captured the images from out in deep space of the mysterious moon like object, which is at the edge of our known solar system. Mr Barnard has also won a scholarship at the University which he is very excited about.

The story went on to say how Lenny had found the 'moon' while searching for other stars in the night sky, coming across the discovery by chance.

Tommy turned to look at Lenny.

"Yeah..." was the response he got in return.

"What happened here Lenny?" Teri asked gently.

Lenny backed away from the wall, "I've seen them."

Tommy spun round, "Seen who Lenny? Seen who?" he pressed.

"Funny looking people took my mummy away."

The three friends all gave each other a knowing look.

"We've seen them too, Lenny," Tommy admitted.

"Have you?"

"Yes, tell me, what do they want?

Lenny started twitching, backing towards the kitchen.

"Trumpets in the sky...!" He exclaimed, shaking his head.

Ray threw up his hands, "Here we go!" giving Teri a look of despair.

"You won't remember, but Lenny remembers, yeah..."

"All this..." Tommy touched the wall, "helps you remember?"

"Yeah and... and..." Lenny looked baffled, "my mummy used to have memories she said she remembered but couldn't place, said it felt like..." He trailed off, his mind transported to another time.

"Déjà vu...!" Teri blurted out.

"Déjà vu, YEAH! Yeah, it's German for remember!" Lenny broke out into a high kicking dance.

"It's French, Lenny." Ray pointed out.

"Yeah...my mummy is German!" Lenny spun around.

Tommy sat on the only available chair, lost in thought. His friends gathered around him.

"Is this all real?" Ray stared back at the decorated wall behind Tommy.

"You start having déjà vu and then get taken away?" Teri put forward, speaking slowly, thinking it through.

"Or you see something you shouldn't have." Tommy added.

"You won't remember, but Lenny remembers." Lenny cooed.

"Well that just about covers us now doesn't it……!" Ray waved his hands dramatically. He checked the time on his watch, "What we going to do… stay here?" scoffing at the thought.

"Not good," Teri viewed the flats interior.

"You could stay upstairs," Lenny suggested. He cocked a head looking up at the ceiling.

"What's up there Lenny??" Tommy asked.

"Empty rooms, yeah…!"

"Really? Bet they're mostly drug dens, or worst." Ray muttered back.

"Alright, Lenny, we'll check it out, and thanks for everything mate."

"Yeah…"

The group vacated Lenny Budgie's bedsit and made their way gingerly back through the building. The only light they had to help them navigate was from the streetlight filtering through the front door's partitioned glass, its weak glow barely lighting the passageways. On the first floor, the landing was large and long, the carpet was ripped up, exposing the concrete canvas underneath, the smell from urine and defecation had permanently soaked into the floor. Four white doors presented themselves. Tommy tried No 5, the nearest one. It was locked. They moved onto the second door opposite, the same. No 7, further down, again locked. Tommy gave this handle a second hard rattle to be sure.

"I'm beginning to think Lenny's flat was the better option," Ray joked, but his eyes said differently.

"Fingers crossed," Tommy looked at his friends before trying the door. He grasped the handle of No 8 and turned the knob. It swung open. All three physically jumped at seeing someone standing before them.

"Whoa!" Ray blurted out.

Teri grabbed Tommy for support, nearly punching him in the process. All three backed away from the entrance of No 8, staring transfixed with dread and alarm.

Inside the doorway, not moving, stood a woman waiting patiently. From the pictures on Lenny's bedsit walls, the group easily guessed the identity of the lady. Marcie Barnard, Lenny's mother.

"Hello," Marcie smiled, sounding strained and false, the voice tinny and distant as if spoken by a person standing behind her.

Chapter Seven

The group retreated, none of them daring to take their eyes from the unsettling evil Marcie. Moving calmly and deliberately, she glided into the landing. Her gaze, hypnotic and intimidating, never wavered.

To the terrified trio it appeared that aging had eluded her, judging from the picture in Lenny's bedsit.

She indicated with a curt nod, implying that the group should enter room No 8.

"Sorry lady, that ain't happening!" Ray managed to find his voice.

"Err, guys!" Teri was staring back the way they had come.

Methodically plodding his way up the stairs was Boiler man, looking less a man now than they remembered. He was now carrying a slim, long, black lance, which appeared heavy, as it had to be dragged up the stairs, a loud thump accompanying every step. He too watched the children impassively, the mouth open, snake tongue flickering.

"Tommy!" Teri cried, her voice cracking.

Inside the doorway of No 8, a kaleidoscopic flash of swirling colours materialized, only the lights never escaping from the room. Where the group was standing, they could identify the depth and complexity of the patterns. It was endless and infinite. A deep undulating humming sound emerged from the room, a sound unlike anything the children had ever heard before.

"What do you want?" screamed Tommy, holding onto both Ray and Teri, who was now crying from abject terror.

Marcie ignored his plea.

Boiler man reached the top of the landing, and without pausing he continued the short distance towards the children, adjusting his grip on the lance which was crackling with incandescent heat.

The door to No 7 suddenly flew open. Two men raced out, both carrying weapons: one with a hammer, the other man holding a baseball bat.

"What the fuck?" the lead man began, switching his gaze from the children to Marcie and then staring at the seemingly impossible yet hypnotic sight emanating from room No 8.

"Is it the police?" a third man, unseen, shouted from the depths of room No 7. The smell of marijuana and other caustic drugs blew out onto the landing with the men's arrival.

The children braced themselves against the wall, instinctively huddling at the appearance of the two men who had emerged, thinking some new terror was about to unfold. It was.

"Nah it's not," the man holding the baseball bat called back into the room, "What the fuck do you want?"

Boiler man was on top of the lead man in seconds, standing before him.

"You don't wanna fuck with...." the man began.

The lance blurred. An arm, still gripping the baseball bat, twitched as if alive on the floor. The man stared idiotically at the space once occupied by his arm, only a charred aroma remained.

"Uhh Uhh Uhh..."

Boiler man twirled the lance again, severing the man's head cleanly from his body; the gaping mouth still gulping words of shock.

"Barry!!" the second man cried out.

Dropping his weapon, he stumbled, arms outstretched, as if to catch the head. The lance flashed again, stabbing the man's guts, stopping him dead in his tracks. With a nimble flick, the lance divided the torso and skull neatly in two. Hitting the ceiling with such force, a shower of white sparks briefly lit up the squalid landing and its occupants.

The second man collapsed to his knees, his lifeless eyes now level with the children's, who were cowering, wide eyed and paralysed.

Boiler Man kicked him over, finishing the job. Marcie stepped sideways, moving in front of room No 8, avoiding contact with the falling body.

"Mummy...!" Lenny cried out, running past the children, arms outstretched, his face a picture of pure joy. No-one had seen or heard his arrival. "Mummy you came back!"

Boiler Man spun around upon hearing Lenny's call, raising the lance for more devastating destruction.

"You muthafucker...!"

The third man had finally joined the party. Jumping out of room No.7, his epic war cry accompanied the swing of a claw hammer detonating Boiler Man's head as easily as ripe pumpkin.

PLOP

Green pulp and fluid decorated the walls. It covered and drenched Marcie face, blinding her.

Lenny lost his footing, kicking Barry's head in the process. Stumbling the last few steps and crashing into Marcie, the pair tumbled through the doorway of No 8 and vanished into the dark swirling vortex, the door slowly swung shut. A fitting closure. Mother and son finally reunited

"WHAT THE HELL JUST HAPPENED? Ray managed to splutter.

The third man pulled the hammer out of Boiler Man's neck, waving it threateningly at the children.

"You fucking want some?" His crazed, blood shot, eyes, ravaged from the crack cocaine, stared wildly at the trio.

All three children scrambled to their feet and ran for their lives.

***

The children didn't stop running. Past the block of rundown flats and shops, down the road, heading back the way they had come. They ran on through the streets, mostly using the middle of the road, until Sanford's glowing hub of activity replaced the shadowy streets of High Field's, and the horror was left behind.

Tommy pulled up first, stopping outside a Scott's Convenience Store near the ring road that circled the town centre. He leant against the glass advertising windows, struggling for breath.

"Tell me we didn't just witness a murder?" He finally panted out.

"Double murder, and that's not including 'reptile man'." Ray countered.

"You ok Teri...? Teri?"

"Yeah, I think so," she began before exploding, "No I'm not ok! What do you think? We've just witnessed...that nightmare!" She waved back up the street. "I should have been practicing football with my dad and settling down to watch 'Britain's got bloody talent' but no, that would be far too normal. Instead, here I am with you two running away from psychopathic crazies from who knows where, chopping people up for fun! Does that answer your question, Tommy? Huh? Does it?"

Two kids emerged from the shop, laughing at a private joke. They stopped laughing at the sight of the trio.

"I didn't mean...what do we do now?" Tommy asked softly.

"God knows, but I don't think I care anymore," Ray disappeared inside the shop.

"Shouldn't we tell someone, like the police?" Teri asked flapping an arm.

Tommy had fallen to his knees, completely exhausted, barely looked up, "And say what exactly Teri?"

"Two people were killed Tommy. Two people...are dead! *They're dead Tommy!*"

"I know, I know…," Tommy grabbed hold of Teri, pulling her down, "I think we should go home and get some rest; it's been so crazy I can't think anymore."

There they sat, looking vacantly up at the sky.

After a while Teri managed to admit, "I'm scared, Tommy, really scared."

Tommy took her hand, gripping it hard, pulling her face kindly round with his other.

"We'll get through this…together," he lifted her chin up.

Their faces now level, eyes locking together, for a second, everything stopped, time stopped.

Teri pulled away, "Sorry I…"

"No, no, it's ok…we should be going anyway," Tommy heaved himself up, finding the strength to do so. He put an arm out and helped Teri up.

The sliding doors opened revealing an angry Ray.

"Can you believe it? They've run out of Mars Bars!" Ray threw his arms up in despair.

Tommy and Teri burst out laughing simultaneously, almost hysterically.

"What I'd say?"

"Nothing mate but, Mars Bars, that's funny."

"Not really, I'm hungry."

"Come on let's get out of here," Teri led the way.

***

Tommy let himself in, carefully turning the latch and closing the front door softly. Slipping off his shoes, noting all was quiet he waited for some retort from his mother, there was none. She had ears that a bat would be jealous of normally. He checked the time; 10.59, she should still be up

The living room door was ajar. Through the crack he could see the room was dark with only the illumination from the TV. Tommy slowly pushed open the door and peered in. The TV was showing a soap opera, it looked like a rerun, one of his mother's favourites. In her armchair his mother watched impassively, motionless, totally still. If she was aware of his presence she showed no sign, staring at the program.

"Mum?" Tommy opened the door wider, expecting the movement to register but his mother ignored his entrance.

"Mum?" he whispered a little louder. She remained frozen. *He'd seen this before, hadn't he?* Now it seemed the phenomenon, the very thing that had started all this, was right here in front of him.

Alarmed, he stepped into the room. "Mum..." this time the word trembled from his quivering lips.

Mrs Martin remained paralysed.

Tommy slumped against the wall, catching and shutting the living room door in the process. Finally, and gratefully, he saw his mother's eyes focus. She blinked, snapping a look over to where he was sitting.

"Oh, Tommy, you made me jump!"

"Sorry... I didn't mean to."

"You're back."

"Yes mum," he answered dutifully but wearily, all of a sudden totally drained, mentally and physically. *So are you.*

"I must have dozed off," Mrs Martin adjusted herself in the chair, arching her back, "How was the film?"

"What? Uh yeah, yeah it was...good."

"You sure? You don't sound certain. How's Ray. Haven't seen him for a while?"

"He's ok...I'm going to bed, mum, I'm knackered."

"Ok, just be quiet, don't wake your sister!"

"I won't. Good night mum," then he added softly without reason, "Love you."

"Good night son."

Tommy stripped quickly, getting into bed, thinking that he'd struggle with sleep, but he was out cold in seconds. His body was exhausted, winning easily the battle over the questions riding his mind.

Failsafe mode was initiated, shutting down all primary functions, backup systems began rebooting, batteries recharging. Only the respiratory circuitries remained in operation, maintaining low output and wattage.

Chapter Eight

Tommy finally dreamt. In the dream was his father, fishing in a lake. Tommy called to him from the bank, a silent hello. His father alerted, turned and waved back, now standing in the river without the need of the boat, not floating not sinking, just... standing in the lake: fishing. Beside him on the bank lay his rod so he picked it up and began fishing too.

Frowning, for he had never fished before, he cast the line hard and expertly over his shoulder and onto the lake, watching as the fine wire and weight zip over and plop into the river, again without sound.

So what do you think? Asked the cat nonchalantly.

He looked down, now in the garden at home, a cat played with a mouse, toying with the rodent, letting it get so far then jabbing it, catching the tail with lightning speed with its claws, holding the creature before releasing it, repeating the game again and again.

You know, space, time and everything. It turned to look up at him, smiling as only a cat would smile.

In the garden some people ran about playing, children now, laughing, friends, yes, they were friends with no names and yet they were familiar, he knew them. He wanted to join in but stayed, waiting with the cat.

I could tell you.... But it'll probably blow your mind.

The children were gone. Now he was somewhere strange, foreign to him. Instinctively he ran, anywhere. The children reappeared, running beside him. Confused, he continued to run anyway, now into a large house, each room leading to another identical room, some children ran with him. The doors flying open before him, he could see a window in one room. The cat peered in; its face larger than the window frame itself. Now frightened, he ran away, but the next room was the same.

Wherever he ran, the same room presented itself. Then he was in a gigantic auditorium. The seats were filling up as he was being led by an attendant, carrying a bag of possessions.

Ray was with him, then he was gone, promising to meet later. *Save me a seat.* The theatre was opulent and grandiose, the attendant still leading the way, crisscrossing the aisles, making their ascent to the upper levels slowly. On stage, preparations were being made. The show looked extravagant and complicated, and yet he couldn't make out a single set piece.

He came across some security guards at a check point. They inspected his ticket. *"Have you searched him?"* came through on the earpiece of one guard. Without waiting, he carried on, presenting the ticket again to an automaton who inspected the ticket which turned out to be fake. The robot explained that they were aware of the issue but not to worry they would still validate the purchase. Again, he was led away, this time to the far side, the view of the show incredibly poor. *This is no good.* The robot shrugged as if to say *'not my problem'*. Its strange mechanical body all legs and arms, rotated on the spot, heading back the way it came.

Giving up on the show in disgust, he found a spot to inspect the contents of the bag. Inside he found various items of nonsensical use. None of them made sense, what were they?

Come I'll show you.

The cat was back. He was also back in his home. A door to the back garden opened, inviting him to leave. Bright lights emanated from outside. In the garden was...

Tommy woke up. The dream was still very real and vivid. He tried to hang on to the memory of it all, piecing together the puzzling meaning, but failing. Last night's incident invaded his thoughts instead, overriding the dream and the luxury that sleep had had of cushioning the inevitable horror.

It was still early, but he got up anyway, unable to clear his mind. Turning on his computer, Tommy left the bedroom for the bathroom, taking a quick shower before his mum and Abby took their turns, enjoying the privacy and solitude. He managed a smile at the thought of nearly kissing Teri outside the shop.

Boiler Man swung the lance, slicing Barry's head clean off...

Tommy twitched, the image of the horror, barging viciously into his fond memories of holding Teri's face in his hands and of nearly kissing her. He grabbed a bowl of cornflakes, taking his breakfast back to his bedroom. At the computer he logged onto the social media sites, scrolling through the home pages, trying to dislodge last night's terrible bloodshed and carnage. It was in vain.

Pulling his phone from his jeans pocket, Tommy reached out to his friends.

Struggling to deal with what happened last night
Ping, he sent it on to both Ray and Teri.

He got an immediate response from Ray.

Tell me about it bro, had proper nightmares last night. Couldn't sleep... you?

Same... something tells me this isn't over

What?

Well, think about it

I try not to

Well, think about it dude, maybe there's more of them

Great... does Teri know?

Hasn't answered

I'll call her

No wait, I've texted her, she might be sleeping

Tommy what we going to do mate?

Tommy sat back staring at the mobile. He didn't have an answer to give.

Ping. Teri answered.

Hey Tommy

Morning, you ok?

Not really

Nightmares...?

And some

You had breakfast yet

I can't eat!

Wanna meet up

Sure

I think it'll be best if we're together, I'll text Ray

Ok

Have you said anything to your mum and dad?

No, are you crazy!

Sorry, yeah, stupid thing to say

They wouldn't believe a word and if they did, they would have called the police

Right, I'll let Ray know, be careful Teri

Tommy messaged Ray. They all agreed to meet up in one hour over at Benson's Park, behind Tommy's house. It was a long hour to wait.

The children convened in Benson's Park and Bowling Green overlooking the back of Tommy's house as agreed, all on time, all looking decidedly apprehensive. In the distance some dog walkers were chatting together, their dogs having done the business of smelling each other's bits and were now sitting impatiently waiting for their owners to finish gossiping and get on with the job of walking.

The Park was long and oval shaped. A couple of tennis courts sat near the car park by the West gate entrance. After the tennis courts, a small children's play area was cordoned off with traditional swings, see-saw etc. From there, a winding lane split north and south, surrounding the large green in the middle and finally coming together again, creating the oval shape. At the opposite end of the park were two bowling greens and a club house, joined by the East gate car park.

"Tell me you've got a plan, Tommy?" Ray sat on the grass, "'Cause the next time any mad baldy comes running at me, we're going straight to the police."

"Amen to that," Teri chipped in.

"They can lock me up and throw away the key!" Ray continued, "So, any idea what's going on buddy? What we going to do? What can we do?"

Tommy sat next to his friend, double checking for dog mess before hunkering down, "I think Lenny spotted something with his telescope, and that something found Lenny and took his mother away after they started finding out about what's really happening around the world."

Teri sighed, staring up at the storm clouds now rolling in.

"Tommy..." she spoke carefully, "that's a crazy story, but I got to admit, after everything last night I'm ready to believe in almost anything now, including spaceships and aliens."

A low rumbling echoed in the distance; its timing not lost on the three children.

"Can you believe that? We go to Popeye's when it's boiling and then go to the park when it's about to rain! Are we cursed or what?" Ray stared at the sky, shaking his head in wonder.

"Rain?" Tommy queried, "We're supposed to be having a heat wave!"

"Check it out dude, clouds don't lie!"

"They're moving real fast, never seen that before!" Teri remarked, still studying the skies.

All three watched as the billowing formations spread, cancelling out the blue when the sounds came. At first the noise was quiet, subtle, even expected, as the density of the clouds grew and grew, rapidly darkening the area.

Thunder and lightning would surely follow such impressive displays from the towering cumulus.

Ray and Tommy stood up.

"My mum said never be in the open when there's a storm," Teri said.

"Don't you have to lie down or something?" Ray asked, questioning Teri.

"That is ridiculous, lying down in the pouring rain?"

"No, it's don't get caught under a tree...I remember now. Whoa! Did you see that?"

Ray pointed up at the clouds.

Deep within the layers of grey masses, explosions of colour like flash bulbs sequenced to detonate repeated over and over.

Then it came, loud distorted sirens, alternating from low frequency to a high-pitched wailing, undulating sounds, ranging from bass to soprano, unusual harmonies, as if a school of whales were being conducted, an amplified orchestra with an orca section.

"That ain't any thunder I've ever heard before?" Ray muttered.

Tommy stared at his friends, open mouthed.

"It sounds like...*trumpets in the sky.*"

Teri and Ray stared back.

"Holy shit...!"

"Come on, we better get out of here!" Tommy pulled Teri away, running for the car park entrance. Ray followed, hot on their heels.

"WHERE TO?" he shouted.

"THERE!" Tommy pointed to the Clubhouse.

The trumpeting sound had steadily grown and was now deafening. The noise had escalated as quickly as it had begun and was still increasing in volume.

As they crashed onto the club's steps, a bird dropped stone dead, hitting the porch roof with such force, the impact bounced the animal over the gutter, narrowly missing the children.

They raced up to the doors.

Please, please, please be open, Tommy prayed.

They were. The three friends almost tumbled over each in their haste to get inside. Outside the trumpeting had reached near ear splitting levels.

"My God, what is that sound?!" Arthur Stapleton appeared from the clubhouse office, looking suspiciously at the children. He tapped his hearing aid, pulling it out quickly. He was the bowling club's secretary-cum-groundsman, and was normally on site, even on quiet days, pottering about the place.

Arthur was a large retiree of a man; a man dedicated to the natural order things, having spent 30 years of his life in the British Army, reaching the rank of Staff Sergeant and finishing his career at Colchester Garrison.

A position in the MCTC (Military Corrective Training Centre) had arisen, and Arthur had jumped at the chance to extend his career, the only life he'd ever known. For the last fifteen years, since leaving the Forces, he had devoted his time and energy to Benson's, making the bowling club his own. In his hands he wielded a Ben Sayers antique 9 iron golf club. After a spate of vandalism to the lawns and windows had occurred, he was predominantly around and ready for action, itching to catch the little bastards who had desecrated the club's integrity and honour and ready to give pay back.

"It's not us!" Teri shouted.

"I don't believe you. I'm calling the police!" he shouted back.

"Go ahead mate," Tommy encouraged, "You do that."

The three friends moved further into the club house hall, ignoring Arthur, looking for sanctuary. Passing the notice board and trophy cabinet, the group pushed open the nearest double swing doors into the lounge room.

"You can't be in here!" Arthur was nearly spitting, foam forming at the corners of his mouth.

"We ain't going nowhere!" Ray shouted back over his shoulder. The double doors swung back, cutting his last words short. Arthur turned and made good his promise, picking up the phone in the office, jabbing the keypad.

"I'm not going to put up with this!!" He put the receiver to his ear, his face flushed with anger.

"What? Why's there no dial tone?" Frowning at the phone, it dawned on him, "You cut the lines!" He shouted, "You're gonna pay for that."

Looking at the picture of the club's founder and four-time president above the desk, he muttered. "Don't you worry, Reg, they're not gonna get away with it this time! No Sirree!"

The old man picked up the Ben Sayers golf club again, hefting it between his hands for balance and weight.

The audacity of the little shits was astonishing. Well, I'm not going to put up with it, not this time

"Come on, Sally, time to go to work," he set off for the main lounge room.

The children fanned out across the room. Tommy ran to the windows facing the west lawn. Some patio doors opened onto the bowling green; he tried the handles. They were locked. He rattled them to be sure. They looked decidedly on the old side of new.

Ray peered into a serving hatch at the far corner of the room. A kitchen lay beyond, smelling slightly stale, the units and stove in dire need of a makeover. Teri had dropped onto a set of red velvet cushioned seats against the wall, hands covering her face, rocking back and forth, a small moan escaping.

Tommy searched the skies through the glass. He had just made out something unexplainable materialising from the grey clouds when Arthur burst into the room. He turned in time to see Arthur swing Sally the 9 iron with terminal force at Teri's head.

"Noooooo....!!" Tommy screamed.

The impact smashed Teri's fingers but wasn't enough to soften the blow to the head. Her skull cracked from the force, snapping back, hitting the wall. She was brain dead before her body hit the floor. Arthur stared at the body on the floor, not sure if he should hit her again.

"You old..." Ray went to rugby tackle the old man who swung Sally again, this time at Ray.

Unable to complete the job, they both crashed to the floor in a heap, hitting a serving table on the way down, the old man taking the brunt of the fall. Ray wrestled for the club, gaining the upper hand as the pair rolled about.

Tommy ran blindly, crashing into chairs to get to Teri, falling to his knees, crying her name. He gathered her body, lifting her up and resting her head in the crook of his arm. Her eyes were open, staring into the distance beyond, seeing nothing anymore.

On her forehead a lump already the size of a ping pong ball could be seen, as if seeking a way out, forming into a darkening protuberance.

"Teri, wake up! *WAKE UP!*"

Ray fought and won the 9 iron from the old man's clutching hands, and stood above him threateningly. He turned, alarmed when Tommy screamed at Teri, stepping away from Arthur, who was holding his chest struggling for breath.

"Wake up," Tom cried quieter this time.

"Ah...ah, I can't breathe," Arthur spluttered.

Both the boys ignored him, with Ray dropping down beside Tommy, tears now falling from him too.

"SHE'S DEAD RAY!"

"No, she can't be...she can't be!"

Tommy rocked their bodies, crushing Teri's with his arms, squeezing her in a vain desperate attempt to pass on energy and life.

Outside the trumpeting din abruptly ceased.

Chapter Nine

Tommy felt a tap on his shoulder. Reluctantly he made eye contact with Ray, the effort almost too much. Both boys' eyes were red and swollen, the tears still falling.

He looked questioningly at his friend.

Ray was staring over his shoulder at something or someone beyond with a resigned look of total defeat. He guessed that it wasn't Bruce Willis and the cavalry.

Marcie and Co. were back, en-masse. Everywhere from within the saloon, strange looking people stood watching them, dotted here and there and even a few outside. No more the bizarre and aberrant Boiler men, but people, normal, typical, every day walk of life people, all staring impassively. Some even had their heads cocked, almost as if listening to a distant sound or trying to see the children better. All were silent; just calmly staring, waiting.

Arthur, prostrate on the floor, continued making complicated noises, managing to turn his head, squinting at the new development in his beloved club house.

"What...?" he mumbled in between breaths.

Tommy sighed, a long sigh of resignation. He managed to smile at his best friend. "I'm sorry I got you into all this mess Ray." Looking down he whispered, "I'm so sorry Teri."

He pushed a lock of hair back that had dropped forward, and stroked her head, laying her body as gently and respectfully as he could to the floor, he folded her arms across her body before getting to his feet.

Ray stood up with him. Together, shoulder to shoulder, to face the music and whatever may come.

Marcie looked at each boy separately. Finally, a half-smile broke out over her impassive and impenetrable mask.

"It's time to reset." Again that, voice tinny and strange. Tommy doubted that it was her original voice, the voice that Lenny once knew and adored.

He gave Ray a look, tightening his lip, finding a new resolve.

"Why us?" He spoke loudly, "Why me?"

Marcie cocked her head. Looking directly at Tommy, the smile remained.

"You both know why...don't you?"

"Not really, no..."

Marcie smiled an even bigger smile.

"You've seen too much. I must say for three young children, we have been quite impressed with your exemplary efforts," her head returned to its normal position, "Quite impressed."

"We...?"

"Yes...we."

"Who are we?" Tommy pressed.

Instead of answering, Marcie walked towards Arthur, kneeling beside the injured man, she reached down to touch his chest.

His wide eyes blinking uncontrollably at her approach now ceased their fluttering. He stared past her at the clubhouse ceiling, no longer breathing.

"Jesus!" Ray croaked.

"He was in pain. I stopped the pain." Marcie stood and returned to face the boys once more.

"Is he reset?" Tommy ventured boldly.

Again the weird smile. Tommy was beginning to really, really hate that smile.

"Do we have time?" Marcie asked out loud, looking at the boys but speaking as if to someone beyond them.

Tommy managed to give Ray a last desperate look before everything he knew evaporated before his very eyes.

"Ray, whatever..."

The room disappeared, only nothingness remained.

Come with me. I'll show you, a voice deep inside his head said.

The clubhouse was gone, Ray and Teri, gone. Everything was gone. Before Tommy was only blackness, below only the same, but he didn't suffer any vertigo. No sickness churning his stomach, his balance steady and still. He only had a moment to input this unsettling phenomenon when an explosion of matter, sparkling orbs from out of nothing, erupted ahead, lighting the distant darkness into a spectacular firework display. Expanding forever outwards, the shooting rays rushed towards him, stretching out. They enveloped Tommy, passing through him.

Looking down he realised he had no body anymore just a...consciousness of thought and reason, and an understanding of the spectacle before him.

The lights formed into crude shapes, still accelerating at implausible speeds, too fast to comprehend. He travelled with one star as it tumbled and formed, growing bigger and brighter. A swirling nebula of multi coloured gases began forming nearby, and as he watched they too began forming, not into crude planetoid shapes but rather a liquid matter, sparkling with electro impulses, blinking and glistening, a dazzling luminescent show of incredible and ultimate power. Too vast to calculate in size, an immeasurable mass, forever infinite.

Home, Marcie's voice spoke from nowhere and yet everywhere, swirling back and forth, panning from side to side.

Then the nebula was gone. Sucked into a distant supermassive black hole, pulling other galaxies and stars towards the vortex; an event horizon of beautiful and catastrophic displays of destruction, refracting and circulating light, bending, and disappearing over the black hole.

We travel through here into dimensional worlds, galaxies.......and to yours

The voice continued.

Our engineers designed your world to be a template, an example of genetic programming, stimulating life where and when necessary.

Each stage of development is analysed and documented. Where needed, we removed and improved the formula of genetics, allowing reproduction to continue or to cease.

Yours is the latest in a line of mapping. A very young and adolescent race, sometimes we control the output with various tests of...ascendancy. You might call these influences...cataclysms, or wars

Why? The voice asked Tommy's consciousness as if reading his thoughts.

This is how all worlds are developed before you may become part of the universe. Every now and then your young race has detected signs, stumbling upon something disorienting or apparent...something it can't explain

Marcie, more heterogeneous than previously, stood in front of Tommy, her eyes inches from his.

That's when we step in and reset what you call the matrix

Tommy blinked. Outside his window his neighbour, Mr Cartwright was busily working his lawnmower up and down the garden. The grass looked immaculate and precisely cut. Still the old man soldiered on, dedicated and obsessed.

"What a weirdo!"

"What you looking at?" Taunted his sister, she had just appeared in the doorway.

"Mind your own business," Tommy muttered hopelessly.

"I'm telling mummy you're being nosey!"

"Yeah, so what?"

"MUMMY...! TOMMY'S BEING A NOSEY PARKER!" shouted Abby at ear splitting levels.

"Hey Abby, I'll tell you something."

"What?" Abby looked suspiciously at her older sibling. She knew the game off by heart, but fell for it all the same.

"Wanna see the bogie man!"

"No!"

"It's Mr Carty!"

"No he's not!"

"Wanna bet!"

"MUMMY, Tommy's telling lies!"

"And he's coming for...YOU!" Tommy lunged at his sister.

Abby ran from the bedroom, shrieking with high pitched delight.

Tommy smiled at the empty doorway... but then frowned. Something...something he couldn't quite put his finger on stopped him from enjoying the moment. It was almost as if...? It passed. Dismissing the notion entirely, he grabbed his rucksack and followed his sister down for breakfast.

Friday morning and school assembly's feast of the terribles. The hall was beginning to fill up.

Ray plonked himself down next to his best friend, eyes only for the girls as they entered the hall.

"Thanks for saving me a seat squire! So, how was your weekend dude?" he smirked.

"The usual, wanted to go see that film Trashcan Man 2. Gonna have to sell some games as I don't have any money, bro. Depressing,"

"I hear yah! Me, I've got a job working down the market, setting stalls up before school on Wednesday's and Friday', working all day Saturday as well!" Ray beamed proudly, "Tell you what, I'll treat you this Saturday night,"

"Really? Nice one dude."

"Yeah, not bad... the stall I mean. Geezer who runs it might be a woofer though. Have to watch my back," Ray laughed loudly.

"Go on then, what you selling?"

"Ladies clothing." Ray mumbled.

"What? Can't hear you?"

"Ladies clothing." Slightly louder this time.

"Oh. For a minute there I thought you said 'LADIES CLOTHING'!" Tommy shouted, ribbing his friend. The pair jostled playfully, annoying a boy next to Tommy.

"Look, there's Tracy Collins," Ray pointed out the girl as she entered the hall giggling with what the boys liked to call 'her pre-tards' a small troupe of identical clones. The strut she performed - well-rehearsed for maximum affect - was turning heads left, right, and centre, including those of the teachers.

"She's a sort or what," Roy drooled.

"Really dude, thought you had better taste than that!"

"Come on man, look at those *bazookas!*"

Tommy wasn't listening anymore. He'd spotted another girl entering the hall. A girl on her own, cropped hair, almost boyish, cut that way so as not to interfere with her training, her football training.

"Who you looking at?" Ray realised he'd been talking to himself.

"No-one in particular," Tommy peered past Ray, pretending to look at someone else.

"Look, there's Teri." Ray waved, trying to get her attention, but Teri was miles away in her own world.

"Really, where?" Tommy looked around, faking.

At that moment in strode Mr Gray, storming past the children and teachers alike. His no nonsense stride, parting the sea of bodies, as only Moses could command, heading directly for the stage.

"Crap, it's Gray," Ray muttered, sinking down into his chair

"Guess you won't be taking part in this morning's competition, then?"

"You guessed right dude!"

Mr Gray placed a few notes onto the speaker's stand and glanced briefly down his nose at the sea of faces in the hall. Everybody hurriedly took their seats, including a few teachers. Mr Gray couldn't wait to deliver his speech; his impatience rising by the second.

"It has unfortunately come..."

Tommy blinked, Mr Gray's monotonic grumble fading away into a background noise no longer audible. He leant forward feeling peculiar.

"SLUGS!" bellowed Mr Gray.

Tommy gasped as if punched. The school assembly; Mr Gray, the setting, everything felt replayed, done before. He felt nauseous, faint headed.

"Wow, mate, that's the strongest déjà vu I've ever had before!" he whispered.

Tommy had to swallow back a small lump of bile that had shot up into his mouth suddenly.

"Dude, did you hear me?" Tommy appealed, turning to his friend.

Only it was Boiler man who stared back, his eyes blacker than night, his mouth rippling crazily, the forked tongue flickering unnaturally.

Someone began to scream. It was Tommy. Screaming over and over and over……

Printed in Great Britain
by Amazon